A world man has never known . . .

Pal-ul-don is separated from the rest of Africa by a vast range of mountains and by bottomless morasses in whose slimy depths lurk monstrous reptiles, the forgotten serpents from an age before the dawn of recorded history. Surmounting all these dangers, Tarzan at last encounters the inhabitants of Pal-ul-don, the ferocious tailed warriors of the Ho-don and Wazdon tribes. Worse even than these are the murderous dwellers in the strange and sinister city of A-lur—and it is here that Tarzan at last finds traces of his beloved Jane.

Edgar Rice Burroughs

TARZAN BOOKS

Available now from Ballantine Books

TARZAN THE TERRIBLE

Edgar Rice Burroughs

BALLANTINE BOOKS • NEW YORK
An Intext Publisher

Edgar Rice Burroughs, Inc. Authorized Edition published
by Ballantine Books, Inc.

SBN 345-03006-0-095

First Printing: July, 1963
Second Printing: November, 1963
Third Printing: October, 1969
Fourth Printing: December, 1972

First Canadian Printing: December, 1963

Printed in the United States of America

Cover Painting: Robert Abbett

BALLANTINE BOOKS, INC.
101 Fifth Avenue, New York, New York 10003

CONTENTS

1

The Pithecanthropus

SILENT as the shadows through which he moved, the great beast slunk through the midnight jungle, his yellow-green eyes round and staring, his sinewy tail undulating behind him, his head lowered and flattened, and every muscle vibrant to the thrill of the hunt. The jungle moon dappled an occasional clearing which the great cat was always careful to avoid. Though he moved through thick verdure across a carpet of innumerable twigs, broken branches, and leaves, his passing gave forth no sound that might have been apprehended by dull human ears.

Apparently less cautious was the hunted thing moving even as silently as the lion a hundred paces ahead of the tawny carnivore, for instead of skirting the moon-splashed natural clearings it passed directly across them, and by the tortuous record of its spoor it might indeed be guessed that it sought these avenues of least resistance, as well it might, since, unlike its grim stalker, it walked erect upon two feet—it walked upon two feet and was hairless except for a black thatch upon its head; its arms were well shaped and muscular; its hands powerful and slender with long tapering fingers and thumbs reaching almost to the first joint of the index fingers. Its legs too were shapely but its feet departed from the standards of all races of men, except possibly a few of the lowest races, in that the great toes protruded at right angles from the foot.

Pausing momentarily in the full light of the gorgeous African moon the creature turned an attentive ear to the rear and then, his head lifted, his features might readily have been discerned in the moonlight. They were strong, clean cut, and regular—features that would have attracted attention for their masculine beauty in any of the great capitals of the world. But was this thing a man? It would have been hard for a watcher in the trees to have decided as the lion's prey resumed its way across the silver tapestry that Luna had laid upon the floor of the dismal jungle, for from beneath the loin cloth of black fur that girdled its thighs there depended a long hairless, white tail.

In one hand the creature carried a stout club, and suspended at its left side from a shoulder belt was a short, sheathed knife, while a cross belt supported a pouch at its right hip. Confining these straps to the body and also apparently supporting the loin cloth was a broad girdle which glittered in the moonlight as though encrusted with virgin gold, and was clasped in the center of the belly with a huge buckle of ornate design that scintillated as with precious stones.

Closer and closer crept Numa, the lion, to his intended victim, and that the latter was not entirely unaware of his danger was evidenced by the increasing frequency with which he turned his ear and his sharp black eyes in the direction of the cat upon his trail. He did not greatly increase his speed, a long swinging walk where the open places permitted, but he loosened the knife in its scabbard and at all times kept his club in readiness for instant action.

Forging at last through a narrow strip of dense jungle vegetation the man-thing broke through into an almost treeless area of considerable extent. For an instant he hesitated, glancing quickly behind him and then up at the security of the branches of the great trees waving overhead, but some greater urge than fear or caution influenced his decision apparently, for he moved off again across the little plain leaving the safety of the trees behind him. At greater or less intervals leafy sanctuaries dotted the grassy expanse ahead of him and the route he took, leading from one to another, indicated that he had not entirely cast discretion to the winds. But after the second tree had been left behind the distance to the next was considerable, and it was then that Numa walked from the concealing cover of the jungle and, seeing his quarry apparently helpless before him, raised his tail stiffly erect and charged.

Two months—two long, weary months filled with hunger, with thirst, with hardships, with disappointment, and, greater than all, with gnawing pain—had passed since Tarzan of the Apes learned from the diary of the dead German captain that his wife still lived. A brief investigation in which he was enthusiastically aided by the Intelligence Department of the British East African Expedition revealed the fact that an attempt had been made to keep Lady Jane in hiding in the interior, for reasons of which only the German High Command might be cognizant.

In charge of Lieutenant Obergatz and a detachment of native German troops she had been sent across the border into the Congo Free State.

Starting out alone in search of her, Tarzan had succeeded in finding the village in which she had been incarcerated only to learn that she had escaped months before, and that the German officer had disappeared at the same time. From there on the stories of the chiefs and the warriors whom he quizzed, were vague and often contradictory. Even the direction that the fugitives had taken Tarzan could only guess at by piecing together bits of fragmentary evidence gleaned from various sources.

Sinister conjectures were forced upon him by various observations which he made in the village. One was incontrovertible proof that these people were man-eaters; the other, the presence in the village of various articles of native German uniforms and equipment. At great risk and in the face of surly objection on the part of the chief, the ape-man made a careful inspection of every hut in the village from which at least a little ray of hope resulted from the fact that he found no article that might have belonged to his wife.

Leaving the village he had made his way toward the southwest, crossing, after the most appalling hardships, a vast waterless steppe covered for the most part with dense thorn, coming at last into a district that had probably never been previously entered by any white man and which was known only in the legends of the tribes whose country bordered it. Here were precipitous mountains, well-watered plateaus, wide plains, and vast swampy morasses, but neither the plains, nor the plateaus, nor the mountains were accessible to him until after weeks of arduous effort he succeeded in finding a spot where he might cross the morasses—a hideous stretch infested by venomous snakes and other larger dangerous reptiles. On several occasions he glimpsed at distances or by night what might have been titanic reptilian monsters, but as there were hippopotami, rhinoceri, and elephants in great numbers in and about the marsh he was never positive that the forms he saw were not of these.

When at last he stood upon firm ground after crossing the morasses he realized why it was that for perhaps countless ages this territory had defied the courage and hardihood of the heroic races of the outer world that had, after innumerable reverses and unbelievable suffering penetrated to practically every other region, from pole to pole.

From the abundance and diversity of the game it might have appeared that every known species of bird and beast and reptile had sought here a refuge wherein they might take their last stand against the encroaching multitudes of men that had steadily spread themselves over the surface of the earth, wresting the hunting grounds from the lower orders, from the moment that the first ape shed his hair and ceased to walk upon his knuckles. Even the species with which Tarzan was familiar showed here either the results of a divergent line of evolution or an unaltered form that had been transmitted without variation for countless ages.

Too, there were many hybrid strains, not the least interesting of which to Tarzan was a yellow and black striped lion. Smaller than the species with which Tarzan was familiar, but still a most formidable beast, since it possessed in addition to sharp saber-like canines the disposition of a devil. To Tarzan it presented evidence that tigers had once roamed the jungles of Africa, possibly giant saber-tooths of another epoch, and these apparently had crossed with lions with the resultant terrors that he occasionally encountered at the present day.

The true lions of this new, Old World differed but little from those with which he was familiar; in size and conformation they were almost identical, but instead of shedding the leopard spots of cubhood, they retained them through life as definitely marked as those of the leopard.

Two months of effort had revealed no slightest evidence that she he sought had entered this beautiful yet forbidding land. His investigation, however, of the cannibal village and his questioning of other tribes in the neighborhood had convinced him that if Lady Jane still lived it must be in this direction that he seek her, since by a process of elimination he had reduced the direction of her flight to only this possibility. How she had crossed the morass he could not guess and yet something within seemed to urge upon him belief that she had crossed it, and that if she still lived it was here that she must be sought. But this unknown, untraversed wild was of vast extent; grim, forbidding mountains blocked his way, torrents tumbling from rocky fastnesses impeded his progress, and at every turn he was forced to match wits and muscles with the great carnivora that he might procure sustenance.

Time and again Tarzan and Numa stalked the same quarry and now one, now the other bore off the prize. Seldom however did the ape-man go hungry for the country was rich in game animals and birds and fish, in fruit and the countless other forms of vegetable life upon which the jungle-bred man may subsist.

Tarzan often wondered why in so rich a country he found no evidences of man and had at last come to the conclusion that the parched, thorn-covered steppe and the hideous morasses had formed a sufficient barrier to protect this country effectively from the inroads of mankind.

After days of searching he had succeeded finally in discovering a pass through the mountains and, coming down upon the opposite side, had found himself in a country practically identical with that which he had left. The hunting was good and at a water hole in the mouth of a cañon where it debouched upon a tree-covered plain Bara, the deer, fell an easy victim to the ape-man's cunning.

It was just at dusk. The voices of great four-footed hunters rose now and again from various directions, and as the cañon afforded among its trees no comfortable retreat the ape-man shouldered the carcass of the deer and started downward onto the plain. At its opposite side rose lofty trees—a great forest which suggested to his practised eye a mighty jungle. Toward this the ape-man bent his step, but when midway of the plain he discovered standing alone such a tree as best suited him for a night's abode, swung lightly to its branches and, presently, a comfortable resting place.

Here he ate the flesh of Bara and when satisfied carried the balance of the carcass to the opposite side of the tree where he deposited it far above the ground in a secure place. Returning to his crotch he settled himself for sleep and in another moment the roars of the lions and the howlings of the lesser cats fell upon deaf ears.

The usual noises of the jungle composed rather than disturbed the ape-man but an unusual sound, however imperceptible to the awakened ear of civilized man, seldom failed to impinge upon the consciousness of Tarzan, however deep his slumber, and so it was that when the moon was high a sudden rush of feet across the grassy carpet in the vicinity of his tree brought him to alert and ready activity. Tarzan does not awaken as you and I with the weight of slumber still upon his eyes and brain, for did the creatures of the wild awaken thus, their awakenings would be few. As his eyes snapped open, clear and bright, so, clear and bright upon the nerve centers of his brain, were registered the various perceptions of all his senses.

Almost beneath him, racing toward his tree was what at first glance appeared to be an almost naked white man, yet even at the first instant of discovery the long, white tail projecting rearward did not escape the ape-man. Behind the fleeing figure, and now so close as to preclude the possibility of its quarry escaping, came Numa, the lion, in full charge. Voiceless the prey, voiceless the killer; as two spirits in a dead world the two moved in silent swiftness toward the culminating tragedy of this grim race.

Even as his eyes opened and took in the scene beneath him —even in that brief instant of perception, followed reason, judgment, and decision, so rapidly one upon the heels of the other that almost simultaneously the ape-man was in mid-air, for he had seen a white-skinned creature cast in a mold similar to his own, pursued by Tarzan's hereditary enemy. So close was the lion to the fleeing man-thing that Tarzan had no time carefully to choose the method of his attack. As a diver leaps from the springboard headforemost into the waters beneath, so Tarzan of the Apes dove straight for Numa, the lion; naked in his right hand the blade of his father that so many times before had tasted the blood of lions.

A raking talon caught Tarzan on the side, inflicting a long, deep wound and then the ape-man was on Numa's back and the blade was sinking again and again into the savage side. Nor was the man-thing either longer fleeing, or idle. He too, creature of the wild, had sensed on the instant the truth of the miracle of his saving, and turning in his tracks, had leaped forward with raised bludgeon to Tarzan's assistance and Numa's undoing. A single terrific blow upon the flattened skull of the beast laid him insensible and then as Tarzan's knife found the wild heart a few convulsive shudders and a sudden relaxation marked the passing of the carnivore.

Leaping to his feet the ape-man placed his foot upon the carcass of his kill and, raising his face to Goro, the moon, voiced the savage victory cry that had so often awakened the echoes of his native jungle.

As the hideous scream burst from the ape-man's lips the man-thing stepped quickly back as in sudden awe, but when Tarzan returned his hunting knife to its sheath and turned toward him the other saw in the quiet dignity of his demeanor no cause for apprehension.

For a moment the two stood appraising each other, and then the man-thing spoke. Tarzan realized that the creature before him was uttering articulate sounds which expressed in speech, though in a language with which Tarzan was unfamiliar, the thoughts of a man possessing to a greater or less extent the same powers of reason that he possessed. In other words, that though the creature before him had the tail and thumbs and great toes of a monkey, it was, in all other respects, quite evidently a man.

The blood, which was now flowing down Tarzan's side,

caught the creature's attention. From the pocket-pouch at his side he took a small bag and approaching Tarzan indicated by signs that he wished the ape-man to lie down that he might treat the wound, whereupon, spreading the edges of the cut apart, he sprinkled the raw flesh with powder from the little bag. The pain of the wound was as nothing to the exquisite torture of the remedy but, accustomed to physical suffering, the ape-man withstood it stoically and in a few moments not only had the bleeding ceased but the pain as well.

In reply to the soft and far from unpleasant modulations of the other's voice, Tarzan spoke in various tribal dialects of the interior as well as in the language of the great apes, but it was evident that the man understood none of these. Seeing that they could not make each other understood, the pithecanthropus advanced toward Tarzan and placing his left hand over his own heart laid the palm of his right hand over the heart of the ape-man. To the latter the action appeared as a form of friendly greeting and, being versed in the ways of uncivilized races, he responded in kind as he realized it was doubtless intended that he should. His action seemed to satisfy and please his new-found acquaintance, who immediately fell to talking again and finally, with his head tipped back, sniffed the air in the direction of the tree above them and then suddenly pointing toward the carcass of Bara, the deer, he touched his stomach in a sign language which even the densest might interpret. With a wave of his hand Tarzan invited his guest to partake of the remains of his savage repast, and the other, leaping nimbly as a little monkey to the lower branches of the tree, made his way quickly to the flesh, assisted always by his long, strong sinuous tail.

The pithecanthropus ate in silence, cutting small strips from the deer's loin with his keen knife. From his crotch in the tree Tarzan watched his companion, noting the preponderance of human attributes which were doubtless accentuated by the paradoxical thumbs, great toes, and tail.

He wondered if this creature was representative of some strange race or if, what seemed more likely, but an atavism. Either supposition would have seemed preposterous enough did he not have before him the evidence of the creature's existence. There he was, however, a tailed man with distinctly arboreal hands and feet. His trappings, gold encrusted and jewel studded, could have been wrought only by skilled artisans; but whether they were the work of this individual or of others like him, or of an entirely different race, Tarzan could not, of course, determine.

His meal finished, the guest wiped his fingers and lips with

leaves broken from a nearby branch, looked up at Tarzan
with a pleasant smile that revealed a row of strong white
teeth, the canines of which were no longer than Tarzan's own,
spoke a few words which Tarzan judged were a polite expression of thanks and then sought a comfortable place in the
tree for the night.

The earth was shadowed in the darkness which precedes
the dawn when Tarzan was awakened by a violent shaking
of the tree in which he had found shelter. As he opened his
eyes he saw that his companion was also astir, and glancing
around quickly to apprehend the cause of the disturbance,
the ape-man was astounded at the sight which met his eyes.

The dim shadow of a colossal form reared close beside
the tree and he saw that it was the scraping of the giant body
against the branches that had awakened him. That such a
tremendous creature could have approached so closely without disturbing him filled Tarzan with both wonderment and
chagrin. In the gloom the ape-man at first conceived the intruder to be an elephant; yet, if so, one of greater proportions
than any he had ever before seen, but as the dim outlines became less indistinct he saw on a line with his eyes and twenty
feet above the ground the dim silhouette of a grotesquely
serrated back that gave the impression of a creature whose
each and every spinal vertebra grew a thick, heavy horn.
Only a portion of the back was visible to the ape-man, the
rest of the body being lost in the dense shadows beneath the
tree, from whence there now arose the sound of giant jaws
powerfully crunching flesh and bones. From the odors that
rose to the ape-man's sensitive nostrils he presently realized
that beneath him was some huge reptile feeding upon the
carcass of the lion that had been slain there earlier in the
night.

As Tarzan's eyes, straining with curiosity, bored futilely
into the dark shadows he felt a light touch upon his shoulder,
and, turning, saw that his companion was attempting to attract his attention. The creature, pressing a forefinger to his
own lips as to enjoin silence, attempted by pulling on Tarzan's arm to indicate that they should leave at once.

Realizing that he was in a strange country, evidently infested by creatures of titanic size, with the habits and powers
of which he was entirely unfamiliar, the ape-man permitted
himself to be drawn away. With the utmost caution the
pithecanthropus descended the tree upon the opposite side
from the great nocturnal prowler, and, closely followed by
Tarzan, moved silently away through the night across the
plain.

The ape-man was rather loath thus to relinquish an opportunity to inspect a creature which he realized was probably entirely different from anything in his past experience; yet he was wise enough to know when discretion was the better part of valor and now, as in the past, he yielded to that law which dominates the kindred of the wild, preventing them from courting danger uselessly, whose lives are sufficiently filled with danger in their ordinary routine of feeding and mating.

As the rising sun dispelled the shadows of the night, Tarzan found himself again upon the verge of a great forest into which his guide plunged, taking nimbly to the branches of the trees through which he made his way with the celerity of long habitude and hereditary instinct, but though aided by a prehensile tail, fingers, and toes, the man-thing moved through the forest with no greater ease or surety than did the giant ape-man.

It was during this journey that Tarzan recalled the wound in his side inflicted upon him the previous night by the raking talons of Numa, the lion, and examining it was surprised to discover that not only was it painless but along its edges were no indications of inflamation, the results doubtless of the antiseptic powder his strange companion had sprinkled upon it.

They had proceeded for a mile or two when Tarzan's companion came to earth upon a grassy slope beneath a great tree whose branches overhung a clear brook. Here they drank and Tarzan discovered the water to be not only deliciously pure and fresh but of an icy temperature that indicated its rapid descent from the lofty mountains of its origin.

Casting aside his loin cloth and weapons Tarzan entered the little pool beneath the tree and after a moment emerged, greatly refreshed and filled with a keen desire to breakfast. As he came out of the pool he noticed his companion examining him with a puzzled expression upon his face. Taking the ape-man by the shoulder he turned him around so that Tarzan's back was toward him and then, touching the end of Tarzan's spine with his forefinger, he curled his own tail up over his shoulder and, wheeling the ape-man about again, pointed first at Tarzan and then at his own caudal appendage, a look of puzzlement upon his face, the while he jabbered excitedly in his strange tongue.

The ape-man realized that probably for the first time his companion had discovered that he was tailless by nature rather than by accident, and so he called attention to his own great toes and thumbs to further impress upon the creature that they were of different species.

The fellow shook his head dubiously as though entirely unable to comprehend why Tarzan should differ so from him but at last, apparently giving the problem up with a shrug, he laid aside his own harness, skin, and weapons and entered the pool.

His ablutions completed and his meager apparel redonned he seated himself at the foot of the tree and motioning Tarzan to a place beside him, opened the pouch that hung at his right side taking from it strips of dried flesh and a couple of handfuls of thin-shelled nuts with which Tarzan was unfamiliar. Seeing the other break them with his teeth and eat the kernel, Tarzan followed the example thus set him, discovering the meat to be rich and well flavored. The dried flesh also was far from unpalatable, though it had evidently been jerked without salt, a commodity which Tarzan imagined might be rather difficult to obtain in this locality.

As they ate Tarzan's companion pointed to the nuts, the dried meat, and various other nearby objects, in each instance repeating what Tarzan readily discovered must be the names of these things in the creature's native language. The apeman could but smile at this evident desire upon the part of his new-found acquaintance to impart to him instructions that eventually might lead to an exchange of thoughts between them. Having already mastered several languages and a multitude of dialects the ape-man felt that he could readily assimilate another even though this appeared one entirely unrelated to any with which he was familiar.

So occupied were they with their breakfast and the lesson that neither was aware of the beady eyes glittering down úpon them from above; nor was Tarzan cognizant of any impending danger until the instant that a huge, hairy body leaped full upon his companion from the branches above them.

2

"To the Death!"

IN THE moment of discovery Tarzan saw that the creature
was almost a counterpart of his companion in size and
conformation, with the exception that his body was entirely clothed with a coat of shaggy black hair which almost concealed his features, while his harness and weapons were similar
to those of the creature he had attacked. Ere Tarzan could
prevent the creature had struck the ape-man's companion a
blow upon the head with his knotted club that felled him, unconscious, to the earth; but before he could inflict further injury upon his defenseless prey the ape-man had closed with
him.

Instantly Tarzan realized that he was locked with a creature of almost superhuman strength. The sinewy fingers of
a powerful hand sought his throat while the other lifted the
bludgeon above his head. But if the strength of the hairy
attacker was great, great too was that of his smooth-skinned
antagonist. Swinging a single terrific blow with clenched fist
to the point of the other's chin, Tarzan momentarily staggered
his assailant and then his own fingers closed upon the shaggy
throat, as with the other hand he seized the wrist of the arm
that swung the club. With equal celerity he shot his right leg
behind the shaggy brute and throwing his weight forward
hurled the thing over his hip heavily to the ground, at the
same time precipitating his own body upon the other's chest.

With the shock of the impact the club fell from the brute's
hand and Tarzan's hold was wrenched from its throat. Instantly the two were locked in a deathlike embrace. Though
the creature bit at Tarzan the latter was quickly aware that
this was not a particularly formidable method of offense or
defense, since its canines were scarcely more developed than
his own. The thing that he had principally to guard against
was the sinuous tail which sought steadily to wrap itself about
his throat and against which experience had afforded him no
defense.

Struggling and snarling the two rolled growling about the sward at the foot of the tree, first one on top and then the other but each more occupied at present in defending his throat from the other's choking grasp than in aggressive, offensive tactics. But presently the ape-man saw his opportunity and as they rolled about he forced the creature closer and closer to the pool, upon the banks of which the battle was progressing. At last they lay upon the very verge of the water and now it remained for Tarzan to precipitate them both beneath the surface but in such a way that he might remain on top.

At the same instant there came within range of Tarzan's vision, just behind the prostrate form of his companion, the crouching, devil-faced figure of the striped saber-tooth hybrid, eyeing him with snarling, malevolent face.

Almost simultaneously Tarzan's shaggy antagonist discovered the menacing figure of the great cat. Immediately he ceased his belligerent activities against Tarzan and, jabbering and chattering to the ape-man, he tried to disengage himself from Tarzan's hold but in such a way that indicated that as far as he was concerned their battle was over. Appreciating the danger to his unconscious companion and being anxious to protect him from the saber-tooth the ape-man relinquished his hold upon his adversary and together the two rose to their feet.

Drawing his knife Tarzan moved slowly toward the body of his companion, expecting that his recent antagonist would grasp the opportunity for escape. To his surprise, however, the beast, after regaining its club, advanced at his side.

The great cat, flattened upon its belly, remained motionless except for twitching tail and snarling lips where it lay perhaps fifty feet beyond the body of the pithecanthropus. As Tarzan stepped over the body of the latter he saw the eyelids quiver and open, and in his heart he felt a strange sense of relief that the creature was not dead and a realization that without his suspecting it there had arisen within his savage bosom a bond of attachment for this strange new friend.

Tarzan continued to approach the saber-tooth, nor did the shaggy beast at his right lag behind. Closer and closer they came until at a distance of about twenty feet the hybrid charged. Its rush was directed toward the shaggy manlike ape who halted in his tracks with upraised bludgeon to meet the assault. Tarzan, on the contrary, leaped forward and with a celerity second not even to that of the swift-moving cat, he threw himself headlong upon him as might a Rugby tackler on an American gridiron. His right arm circled the beast's neck in front of the right shoulder, his left behind the left foreleg, and so great was the force of the impact that the two rolled over and over several times upon the ground, the cat screaming and clawing to liberate itself that it might turn upon its attacker, the man clinging desperately to his hold.

Seemingly the attack was one of mad, senseless ferocity unguided by either reason or skill. Nothing, however, could have been farther from the truth than such an assumption since every muscle in the ape-man's giant frame obeyed the dictates of the cunning mind that long experience had trained to meet every exigency of such an encounter. The long, powerful legs, though seemingly inextricably entangled with the hind feet of the clawing cat, ever as by a miracle, escaped the raking talons and yet at just the proper instant in the midst of all the rolling and tossing they were where they should be to carry out the ape-man's plan of offense. So that on the instant that the cat believed it had won the mastery of its antagonist it was jerked suddenly upward as the ape-man rose to his feet, holding the striped back close against his body as he rose and forcing it backward until it could but claw the air helplessly.

Instantly the shaggy black rushed in with drawn knife which it buried in the beast's heart. For a few moments Tarzan retained his hold but when the body had relaxed in final dissolution he pushed it from him and the two who had formerly been locked in mortal combat stood facing each other across the body of the common foe.

Tarzan waited, ready either for peace or war. Presently two shaggy black hands were raised; the left was laid upon its own heart and the right extended until the palm touched Tarzan's breast. It was the same form of friendly salutation with which the pithecanthropus had sealed his alliance with the ape-man and Tarzan, glad of every ally he could win in this strange and savage world, quickly accepted the proffered friendship.

At the conclusion of the brief ceremony Tarzan, glancing in the direction of the hairless pithecanthropus, discovered that the latter had recovered consciousness and was sitting erect watching them intently. He now rose slowly and at the same time the shaggy black turned in his direction and addressed him in what evidently was their common language. The hairless one replied and the two approached each other slowly. Tarzan watched interestedly the outcome of their meeting. They halted a few paces apart, first one and then the other speaking rapidly but without apparent excitement, each oc-

casionally glancing or nodding toward Tarzan, indicating
that he was to some extent the subject of their conversation.

Presently they advanced again until they met, whereupon
was repeated the brief ceremony of alliance which had previously marked the cessation of hostilities between Tarzan and
the black. They then advanced toward the ape-man addressing him earnestly as though endeavoring to convey to him some
important information. Presently, however, they gave it up
as an unprofitable job and, resorting to sign language, conveyed to Tarzan that they were proceeding upon their way
together and were urging him to accompany them.

As the direction they indicated was a route which Tarzan
had not previously traversed he was extremely willing to accede to their request, as he had determined thoroughly to
explore this unknown land before definitely abandoning search
for Lady Jane therein.

For several days their way led through the foothills parallel to the lofty range towering above. Often were they menaced by the savage denizens of this remote fastness, and occasionally Tarzan glimpsed weird forms of gigantic proportions amidst the shadows of the nights.

On the third day they came upon a large natural cave in
the face of a low cliff at the foot of which tumbled one of the
numerous mountain brooks that watered the plain below and
fed the morasses in the lowlands at the country's edge. Here
the three took up their temporary abode where Tarzan's instruction in the language of his companions progressed more
rapidly than while on the march.

The cave gave evidence of having harbored other manlike
forms in the past. Remnants of a crude, rock fireplace remained and the walls and ceiling were blackened with the
smoke of many fires. Scratched in the soot, and sometimes
deeply into the rock beneath, were strange hieroglyphics and
the outlines of beasts and birds and reptiles, some of the latter
of weird form suggesting the extinct creatures of Jurassic
times. Some of the more recently made hieroglyphics Tarzan's companions read with interest and commented upon,
and then with the points of their knives they too added to
the possibly age-old record of the blackened walls.

Tarzan's curiosity was aroused, but the only explanation
at which he could arrive was that he was looking upon possibly the world's most primitive hotel register. At least it
gave him a further insight into the development of the strange
creatures with which Fate had thrown him. Here were men
with the tails of monkeys, one of them as hair covered as
any fur-bearing brute of the lower orders, and yet it was evi-

dent that they possessed not only a spoken, but a written language. The former he was slowly mastering and at this new evidence of unlooked-for civilization in creatures possessing so many of the physical attributes of beasts, Tarzan's curiosity was still further piqued and his desire quickly to master their tongue strengthened, with the result that he fell to with even greater assiduity to the task he had set himself. Already he knew the names of his companions and the common names of the fauna and flora with which they had most often come in contact.

Ta-den, he of the hairless, white skin, having assumed the rôle of tutor, prosecuted his task with a singleness of purpose that was reflected in his pupil's rapid mastery of Ta-den's mother tongue. Om-at, the hairy black, also seemed to feel that there rested upon his broad shoulders a portion of the burden of responsibility for Tarzan's education, with the result that either one or the other of them was almost constantly coaching the ape-man during his waking hours. The result was only what might have been expected—a rapid assimilation of the teachings to the end that before any of them realized it, communication by word of mouth became an accomplished fact.

Tarzan explained to his companions the purpose of his mission but neither could give him any slightest thread of hope to weave into the fabric of his longing. Never had there been in their country a woman such as he described, nor any tailless man other than himself that they ever had seen.

"I have been gone from A-lur while Bu, the moon, has eaten seven times," said Ta-den. "Many things may happen in seven times twenty-eight days; but I doubt that your woman could have entered our country across the terrible morasses which even you found an almost insurmountable obstacle, and if she had, could she have survived the perils that you already have encountered beside those of which you have yet to learn? Not even our own women venture into the savage lands beyond the cities."

"'A-lur,' Light-city, City of Light," mused Tarzan, translating the word into his own tongue. "And where is A-lur?" he asked. "Is it your city, Ta-den, and Om-at's?"

"It is mine," replied the hairless one; "but not Om-at's. The Waz-don have no cities—they live in the trees of the forests and the caves of the hills—is it not so, *black man?*" he concluded, turning toward the hairy giant beside him.

"Yes," replied Om-at, "We Waz-don are free—only the Ho-don imprison themselves in cities. I would not be a white man!"

Tarzan smiled. Even here was the racial distinction between white man and black man—Ho-don and Waz-don. Not even the fact that they appeared to be equals in the matter of intelligence made any difference—one was white and one was black, and it was easy to see that the white considered himself superior to the other—one could see it in his quiet smile.

"Where is A-lur?" Tarzan asked again. "You are returning to it?"

"It is beyond the mountains," replied Ta-den. "I do not return to it—not yet. Not until Ko-tan is no more."

"Ko-tan?" queried Tarzan.

"Ko-tan is king," explained the pithecanthropus. "He rules this land. I was one of his warriors. I lived in the palace of Ko-tan and there I met O-lo-a, his daughter. We loved, Like-star-light, and I; but Ko-tan would have none of me. He sent me away to fight with the men of the village of Dak-at, who had refused to pay his tribute to the king, thinking that I would be killed, for Dak-at is famous for his many fine warriors. And I was not killed. Instead I returned victorious with the tribute and with Dak-at himself my prisoner; but Ko-tan was not pleased because he saw that O-lo-a loved me even more than before, her love being strengthened and fortified by pride in my achievement.

"Powerful is my father, Ja-don, the Lion-man, chief of the largest village outside of A-lur. Him Ko-tan hesitated to affront and so he could not but praise me for my success, though he did it with half a smile. But you do not understand! It is what we call a smile that moves only the muscles of the face and effects not the light of the eyes—it means hypocrisy and duplicity. I must be praised and rewarded. What better than that he reward me with the hand of O-lo-a, his daughter? But no, he saves O-lo-a for Bu-lot, son of Mo-sar, the chief whose great-grandfather was king and who thinks that he should be king. Thus would Ko-tan appease the wrath of Mo-sar and win the friendship of those who think with Mo-sar that Mo-sar should be king.

"But what reward shall repay the faithful Ta-den? Greatly do we honor our priests. Within the temples even the chiefs and the king himself bow down to them. No greater honor could Ko-tan confer upon a subject—who wished to be a priest; but I did not so wish. Priests other than the high priest must become eunuchs for they may never marry.

"It was O-lo-a herself who brought word to me that her father had given the commands that would set in motion the machinery of the temple. A messenger was on his way in search of me to summon me to Ko-tan's presence. To have refused the priesthood once it was offered me by the king would have been to have affronted the temple and the gods —that would have meant death; but if I did not appear before Ko-tan I would not have to refuse anything. O-lo-a and I decided that I must not appear. It was better to fly, carrying in my bosom a shred of hope, than to remain and, with my priesthood, abandon hope forever.

"Beneath the shadows of the great trees that grow within the palace grounds I pressed her to me for, perhaps, the last time and then, lest by ill-fate I meet the messenger, I scaled the great wall that guards the palace and passed through the darkened city. My name and rank carried me beyond the city gate. Since then I have wandered far from the haunts of the Ho-don but strong within me is the urge to return if even but to look from without her walls upon the city that holds her most dear to me and again to visit the village of my birth, to see again my father and my mother."

"But the risk is too great?" asked Tarzan.

"It is great, but not too great," replied Ta-den. "I shall go."

"And I shall go with you, if I may," said the ape-man, "for I must see this City of Light, this A-lur of yours, and search there for my lost mate even though you believe that there is little chance that I find her. And you, Om-at, do you come with us?"

"Why not?" asked the hairy one. "The lairs of my tribe lie in the crags above A-lur and though Es-sat, our chief, drove me out I should like to return again, for there is a she there upon whom I should be glad to look once more and who would be glad to look upon me. Yes, I will go with you. Es-sat feared that I might become chief and who knows but that Es-sat was right. But Pan-at-lee! it is she I seek first even before a chieftainship."

"We three, then, shall travel together," said Tarzan.

"And fight together," added Ta-den; "the three as one," and as he spoke he drew his knife and held it above his head.

"The three as one," repeated Om-at, drawing his weapon and duplicating Ta-den's act. "It is spoken!"

"The three as one!" cried Tarzan of the Apes. "To the death!" and his blade flashed in the sunlight.

"Let us go, then," said Om-at; "my knife is dry and cries aloud for the blood of Es-sat."

The trail over which Ta-den and Om-at led and which scarcely could be dignified even by the name of trail was suited more to mountain sheep, monkeys, or birds than to man; but the three that followed it were trained to ways which no ordinary man might essay. Now, upon the lower slopes, it led through dense forests where the ground was so matted with fallen trees and over-rioting vines and brush that the way held always to the swaying branches high above the tangle; again it skirted yawning gorges whose slippery-faced rocks gave but momentary foothold even to the bare feet that lightly touched them as the three leaped chamois-like from one precarious foothold to the next. Dizzy and terrifying was the way that Om-at chose across the summit as he led them around the shoulder of a towering crag that rose a sheer two thousand feet of perpendicular rock above a tumbling river. And when at last they stood upon comparatively level ground again Om-at turned and looked at them both intently and especially at Tarzan of the Apes.

"You will both do," he said. "You are fit companions for Om-at, the Waz-don."

"What do you mean?" asked Tarzan.

"I brought you this way," replied the black, "to learn if either lacked the courage to follow where Om-at led. It is here that the young warriors of Es-sat come to prove their courage. And yet, though we are born and raised upon cliff sides, it is considered no disgrace to admit that Pastar-ul-ved, the Father of Mountains, has defeated us, for of those who try it only a few succeed—the bones of the others lie at the feet of Pastar-ul-ved."

Ta-den laughed. "I would not care to come this way often," he said.

"No," replied Om-at; "but it has shortened our journey by at least a full day. So much the sooner shall Tarzan look upon the Valley of Jad-ben-Otho. Come!" and he led the way upward along the shoulder of Pastar-ul-ved until there lay spread below them a scene of mystery and of beauty—a green valley girt by towering cliffs of marble whiteness—a green valley dotted by deep blue lakes and crossed by the blue trail of a winding river. In the center a city of the whiteness of the marble cliffs—a city which even at so great a distance evidenced a strange, yet artistic architecture. Outside the city there were visible about the valley isolated groups of buildings—sometimes one, again two and three and four in a cluster—but always of the same glaring whiteness, and always in some fantastic form.

About the valley the cliffs were occasionally cleft by deep gorges, verdure filled, giving the appearance of green rivers rioting downward toward a central sea of green.

"Jad Pele ul Jad-ben-Otho," murmured Tarzan in the

tongue of the pithecanthropi; *"The Valley of the Great God* —it is beautiful!"

"Here, in A-lur, lives Ko-tan, the king, ruler over all Pal-ul-don," said Ta-den.

"And here in these gorges live the Waz-don," exclaimed Om-at, "who do not acknowledge that Ko-tan is the ruler over all the *Land-of-man.*"

Ta-den smiled and shrugged. "We will not quarrel, you and I," he said to Om-at, "over that which all the ages have not proved sufficient time in which to reconcile the Ho-don and Waz-don; but let me whisper to you a secret, Om-at. The Ho-don live together in greater or less peace under one ruler so that when danger threatens them they face the enemy with many warriors, for every fighting Ho-don of Pal-ul-don is there. But you Waz-don, how is it with you? You have a dozen kings who fight not only with the Ho-don but with one another. When one of your tribes goes forth upon the fighting trail, even against the Ho-don, it must leave behind sufficient warriors to protect its women and its children from the neighbors upon either hand. When we want eunuchs for the temples or servants for the fields or the homes we march forth in great numbers upon one of your villages. You cannot even flee, for upon either side of you are enemies and though you fight bravely we come back with those who will presently be eunuchs in the temples and servants in our fields and homes. So long as the Waz-don are thus foolish the Ho-don will dominate and their king will be king of Pal-ul-don."

"Perhaps you are right," admitted Om-at. "It is because our neighbors are fools, each thinking that his tribe is the greatest and should rule among the Waz-don. They will not admit that the warriors of my tribe are the bravest and our shes the most beautiful."

Ta-den grinned. "Each of the others presents precisely the same arguments that you present, Om-at," he said, "which, my friend, is the strongest bulwark of defense possessed by the Ho-don."

"Come!" exclaimed Tarzan; "such discussions often lead to quarrels and we three must have no quarrels. I, of course, am interested in learning what I can of the political and economic conditions of your land; I should like to know something of your religion; but not at the expense of bitterness between my only friends in Pal-ul-don. Possibly, however, you hold to the same god?"

"There indeed we do differ," cried Om-at, somewhat bitterly and with a trace of excitement in his voice.

"Differ!" almost shouted Ta-den; "and why should we not differ? Who could agree with the preposterous——"

"Stop!" cried Tarzan. "Now, indeed, have I stirred up a hornets' nest. Let us speak no more of matters political or religious."

"That is wiser," agreed Om-at; "but I might mention, for your information, that the one and only god has a long tail."

"It is sacrilege," cried Ta-den, laying his hand upon his knife; "Jad-ben-Otho has no tail!"

"Stop!" shrieked Om-at, springing forward; but instantly Tarzan interposed himself between them.

"Enough!" he snapped. "Let us be true to our oaths of friendship that we may be honorable in the sight of God in whatever form we conceive Him."

"You are right, Tailless One," said Ta-den. "Come, Om-at, let us look after our friendship and ourselves, secure in the conviction that Jad-ben-Otho is sufficiently powerful to look after himself."

"Done!" agreed Om-at, "but——"

"No 'buts,' Om-at," admonished Tarzan.

The shaggy black shrugged his shoulders and smiled. "Shall we make our way down toward the valley?" he asked. "The gorge below us is uninhabited; that to the left contains the caves of my people. I would see Pan-at-lee once more. Ta-den would visit his father in the valley below and Tarzan seeks entrance to A-lur in search of the mate that would be better dead than in the clutches of the Ho-don priests of Jad-ben-Otho. How shall we proceed?"

"Let us remain together as long as possible," urged Ta-den. "You, Om-at, must seek Pan-at-lee by night and by stealth, for three, even we three, may not hope to overcome Es-sat and all his warriors. At any time may we go to the village where my father is chief, for Ja-don always will welcome the friends of his son. But for Tarzan to enter A-lur is another matter, though there is a way and he has the courage to put it to the test—listen, come close for Jad-ben-Otho has keen ears and this he must not hear," and with his lips close to the ears of his companions Ta-den, the Tall-tree, son of Ja-don, the Lion-man, unfolded his daring plan.

And at the same moment, a hundred miles away, a lithe figure, naked but for a loin cloth and weapons, moved silently across a thorn-covered, waterless steppe, searching always along the ground before him with keen eyes and sensitive nostrils.

3

Pan-at-lee

Night had fallen upon unchartered Pal-ul-don. A slender
moon, low in the west, bathed the white faces of the
chalk cliffs presented to her, in a mellow, unearthly
glow. Black were the shadows in Kor-ul-ja, Gorge-of-lions,
where dwelt the tribe of the same name under Es-sat, their
chief. From an aperture near the summit of the lofty escarpment a hairy figure emerged—the head and shoulders first—
and fierce eyes scanned the cliff side in every direction.

It was Es-sat, the chief. To right and left and below he
looked as though to assure himself that he was unobserved,
but no other figure moved upon the cliff face, nor did another
hairy body protrude from any of the numerous cave mouths
from the high-flung abode of the chief to the habitations of
the more lowly members of the tribe nearer the cliff's base.
Then he moved outward upon the sheer face of the white
chalk wall. In the half-light of the baby moon it appeared
that the heavy, shaggy black figure moved across the face
of the perpendicular wall in some miraculous manner, but
closer examination would have revealed stout pegs, as large
around as a man's wrist protruding from holes in the cliff
into which they were driven. Es-sat's four handlike members and his long, sinuous tail permitted him to move with
consummate ease whither he chose—a gigantic rat upon a
mighty wall. As he progressed upon his way he avoided the
cave mouths, passing either above or below those that lay in
his path.

The outward appearance of these caves was similar. An
opening from eight to as much as twenty feet long by eight
high and four to six feet deep was cut into the chalklike rock
of the cliff, in the back of this large opening, which formed
what might be described as the front veranda of the home,
was an opening about three feet wide and six feet high, evidently forming the doorway to the interior apartment or
apartments. On either side of this doorway were smaller

openings which it were easy to assume were windows through which light and air might find their way to the inhabitants. Similar windows were also dotted over the cliff face between the entrance porches, suggesting that the entire face of the cliff was honeycombed with apartments. From many of these smaller apertures small streams of water trickled down the escarpment, and the walls above others was blackened as by smoke. Where the water ran the wall was eroded to a depth of from a few inches to as much as a foot, suggesting that some of the tiny streams had been trickling downward to the green carpet of vegetation below for ages.

In this primeval setting the great pithecanthropus aroused no jarring discord for he was as much a part of it as the trees that grew upon the summit of the cliff or those that hid their feet among the dank ferns in the bottom of the gorge.

Now he paused before an entrance-way and listened and then, noiselessly as the moonlight upon the trickling waters, he merged with the shadows of the outer porch. At the doorway leading into the interior he paused again, listening, and then quietly pushing aside the heavy skin that covered the aperture he passed within a large chamber hewn from the living rock. From the far end, through another doorway, shone a light, dimly. Toward this he crept with utmost stealth, his naked feet giving forth no sound. The knotted club that had been hanging at his back from a thong about his neck he now removed and carried in his left hand.

Beyond the second doorway was a corridor running parallel with the cliff face. In this corridor were three more doorways, one at each end and a third almost opposite that in which Es-sat stood. The light was coming from an apartment at the end of the corridor at his left. A sputtering flame rose and fell in a small stone receptacle that stood upon a table or bench of the same material, a monolithic bench fashioned at the time the room was excavated, rising massively from the floor, of which it was a part.

In one corner of the room beyond the table had been left a dais of stone about four feet wide and eight feet long. Upon this were piled a foot or so of softly tanned pelts from which the fur had not been removed. Upon the edge of this dais sat a young female Waz-don. In one hand she held a thin piece of metal, apparently of hammered gold, with serrated edges, and in the other a short, stiff brush. With these she was occupied in going over her smooth, glossy coat which bore a remarkable resemblance to plucked sealskin. Her loin cloth of yellow and black striped *jato*-skin lay on the couch beside her with the circular breastplates of beaten gold, revealing the symmetrical lines of her nude figure in all its beauty and harmony of contour, for even though the creature was jet black and entirely covered with hair yet she was undeniably beautiful.

That she was beautiful in the eyes of Es-sat, the chief, was evidenced by the gloating expression upon his fierce countenance and the increased rapidity of his breathing. Moving quickly forward he entered the room and as he did so the young she looked up. Instantly her eyes filled with terror and as quickly she seized the loin cloth and with a few deft movements adjusted it about her. As she gathered up her breastplates Es-sat rounded the table and moved quickly toward her.

"What do you want?" she whispered, though she knew full well.

"Pan-at-lee," he said, "your chief has come for you."

"It was for this that you sent away my father and my brothers to spy upon the Kor-ul-lul? I will not have you. Leave the cave of my ancestors!"

Es-sat smiled. It was the smile of a strong and wicked man who knows his power—not a pleasant smile at all. "I will leave, Pan-at-lee," he said; "but you shall go with me—to the cave of Es-sat, the chief, to be the envied of the shes of Kor-ul-ja. Come!"

"Never!" cried Pan-at-lee. "I hate you. Sooner would I mate with a Ho-don than with you, beater of women, murderer of babes."

A frightful scowl distorted the features of the chief. "She-jato!" he cried. "I will tame you! I will break you! Es-sat, the chief, takes what he will and who dares question his right, or combat his least purpose, will first serve that purpose and then be broken as I break this," and he picked a stone platter from the table and broke it in his powerful hands. "You might have been first and most favored in the cave of the ancestors of Es-sat; but now shall you be last and least and when I am done with you you shall belong to all of the men of Es-sat's cave. Thus for those who spurn the love of their chief!"

He advanced quickly to seize her and as he laid a rough hand upon her she struck him heavily upon the side of his head with her golden breastplates. Without a sound Es-sat, the chief, sank to the floor of the apartment. For a moment Pan-at-lee bent over him, her improvised weapon raised to strike again should he show signs of returning consciousness, her glossy breasts rising and falling with her quickened breathing. Suddenly she stooped and removed Es-sat's knife

with its scabbard and shoulder belt. Slipping it over her own
shoulder she quickly adjusted her breastplates and keeping
a watchful glance upon the figure of the fallen chief, backed
from the room.

In a niche in the outer room, just beside the doorway leading to the balcony, were neatly piled a number of rounded
pegs from eighteen to twenty inches in length. Selecting five
of these she made them into a little bundle about which she
twined the lower extremity of her sinuous tail and thus carrying them made her way to the outer edge of the balcony.
Assuring herself that there was none about to see, or hinder
her, she took quickly to the pegs already set in the face of
the cliff and with the celerity of a monkey clambered swiftly
aloft to the highest row of pegs which she followed in the
direction of the lower end of the gorge for a matter of some
hundred yards. Here, above her head, were a series of small
round holes placed one above another in three parallel rows.
Clinging only with her toes she removed two of the pegs from
the bundle carried in her tail and taking one in either hand
she inserted them in two opposite holes of the outer rows
as far above her as she could reach. Hanging by these new
holds she now took one of the three remaining pegs in each
of her feet, leaving the fifth grasped securely in her tail.
Reaching above her with this member she inserted the fifth
peg in one of the holes of the center row and then, alternately
hanging by her tail, her feet, or her hands, she moved the
pegs upward to new holes, thus carrying her stairway with her
as she ascended.

At the summit of the cliff a gnarled tree exposed its time-
worn roots above the topmost holes forming the last step from
the sheer face of the precipice to level footing. This was the
last avenue of escape for members of the tribe hard pressed
by enemies from blow. There were three such emergncy
exits from the village and it were death to use them in other
than an emergency. This Pan-at-lee well knew; but she knew,
too, that it were worse than death to remain where the angered
Es-sat might lay hands upon her.

When she had gained the summit, the girl moved quickly
through the darkness in the direction of the next gorge which
cut the mountain-side a mile beyond Kor-ul-ja. It was the
Gorge-of-water, Kor-ul-lul, to which her father and two brothers had been sent by Es-sat ostensibly to spy upon the neighboring tribe. There was a chance, a slender chance, that she
might find them; if not there was the deserted Kor-ul-gryf
several miles beyond, where she might hide indefinitely from
man if she could elude the frightful monster from which the

gorge derived its name and whose presence there had rendered its caves uninhabitable for generations.

Pan-at-lee crept stealthily along the rim of the Kor-ul-lul. Just where her father and brothers would watch she did not know. Sometimes their spies remained upon the rim, sometimes they watched from the gorge's bottom. Pan-at-lee was at a loss to know what to do or where to go. She felt very small and helpless alone in the vast darkness of the night. Strange noises fell upon her ears. They came from the lonely reaches of the towering mountains above her, from far away in the invisible valley and from the nearer foothills and once, in the distance, she heard what she thought was the bellow of a bull *gryf*. It came from the direction of the Kor-ul-gryf. She shuddered.

Presently there came to her keen ears another sound. Something approached her along the rim of the gorge. It was coming from above. She halted, listening. Perhaps it was her father, or a brother. It was coming closer. She strained her eyes through the darkness. She did not move—she scarcely breathed. And then, of a sudden, quite close it seemed, there blazed through the black night two yellow-green spots of fire.

Pan-at-lee was brave, but as always with the primitive, the darkness held infinite terrors for her. Not alone the terrors of the known but more frightful ones as well—those of the unknown. She had passed through much this night and her nerves were keyed to the highest pitch—raw, taut nerves, they were, ready to react in an exaggerated form to the slightest shock.

But this was no slight shock. To hope for a father and a brother and to see death instead glaring out of the darkness! Yes, Pan-at-lee was brave, but she was not of iron. With a shriek that reverberated among the hills she turned and fled along the rim of Kor-ul-lul and behind her, swiftly, came the devil-eyed lion of the mountains of Pal-ul-don.

Pan-at-lee was lost. Death was inevitable. Of this there could be no doubt, but to die beneath the rending fangs of the carnivore, congenital terror of her kind—it was unthinkable. But there was an alternative. The lion was almost upon her—another instant and he would seize her. Pan-at-lee turned sharply to her left. Just a few steps she took in the new direction before she disappeared over the rim of Kor-ul-lul. The baffled lion, planting all four feet, barely stopped upon the verge of the abyss. Glaring down into the black shadows beneath he mounted an angry roar.

Through the darkness at the bottom of Kor-ul-ja, Om-at led

the way toward the caves of his people. Behind him came
Tarzan and Ta-den. Presently they halted beneath a great
tree that grew close to the cliff.

"First," whispered Om-at, "I will go to the cave of Pan-at-
lee. Then will I seek the cave of my ancestors to have speech
with my own blood. It will not take long. Wait here—I shall
return soon. Afterward shall we go together to Ta-den's
people."

He moved silently toward the foot of the cliff up which
Tar an could presently see him ascending like a great fly on
a wall. In the dim light the ape-man could not see the pegs
set in the face of the cliff. Om-at moved warily. In the lower
tier of caves there should be a sentry. His knowledge of his
people and their customs told him, however, that in all proba-
bility the sentry was asleep. In this he was not mistaken, yet
he did not in any way abate his wariness. Smoothly and
swiftly he ascended toward the cave of Pan-at-lee while from
below Tarzan and Ta-den watched him.

"How does he do it?" asked Tarzan. "I can see no foothold
upon that vertical surface and yet he appears to be climbing
with the utmost ease."

Ta-den explained the stairway of pegs. "You could ascend
easily," he said, "although a tail would be of great assistance."

They watched until Om-at was about to enter the cave of
Pan-at-lee without seeing any indication that he had been
observed and then, simultaneously, both saw a head appear
in the mouth of one of the lower caves. It was quickly evident
that its owner had discovered Om-at for immediately he started
upward in pursuit. Without a word Tarzan and Ta-den sprang
forward toward the foot of the cliff. The pithecanthropus was
the first to reach it and the ape-man saw him spring upward
for a handhold on the lowest peg above him. Now Tarzan saw
other pegs roughly paralleling each other in zigzag rows up the
cliff face. He sprang and caught one of these, pulled himself
upward by one hand until he could reach a second with his
other hand; and when he had ascended far enough to use his
feet, discovered that he could make rapid progress. Ta-den
was outstripping him, however, for these precarious ladders
were no novelty to him and, further, he had an advantage in
possessing a tail.

Nevertheless, the ape-man gave a good account of himself,
being presently urged to redoubled efforts by the fact that the
Waz-don above Ta-den glanced down and discovered his pursuers just before the Ho-don overtook him. Instantly a wild
cry shattered the silence of the gorge—a cry that was imme-

diately answered by hundreds of savage throats as warrior after warrior emerged from the entrance to his cave.

The creature who had raised the alarm had now reached the recess before Pan-at-lee's cave and here he halted and turned to give battle to Ta-den. Unslinging his club which had hung down his back from a thong about his neck he stood upon the level floor of the entrance-way effectually blocking Ta-den's ascent. From all directions the warriors of Kor-ul-ja were swarming toward the interlopers. Tarzan, who had reached a point on the same level with Ta-den but a little to the latter's left, saw that nothing short of a miracle could save them. Just at the ape-man's left was the entrance to a cave that either was deserted or whose occupants had not as yet been aroused, for the level recess remained unoccupied. Resourceful was the alert mind of Tarzan of the Apes and quick to respond were the trained muscles. In the time that you or I might give to debating an action he would accomplish it and now, though only seconds separated his nearest antagonist from him, in the brief span of time at his disposal he had stepped into the recess, unslung his long rope and leaning far out shot the sinuous noose, with the precision of long habitude, toward the menacing figure wielding its heavy club above Ta-den. There was a momentary pause of the rope-hand as the noose sped toward its goal, a quick movement of the right wrist that closed it upon its victim as it settled over his head and then a surging tug as, seizing the rope in both hands, Tarzan threw back upon it all the weight of his great frame.

Voicing a terrified shriek, the Waz-don lunged headforemost from the recess above Ta-den. Tarzan braced himself for the coming shock when the creature's body should have fallen the full length of the rope and as it did there was a snap of the vertebrae that rose sickeningly in the momentary silence that had followed the doomed man's departing scream. Unshaken by the stress of the suddenly arrested weight at the end of the rope, Tarzan quickly pulled the body to his side that he might remove the noose from about its neck, for he could not afford to lose so priceless a weapon.

During the several seconds that had elapsed since he cast the rope the Waz-don warriors had remained inert as though paralyzed by wonder or by terror. Now, again, one of them found his voice and his head and straightway, shrieking invectives at the strange intruder, started upward for the ape-man, urging his fellows to attack. This man was the closest to Tarzan. But for him the ape-man could easily have reached Ta-den's side as the latter was urging him to do. Tarzan raised the body of the dead Waz-don above his head, held it poised there for a moment as with face raised to the heavens he screamed forth the horrid challenge of the bull apes of the tribe of Kerchak, and with all the strength of his giant sinews he hurled the corpse heavily upon the ascending warrior. So great was the force of the impact that not only was the Waz-don torn from his hold but two of the pegs to which he clung were broken short in their sockets.

As the two bodies, the living and the dead, hurtled downward toward the foot of the cliff a great cry arose from the Waz-don. "Jad-guru-don! Jad-guru-don!" they screamed, and then: "Kill him! Kill him!"

And now Tarzan stood in the recess beside Ta-den. "Jad-guru-don!" repeated the latter, smiling—"The terrible man! Tarzan the Terrible! They may kill you, but they will never forget you."

"They shall not ki—What have we here?" Tarzan's statement as to what "they" should not do was interrupted by a sudden ejaculation as two figures, locked in deathlike embrace, stumbled through the doorway of the cave to the outer porch. One was Om-at, the other a creature of his own kind but with a rough coat, the hairs of which seemed to grow straight outward from the skin, stiffly, unlike Om-at's sleek covering. The two were quite evidently well matched and equally evident was the fact that each was bent upon murder. They fought almost in silence except for an occasional low growl as one or the other acknowledged thus some new hurt.

Tarzan, following a natural impulse to aid his ally, leaped forward to enter the dispute only to be checked by a grunted admonition from Om-at. "Back!" he said. "This fight is mine, alone."

The ape-man understood and stepped aside.

"It is a *gund-bar*," explained Taden, "a *chief-battle*. This fellow must be Es-sat, the chief. If Om-at kills him without assistance Om-at may become chief."

Tarzan smiled. It was the law of his own jungle—the law of the tribe of Kerchak, the bull ape—the ancient law of primitive man that needed but the refining influences of civilization to introduce the hired dagger and the poison cup. Then his attention was drawn to the outer edge of the vestibule. Above it appeared the shaggy face of one of Es-sat's warriors. Tarzan sprang to intercept the man; but Ta-den was there ahead of him. "Back!" cried the Ho-don to the newcomer. "It is *gund-bar*." The fellow looked scrutinizingly at the two fighters, then turned his face downward toward his fellows. "Back!" he cried, "it is *gund-bar* between Es-sat and

Om-at." Then he looked back at Ta-den and Tarzan. "Who
are you?" he asked.

"We are Om-at's friends," replied Ta-den.

The fellow nodded. "We will attend to you later," he said
and disappeared below the edge of the recess.

The battle upon the ledge continued with unabated ferocity,
Tarzan and Ta-den having difficulty in keeping out of the way
of the contestants who tore and beat at each other with hands
and feet and lashing tails. Es-sat was unarmed—Pan-at-lee
had seen to that—but at Om-at's side swung a sheathed knife
which he made no effort to draw. That would have been
contrary to their savage and primitive code for the chief-battle
must be fought with nature's weapons.

Sometimes they separated for an instant only to rush upon
each other again with all the ferocity and nearly the strength
of mad bulls. Presently one of them tripped the other but in
that viselike embrace one could not fall alone—Es-sat dragged
Om-at with him, toppling upon the brink of the niche. Even
Tarzan held his breath. There they surged to and fro perilously for a moment and then the inevitable happened—the
two, locked in murderous embrace, rolled over the edge and
disappeared from the ape-man's view.

Tarzan voiced a suppressed sigh for he had liked Om-at
and then, with Ta-den, approached the edge and looked over.
Far below, in the dim light of the coming dawn, two inert
forms should be lying stark in death; but, to Tarzan's amazement, such was far from the sight that met his eyes. Instead,
there were the two figures still vibrant with life and still battling only a few feet below him. Clinging always to the pegs
with two holds—a hand and a foot, or a foot and a tail, they
seemed as much at home upon the perpendicular wall as upon
the level surface of the vestibule; but now their tactics were
slightly altered, for each seemed particularly bent upon dis-
lodging his antagonist from his holds and precipitating him to
certain death below. It was soon evident that Om-at, younger
and with greater powers of endurance than Es-sat, was gaining
an advantage. Now was the chief almost wholly on the de-
fensive. Holding him by the cross belt with one mighty hand
Om-at was forcing his foeman straight out from the cliff, and
with the other hand and one foot was rapidly breaking first one
of Es-sat's holds and then another, alternating his efforts, or
rather punctuating them, with vicious blows to the pit of his
adversary's stomach. Rapidly was Es-sat weakening and with
the knowledge of impending death there came, as there comes
to every coward and bully under similar circumstances, a
crumbling of the veneer of bravado which had long masquer-

aded as courage and with it crumbled his code of ethics. Now was Es-sat no longer chief of Kor-ul-ja—instead he was a whimpering craven battling for life. Clutching at Om-at, clutching at the nearest pegs he sought any support that would save him from that awful fall, and as he strove to push aside the hand of death, whose cold fingers he already felt upon his heart, his tail sought Om-at's side and the handle of the knife that hung there.

Tarzan saw and even as Es-sat drew the blade from its sheath he dropped catlike to the pegs beside the battling men. Es-sat's tail had drawn back for the cowardly fatal thrust. Now many others saw the perfidious act and a great cry of rage and disgust arose from savage throats; but as the blade sped toward its goal, the ape-man seized the hairy member that wielded it, and at the same instant Om-at thrust the body of Es-sat from him with such force that its weakened holds were broken and it hurtled downward, a brief meteor of screaming fear, to death.

4

Tarzan-jad-guru

A s TARZAN and Om-at clambered back to the vestibule of Pan-at-lee's cave and took their stand beside Ta-den in readiness for whatever eventuality might follow the death of Es-sat, the sun that topped the eastern hills touched also the figure of a sleeper upon a distant, thorn-covered steppe awakening him to another day of tireless tracking along a faint and rapidly disappearing spoor.

For a time silence reigned in the Kor-ul-ja. The tribesmen waited, looking now down upon the dead thing that had been their chief, now at one another, and now at Om-at and the two who stood upon his either side. Presently Om-at spoke. "I am Om-at," he cried. "Who will say that Om-at is not *gund* of Kor-ul-ja?"

He waited for a taker of his challenge. One or two of the

larger young bucks fidgeted restlessly and eyed him; but there was no reply.

"Then Om-at is *gund*," he said with finality. "Now tell me, where are Pan-at-lee, her father, and her brothers?"

An old warrior spoke. "Pan-at-lee should be in her cave. Who should know that better than you who are there now? Her father and her brothers were sent to watch Kor-ul-lul; but neither of these questions arouse any tumult in our breasts. There is one that does: Can Om-at be chief of Kor-ul-ja and yet stand at bay against his own people with a Ho-don and that terrible man at his side—that terrible man who has no tail? Hand the strangers over to your people to be slain as is the way of the Waz-don and then may Om-at be *gund*."

Neither Tarzan nor Ta-den spoke then; they but stood watching Om-at and waiting for his decision, the ghost of a smile upon the lips of the ape-man. Ta-den, at least, knew that the old warrior had spoken the truth—the Waz-don entertain no strangers and take no prisoners of an alien race.

Then spoke Om-at. "Always there is change," he said. "Even the old hills of Pal-ul-don appear never twice alike —the brilliant sun, a passing cloud, the moon, a mist, the changing seasons, the sharp clearness following a storm; these things bring each a new change in our hills. From birth to death, day by day, there is constant change in each of us. Change, then, is one of Jad-ben-Otho's laws.

"And now I, Om-at, your *gund*, bring another change. Strangers who are brave men and good friends shall no longer be slain by the Waz-don of Kor-ul-ja!"

There were growls and murmurings and a restless moving among the warriors as each eyed the others to see who would take the initiative against Om-at, the iconoclast.

"Cease your mutterings," admonished the new *gund*. "I am your chief. My word is your law. You had no part in making me chief. Some of you helped Es-sat to drive me from the cave of my ancestors; the rest of you permitted it. I owe you nothing. Only these two, whom you would have me kill, were loyal to me. I am *gund* and if there be any who doubts it let him speak—he cannot die younger."

Tarzan was pleased. Here was a man after his own heart. He admired the fearlessness of Om-at's challenge and he was a sufficiently good judge of men to know that he had listened to no idle bluff. Om-at would back up his words to the death, if necessary, and the chances were that he would not be the one to die. Evidently the majority of the Kor-ul-jaians entertained the same conviction.

"I will make you a good *gund*," said Om-at, seeing that no

one appeared inclined to dispute his rights. "Your wives and daughters will be safe—they were not safe while Es-sat ruled. Go now to your crops and your hunting. I leave to search for Pan-at-lee. Ab-on will be *gund* while I am away—look to him for guidance and to me for an accoutting when I return—and may Jad-ben-Otho smile upon you."

He turned toward Tarzan and the Ho-don. "And you, my friends," he said, "are free to go among my people; the cave of my ancestors is yours; do what you will."

"I," said Tarzan, "will go with Om-at to search for Pan-at-lee."

"And I," said Ta-den.

Om-at smiled. "Good!" he exclaimed. "And when we have found her we shall go together upon Tarzan's business and Ta-den's. Where first shall we search?" He turned toward his warriors. "Who knows where she may be?"

None knew other than that Pan-at-lee had gone to her cave with the others the previous evening—there was no clew, no suggestion as to her whereabouts.

"Show me where she sleeps," said Tarzan; "let me see something that belongs to her—an article of her apparel—then, doubtless, I can help you."

Two young warriors climbed closer to the ledge upon which Om-at stood. They were In-sad and O-dan. It was the latter who spoke.

"*Gund* of Kor-ul-ja," he said, "we would go with you to search for Pan-at-lee."

It was the first acknowledgment of Om-at's chieftainship and immediately following it the tenseness that had prevailed seemed to relax—the warriors spoke aloud instead of in whispers, and the women appeared from the mouths of caves as with the passing of a sudden storm. In-sad and O-dan had taken the lead and now all seemed glad to follow. Some came to talk with Om-at and to look more closely at Tarzan; others, heads of caves, gathered their hunters and discussed the business of the day. The women and children prepared to descend to the fields with the youths and the old men, whose duty it was to guard them.

"O-dan and In-sad shall go with us," announced Om-at, "we shall not need more. Tarzan, come with me and I shall show you where Pan-at-lee sleeps, though why you should wish to know I cannot guess—she is not there. I have looked for myself."

The two entered the cave where Om-at led the way to the apartment in which Es-sat had surprised Pan-at-lee the previous night.

"All here are hers," said Om-at, "except the war club lying on the floor—that was Es-sat's."

The ape-man moved silently about the apartment, the quivering of his sensitive nostrils scarcely apparent to his companion who only wondered what good purpose could be served here and chafed at the delay.

"Come!" said the ape-man, presently, and led the way toward the outer recess.

Here their three companions were awaiting them. Tarzan passed to the left side of the niche and examined the pegs that lay within reach. He looked at them but it was not his eyes that were examining them. Keener than his keen eyes was that marvelously trained sense of scent that had first been developed in him during infancy under the tutorage of his foster mother, Kala, the she-ape, and further sharpened in the grim jungles by that master teacher—the instinct of self-preservation.

From the left side of the niche he turned to the right. Om-at was becoming impatient.

"Let us be off," he said. "We must search for Pan-at-lee if we would ever find her."

"Where shall we search?" asked Tarzan.

Om-at scratched his head. "Where?" he repeated. "Why all Pal-ul-don, if necessary."

"A large job," said Tarzan. "Come," he added, "she went this way," and he took to the pegs that led aloft toward the summit of the cliff. Here he followed the scent easily since none had passed that way since Pan-at-lee had fled. At the point at which she had left the permanent pegs and resorted to those carried with her Tarzan came to an abrupt halt. "She went this way to the summit," he called back to Om-at who was directly behind him; "but there are no pegs here."

"I do not know how you know that she went this way," said Om-at; "but we will get pegs. In-sad, return and fetch climbing pegs for five."

The young warrior was soon back and the pegs distributed. Om-at handed five to Tarzan and explained their use. The ape-man returned one. "I need but four," he said.

Om-at smiled. "What a wonderful creature you would be if you were not deformed," he said, glancing with pride at his own strong tail.

"I admit that I am handicapped," replied Tarzan. "You others go ahead and leave the pegs in place for me. I am afraid that otherwise it will be slow work as I cannot hold the pegs in my toes as you do."

"All right," agreed Om-at; "Ta-den, In-sad, and I will go

first, you follow and O-dan bring up the rear and collect the pegs—we cannot leave them here for our enemies."

"Can't your enemies bring their own pegs?" asked Tarzan.

"Yes; but it delays them and makes easier our defense and —they do not know which of all the holes you see are deep enough for pegs—the others are made to confuse our enemies and are too shallow to hold a peg."

At the top of the cliff beside the gnarled tree Tarzan again took up the trail. Here the scent was fully as strong as upon the pegs and the ape-man moved rapidly across the ridge in the direction of the Kor-ul-lul.

Presently he paused and turned toward Om-at. "Here she moved swiftly, running at top speed, and, Om-at, she was pursued by a lion."

"You can read that in the grass?" asked O-dan as the others gathered about the ape-man.

Tarzan nodded. "I do not think the lion got her," he added; "but that we shall determine quickly. No, he did not get her —look!" and he pointed toward the southwest, down the ridge.

Following the direction indicated by his finger, the others presently detected a movement in some bushes a couple of hundred yards away.

"What is it?" asked Om-at. "It is she?" and he started toward the spot.

"Wait," advised Tarzan. "It is the lion which pursued her."

"You can see him?" asked Ta-den.

"No, I can smell him."

The others looked their astonishment and incredulity; but of the fact that it was indeed a lion they were not left long in doubt. Presently the bushes parted and the creature stepped out in full view, facing them. It was a magnificent beast, large and beautifully maned, with the brilliant leopard spots of its kind well marked and symmetrical. For a moment it eyed them and then, still chafing at the loss of its prey earlier in the morning, it charged.

The Pal-ul-donians unslung their clubs and stood waiting the onrushing beast. Tarzan of the Apes drew his hunting knife and crouched in the path of the fanged fury. It was almost upon him when it swerved to the right and leaped for Om-at only to be sent to earth with a staggering blow upon the head. Almost instantly it was up and though the men rushed fearlessly in, it managed to sweep aside their weapons with its mighty paws. A single blow wrenched O-dan's club from his hand and sent it hurtling against Ta-den, knocking him from his feet. Taking advantage of its opportunity the lion rose to throw itself upon O-dan and at the same instant Tarzan flung himself upon its back. Strong, white teeth buried themselves in the spotted neck, mighty arms encircled the savage throat and the sinewy legs of the ape-man locked themselves about the gaunt belly.

The others, powerless to aid, stood breathlessly about as the great lion lunged hither and thither, clawing and biting fearfully and futilely at the savage creature that had fastened itself upon him. Over and over they rolled and now the on-lookers saw a brown hand raised above the lion's side—a brown hand grasping a keen blade. They saw it fall and rise and fall again—each time with terrific force and in its wake they saw a crimson stream trickling down *ja's* gorgeous coat.

Now from the lion's throat rose hideous screams of hate and rage and pain as he redoubled his efforts to dislodge and punish his tormentor; but always the tousled black head remained half .buried in the dark brown mane and the mighty arm rose and fell to plunge the knife again and again into the dying beast.

The Pal-ul-donians stood in mute wonder and admiration. Brave men and mighty hunters they were and as such the first to accord honor to a mightier.

"And you would have had me slay him!" cried Om-at, glancing at In-sad and O-dan.

"Jad-ben-Otho reward you that you did not," breathed In-sad.

And now the lion lunged suddenly to earth and with a few spasmodic quiverings lay still. The ape-man rose and shook himself, even as might *ja*, the leopard-coated lion of Pal-ul-don, had he been the one to survive.

O-dan advanced quickly toward Tarzan. Placing a palm upon his own breast and the other on Tarzan's. "Tarzan the Terrible," he said, "I ask no greater honor than your friend-ship."

"And I no more than the friendship of Om-at's friends," replied the ape-man simply, returning the other's salute.

"Do you think," asked Om-at, coming close to Tarzan and laying a hand upon the other's shoulder, "that he got her?"

"No, my friend; it was a hungry lion that charged us."

"You seem to know much of lions," said In-sad.

"Had I a brother I could not know him better," replied Tarzan.

"Then where can she be?" continued Om-at.

"We can but follow while the spoor is fresh," answered the ape-man and again taking up his interrupted tracking he led them down the ridge and at a sharp turning of the trail to the left brought them to the verge of the cliff that dropped into the Kor-ul-lul. For a moment Tarzan examined the ground to the right and to the left, then he stood erect and looking at Om-at pointed into the gorge.

For a moment the Waz-don gazed down into the green rift at the bottom of which a tumultuous river tumbled downward along its rocky bed, then he closed his eyes as to a sudden spasm of pain and turned away.

"You—mean—she jumped?" he asked.

"To escape the lion," replied Tarzan. "He was right behind her—look, you can see where his four paws left their impress in the turf as he checked his charge upon the very verge of the abyss."

"Is there any chance—" commenced Om-at, to be suddenly silenced by a warning gesture from Tarzan.

"Down!" whispered the ape-man, "many men are coming. They are running—from down the ridge." He flattened himself upon his belly in the grass, the others following his example.

For some minutes they waited thus and then the others, too, heard the sound of running feet and now a hoarse shout followed by many more.

"It is the war cry of the Kor-ul-lul," whispered Om-at— "the hunting cry of men who hunt men. Presently shall we see them and if Jad-ben-Otho is pleased with us they shall not too greatly outnumber us."

"They are many," said Tarzan, "forty or fifty, I should say; but how many are the pursued and how many the pursuers we cannot even guess, except that the latter must greatly outnumber the former, else these would not run so fast."

"Here they come," said Ta-den.

"It is An-un, father of Pan-at-lee, and his two sons," exclaimed O-dan. "They will pass without seeing us if we do not hurry," he added looking at Om-at, the chief, for a sign.

"Come!" cried the latter, springing to his feet and running rapidly to intercept the three fugitives. The others followed him.

"Five friends!" shouted Om-at as An-un and his sons discovered them.

"*Adenen yo!*" echoed O-dan and In-sad.

The fugitives scarcely paused as these unexpected reinforcements joined them but they eyed Ta-den and Tarzan with puzzled glances.

"The Kor-ul-lul are many," shouted An-un. "Would that we might pause and fight; but first we must warn Es-sat and our people."

"Yes," said Om-at, "we must warn our people."

"Es-sat is dead," said In-sad.

"Who is chief?" asked one of An-un's sons.

"Om-at," replied O-dan.

"It is well," cried An-un. "Pan-at-lee said that you would come back and slay Es-sat."

Now the enemy broke into sight behind them.

"Come!" cried Tarzan," let us turn and charge them, raising a great cry. They pursued but three and when they see eight charging upon them they will think that many men have come to do battle. They will believe that there are more even than they see and then one who is swift will have time to reach the gorge and warn your people."

"It is well," said Om-at. "Id-an, you are swift—carry word to the warriors of Kor-ul-ja that we fight the Kor-ul-lul upon the ridge and that Ab-on shall send a hundred men."

Id-an, the son of An-un, sped swiftly toward the cliff-dwellings of the Kor-ul-ja while the others charged the oncoming Kor-ul-lul, the war cries of the two tribes rising and falling in a certain grim harmony. The leaders of the Kor-ul-lul paused at sight of the reinforcements, waiting apparently for those behind to catch up with them and, possibly, also to learn how great a force confronted them. The leaders, swifter runners than their fellows, perhaps, were far in advance while the balance of their number had not yet emerged from the brush; and now as Om-at and his companions fell upon them with a ferocity born of necessity they fell back, so that when their companions at last came in sight of them they appeared to be in full rout. The natural result was that the others turned and fled.

Encouraged by this first success Om-at followed them into the brush, his little company charging valiantly upon his either side, and loud and terrifying were the savage yells with which they pursued the fleeing enemy. The brush, while not growing so closely together as to impede progress, was of such height as to hide the members of the party from one another when they became separated by even a few yards. The result was that Tarzan, always swift and always keen for battle, was soon pursuing the enemy far in the lead of the others—a lack of prudence which was to prove his undoing.

The warriors of Kor-ul-lul, doubtless as valorous as their foemen, retreated only to a more strategic position in the brush, nor were they long in guessing that the number of their pursuers was fewer than their own. They made a stand then where the brush was densest—an ambush it was, and into this ran Tarzan of the Apes. They tricked him neatly. Yes, sad as is the narration of it, they tricked the wily jungle lord. But then they were fighting on their own ground, every foot of which they knew as you know your front parlor, and they were following their own tactics, of which Tarzan knew nothing.

A single black warrior appeared to Tarzan a laggard in the rear of the retreating enemy and thus retreating he lured Tarzan on. At last he turned at bay confronting the ape-man with bludgeon and drawn knife and as Tarzan charged him a score of burly Waz-don leaped from the surrounding brush. Instantly, but too late, the giant Tarmangani realized his peril. There flashed before him a vision of his lost mate and a great and sickening regret surged through him with the realization that if she still lived she might no longer hope, for though she might never know of the passing of her lord the fact of it must inevitably seal her doom.

And consequent to this thought there enveloped him a blind frenzy of hatred for these creatures who dared thwart his purpose and menace the welfare of his wife. With a savage growl he threw himself upon the warrior before him twisting the heavy club from the creature's hand as if he had been a little child, and with his left fist backed by the weight and sinew of his giant frame, he crashed a shattering blow to the center of the Waz-don's face—a blow that crushed the bones and dropped the fellow in his tracks. Then he swung upon the others with their fallen comrade's bludgeon striking to right and left mighty, unmerciful blows that drove down their own weapons until that wielded by the ape-man was splintered and shattered. On either hand they fell before his cudgel; so rapid the delivery of his blows, so catlike his recovery that in the first few moments of the battle he seemed invulnerable to their attack; but it could not last—he was outnumbered twenty to one and his undoing came from a thrown club. It struck him upon the back of the head. For a moment he stood swaying and then like a great pine beneath the woodsman's ax he crashed to earth.

Others of the Kor-ul-lul had rushed to engage the balance of Om-at's party. They could be heard fighting at a short distance and it was evident that the Kor-ul-ja were falling slowly back and as they fell Om-at called to the missing one: "Tarzan the Terrible! Tarzan the Terrible!"

"Jad-guru, indeed," repeated one of the Kor-ul-lul rising from where Tarzan had dropped him. "Tarzan-jad-guru! He was worse than that."

5

In the Kor-ul-gryf

As TARZAN fell among his enemies a man halted many miles away upon the outer verge of the morass that encircles Pal-ul-don. Naked he was except for a loin cloth and three belts of cartridges, two of which passed over his shoulders, crossing upon his chest and back, while the third encircled his waist. Slung to his back by its leathern sling-strap was an Enfield, and he carried too a long knife, a bow and a quiver of arrows. He had come far, through wild and savage lands, menaced by fierce beasts and fiercer men, yet intact to the last cartridge was the ammunition that had filled his belts the day that he set out.

The bow and the arrows and the long knife had brought him thus far safely, yet often in the face of great risks that could have been minimized by a single shot from the well-kept rifle at his back. What purpose might he have for conserving this precious ammunition? in risking his life to bring the last bright shining missile to his unknown goal? For what, for whom were these death-dealing bits of metal preserved? In all the world only he knew.

When Pan-at-lee stepped over the edge of the cliff above Kor-ul-lul she expected to be dashed to instant death upon the rocks below; but she had chosen this in preference to the rending fangs of *ja*. Instead, chance had ordained that she make the frightful plunge at a point where the tumbling river swung close beneath the overhanging cliff to eddy for a slow moment in a deep pool before plunging madly downward again in a cataract of boiling foam, and water thundering against rocks.

Into this icy pool the girl shot, and down and down beneath the watery surface until, half choked, yet fighting bravely, she battled her way once more to air. Swimming strongly she made the opposite shore and there dragged herself out upon the bank to lie panting and spent until the approaching dawn warned her to seek concealment, for she was in the country of her people's enemies.

Rising, she moved into the concealment of the rank vegetation that grows so riotously in the well-watered *kors* [1] of Pal-ul-don.

Hidden amidst the plant life from the sight of any who might chance to pass along the well-beaten trail that skirted the river Pan-at-lee sought rest and food, the latter growing in abundance all about her in the form of fruits and berries and succulent tubers which she scooped from the earth with the knife of the dead Es-sat.

Ah! if she had but known that he was dead! What trials and risks and terrors she might have been saved; but she thought that he still lived and so she dared not return to Kor-ul-ja. At least not yet while his rage was at white heat. Later, perhaps, her father and brothers returned to their cave, she might risk it; but not now—not now. Nor could she for long remain here in the neighborhood of the hostile Kor-ul-lul and somewhere she must find safety from beasts before the night set in.

As she sat upon the bole of a fallen tree seeking some solution of the problem of existence that confronted her, there broke upon her ears from up the gorge the voices of shouting men—a sound that she recognized all too well. It was the war cry of the Kor-ul-lul. Closer and closer it approached her hiding place. Then, through the veil of foliage she caught glimpses of three figures fleeing along the trail, and behind them the shouting of the pursuers rose louder and louder as they neared her. Again she caught sight of the fugitives crossing the river below the cataract and again they were lost to sight. And now the pursuers came into view—shouting Kor-ul-lul warriors, fierce and implacable. Forty, perhaps fifty of them. She waited breathless; but they did not swerve from the trail and passed her, unguessing that an enemy she lay hid within a few yards of them.

Once again she caught sight of the pursued—three Waz-don warriors clambering the cliff face at a point where portions of

---

[1] I have used the Pal-ul-don word for *gorge* with the English plural, which is not the correct native plural form. The latter, it seems to me, is awkward for us and so I have generally ignored it throughout my manuscript, permitting, for example, Kor-ul-ja to answer for both singular and plural. However, for the benefit of those who may be interested in such things I may say that the plurals are formed simply for all words in the Pal-ul-don language by doubling the initial letter of the word, as *k'kor*, gorges, pronounced as though written *kakor*, the *a* having the sound of *a* in *sofa*. Lions, then, would be *j'ja*, or *men d' don*.

the summit had fallen away presenting a steep slope that might be ascended by such as these. Suddenly her attention was riveted upon the three. Could it be? O Jad-ben-Otho! had she but known a moment before. When they passed she might have joined them, for they were her father and two brothers. Now it was too late. With bated breath and tense muscles she watched the race. Would they reach the summit? Would the Kor-ul-lul overhaul them? They climbed well, but, oh, so slowly. Now one lost his footing in the loose shale and slipped back! The Kor-ul-lul were ascending—one hurled his club at the nearest fugitive. The Great God was pleased with the brother of Pan-at-lee, for he caused the club to fall short of its target, and to fall, rolling and bounding, back upon its owner carrying him from his feet and precipitating him to the bottom of the gorge.

Standing now, her hands pressed tight above her golden breastplates, Pan-at-lee watched the race for life. Now one, her older brother, reached the summit and clinging there to something that she could not see he lowered his body and his long tail to the father beneath him. The latter, seizing this support, extended his own tail to the son below—the one who had slipped back—and thus, upon a living ladder of their own making, the three reached the summit and disappeared from view before the Kor-ul-lul overtook them. But the latter did not abandon the chase. On they went until they too had disappeared from sight and only a faint shouting came down to Pan-at-lee to tell her that the pursuit continued.

The girl knew that she must move on. At any moment now might come a hunting party, combing the gorge for the smaller animals that fed or bedded there.

Behind her were Es-sat and the returning party of Kor-ul-lul that had pursued her kin; before her, across the next ridge, was the Kor-ul-gryf, the lair of the terrifying monsters that brought the chill of fear to every inhabitant of Pal-ul-don; below her, in the valley, was the country of the Ho-don, where she could look for only slavery, or death; here were the Kor-ul-lul, the ancient enemies of her people and everywhere were the wild beasts that eat the flesh of man.

For but a moment she debated and then turning her face toward the southeast she set out across the gorge of water toward the Kor-ul-gryf—at least there were no men there. As it is now, so it was in the beginning, back to the primitive progenitor of man which is typified by Pan-at-lee and her kind today, of all the hunters that woman fears, man is the most relentless, the most terrible. To the dangers of man she preferred the dangers of the *gryf*.

Moving cautiously she reached the foot of the cliff at the far side of Kor-ul-lul and here, toward noon, she found a comparatively easy ascent. Crossing the ridge she stood at last upon the brink of Kor-ul-gryf—the horror place of the folklore of her race. Dank and mysterious grew the vegetation below; giant trees waved their plumed tops almost level with the summit of the cliff; and over all brooded an ominous silence.

Pan-at-lee lay upon her belly and stretching over the edge scanned the cliff face below her. She could see caves there and the stone pegs which the ancients had fashioned so laboriously by hand. She had heard of these in the firelight tales of her childhood and of how the *gryfs* had come from the morasses across the mountains and of how at last the people had fled after many had been seized and devoured by the hideous creatures, leaving their caves untenanted for no man living knew how long. Some said that Jad-ben-Otho, who has lived forever, was still a little boy. Pan-at-lee shuddered; but there were caves and in them she would be safe even from the *gryfs*.

She found a place where the stone pegs reached to the very summit of the cliff, left there no doubt in the final exodus of the tribe when there was no longer need of safeguarding the deserted caves against invasion. Pan-at-lee clambered slowly down toward the uppermost cave. She found the recess in front of the doorway almost identical with those of her own tribe. The floor of it, though, was littered with twigs and old nests and the droppings of birds, until it was half choked. She moved along to another recess and still another, but all were alike in the accumulated filth. Evidently there was no need in looking further. This one seemed large and commodious. With her knife she fell to work cleaning away the débris by the simple expedient of pushing it over the edge, and always her eyes turned constantly toward the silent gorge where lurked the fearsome creatures of Pal-ul-don. And other eyes there were, eyes she did not see, but that saw her and watched her every move—fierce eyes, greedy eyes, cunning and cruel. They watched her, and a red tongue licked flabby, pendulous lips. They watched her, and a half-human brain laboriously evolved a brutish design.

As in her own Kor-ul-ja, the natural springs in the cliff had been developed by the long-dead builders of the caves so that fresh, pure water trickled now, as it had for ages, within easy access to the cave entrances. Her only difficulty would be in procuring food and for that she must take the risk at least once in two days, for she was sure that she could find fruits and tubers and perhaps small animals, birds, and eggs near the foot of the cliff, the last two, possibly, in the caves themselves.

Thus might she live on here indefinitely. She felt now a certain sense of security imparted doubtless by the impregnability of her high-flung sanctuary that she knew to be safe from all the more dangerous beasts, and this one from men, too, since it lay in the abjured Kor-ul-gryf.

Now she determined to inspect the interior of her new home. The sun still in the south, lighted the interior of the first apartment. It was similar to those of her experience—the same beasts and men were depicted in the same crude fashion in the carvings on the walls—evidently there had been little progress in the race of Waz-don during the generations that had come and departed since Kor-ul-gryf had been abandoned by men. Of course Pan-at-lee thought no such thoughts, for evolution and progress existed not for her, or her kind. Things were as they had always been and would always be as they were.

That these strange creatures have existed thus for incalculable ages it can scarce be doubted, so marked are the indications of antiquity about their dwellings—deep furrows worn by naked feet in living rock; the hollow in the jamb of a stone doorway where many arms have touched in passing; the endless carvings that cover, ofttimes, the entire face of a great cliff and all the walls and ceilings of every cave and each carving wrought by a different hand, for each is the coat of arms, one might say, of the adult male who traced it.

And so Pan-at-lee found this ancient cave homelike and familiar. There was less litter within than she had found without and what there was was mostly an accumulation of dust. Beside the doorway was the niche in which wood and tinder were kept, but there remained nothing now other than mere dust. She had however saved a little pile of twigs from the débris on the porch. In a short time she had made a light by firing a bundle of twigs and lighting others from this fire she explored some of the inner rooms. Nor here did she find aught that was new or strange nor any relic of the departed owners other than a few broken stone dishes. She had been looking for something soft to sleep upon, but was doomed to disappointment as the former owners had evidently made a leisurely departure, carrying all their belongings with them. Below, in the gorge were leaves and grasses and fragrant branches, but Pan-at-lee felt no stomach for descending into that horrid abyss for the gratification of mere creature comfort—only the necessity for food would drive her there.

And so, as the shadows lengthened and night approached she prepared to make as comfortable a bed as she could by gathering the dust of ages into a little pile and spreading it

between her soft body and the hard floor—at best it was only
better than nothing. But Pan-at-lee was very tired. She had
not slept since two nights before and in the interval she had
experienced many dangers and hardships. What wonder then
that despite the hard bed, she was asleep almost immediately
she had composed herself for rest.

She slept and the moon rose, casting its silver light upon the
cliff's white face and lessening the gloom of the dark forest
and the dismal gorge. In the distance a lion roared. There
was a long silence. From the upper reaches of the gorge came
a deep bellow. There was a movement in the trees at the
cliff's foot. Again the bellow, low and ominous. It was answered from below the deserted village. Something dropped
from the foliage of a tree directly below the cave in which
Pan-at-lee slept—it dropped to the ground among the dense
shadows. Now it moved, cautiously. It moved toward the
foot of the cliff, taking form and shape in the moonlight. It
moved like the creature of a bad dream—slowly, sluggishly.
It might have been a huge sloth—it might have been a man,
with so grotesque a brush does the moon paint—master cubist.

Slowly it moved up the face of the cliff—like a great grubworm it moved; but now the moon-brush touched it again and
it had hands and feet and with them it clung to the stone pegs
and raised itself laboriously aloft toward the cave where Pan-
at-lee slept. From the lower reaches of the gorge came again
the sound of bellowing, and it was answered from above the
village.

Tarzan of the Apes opened his eyes. He was conscious of
a pain in his head, and at first that was about all. A moment
later grotesque shadows, rising and falling, focused his arousing perceptions. Presently he saw that he was in a cave. A
dozen Waz-don warriors squatted about, talking. A rude
stone cresset containing burning oil lighted the interior and as
the flame rose and fell the exaggerated shadows of the warriors danced upon the walls behind them.

"We brought him to you alive, *Gund*," he heard one of them
saying, "because never before was Ho-don like him seen. He
has no tail—he was born without one, for there is no scar to
mark where a tail had been cut off. The thumbs upon his
hands and feet are unlike those of the races of Pal-ul-don. He
is more powerful than many men put together and he attacks
with the fearlessness of *ja*. We brought him alive, that you
might see him before he is slain."

The chief rose and approached the ape-man, who closed his
eyes and feigned unconsciousness. He felt hairy hands upon

him as he was turned over, none too gently. The *gund* examined him from head to foot, making comments, especially upon the shape and size of his thumbs and great toes.

"With these and with no tail," he said, "it cannot climb."

"No," agreed one of the warriors, "it would surely fall even from the cliff pegs."

"I have never seen a thing like it," said the chief. "It is neither Waz-don nor Ho-don. I wonder from whence it came and what it is called."

"The Kor-ul-ja shouted aloud, 'Tarzan-jad-guru!' and we thought that they might be calling this one," said a warrior. "Shall we kill it now?"

"No," replied the chief, "we will wait until it's life returns into its head that I may question it. Remain here, In-tan, and watch it. When it can again hear and speak call me."

He turned and departed from the cave, the others, except In-tan, following him. As they moved past him and out of the chamber Tarzan caught snatches of their conversation which indicated that the Kor-ul-ja reinforcements had fallen upon their little party in great numbers and driven them away. Evidently the swift feet of Id-an had saved the day for the warriors of Om-at. The ape-man smiled, then he partially opened an eye and cast it upon In-tan. The warrior stood at the entrance to the cave looking out—his back was toward his prisoner. Tarzan tested the bonds that secured his wrists. They seemed none too stout and they had tied his hands in front of him! Evidence indeed that the Waz-don took few prisoners—if any.

Cautiously he raised his wrists until he could examine the thongs that confined them. A grim smile lighted his features. Instantly he was at work upon the bonds with his strong teeth, but ever a wary eye was upon In-tan, the warrior of Kor-ul-lul. The last knot had been loosened and Tarzan's hands were free when In-tan turned to cast an appraising eye upon his ward. He saw that the prisoner's position was changed—he no longer lay upon his back as they had left him, but upon his side and his hands were drawn up against his face. In-tan came closer and bent down. The bonds seemed very loose upon the prisoner's wrists. He extended his hand to examine them with his fingers and instantly the two hands leaped from their bonds —one to seize his own wrist, the other his throat. So unexpected the catlike attack that In-tan had not even time to cry out before steel fingers silenced him. The creature pulled him suddenly forward so that he lost his balance and rolled over upon the prisoner and to the floor beyond to stop with Tarzan upon his breast. In-tan struggled to release himself—struggled to draw his knife; but Tarzan found it before him. The Waz-don's tail leaped to the other's throat, encircling it—he too could choke; but his own knife, in the hands of his antagonist, severed the beloved member close to its root.

The Waz-don's struggles became weaker—a film was obscuring his vision. He knew that he was dying and he was right. A moment later he was dead. Tarzan rose to his feet and placed one foot upon the breast of his dead foe. How the urge seized him to roar forth the victory cry of his kind! But he dared not. He discovered that they had not removed his rope from his shoulders and that they had replaced his knife in its sheath. It had been in his hand when he was felled. Strange creatures! He did not know that they held a superstitious fear of the weapons of a dead enemy, believing that if buried without them he would forever haunt his slayers in search of them and that when he found them he would kill the man who killed him. Against the wall leaned his bow and quiver of arrows.

Tarzan stepped toward the doorway of the cave and looked out. Night had just fallen. He could hear voices from the nearer caves and there floated to his nostrils the odor of cooking food. He looked down and experienced a sensation of relief. The cave in which he had been held was in the lowest tier—scarce thirty feet from the base of the cliff. He was about to chance an immediate descent when there occurred to him a thought that brought a grin to his savage lips—a thought that was born of the name the Waz-don had given him —Tarzan-jad-guru—Tarzan the Terrible—and a recollection of the days when he had delighted in baiting the blacks of the distant jungle of his birth. He turned back into the cave where lay the dead body of In-tan. With his knife he severed the warrior's head and carrying it to the outer edge of the recess tossed it to the ground below, then he dropped swiftly and silently down the ladder of pegs in a way that would have surprised the Kor-ul-lul who had been so sure that he could not climb.

At the bottom he picked up the head of In-tan and disappeared among the shadows of the trees carrying the grisly trophy by its shock of shaggy hair. Horrible? But you are judging a wild beast by the standards of civilization. You may teach a lion tricks, but he is still a lion. Tarzan looked well in a Tuxedo, but he was still a Tarmangani and beneath his pleated shirt beat a wild and savage heart.

Nor was his madness lacking in method. He knew that the hearts of the Kor-ul-lul would be filled with rage when they discovered the thing that he had done and he knew too, that

mixed with the rage would be a leaven of fear and it was fear
of him that had made Tarzan master of many jungles—one
does not win the respect of the killers with bonbons.

Below the village Tarzan returned to the foot of the cliff
searching for a point where he could make the ascent to the
ridge and thus back to the village of Om-at, the Kor-ul-ja. He
came at last to a place where the river ran so close to the rocky
wall that he was forced to swim it in search of a trail upon
the opposite side and here it was that his keen nostrils detected a familiar spoor. It was the scent of Pan-at-lee at the
spot where she had emerged from the pool and taken to the
safety of the jungle.

Immediately the ape-man's plans were changed. Pan-at-lee
lived, or at least she had lived after the leap from the cliff's
summit. He had started in search of her for Om-at, his friend,
and for Om-at he would continue upon the trail he had picked
up thus fortuitously by accident. It led him into the jungle
and across the gorge and then to the point at which Pan-at-lee
had commenced the ascent of the opposite cliffs. Here Tarzan
abandoned the head of In-tan, tying it to the lower branch of a
tree, for he knew that it would handicap him in his ascent of
the steep escarpment. Apelike he ascended, following easily
the scent spoor of Pan-at-lee. Over the summit and across the
ridge the trail lay, plain as a printed page to the delicate senses
of the jungle-bred tracker.

Tarzan knew naught of the Kor-ul-gryf. He had seen, dimly
in the shadows of the night, strange, monstrous forms and
Ta-den and Om-at had spoken of great creatures that all men
feared; but always, everywhere, by night and by day, there
were dangers. From infancy death had stalked, grim and terrible, at his heels. He knew little of any other existence. To
cope with danger was his life and he lived his life as simply
and as naturally as you live yours amidst the dangers of the
crowded city streets. The black man who goes abroad in the
jungle by night is afraid, for he has spent his life since infancy
surrounded by numbers of his own kind and safeguarded, especially at night, by such crude means as lie within his powers.
But Tarzan had lived as the lion lives and the panther and the
elephant and the ape—a true jungle creature dependent solely
upon his prowess and his wits, playing a lone hand against
creation. Therefore he was surprised at nothing and feared
nothing and so he walked through the strange night as undis-
turbed and unapprehensive as the farmer to the cow lot in the
darkness before the dawn.

Once more Pan-at-lee's trail ended at the verge of a cliff; but
this time there was no indication that she had leaped over the

edge and a moment's search revealed to Tarzan the stone pegs upon which she had made her descent. As he lay upon his belly leaning over the top of the cliff examining the pegs his attention was suddenly attracted by something at the foot of the cliff. He could not distinguish its identity, but he saw that it moved and presently that it was ascending slowly, apparently by means of pegs similar to those directly below him. He watched it intently as it rose higher and higher until he was able to distinguish its form more clearly, with the result that he became convinced that it more nearly resembled some form of great ape than a lower order. It had a tail, though, and in other respects it did not seem a true ape.

Slowly it ascended to the upper tier of caves, into one of which it disappeared. Then Tarzan took up again the trail of Pan-at-lee. He followed it down the stone pegs to the nearest cave and then further along the upper tier. The ape-man raised his eyebrows when he saw the direction in which it led, and quickened his pace. He had almost reached the third cave when the echoes of Kor-ul-gryf were awakened by a shrill scream of terror.

6

The Tor-o-don

PAN-AT-LEE slept—the troubled sleep, of physical and nervous exhaustion, filled with weird dreamings. She dreamed that she slept beneath a great tree in the bottom of the Kor-ul-gryf and that one of the fearsome beasts was creeping upon her but she could not open her eyes nor move. She tried to scream but no sound issued from her lips. She felt the thing touch her throat, her breast, her arm, and there it closed and seemed to be dragging her toward it. With a superhuman effort of will she opened her eyes. In the instant she knew that she was dreaming and that quickly the hallucination of the dream would fade—it had happened to her many times before. But it persisted. In the dim light that filtered into the dark chamber she saw a form beside her, she felt hairy fingers upon her and a hairy breast against which she was being drawn. Jad-ben-Otho! this was no dream. And then she screamed and tried to fight the thing from her; but her scream was answered by a low growl and another hairy hand seized her by the hair of the head. The beast rose now upon its hind legs and dragged her from the cave to the moonlit recess without and at the same instant she saw the figure of what she took to be a Ho-don rise above the outer edge of the niche.

The beast that held her saw it too and growled ominously but it did not relinquish its hold upon her hair. It crouched as though waiting an attack, and it increased the volume and frequency of its growls until the horrid sounds reverberated through the gorge, drowning even the deep bellowings of the beasts below, whose mighty thunderings had broken out anew with the sudden commotion from the high-flung cave. The beast that held her crouched and the creature that faced it crouched also, and growled—as hideously as the other. Pan-at-lee trembled. This was no Ho-don and though she feared the Ho-don she feared this thing more, with its catlike crouch and its beastly growls. She was lost—that Pan-at-lee knew. The two things might fight for her, but whichever won she was lost. Perhaps, during the battle, if it came to that, she might find the opportunity to throw herself over into the Kor-ul-gryf.

The thing that held her she had recognized now as a Tor-o-don, but the other thing she could not place, though in the moonlight she could see it very distinctly. It had no tail. She could see its hands and its feet, and they were not the hands and feet of the races of Pal-ul-don. It was slowly closing upon the Tor-o-don and in one hand it held a gleaming knife. Now it spoke and to Pan-at-lee's terror was added an equal weight of consternation.

"When it leaves go of you," it said, "as it will presently to defend itself, run quickly behind me, Pan-at-lee, and go to the cave nearest the pegs you descended from the cliff top. Watch from there. If I am defeated you will have time to escape this slow thing; if I am not I will come to you there. I am Om-at's friend and yours."

The last words took the keen edge from Pan-at-lee's terror; but she did not understand. How did this strange creature know her name? How did it know that she had descended the pegs by a certain cave? It must, then, have been here when she came. Pan-at-lee was puzzled.

"Who are you?" she asked, "and from whence do you come?"

"I am Tarzan," he replied, "and just now I came from Om-at, of Kor-ul-ja, in search of you."

Om-at, *gund* of Kor-ul-ja! What wild talk was this? She

would have questioned him further, but now he was approaching the Tor-o-don and the latter was screaming and growling so loudly as to drown the sound of her voice. And then it did what the strange creature had said that it would do—it released its hold upon her hair as it prepared to charge. Charge it did and in those close quarters there was no room to fence for openings. Instantly the two beasts locked in deadly embrace, each seeking the other's throat. Pan-at-lee watched, taking no advantage of the opportunity to escape which their preoccupation gave her. She watched and waited, for into her savage little brain had come the resolve to pin her faith to this strange creature who had unlocked her heart with those four words—"I am Om-at's friend!" And so she waited, with drawn knife, the opportunity to do her bit in the vanquishing of the Tor-o-don. That the newcomer could do it unaided she well knew to be beyond the realms of possibility, for she knew well the prowess of the *beastlike man* with whom it fought. There were not many of them in Pal-ul-don, but what few there were were a terror to the women of the Waz-don and the Ho-don, for the old Tor-o-don bulls roamed the mountains and the valleys of Pal-ul-don between rutting seasons and woe betide the women who fell in their paths.

With his tail the Tor-o-don sought one of Tarzan's ankles, and finding it, tripped him. The two fell heavily, but so agile was the ape-man and so quick his powerful muscles that even in falling he twisted the beast beneath him, so that Tarzan fell on top and now the tail that had tripped him sought his throat as had the tail of In-tan, the Kor-ul-lul. In the effort of turning his antagonist's body during the fall Tarzan had had to relinquish his knife that he might seize the shaggy body with both hands and now the weapon lay out of reach at the very edge of the recess. Both hands were occupied for the moment in fending off the clutching fingers that sought to seize him and drag his throat within reach of his foe's formidable fangs and now the tail was seeking its deadly hold with a formidable persistence that would not be denied.

Pan-at-lee hovered about, breathless, her dagger ready, but there was no opening that did not also endanger Tarzan, so constantly were the two duelists changing their positions. Tarzan felt the tail slowly but surely insinuating itself about his neck though he had drawn his head down between the muscles of his shoulders in an effort to protect this vulnerable part. The battle seemed to be going against him for the giant beast against which he strove would have been a fair match in weight and strength for Bolgani, the gorilla. And knowing this he suddenly exerted a single super-human effort, thrust far apart the giant hands and with the swiftness of a striking snake buried his fangs in the jugular of the Tor-o-don. At the same instant the creature's tail coiled about his own throat and then commenced a battle royal of turning and twisting bodies as each sought to dislodge the fatal hold of the other, but the acts of the ape-man were guided by a human brain and thus it was that the rolling bodies rolled in the direction that Tarzan wished—toward the edge of the recess.

The choking tail had shut the air from his lungs, he knew that his gasping lips were parted and his tongue protruding; and now his brain reeled and his sight grew dim; but not before he reached his goal and a quick hand shot out to seize the knife that now lay within reach as the two bodies tottered perilously upon the brink of the chasm.

With all his remaining strength the ape-man drove home the blade—once, twice, thrice, and then all went black before him as he felt himself, still in the clutches of the Tor-o-don, topple from the recess.

Fortunate it was for Tarzan that Pan-at-lee had not obeyed his injunction to make good her escape while he engaged the Tor-o-don, for it was to this fact that he owed his life. Close beside the struggling forms during the brief moments of the terrific climax she had realized every detail of the danger to Tarzan with which the emergency was fraught and as she saw the two rolling over the outer edge of the niche she seized the ape-man by an ankle at the same time throwing herself prone upon the rocky floor. The muscles of the Tor-o-don relaxed in death with the last thrust of Tarzan's knife and with its hold upon the ape-man released it shot from sight into the gorge below.

It was with infinite difficulty that Pan-at-lee retained her hold upon the ankle of her protector, but she did so and then, slowly, she sought to drag the dead weight back to the safety of the niche. This, however, was beyond her strength and she could but hold on tightly, hoping that some plan would suggest itself before her powers of endurance failed. She wondered if, after all, the creature was already dead, but that she could not bring herself to believe—and if not dead how long it would be before he regained consciousness. If he did not regain it soon he never would regain it, that she knew, for she felt her fingers numbing to the strain upon them and slipping, slowly, slowly, from their hold. It was then that Tarzan regained consciousness. He could not know what power upheld him, but he felt that whatever it was it was slowly releasing its hold upon his ankle. Within easy reach of his hands were two pegs and these he seized upon just as Pan-at-lee's fingers slipped from their hold.

As it was he came near to being precipitated into the gorge —only his great strength saved him. He was upright now and his feet found other pegs. His first thought was of his foe. Where was he? Waiting above there to finish him? Tarzan looked up just as the frightened face of Pan-at-lee appeared over the threshold of the recess.

"You live?" she cried.

"Yes," replied Tarzan. "Where is the shaggy one?"

Pan-at-lee pointed downward. "There," she said, "dead."

"Good!" exclaimed the ape-man, clambering to her side. "You are unharmed?" he asked.

"You came just in time," replied Pan-at-lee; "but who are you and how did you know that I was here and what do you know of Om-at and where did you come from and what did you mean by calling Om-at, *gund?*"

"Wait, wait," cried Tarzan; "one at a time. My, but you are all alike—the shes of the tribe of Kerchak, the ladies of England, and their sisters of Pal-ul-don. Have patience and I will try to tell you all that you wish to know. Four of us set out with Om-at from Kor-ul-ja to search for you. We were attacked by the Kor-ul-lul and separated. I was taken prisoner, but escaped. Again I stumbled upon your trail and followed it, reaching the summit of this cliff just as the hairy one was climbing up after you. I was coming to investigate when I heard your scream—the rest you know."

"But you called Om-at, *gund* of Kor-ul-ja," she insisted. "Es-sat is *gund.*"

"Es-sat is dead," explained the ape-man. "Om-at slew him and now Om-at is *gund.* Om-at came back seeking you. He found Es-sat in your cave and killed him."

"Yes," said the girl, "Es-sat came to my cave and I struck him down with my golden breastplates and escaped."

"And a lion pursued you," continued Tarzan, "and you leaped from the cliff into Kor-ul-lul, but why you were not killed is beyond me."

"Is there anything beyond you?" exclaimed Pan-at-lee. "How could you know that a lion pursued me and that I leaped from the cliff and not know that it was the pool of deep water below that saved me?"

"I would have known that, too, had not the Kor-ul-lul come then and prevented me continuing upon your trail. But now I would ask you a question—by what name do you call the thing with which I just fought?"

"It was a Tor-o-don," she replied. "I have seen but one be-

fore. They are terrible creatures with the cunning of man
and the ferocity of a beast. Great indeed must be the warrior
who slays one single-handed." She gazed at him in open admiration.

"And now," said Tarzan, "you must sleep, for tomorrow we
shall return to Kor-ul-ja and Om-at, and I doubt that you have
had much rest these two nights."

Pan-at-lee, lulled by a feeling of security, slept peacefully
into the morning while Tarzan stretched himself upon the
hard floor of the recess just outside her cave.

The sun was high in the heavens when he awoke; for two
hours it had looked down upon another heroic figure miles
away—the figure of a godlike man fighting his way through the
hideous morass that lies like a filthy moat defending Pal-ul-don
from the creatures of the outer world. Now waist deep in the
sucking ooze, now menaced by loathsome reptiles, the man advanced only by virtue of Herculean efforts gaining laboriously
by inches along the devious way that he was forced to choose
in selecting the least precarious footing. Near the center of
the morass was open water—slimy, green-hued water. He
reached it at last after more than two hours of such effort as
would have left an ordinary man spent and dying in the
sticky mud, yet he was less than halfway across the marsh.
Greasy with slime and mud was his smooth, brown hide, and
greasy with slime and mud was his beloved Enfield that had
shone so brightly in the first rays of the rising sun.

He paused a moment upon the edge of the open water and
then throwing himself forward struck out to swim across. He
swam with long, easy, powerful strokes calculated less for
speed than for endurance, for his was, primarily, a test of the
latter, since beyond the open water was another two hours or
more of gruelling effort between it and solid ground. He was,
perhaps, halfway across and congratulating himself upon the
ease of the achievement of this portion of his task when there
arose from the depths directly in his path a hideous reptile,
which, with wide-distended jaws, bore down upon him, hissing shrilly.

Tarzan arose and stretched, expanded his great chest and
drank in deep draughts of the fresh morning air. His clear
eyes scanned the wondrous beauties of the landscape spread
out before them. Directly below lay Kor-ul-gryf, a dense,
somber green of gently moving tree tops. To Tarzan it was
neither grim, nor forbidding—it was jungle, beloved jungle.
To his right there spread a panorama of the lower reaches of
the Valley of Jad-ben-Otho, with its winding streams and its

blue lakes. Gleaming whitely in the sunlight were scattered
groups of dwellings—the feudal strongholds of the lesser chiefs
of the Ho-don. A-lur, the City of Light, he could not see as it
was hidden by the shoulder of the cliff in which the deserted
village lay.

For a moment Tarzan gave himself over to that spiritual
enjoyment of beauty that only the man-mind may attain and
then Nature asserted herself and the belly of the beast called
aloud that it was hungry. Again Tarzan looked down at
Kor-ul-gryf. There was the jungle! Grew there a jungle that
would not feed Tarzan? The ape-man smiled and commenced
the descent to the gorge. Was there danger there? Of course.
Who knew it better than Tarzan? In all jungles lies death,
for life and death go hand in hand and where life teems death
reaps his fullest harvest. Never had Tarzan met a creature of
the jungle with which he could not cope—sometimes by virtue
of brute strength alone, again by a combination of brute
strength and the cunning of the man-mind; but Tarzan had
never met a *gryf*.

He had heard the bellowings in the gorge the night before
after he had lain down to sleep and he had meant to ask Pan-
at-lee this morning what manner of beast so disturbed the
slumbers of its betters. He reached the foot of the cliff and
strode into the jungle and here he halted, his keen eyes and
ears watchful and alert, his sensitive nostrils searching each
shifting air current for the scent spoor of game. Again he advanced deeper into the wood, his light step giving forth no
sound, his bow and arrows in readiness. A light morning
breeze was blowing from up the gorge and in this direction
he bent his steps. Many odors impinged upon his organs of
scent. Some of these he classified without effort, but others
were strange—the odors of beasts and of birds, of trees and
shrubs and flowers with which he was unfamiliar. He sensed
faintly the reptilian odor that he had learned to connect with
the strange, nocturnal forms that had loomed dim and bulky
on several occasions since his introduction to Pal-ul-don.

And then, suddenly he caught plainly the strong, sweet odor
of Bara, the deer. Were the belly vocal, Tarzan's would have
given a little cry of joy, for it loved the flesh of Bara. The
ape-man moved rapidly, but cautiously forward. The prey
was not far distant and as the hunter approached it, he took
silently to the trees and still in his nostrils was the faint reptilian odor that spoke of a great creature which he had never
yet seen except as a denser shadow among the dense shadows
of the night; but the odor was of such a faintness as suggests
to the jungle bred the distance of absolute safety.

And now, moving noiselessly, Tarzan came within sight of Bara drinking at a pool where the stream that waters Kor-ul-gryf crosses an open place in the jungle. The deer was too far from the nearest tree to risk a charge, so the ape-man must depend upon the accuracy and force of his first arrow, which must drop the deer in its tracks or forfeit both deer and shaft. Far back came the right hand and the bow, that you or I might not move, bent easily beneath the muscles of the forest god. There was a singing twang and Bara, leaping high in air, collapsed upon the ground, an arrow through his heart. Tarzan dropped to earth and ran to his kill, lest the animal might even yet rise and escape; but Bara was safely dead. As Tarzan stooped to lift it to his shoulder there fell upon his ears a thunderous bellow that seemed almost at his right elbow, and as his eyes shot in the direction of the sound, there broke upon his vision such a creature as paleontologists have dreamed as having possibly existed in the dimmest vistas of Earth's infancy—a gigantic creature, vibrant with mad rage, that charged, bellowing, upon him.

When Pan-at-lee awoke she looked out upon the niche in search of Tarzan. He was not there. She sprang to her feet and rushed out, looking down into Kor-ul-gryf guessing that he had gone down in search of food and there she caught a glimpse of him disappearing into the forest. For an instant she was panic-stricken. She knew that he was a stranger in Pal-ul-don and that, so, he might not realize the dangers that lay in that gorge of terror. Why did she not call to him to return? You or I might have done so, but no Pal-ul-don, for they know the ways of the *gryf*—they know the weak eyes and the keen ears, and that at the sound of a human voice they come. To have called to Tarzan, then, would but have been to invite disaster and so she did not call. Instead, afraid though she was, she descended into the gorge for the purpose of overhauling Tarzan and warning him in whispers of his danger. It was a brave act, since it was performed in the face of countless ages of inherited fear of the creatures that she might be called upon to face. Men have been decorated for less.

Pan-at-lee, descended from a long line of hunters, assumed that Tarzan would move up wind and in this direction she sought his tracks, which she soon found well marked, since he had made no effort to conceal them. She moved rapidly until she reached the point at which Tarzan had taken to the trees. Of course she knew what had happened; since her own people were semi-arboreal; but she could not track him through the trees, having no such well-developed sense of scent as he.

She could but hope that he had continued on up wind and in this direction she moved, her heart pounding in terror against her ribs, her eyes glancing first in one direction and then another. She had reached the edge of a clearing when two things happened—she caught sight of Tarzan bending over a dead deer and at the same instant a deafening roar sounded almost beside her. It terrified her beyond description, but it brought no paralysis of fear. Instead it galvanized her into instant action with the result that Pan-at-lee swarmed up the nearest tree to the very loftiest branch that would sustain her weight. Then she looked down.

The thing that Tarzan saw charging him when the warning bellow attracted his surprised eyes loomed terrifically monstrous before him—monstrous and awe-inspiring; but it did not terrify Tarzan, it only angered him, for he saw that it was beyond even his powers to combat and that meant that it might cause him to lose his kill, and Tarzan was hungry. There was but a single alternative to remaining for annihilation and that was flight—swift and immediate. And Tarzan fled, but he carried the carcass of Bara, the deer, with him. He had not more than a dozen paces start, but on the other hand the nearest tree was almost as close. His greatest danger lay, he imagined, in the great, towering height of the creature pursuing him, for even though he reached the tree he would have to climb high in an incredibly short time as, unless appearances were deceiving, the thing could reach up and pluck him down from any branch under thirty feet above the ground, and possibly from those up to fifty feet, if it reared up on its hind legs.

But Tarzan was no sluggard and though the *gryf* was incredibly fast despite its great bulk, it was no match for Tarzan, and when it comes to climbing, the little monkeys gaze with envy upon the feats of the ape-man. And so it was that the bellowing *gryf* came to a baffled stop at the foot of the tree and even though he reared up and sought to seize his prey among the branches, as Tarzan had guessed he might, he failed in this also. And then, well out of reach, Tarzan came to a stop and there, just above him, he saw Pan-at-lee sitting, wide-eyed and trembling.

"How came you here?" he asked.

She told him. "You came to warn me!" he said. "It was very brave and unselfish of you. I am chagrined that I should have been thus surprised. The creature was up wind from me and yet I did not sense its near presence until it charged. I cannot understand it."

"It is not strange," said Pan-at-lee. "That is one of the peculiarities of the *gryf*—it is said that man never knows of its presence until it is upon him—so silently does it move despite its great size."

"But I should have smelled it," cried Tarzan, disgustedly.

"Smelled it!" ejaculated Pan-at-lee. "Smelled it?"

"Certainly. How do you suppose I found this deer so quickly? And I sensed the *gryf*, too, but faintly as at a great distance." Tarzan suddenly ceased speaking and looked down at the bellowing creature below them—his nostrils quivered as though searching for a scent. "Ah!" he exclaimed. "I have it!"

"What?" asked Pan-at-lee.

"I was deceived because the creature gives off practically no odor," explained the ape-man. "What I smelled was the faint aroma that doubtless permeates the entire jungle because of the long presence of many of the creatures—it is the sort of odor that would remain for a long time, faint as it is.

"Pan-at-lee, did you ever hear of a triceratops? No? Well this thing that you call a *gryf* is a triceratops and it has been extinct for hundreds of thousands of years. I have seen its skeleton in the museum in London and a figure of one restored. I always thought that the scientists who did such work depended principally upon an overwrought imagination, but I see that I was wrong. This living thing is not an exact counterpart of the restoration that I saw; but it is so similar as to be easily recognizable, and then, too, we must remember that during the ages that have elapsed since the paleontologist's specimen lived many changes might have been wrought by evolution in the living line that has quite evidently persisted in Pal-ul-don."

"Triceratops, London, paleo—I don't know what you are talking about," cried Pan-at-lee.

Tarzan smiled and threw a piece of dead wood at the face of the angry creature below them. Instantly the great bony hood over the neck was erected and a mad bellow rolled upward from the gigantic body. Full twenty feet at the shoulder the thing stood, a dirty slate-blue in color except for its yellow face with the blue bands encircling the eyes, the red hood with the yellow lining and the yellow belly. The three parallel lines of bony protuberances down the back gave a further touch of color to the body, those following the line of the spine being red, while those on either side are yellow. The five- and three-toed hoofs of the ancient horned dinosaurs had become talons in the *gryf*, but the three horns, two large ones above the eyes and a median horn on the nose, had persisted through all the ages. Weird and terrible as was its appearance Tarzan could not but admire the mighty creature looming big below him, its seventy-five feet of length majestically typifying those things which all his life the ape-man had admired—courage and strength. In that massive tail alone was the strength of an elephant.

The wicked little eyes looked up at him and the horny beak opened to disclose a full set of powerful teeth.

"Herbivorous!" murmured the ape-man. "Your ancestors may have been, but not you," and then to Pan-at-lee: "Let us go now. At the cave we will have deer meat and then—back to Kor-ul-ja and Om-at."

The girl shuddered. "Go?" she repeated. "We will never go from here."

"Why not?" asked Tarzan.

For answer she but pointed to the *gryf*.

"Nonsense!" exclaimed the man. "It cannot climb. We can reach the cliff through the trees and be back in the cave before it knows what has become of us."

"You do not know the *gryf*," replied Pan-at-lee gloomily. "Wherever we go it will follow and always it will be ready at the foot of each tree when we would descend. It will never give us up."

"We can live in the trees for a long time if necessary," replied Tarzan, "and sometime the thing will leave."

The girl shook her head. "Never," she said, "and then there are the Tor-o-don. They will come and kill us and after eating a little will throw the balance to the *gryf*—the *gryf* and Tor-o-don are friends, because the Tor-o-don shares his food with the *gryf*."

"You may be right," said Tarzan; "but even so I don't intend waiting here for someone to come along and eat part of me and then feed the balance to that beast below. If I don't get out of this place whole it won't be my fault. Come along now and we'll make a try at it," and so saying he moved off through the tree tops with Pan-at-lee close behind. Below them, on the ground, moved the horned dinosaur and when they reached the edge of the forest where there lay fifty yards of open ground to cross to the foot of the cliff he was there with them, at the bottom of the tree, waiting.

Tarzan looked ruefully down and scratched his head.

7

Jungle Craft

PRESENTLY he looked up and at Pan-at-lee. "Can you cross the gorge through the trees very rapidly?" he questioned.

"Alone?" she asked.

"No," relied Tarzan.

"I can follow wherever you can lead," she said then.

"Across and back again?"

"Yes."

"Then come, and do exactly as I bid." He started back again through the trees, swiftly, swinging monkey-like from limb to limb, following a zigzag course that he tried to select with an eye for the difficulties of the trail beneath. Where the underbrush was heaviest, where fallen trees blocked the way, he led the footsteps of the creature below them; but all to no avail. When they reached the opposite side of the gorge the *gryf* was with them.

"Back again," said Tarzan, and, turning, the two retraced their high-flung way through the upper terraces of the ancient forest of Kor-ul-gryf. But the result was the same—no, not quite; it was worse, for another *gryf* had joined the first and now two waited beneath the tree in which they stopped.

The cliff looming high above them with its innumerable cave mouths seemed to beckon and to taunt them. It was so near, yet eternity yawned between. The body of the Tor-o-don lay at the cliff's foot where it had fallen. It was in plain view of the two in the tree. One of the *gryfs* walked over and sniffed about it, but did not offer to devour it. Tarzan had examined it casually as he had passed earlier in the morning. He guessed that it represented either a very high order of ape or a very low order of man—something akin to the Java man, perhaps; a truer example of the pithecanthropi than either the Ho-don or the Waz-don; possibly the precursor of them both. As his eyes wandered idly over the scene below his active brain was working out the details of the plan that he had made to permit Pan-at-lee's escape from the gorge. His thoughts were interrupted by a strange cry from above them in the gorge.

"Whee-oo! Whee-oo!" it sounded, coming closer.

The *gryfs* below raised their heads and looked in the direction of the interruption. One of them made a low, rumbling sound in its throat. It was not a bellow and it did not indicate anger. Immediately the "Whee-oo!" responded. The *gryfs* repeated the rumbling and at intervals the "Whee-oo!" was repeated, coming ever closer.

Tarzan looked at Pan-at-lee. "What is it?" he asked.

"I do not know," she replied. "Perhaps a strange bird, or another horrid beast that dwells in this frightful place."

"Ah," exclaimed Tarzan; "there it is. Look!"

Pan-at-lee voiced a cry of despair. "A Tor-o-don!"

The creature, walking erect and carrying a stick in one hand, advanced at a slow, lumbering gait. It walked directly toward the *gryfs,* who moved aside, as though afraid. Tarzan watched intently. The Tor-o-don was now quite close to one of the triceratops. It swung its head and snapped at him viciously. Instantly the Tor-o-don sprang in and commenced to belabor the huge beast across the face with his stick. To the apeman's amazement the *gryf,* that might have annihilated the comparatively puny Tor-o-don instantly in any of a dozen ways, cringed like a whipped cur.

"Whee-oo! Whee-oo!" shouted the Tor-o-don and the *gryf* came slowly toward him. A whack on the median horn brought it to a stop. Then the Tor-o-don walked around behind it, clambered up its tail and seated himself astraddle of the huge back. "Whee-oo!" he shouted and prodded the beast with a sharp point of his stick. The *gryf* commenced to move off.

So rapt had Tarzan been in the scene below him that he had given no thought to escape, for he realized that for him and Pan-at-lee time had in these brief moments turned back countless ages to spread before their eyes a page of the dim and distant past. They two had looked upon the first man and his primitive beasts of burden.

And now the ridden *gryf* halted and looked up at them, bellowing. It was sufficient. The creature had warned its master of their presence. Instantly the Tor-o-don urged the beast close beneath the tree which held them, at the same time leaping to his feet upon the horny back. Tarzan saw the bestial face, the great fangs, the mighty muscles. From the loins of such had sprung the human race—and only from such could it have sprung, for only such as this might have survived the horrid dangers of the age that was theirs.

The Tor-o-don beat upon his breast and growled horribly —hideous, uncouth, beastly. Tarzan rose to his full height upon a swaying branch—straight and beautiful as a demigod —unspoiled by the taint of civilization—a perfect specimen of what the human race might have been had the laws of man not interfered with the laws of nature.

The Present fitted an arrow to his bow and drew the shaft far back. The Past basing its claims upon brute strength sought to reach the other and drag him down; but the loosed arrow sank deep into the savage heart and the Past sank back into the oblivion that had claimed his kind.

"Tarzan-jad-guru!" murmured Pan-at-lee, unknowingly giving him out of the fullness of her admiration the same title that the warriors of her tribe had bestowed upon him.

The ape-man turned to her. "Pan-at-lee," he said, "these beasts may keep us treed here indefinitely. I doubt if we can escape together, but I have a plan. You remain here, hiding yourself in the foliage, while I start back across the gorge in sight of them and yelling to attract their attention. Unless they have more brains than I suspect they will follow me. When they are gone you make for the cliff. Wait for me in the cave not longer than today. If I do not come by tomorrow's sun you will have to start back for Kor-ul-ja alone. Here is a joint of deer meat for you." He had severed one of the deer's hind legs and this he passed up to her.

"I cannot desert you," she said simply; "it is not the way of my people to desert a friend and ally. Om-at would never forgive me."

"Tell Om-at that I commanded you to go," replied Tarzan.

"It is a command?" she asked.

"It is! Good-bye, Pan-at-lee. Hasten back to Om-at—you are a fitting mate for the chief of Kor-ul-ja." He moved off slowly through the trees.

"Good-bye, Tarzan-jad-guru!" she called after him. "Fortunate are my Om-at and his Pan-at-lee in owning such a friend."

Tarzan, shouting aloud, continued upon his way and the great *gryfs*, lured by his voice, followed beneath. His ruse was evidently proving successful and he was filled with elation as he led the bellowing beasts farther and farther from Pan-at-lee. He hoped that she would take advantage of the opportunity afforded her for escape, yet at the same time he was filled with concern as to her ability to survive the dangers which lay between Kor-ul-gryf and Kor-ul-ja. There were lions and Tor-o-dons and the unfriendly tribe of Kor-ul-lul to

hinder her progress, though the distance in itself to the cliffs
of her people was not great.

He realized her bravery and understood the resourcefulness
that she must share in common with all primitive people who,
day by day, must contend face to face with nature's law of the
survival of the fittest, unaided by any of the numerous artificial
protections that civilization has thrown around its brood of
weaklings.

Several times during this crossing of the gorge Tarzan en-
deavored to outwit his keen pursuers, but all to no avail.
Double as he would he could not throw them off his track and
ever as he changed his course they changed theirs to conform.
Along the verge of the forest upon the southeastern side of
the gorge he sought some point at which the trees touched
some negotiable portion of the cliff, but though he traveled
far both up and down the gorge he discovered no such easy
avenue of escape. The ape-man finally commenced to entertain an idea of the hopelessness of his case and to realize to the
full why the Kor-ul-gryf had been religiously abjured by the
races of Pal-ul-don for all these many ages.

Night was falling and though since early morning he had
sought diligently a way out of this cul-de-sac he was no nearer
to liberty than at the moment the first bellowing *gryf* had
charged him as he stooped over the carcass of his kill: but
with the falling of night came renewed hope for, in common
with the great cats, Tarzan was, to a greater or lesser extent, a
nocturnal beast. It is true he could not see by night as well
as they, but that lack was largely recompensed for by the
keenness of his scent and the highly developed sensitiveness
of his other organs of perception. As the blind follow and
interpret their *Braille* characters with deft fingers, so Tarzan
reads the book of the jungle with feet and hands and eyes and
ears and nose; each contributing its share to the quick and
accurate translation of the text.

But again he was doomed to be thwarted by one vital weakness—he did not know the *gryf,* and before the night was
over he wondered if the things never slept, for wheresoever
he moved they moved also, and always they barred his road to
liberty. Finally, just before dawn, he relinquished his immediate effort and sought rest in a friendly tree crotch in the
safety of the middle terrace.

Once again was the sun high when Tarzan awoke, rested
and refreshed. Keen to the necessities of the moment he made
no effort to locate his jailers lest in the act he might apprise
them of his movements. Instead he sought cautiously and si-

lently to melt away among the foliage of the trees. His first move, however, was heralded by a deep bellow from below.

Among the numerous refinements of civilization that Tarzan had failed to acquire was that of profanity, and possibly it is to be regretted since there are circumstances under which it is at least a relief to pent emotion. And it may be that in effect Tarzan resorted to profanity if there can be physical as well as vocal swearing, since immediately the bellow announced that his hopes had been again frustrated, he turned quickly and seeing the hideous face of the *gryf* below him seized a large fruit from a nearby branch and hurled it viciously at the horned snout. The missile struck full between the creature's eyes, resulting in a reaction that surprised the ape-man; it did not arouse the beast to a show of revengeful rage as Tarzan had expected and hoped; instead the creature gave a single vicious side snap at the fruit as it bounded from his skull and then turned sulkily away, walking off a few steps.

There was that in the act that recalled immediately to Tarzan's mind similar action on the preceding day when the Tor-o-don had struck one of the creatures across the face with his staff, and instantly there sprung to the cunning and courageous brain a plan of escape from his predicament that might have blanched the cheek of the most heroic.

The gambling instinct is not strong among creatures of the wild; the chances of their daily life are sufficient stimuli for the beneficial excitement of their nerve centers. It has remained for civilized man, protected in a measure from the natural dangers of existence, to invent artificial stimulants in the form of cards and dice and roulette wheels. Yet when necessity bids there are no greater gamblers than the savage denizens of the jungle, the forest, and the hills, for as lightly as you roll the ivory cubes upon the green cloth they will gamble with death—their own lives the stake.

And so Tarzan would gamble now, pitting the seemingly wild deductions of his shrewd brain against all the proofs of the bestial ferocity of his antagonists that his experience of them had adduced—against all the age-old folklore and legend that had been handed down for countless generations and passed on to him through the lips of Pan-at-lee.

Yet as he worked in preparation for the greatest play that man can make in the game of life, he smiled; nor was there any indication of haste or excitement or nervousness in his demeanor.

First he selected a long, straight branch about two inches in diameter at its base. This he cut from the tree with his knife, removed the smaller branches and twigs until he had fashioned

a pole about ten feet in length. This he sharpened at the
smaller end. The staff finished to his satisfaction he looked
down upon the triceratops.

"Whee-oo!" he cried.

Instantly the beasts raised their heads and looked at him.
From the throat of one of them came faintly a low rumbling
sound.

"Whee-oo!" repeated Tarzan and hurled the balance of the
carcass of the deer to them.

Instantly the *gryfs* fell upon it with much bellowing, one of
them attempting to seize it and keep it from the other: but
finally the second obtained a hold and an instant later it had
been torn asunder and greedily devoured. Once again they
looked up at the ape-man and this time they saw him descending to the ground.

One of them started toward him. Again Tarzan repeated
the weird cry of the Tor-o-don. The *gryf* halted in his track,
aparently puzzled, while Tarzan slipped lightly to the earth
and advanced toward the nearer beast, his staff raised menac-
ingly and the call of the first-man upon his lips.

Would the cry be answered by the low rumbling of the beast
of burden or the horrid bellow of the man-eater? Upon the
answer to this question hung the fate of the ape-man.

Pan-at-lee was listening intently to the sounds of the departing *gryfs* as Tarzan led them cunningly from her, and
when she was sure that they were far enough away to insure
her safe retreat she dropped swiftly from the branches to the
ground and sped like a frightened deer across the open space
to the foot of the cliff, stepped over the body of the Tor-o-don
who had attacked her the night before and was soon climbing
rapidly up the ancient stone pegs of the deserted cliff village.
In the mouth of the cave near that which she had occupied she
kindled a fire and cooked the haunch of venison that Tarzan
had left her, and from one of the trickling streams that ran
down the face of the escarpment she obtained water to satisfy
her thirst.

All day she waited, hearing in the distance, and sometimes
close at hand, the bellowing of the *gryfs* which pursued the
strange creature that had dropped so miraculously into her
life. For him she felt the same keen, almost fanatical loyalty
that many another had experienced for Tarzan of the Apes.
Beast and human, he had held them to him with bonds that
were stronger than steel—those of them that were clean and
courageous, and the weak and the helpless; but never could
Tarzan claim among his admirers the coward, the ingrate or

the scoundrel; from such, both man and beast, he had won fear and hatred.

To Pan-at-lee he was all that was brave and noble and heroic and, too, he was Om-at's friend—the friend of the man she loved. For any one of these reasons Pan-at-lee would have died for Tarzan, for such is the loyalty of the simple-minded children of nature. It has remained for civilization to teach us to weigh the relative rewards of loyalty and its antithesis. The loyalty of the primitive is spontaneous, unreasoning, unselfish and such was the loyalty of Pan-at-lee for the Tarmangani.

And so it was that she waited that day and night, hoping that he would return that she might accompany him back to Om-at, for her experience had taught her that in the face of danger two have a better chance than one. But Tarzan-jad-guru had not come, and so upon the following morning Pan-at-lee set out upon her return to Kor-ul-ja.

She knew the dangers and yet she faced them with the stolid indifference of her race. When they directly confronted and menaced her would be time enough to experience fear or excitement or confidence. In the meantime it was unnecessary to waste nerve energy by anticipating them. She moved therefore through her savage land with no greater show of concern than might mark your sauntering to a corner drug-store for a sundae. But this is your life and that is Pan-at-lee's and even now as you read this Pan-at-lee may be sitting upon the edge of the recess of Om-at's cave while the *ja* and *jato* roar from the gorge below and from the ridge above, and the Kor-ul-lul threaten upon the south and the Ho-don from the Valley of Jad-ben-Otho far below, for Pan-at-lee still lives and preens her silky coat of jet beneath the tropical moonlight of Pal-ul-don.

But she was not to reach Kor-ul-ja this day, nor the next, nor for many days after though the danger that threatened her was neither Waz-don enemy nor savage beast.

She came without misadventure to the Kor-ul-lul and after descending its rocky southern wall without catching the slightest glimpse of the hereditary enemies of her people, she experienced a renewal of confidence that was little short of practical assurance that she would successfully terminate her venture and be restored once more to her own people and the lover she had not seen for so many long and weary moons.

She was almost across the gorge now and moving with an extreme caution abated no wit by her confidence, for wariness is an instinctive trait of the primitive, something which cannot be laid aside even momentarily if one would survive. And so she came to the trail that follows the windings of Kor-ul-lul from its uppermost reaches down into the broad and fertile Valley of Jad-ben-Otho.

And as she stepped into the trail there arose on either side of her from out of the bushes that border the path, as though materialized from thin air, a score of tall, white warriors of the Ho-don. Like a frightened deer Pan-at-lee cast a single startled look at these menacers of her freedom and leaped quickly toward the bushes in an effort to escape; but the warriors were too close at hand. They closed upon her from every side and then, drawing her knife she turned at bay, metamorphosed by the fires of fear and hate from a startled deer to a raging tiger-cat. They did not try to kill her, but only to subdue and capture her; and so it was that more than a single Ho-don warrior felt the keen edge of her blade in his flesh before they had succeeded in overpowering her by numbers. And still she fought and scratched and bit after they had taken the knife from her until it was necessary to tie her hands and fasten a piece of wood between her teeth by means of thongs passed behind her head.

At first she refused to walk when they started off in the direction of the valley but after two of them had seized her by the hair and dragged her for a number of yards she thought better of her original decision and came along with them, though still as defiant as her bound wrists and gagged mouth would permit.

Near the entrance to Kor-ul-lul they came upon another body of their warriors with which were several Waz-don prisoners from the tribe of Kor-ul-lul. It was a raiding party come up from a Ho-don city of the valley after slaves. This Pan-at-lee knew for the occurrence was by no means unusual. During her lifetime the tribe to which she belonged had been sufficiently fortunate, or powerful, to withstand successfully the majority of such raids made upon them, but yet Pan-at-lee had known of friends and relatives who had been carried into slavery by the Ho-don and she knew, too, another thing which gave her hope, as doubtless it did to each of the other captives —that occasionally the prisoners escaped from the cities of the hairless whites.

After they had joined the other party the entire band set forth into the valley and presently, from the conversation of her captors, Pan-at-lee knew that she was headed for A-lur, the City of Light; while in the cave of his ancestors, Om-at, chief of the Kor-ul-ja, bemoaned the loss of both his friend and she that was to have been his mate.

As THE hissing reptile bore down upon the stranger swimming in the open water near the center of the morass on the frontier of Pal-ul-don it seemed to the man that this indeed must be the futile termination of an arduous and danger-filled journey. It seemed, too, equally futile to pit his puny knife against this frightful creature. Had he been attacked on land it is possible that he might as a last resort have used his Enfield, though he had come thus far through all these weary, danger-ridden miles without recourse to it, though again and again had his life hung in the balance in the face of the savage denizens of forest, jungle, and steppe. For whatever it may have been for which he was preserving his precious ammunition he evidently held it more sacred even than his life, for as yet he had not used a single round and now the decision was not required of him, since it would have been impossible for him to have unslung his Enfield, loaded and fired with the necessary celerity while swimming.

Though his chance for survival seemed slender, and hope at its lowest ebb, he was not minded therefore to give up without a struggle. Instead he drew his blade and awaited the oncoming reptile. The creature was like no living thing he ever before had seen although possibly it resembled a crocodile in some respects more than it did anything with which he was familiar.

As this frightful survivor of some extinct progenitor charged upon him with distended jaws there came to the man quickly a full consciousness of the futility of endeavoring to stay the mad rush or pierce the armor-coated hide with his little knife. The thing was almost upon him now and whatever form of defense he chose must be made quickly. There seemed but a single alternative to instant death, and this he took at almost the instant the great reptile towered directly above him.

With the celerity of a seal he dove headforemost beneath the oncoming body and at the same instant, turning upon his back, he plunged his blade into the soft, cold surface of the slimy belly as the momentum of the hurtling reptile carried it swiftly over him; and then with powerful strokes he swam on beneath the surface for a dozen yards before he rose. A glance showed him the stricken monster plunging madly in pain and rage upon the surface of the water behind him. That it was writhing in its death agonies was evidenced by the fact that it made no effort to pursue him, and so, to the accompaniment of the shrill screaming of the dying monster, the man won at last to the farther edge of the open water to take up once more the almost superhuman effort of crossing the last stretch of clinging mud which separated him from the solid ground of Pal-ul-don.

A good two hours it took him to drag his now weary body through the clinging, stinking muck, but at last, mud covered and spent, he dragged himself out upon the soft grasses of the bank. A hundred yards away a stream, winding its way down from the distant mountains, emptied into the morass, and, after a short rest, he made his way to this and seeking a quiet pool, bathed himself and washed the mud and slime from his weapons, accouterments, and loin cloth. Another hour was spent beneath the rays of the hot sun in wiping, polishing, and oiling his Enfield though the means at hand for drying it consisted principally of dry grasses. It was afternoon before he had satisfied himself that his precious weapon was safe from any harm by dirt, or dampness, and then he arose and took up the search for the spoor he had followed to the opposite side of the swamp.

Would he find again the trail that had led into the opposite side of the morass, to be lost there, even to his trained senses? If he found it not again upon this side of the almost impassable barrier he might assume that his long journey had ended in failure. And so he sought up and down the verge of the stagnant water for traces of an old spoor that would have been invisible to your eyes or mine, even had we followed directly in the tracks of its maker.

As Tarzan advanced upon the *gryfs* he imitated as closely as he could recall them the methods and mannerisms of the Toro-don, but up to the instant that he stood close beside one of the huge creatures he realized that his fate still hung in the balance, for the thing gave forth no sign, either menacing or otherwise. It only stood there, watching him out of its cold, reptilian eyes and then Tarzan raised his staff and with a menacing "Whee-oo!" struck the *gryf* a vicious blow across the face.

The creature made a sudden side snap in his direction, a snap that did not reach him, and then turned sullenly away, precisely as it had when the Tor-o-don commanded it. Walking around to its rear as he had seen the shaggy first-man do, Tarzan ran up the broad tail and seated himself upon the creature's back, and then again imitating the acts of the Tor-o-don he prodded it with the sharpened point of his staff, and thus goading it forward and guiding it with blows, first upon one side and then upon the other, he started it down the gorge in the direction of the valley.

At first it had been in his mind only to determine if he could successfully assert any authority over the great monsters, realizing that in this possibility lay his only hope of immediate escape from his jailers. But once seated upon the back of his titanic mount the ape-man experienced the sensation of a new thrill that recalled to him the day in his boyhood that he had first clambered to the broad head of Tantor, the elephant, and this, together with the sense of mastery that was always meat and drink to the lord of the jungle, decided him to put his newly acquired power to some utilitarian purpose.

Pan-at-lee he judged must either have already reached safety or met with death. At least, no longer could he be of service to her, while below Kor-ul-gryf, in the soft green valley, lay A-lur, the City of Light, which, since he had gazed upon it from the shoulder of Pastar-ul-ved, had been his ambition and his goal.

Whether or not its gleaming walls held the secret of his lost mate he could not even guess but if she lived at all within the precincts of Pal-ul-don it must be among the Ho-don, since the hairy black men of this forgotten world took no prisoners. And so to A-lur he would go, and how more effectively than upon the back of this grim and terrible creature that the races of Pal-ul-don held in such awe?

A little mountain stream tumbles down from Kor-ul-gryf to be joined in the foothills with that which empties the waters of Kor-ul-lul into the valley, forming a small river which runs southwest, eventually entering the valley's largest lake at the City of A-lur, through the center of which the stream passes. An ancient trail, well marked by countless generations of naked feet of man and beast, leads down toward A-lur beside the river, and along this Tarzan guided the *gryf*. Once clear of the forest which ran below the mouth of the gorge, Tarzan caught occasional glimpses of the city gleaming in the distance far below him.

The country through which he passed was resplendent with the riotous beauties of tropical verdure. Thick, lush grasses

grew waist high upon either side of the trail and the way was
broken now and again by patches of open park-like forest, or
perhaps a little patch of dense jungle where the trees over-
arched the way and trailing creepers depended in graceful
loops from branch to branch.

At times the ape-man had difficulty in commanding obedience upon the part of his unruly beast, but always in the end
its fear of the relatively puny goad urged it on to obedience.
Late in the afternoon as they approached the confluence of the
stream they were skirting and another which appeared to come
from the direction of Kor-ul-ja the ape-man, emerging from
one of the jungle patches, discovered a considerable party of
Ho-don upon the opposite bank. Simultaneously they saw
him and the mighty creature he bestrode. For a moment they
stood in wide-eyed amazement and then, in answer to the command of their leader, they turned and bolted for the shelter of
the nearby wood.

The ape-man had but a brief glimpse of them but it was
sufficient indication that there were Waz-don with them,
doubtless prisoners taken in one of the raids upon the Waz-don
villages of which Ta-den and Om-at had told him.

At the sound of their voices the *gryf* had bellowed terrifically and started in pursuit even though a river intervened, but
by dint of much prodding and beating, Tarzan had succeeded
in heading the animal back into the path though thereafter for
a long time it was sullen and more intractable than ever.

As the sun dropped nearer the summit of the western hills
Tarzan became aware that his plan to enter A-lur upon the
back of a *gryf* was likely doomed to failure, since the stub-
bornness of the great beast was increasing momentarily, doubtless due to the fact that its huge belly was crying out for food.
The ape-man wondered if the Tor-o-dons had any means of
picketing their beasts for the night, but as he did not know
and as no plan suggested itself, he determined that he should
have to trust to the chance of finding it again in the morning.

There now arose in his mind a question as to what would be
their relationship when Tarzan had dismounted. Would it
again revert to that of hunter and quarry or would fear of the
goad continue to hold its supremacy over the natural instinct
of the hunting flesh-eater? Tarzan wondered but as he could
not remain upon the *gryf* forever, and as he preferred dis-
mounting and putting the matter to a final test while it was
still light, he decided to act at once.

How to stop the creature he did not know, as up to this time
his sole desire had been to urge it forward. By experimen-
tating with his staff, however, he found that he could bring it

to a halt by reaching forward and striking the thing upon its beaklike snout. Close by grew a number of leafy trees, in any one of which the ape-man could have found sanctuary, but it had occurred to him that should he immediately take to the trees it might suggest to the mind of the *gryf* that the creature that had been commanding him all day feared him, with the result that Tarzan would once again be held a prisoner by the triceratops.

And so, when the *gryf* halted, Tarzan slid to the ground, struck the creature a careless blow across the flank as though in dismissal and walked indifferently away. From the throat of the beast came a low rumbling sound and without even a glance at Tarzan it turned and entered the river where it stood drinking for a long time.

Convinced that the *gryf* no longer constituted a menace to him the ape-man, spurred on himself by the gnawing of hunger, unslung his bow and selecting a handful of arrows set forth cautiously in search of food, evidence of the near presence of which was being borne up to him by a breeze from down river.

Ten minutes later he had made his kill, again one of the Pal-ul-don specimens of antelope, all species of which Tarzan had known since childhood as Bara, the deer, since in the little primer that had been the basis of his education the picture of a deer had been the nearest approach to the likeness of the antelope, from the giant eland to the smaller bushbuck of the hunting grounds of his youth.

Cutting off a haunch he cached it in a nearby tree, and throwing the balance of the carcass across his shoulder trotted back toward the spot at which he had left the *gryf*. The great beast was just emerging from the river when Tarzan, seeing it, issued the weird cry of the Tor-o-don. The creature looked in the direction of the sound voicing at the same time the low rumble with which it answered the call of its master. Twice Tarzan repeated his cry before the beast moved slowly toward him, and when it had come within a few paces he tossed the carcass of the deer to it, upon which it fell with greedy jaws.

"If anything will keep it within call," mused the ape-man as he returned to the tree in which he had cached his own portion of his kill, "it is the knowledge that I will feed it." But as he finished his repast and settled himself comfortably for the night high among the swaying branches of his eyrie he had little confidence that he would ride into A-lur the following day upon his prehistoric steed.

When Tarzan awoke early the following morning he dropped lightly to the ground and made his way to the stream. Removing his weapons and loin cloth he entered the cold waters of the little pool, and after his refreshing bath returned to the tree to breakfast upon another portion of Bara, the deer, adding to his repast some fruits and berries which grew in abundance nearby.

His meal over he sought the ground again and raising his voice in the weird cry that he had learned, he called aloud on the chance of attracting the *gryf*, but though he waited for some time and continued calling there was no response, and he was finally forced to the conclusion that he had seen the last of his great mount of the preceding day.

And so he set his face toward A-lur, pinning his faith upon his knowledge of the Ho-don tongue, his great strength and his native wit.

Refreshed by food and rest, the journey toward A-lur, made in the cool of the morning along the bank of the joyous river, he found delightful in the extreme. Differentiating him from his fellows of the savage jungle were many characteristics other than those physical and mental. Not the least of these were in a measure spiritual, and one that had doubtless been as strong as another in influencing Tarzan's love of the jungle had been his appreciation of the beauties of nature. The apes cared more for a grubworm in a rotten log than for all the majestic grandeur of the forest giants waving above them. The only beauties that Numa acknowledged were those of his own person as he paraded them before the admiring eyes of his mate, but in all the manifestations of the creative power of nature of which Tarzan was cognizant he appreciated the beauties.

As Tarzan neared the city his interest became centered upon the architecture of the outlying buildings which were hewn from the chalklike limestone of what had once been a group of low hills, similar to the many grass-covered hillocks that dotted the valley in every direction. Ta-den's explanation of the Ho-don methods of house construction accounted for the ofttimes remarkable shapes and proportions of the buildings which, during the ages that must have been required for their construction, had been hewn from the limestone hills, the exteriors chiseled to such architectural forms as appealed to the eyes of the builders while at the same time following roughly the original outlines of the hills in an evident desire to economize both labor and space. The excavation of the apartments within had been similarly governed by necessity.

As he came nearer Tarzan saw that the waste material from these building operations had been utilized in the construction of outer walls about each building or group of buildings resulting from a single hillock, and later he was to learn that it had also been used for the filling of inequalities between the hills and the forming of paved streets throughout the city, the result, possibly, more of the adoption of an easy method of disposing of the quantities of broken limestone than by any real necessity for pavements.

There were people moving about within the city and upon the narrow ledges and terraces that broke the lines of the buildings and which seemed to be a peculiarity of Ho-don architecture, a concession, no doubt, to some inherent instinct that might be traced back to their early cliff-dwelling progenitors.

Tarzan was not surprised that at a short distance he aroused no suspicion or curiosity in the minds of those who saw him, since, until closer scrutiny was possible, there was little to distinguish him from a native either in his general conformation or his color. He had, of course, formulated a plan of action and, having decided, he did not hesitate in the carrying out his plan.

With the same assurance that you might venture upon the main street of a neighboring city Tarzan strode into the Ho-don city of A-lur. The first person to detect his spuriousness was a little child playing in the arched gateway of one of the walled buildings. "No tail! no tail!" it shouted, throwing a stone at him, and then it suddenly grew dumb and its eyes wide as it sensed that this creature was something other than a mere Ho-don warrior who had lost his tail. With a gasp the child turned and fled screaming into the courtyard of its home.

Tarzan continued on his way, fully realizing that the moment was imminent when the fate of his plan would be decided. Nor had he long to wait since at the next turning of the winding street he came face to face with a Ho-don warrior. He saw the sudden surprise in the latter's eyes, followed instantly by one of suspicion, but before the fellow could speak Tarzan addressed him.

"I am a stranger from another land," he said; "I would speak with Ko-tan, your king."

The fellow stepped back, laying his hand upon his knife. "There are no strangers that come to the gates of A-lur," he said, "other than as enemies or slaves."

"I come neither as a slave nor an enemy," replied Tarzan. "I come directly from Jad-ben-Otho. Look!" and he held out his hands that the Ho-don might see how greatly they differed from his own, and then wheeled about that the other might see that he was tailless, for it was upon this fact that his plan had been based, due to his recollection of the quarrel between

Ta-den and Om-at, in which the Waz-don had claimed that Jad-ben-Otho had a long tail while the Ho-don had been equally willing to fight for his faith in the taillessness of his god.

The warrior's eyes widened and an expression of awe crept into them, though it was still tinged with suspicion. "Jad-ben-Otho!" he murmured, and then, "It is true that you are neither Ho-don nor Waz-don, and it is also true that Jad-ben-Otho has no tail. Come," he said, "I will take you to Ko-tan, for this is a matter in which no common warrior may interfere. Follow me," and still clutching the handle of his knife and keeping a wary side glance upon the ape-man he led the way through A-lur.

The city covered a large area. Sometimes there was a considerable distance between groups of buildings, and again they were quite close together. There were numerous imposing groups, evidently hewn from the larger hills, often rising to a height of a hundred feet or more. As they advanced they met numerous warriors and women, all of whom showed great curiosity in the stranger, but there was no attempt to menace him when it was found that he was being conducted to the palace of the king.

They came at last to a great pile that sprawled over a considerable area, its western front facing upon a large blue lake and evidently hewn from what had once been a natural cliff. This group of buildings was surrounded by a wall of considerably greater height than any that Tarzan had before seen. His guide led him to a gateway before which waited a dozen or more warriors who had risen to their feet and formed a barrier across the entrance-way as Tarzan and his party appeared around the corner of the palace wall, for by this time he had accumulated such a following of the curious as presented to the guards the appearance of a formidable mob.

The guide's story told, Tarzan was conducted into the courtyard where he was held while one of the warriors entered the palace, evidently with the intention of notifying Ko-tan. Fifteen minutes later a large warrior appeared, followed by several others, all of whom examined Tarzan with every sign of curiosity as they approached.

The leader of the party halted before the ape-man. "Who are you?" he asked, "and what do you want of Ko-tan, the king?"

"I am a friend," replied the ape-man, "and I have come from the country of Jad-ben-Otho to visit Ko-tan of Pal-ul-don."

The warrior and his followers seemed impressed. Tarzan could see the latter whispering among themselves.

"How come you here," asked the spokesman, "and what do you want of Ko-tan?"

Tarzan drew himself to his full height. "Enough!" he cried. "Must the messenger of Jad-ben-Otho be subjected to the treatment that might be accorded to a wandering Waz-don? Take me to the king at once lest the wrath of Jad-ben-Otho fall upon you."

There was some question in the mind of the ape-man as to how far he might carry his unwarranted show of assurance, and he waited therefore with amused interest the result of his demand. He did not, however, have long to wait for almost immediately the attitude of his questioner changed. He whitened, cast an apprehensive glance toward the eastern sky and then extended his right palm toward Tarzan, placing his left over his own heart in the sign of amity that was common among the peoples of Pal-ul-don.

Tarzan stepped quickly back as though from a profaning hand, a feigned expression of horror and disgust upon his face.

"Stop!" he cried, "who would dare touch the sacred person of the messenger of Jad-ben-Otho? Only as a special mark of favor from Jad-ben-Otho may even Ko-tan himself receive this honor from me. Hasten! Already now have I waited too long! What manner of reception the Ho-don of A-lur would extend to the son of my father!"

At first Tarzan had been inclined to adopt the rôle of Jad-ben-Otho himself but it occurred to him that it might prove embarrassing and considerable of a bore to be compelled constantly to portray the character of a god, but with the growing success of his scheme it had suddenly occurred to him that the authority of the son of Jad-ben-Otho would be far greater than that of an ordinary messenger of a god, while at the same time giving him some leeway in the matter of his acts and demeanor, the ape-man reasoning that a young god would not be held so strictly accountable in the matter of his dignity and bearing as an older and greater god.

This time the effect of his words was immediately and painfully noticeable upon all those near him. With one accord they shrank back, the spokesman almost collapsing in evident terror. His apologies, when finally the paralysis of his fear would permit him to voice them, were so abject that the ape-man could scarce repress a smile of amused contempt.

"Have mercy, O Dor-ul-Otho," he pleaded, "on poor old Dak-lot. Precede me and I will show you to where Ko-tan, the king, awaits you, trembling. Aside, snakes and vermin," he cried pushing his warriors to right and left for the purpose of forming an avenue for Tarzan.

"Come!" cried the ape-man peremptorily, "lead the way, and let these others follow."

The now thoroughly frightened Dak-lot did as he was bid, and Tarzan of the Apes was ushered into the palace of Kotan, King of Pal-ul-don.

9

Blood-Stained Altars

THE entrance through which he caught his first glimpse of the interior was rather beautifully carved in geometric designs, and within the walls were similarly treated, though as he proceeded from one apartment to another he found also the figures of animals, birds, and men taking their places among the more formal figures of the mural decorator's art. Stone vessels were much in evidence as well as ornaments of gold and the skins of many animals, but nowhere did he see an indication of any woven fabric, indicating that in that respect at least the Ho-don were still low in the scale of evolution, and yet the proportions and symmetry of the corridors and apartments bespoke a degree of civilization.

The way led through several apartments and long corridors, up at least three flights of stone stairs and finally out upon a ledge upon the western side of the building overlooking the blue lake. Along this ledge, or arcade, his guide led him for a hundred yards, to stop at last before a wide entrance-way leading into another apartment of the palace.

Here Tarzan beheld a considerable concourse of warriors in an enormous apartment, the domed ceiling of which was fully fifty feet above the floor. Almost filling the chamber was a great pyramid ascending in broad steps well up under the dome in which were a number of round apertures which let in the light. The steps of the pyramid were occupied by warriors to the very pinnacle, upon which sat a large, imposing figure of a man whose golden trappings shone brightly in the light of the afternoon sun, a shaft of which poured through one of the tiny apertures of the dome.

"Ko-tan!" cried Dak-lot, addressing the resplendent figure at the pinnacle of the pyramid. "Ko-tan and warriors of Pal-ul-don! Behold the honor that Jad-ben-Otho has done you in sending as his messenger his own son," and Dak-lot, stepping aside, indicated Tarzan with a dramatic sweep of his hand.

Ko-tan rose to his feet and every warrior within sight craned his neck to have a better view of the newcomer. Those upon the opposite side of the pyramid crowded to the front as the words of the old warrior reached them. Skeptical were the expressions on most of the faces; but theirs was a skepticism marked with caution. No matter which way fortune jumped they wished to be upon the right side of the fence. For a moment all eyes were centered upon Tarzan and then gradually they drifted to Ko-tan, for from his attitude would they receive the cue that would determine theirs. But Ko-tan was evidently in the same quandary as they—the very attitude of his body indicated it—it was one of indecision and of doubt.

The ape-man stood erect, his arms folded upon his broad breast, an expression of haughty disdain upon his handsome face; but to Dak-lot there seemed to be indications also of growing anger. The situation was becoming strained. Dak-lot fidgeted, casting apprehensive glances at Tarzan and appealing ones at Ko-tan. The silence of the tomb wrapped the great chamber of the throneroom of Pal-ul-don.

At last Ko-tan spoke. "Who says that he is Dor-ul-Otho?" he asked, casting a terrible look at Dak-lot.

"He does!" almost shouted that terrified noble.

"And so it must be true?" queried Ko-tan.

Could it be that there was a trace of irony in the chief's tone? Otho forbid! Dak-lot cast a side glance at Tarzan—a glance that he intended should carry the assurance of his own faith; but that succeeded only in impressing the ape-man with the other's pitiable terror.

"O Ko-tan!" pleaded Dak-lot, "your own eyes must convince you that indeed he is the son of Otho. Behold his god-like figure, his hands, and his feet, that are not as ours, and that he is entirely tailless as is his mighty father."

Ko-tan appeared to be perceiving these facts for the first time and there was an indication that his skepticism was faltering. At that moment a young warrior who had pushed his way forward from the opposite side of the pyramid to where he could obtain a good look at Tarzan raised his voice.

"Ko-tan," he cried, "it must be even as Dak-lot says, for I am sure now that I have seen Dor-ul-Otho before. Yesterday as we were returning with the Kor-ul-lul prisoners we beheld

him seated upon the back of a great *gryf*. We hid in the
woods before he came too near, but I saw enough to make
sure that he who rode upon the great beast was none other
than the messenger who stands here now."

This evidence seemed to be quite enough to convince the
majority of the warriors that they indeed stood in the presence
of deity—their faces showed it only too plainly, and a sudden
modesty that caused them to shrink behind their neighbors.
As their neighbors were attempting to do the same thing, the
result was a sudden melting away of those who stood nearest
the ape-man, until the steps of the pyramid directly before
him lay vacant to the very apex and to Ko-tan. The latter,
possibly influenced as much by the fearful attitude of his
followers as by the evidence adduced, now altered his tone
and his manner in such a degree as might comport with the
requirements if the stranger was indeed the Dor-ul-Otho while
leaving his dignity a loophole of escape should it appear that
he had entertained an impostor.

"If indeed you are the Dor-ul-Otho," he said, addressing
Tarzan, "you will know that our doubts were but natural since
we have received no sign from Jad-ben-Otho that he intended
honoring us so greatly, nor how could we know, even, that the
Great God had a son? If you are he, all Pal-ul-don rejoices to
honor you; if you are not he, swift and terrible shall be the
punishment of your temerity. I, Ko-tan, King of Pal-ul-don,
have spoken."

"And spoken well, as a king should speak," said Tarzan,
breaking his long silence, "who fears and honors the god of his
people. It is well that you insist that I indeed be the Dor-ul-
Otho before you accord me the homage that is my due. Jad-
ben-Otho charged me specially to ascertain if you were fit to
rule his people. My first experience of you indicates that
Jad-ben-Otho chose well when he breathed the spirit of a king
into the babe at your mother's breast."

The effect of this statement, made so casually, was marked
in the expressions and excited whispers of the now awe-struck
assemblage. At last they knew how kings were made! It was
decided by Jad-ben-Otho while the candidate was still a suck-
ling babe! Wonderful! A miracle! and this divine creature
in whose presence they stood knew all about it. Doubtless he
even discussed such matters with their god daily. If there
had been an atheist among them before, or an agnostic, there
was none now, for had they not looked with their own eyes
upon the son of god?

"It is well then," continued the ape-man, "that you should
assure yourself that I am no impostor. Come closer that you

may see that I am not as are men. Furthermore it is not meet that you stand upon a higher level than the son of your god." There was a sudden scramble to reach the floor of the throne-room, nor was Ko-tan far behind his warriors, though he managed to maintain a certain majestic dignity as he descended the broad stairs that countless naked feet had polished to a gleaming smoothness through the ages. "And now," said Tarzan as the king stood before him, "you can have no doubt that I am not of the same race as you. Your priests have told you that Jad-ben-Otho is tailless. Tailless, therefore, must be the race of gods that spring from his loins. But enough of such proofs as these! You know the power of Jad-ben-Otho; how his lightnings gleaming out of the sky carry death as he wills it; how the rains come at his bidding, and the fruits and the berries and the grains, the grasses, the trees and the flowers spring to life at his divine direction; you have witnessed birth and death, and those who honor their god honor him because he controls these things. How would it fare then with an impostor who claimed to be the son of this all-powerful god? This then is all the proof that you require, for as he would strike you down should you deny me, so would he strike down one who wrongfully claimed kinship with him."

This line of argument being unanswerable must needs be convincing. There could be no questioning of this creature's statements without the tacit admission of lack of faith in the omnipotence of Jad-ben-Otho. Ko-tan was satisfied that he was entertaining deity, but as to just what form his entertainment should take he was rather at a loss to know. His conception of god had been rather a vague and hazy affair, though in common with all primitive people his god was a personal one as were his devils and demons. The pleasures of Jad-ben-Otho he had assumed to be the excesses which he himself enjoyed, but devoid of any unpleasant reaction. It therefore occurred to him that the Dor-ul-Otho would be greatly entertained by eating—eating large quantities of everything that Ko-tan liked best and that he had found most injurious; and there was also a drink that the women of the Ho-don made by allowing corn to soak in the juices of succulent fruits, to which they had added certain other ingredients best known to themselves. Ko-tan knew by experience that a single draught of this potent liquor would bring happiness and surcease from worry, while several would cause even a king to do things and enjoy things that he would never even think of doing or enjoying while not under the magical influence of the potion, but unfortunately the next morning brought suffering in direct ratio to the joy of the preceding day. A god,

Ko-tan reasoned, could experience all the pleasure without the headache, but for the immediate present he must think of the necessary dignities and honors to be accorded his immortal guest.

No foot other than a king's had touched the surface of the apex of the pyramid in the throneroom at A-lur during all the forgotten ages through which the kings of Pal-ul-don had ruled from its high eminence. So what higher honor could Ko-tan offer than to give place beside him to the Dor-ul-Otho? And so he invited Tarzan to ascend the pyramid and take his place upon the stone bench that topped it. As they reached the step below the sacred pinnacle Ko-tan continued as though to mount to his throne, but Tarzan laid a detaining hand upon his arm.

"None may sit upon a level with the gods," he admonished, stepping confidently up and seating himself upon the throne. The abashed Ko-tan showed his embarrassment, an embarrassment he feared to voice lest he incur the wrath of the king of kings.

"But," added Tarzan, "a god may honor his faithful servant by inviting him to a place at his side. Come, Ko-tan; thus would I honor you in the name of Jad-ben-Otho."

The ape-man's policy had for its basis an attempt not only to arouse the fearful respect of Ko-tan but to do it without making of him an enemy at heart, for he did not know how strong a hold the religion of the Ho-don had upon them, for since the time that he had prevented Ta-den and Om-at from quarreling over a religious difference the subject had been utterly taboo among them. He was therefore quick to note the evident though wordless resentment of Ko-tan at the suggestion that he entirely relinquish his throne to his guest. On the whole, however, the effect had been satisfactory as he could see from the renewed evidence of awe upon the faces of the warriors.

At Tarzan's direction the business of the court continued where it had been interrupted by his advent. It consisted principally in the settling of disputes between warriors. There was present one who stood upon the step just below the throne and which Tarzan was to learn was the place reserved for the higher chiefs of the allied tribes which made up Ko-tan's kingdom. The one who attracted Tarzan's attention was a stalwart warrior of powerful physique and massive, lion-like features. He was addressing Ko-tan on a question that is as old as government and that will continue in unabated importance until man ceases to exist. It had to do with a boundary dispute with one of his neighbors.

The matter itself held little or no interest for Tarzan, but he was impressed by the appearance of the speaker and when Ko-tan addressed him as Ja-don the ape-man's interest was permanently crystallized, for Ja-don was the father of Ta-den. That the knowledge would benefit him in any way seemed rather a remote possibility since he could not reveal to Ja-don his friendly relations with his son without admitting the falsity of his claims to godship.

When the affairs of the audience were concluded Ko-tan suggested that the son of Jad-ben-Otho might wish to visit the temple in which were performed the religious rites coincident to the worship of the Great God. And so the ape-man was conducted by the king himself, followed by the warriors of his court, through the corridors of the palace toward the northern end of the group of buildings within the royal enclosure.

The temple itself was really a part of the palace and similar in architecture. There were several ceremonial places of varying sizes, the purposes of which Tarzan could only conjecture. Each had an altar in the west end and another in the east and were oval in shape, their longest diameter lying due east and west. Each was excavated from the summit of a small hillock and all were without roofs. The western altars invariably were a single block of stone the top of which was hollowed into an oblong basin. Those at the eastern ends were similar blocks of stone with flat tops and these latter, unlike those at the opposite ends of the ovals were invariably stained or painted a reddish brown, nor did Tarzan need to examine them closely to be assured of what his keen nostrils already had told him—that the brown stains were dried and drying human blood.

Below these temple courts were corridors and apartments reaching far into the bowels of the hills, dim, gloomy passages that Tarzan glimpsed as he was led from place to place on his tour of inspection of the temple. A messenger had been dispatched by Ko-tan to announce the coming visit of the son of Jad-ben-Otho with the result that they were accompanied through the temple by a considerable procession of priests whose distinguishing mark of profession seemed to consist in grotesque headdresses; sometimes hideous faces carved from wood and entirely concealing the countenances of their wearers, or again, the head of a wild beast cunningly fitted over the head of a man. The high priest alone wore no such headdress. He was an old man with close-set, cunning eyes and a cruel, thin-lipped mouth.

At first sight of him Tarzan realized that here lay the greatest danger to his ruse, for he saw at a glance that the man was antagonistic toward him and his pretensions, and he knew too that doubtless of all the people of Pal-ul-don the high priest was most likely to harbor the truest estimate of Jad-ben-Otho, and, therefore, would look with suspicion on one who claimed to be the son of a fabulous god.

No matter what suspicion lurked within his crafty mind, Lu-don, the high priest of A-lur, did not openly question Tarzan's right to the title of Dor-ul-Otho, and it may be that he was restrained by the same doubts which had originally restrained Ko-tan and his warriors—the doubt that is at the bottom of the minds of all blasphemers even and which is based upon the fear that after all there may be a god. So, for the time being at least Lu-don played safe. Yet Tarzan knew as well as though the man had spoken aloud his inmost thoughts that it was in the heart of the high priest to tear the veil from his imposture.

At the entrance to the temple Ko-tan had relinquished the guidance of the guest to Lu-don and now the latter led Tarzan through those portions of the temple that he wished him to see. He showed him the great room where the votive offerings were kept, gifts from the barbaric chiefs of Pal-ul-don and from their followers. These things ranged in value from presents of dried fruits to massive vessels of beaten gold, so that in the great main storeroom and its connecting chambers and corridors was an accumulation of wealth that amazed even the eyes of the owner of the secret of the treasure vaults of Opar.

Moving to and fro throughout the temple were sleek black Waz-don slaves, fruits of the Ho-don raids upon the villages of their less civilized neighbors. As they passed the barred entrance to a dim corridor, Tarzan saw within a great company of pithecanthropi of all ages and of both sexes, Ho-don as well as Waz-don, the majority of them squatted upon the stone floor in attitudes of utter dejection while some paced back and forth, their features stamped with the despair of utter hopelessness.

"And who are these who lie here thus unhappily?" he asked of Lu-don. It was the first question that he had put to the high priest since entering the temple, and instantly he regretted that he had asked it, for Lu-don turned upon him a face upon which the expression of suspicion was but thinly veiled.

"Who should know better than the son of Jad-ben-Otho?" he retorted.

"The questions of Dor-ul-Otho are not with impunity answered with other questions," said the ape-man quietly, "and it may interest Lu-don, the high priest, to know that the blood of a false priest upon the altar of his temple is not displeasing in the eyes of Jad-ben-Otho."

Lu-don paled as he answered Tarzan's question. "They are the offerings whose blood must refresh the eastern altars as the sun returns to your father at the day's end."

"And who told you," asked Tarzan, "that Jad-ben-Otho was pleased that his people were slain upon his altars? What if you were mistaken?"

"Then countless thousands have died in vain," replied Lu-don.

Ko-tan and the surrounding warriors and priests were listening attentively to the dialogue. Some of the poor victims behind the barred gateway had heard and rising, pressed close to the barrier through which one was conducted just before sunset each day, never to return.

"Liberate them!" cried Tarzan with a wave of his hand toward the imprisoned victims of a cruel superstition, "for I can tell you in the name of Jad-ben-Otho that you are mistaken."

10

The Forbidden Garden

L U-DON paled. "It is sacrilege," he cried; "for countless ages have the priests of the Great God offered each night a life to the spirit of Jad-ben-Otho as it returned below the western horizon to its master, and never has the Great God given sign that he was displeased."

"Stop!" commanded Tarzan. "It is the blindness of the priesthood that has failed to read the messages of their god. Your warriors die beneath the knives and clubs of the Waz-don; your hunters are taken by ja and jato; no day goes by but witnesses the deaths of few or many in the villages of the Ho-don, and one death each day of those that die are the toll which Jad-ben-Otho has exacted for the lives you take upon the eastern altar. What greater sign of his displeasure could you require, O stupid priest?"

Lu-don was silent. There was raging within him a great conflict between his fear that this indeed might be the son of god and his hope that it was not, but at last his fear won and he bowed his head. "The son of Jad-ben-Otho has spoken," he said, and turning to one of the lesser priests: "Remove the bars and return these people from whence they came."

He thus addressed did as he was bid and as the bars came down the prisoners, now all fully aware of the miracle that had saved them, crowded forward and throwing themselves upon their knees before Tarzan raised their voices in thanksgiving.

Ko-tan was almost as staggered as the high priest by this ruthless overturning of an age-old religious rite. "But what," he cried, "may we do that will be pleasing in the eyes of Jad-ben-Otho?" turning a look of puzzled apprehension toward the ape-man.

"If you seek to please your god," he replied, "place upon your altars such gifts of food and apparel as are most welcome in the city of your people. These things will Jad-ben-Otho bless, when you may distribute them among those of the city who need them most. With such things are your storerooms filled as I have seen with mine own eyes, and other gifts will be brought when the priests tell the people that in this way they find favor before their god," and Tarzan turned and signified that he would leave the temple.

As they were leaving the precincts devoted to the worship of their deity, the ape-man noticed a small but rather ornate building that stood entirely detached from the others as though it had been cut from a little pinnacle of limestone which had stood out from its fellows. As his interested glance passed over it he noticed that its door and windows were barred.

"To what purpose is that building dedicated?" he asked of Lu-don. "Who do you keep imprisoned there?"

"It is nothing," replied the high priest nervously, "there is no one there. The place is vacant. Once it was used but not now for many years," and he moved on toward the gateway which led back into the palace. Here he and the priests halted while Tarzan with Ko-tan and his warriors passed out from the sacred precincts of the temple grounds.

The one question which Tarzan would have asked he had feared to ask for he knew that in the hearts of many lay a suspicion as to his genuineness, but he determined that before he slept he would put the question to Ko-tan, either directly or indirectly—as to whether there was, or had been recently within the city of A-lur a female of the same race as his.

As their evening meal was being served to them in the

banquet hall of Ko-tan's palace by a part of the army of black slaves upon whose shoulders fell the burden of all the heavy and menial tasks of the city, Tarzan noticed that there came to the eyes of one of the slaves what was apparently an expression of startled recognition, as he looked upon the ape-man for the first time in the banquet hall of Ko-tan. And again later he saw the fellow whisper to another slave and nod his head in his direction. The ape-man did not recall ever having seen this Waz-don before and he was at a loss to account for an explanation of the fellow's interest in him, and presently the incident was all but forgotten.

Ko-tan was surprised and inwardly disgusted to discover that his godly guest had no desire to gorge himself upon rich foods and that he would not even so much as taste the villainous brew of the Ho-don. To Tarzan the banquet was a dismal and tiresome affair, since so great was the interest of the guests in gorging themselves with food and drink that they had no time for conversation, the only vocal sounds being confined to a continuous grunting which, together with their table manners reminded Tarzan of a visit he had once made to the famous Berkshire herd of His Grace, the Duke of Westminster at Woodhouse, Chester.

One by one the diners succumbed to the stupifying effects of the liquor with the result that the grunting gave place to snores, so presently Tarzan and the slaves were the only conscious creatures in the banquet hall.

Rising, the ape-man turned to a tall black who stood behind him. "I would sleep," he said, "show me to my apartment."

As the fellow conducted him from the chamber the slave who had shown surprise earlier in the evening at sight of him, spoke again at length to one of his fellows. The latter cast a half-frightened look in the direction of the departing ape-man. "If you are right," he said, "they should reward us with our liberty, but if you are wrong, O Jad-ben-Otho, what will be our fate?"

"But I am not wrong!" cried the other.

"Then there is but one to tell this to, for I have heard that he looked sour when this Dor-ul-Otho was brought to the temple and that while the so-called son of Jad-ben-Otho was there he gave this one every cause to fear and hate him. I mean Lu-don, the high priest."

"You know him?" asked the other slave.

"I have worked in the temple," replied his companion.

"Then go to him at once and tell him, but be sure to exact the promise of our freedom for the proof."

And so a black Waz-don came to the temple gate and asked

to see Lu-don, the high priest, on a matter of great importance, and though the hour was late Lu-don saw him, and when he had heard his story he promised him and his friend not only their freedom but many gifts if they could prove the correctness of their claims.

And as the slave talked with the high priest in the temple at A-lur the figure of a man groped its way around the shoulder of Pastar-ul-ved and the moonlight glistened from the shiny barrel of an Enfield that was strapped to the naked back, and brass cartridges shed tiny rays of reflected light from their polished cases where they hung in the bandoliers across the broad brown shoulders and the lean waist.

Tarzan's guide conducted him to a chamber overlooking the blue lake where he found a bed similar to that which he had seen in the villages of the Waz-don, merely a raised dais of stone upon which was piled great quantities of furry pelts. And so he lay down to sleep, the question that he most wished to put still unasked and unanswered.

With the coming of a new day he was awake and wandering about the palace and the palace grounds before there was sign of any of the inmates of the palace other than slaves, or at least he saw no others at first, though presently he stumbled upon an enclosure which lay almost within the center of the palace grounds surrounded by a wall that piqued the ape-man's curiosity, since he had determined to investigate as fully as possible every part of the palace and its environs.

This place, whatever it might be, was apparently without doors or windows but that it was at least partially roofless was evidenced by the sight of the waving branches of a tree which spread above the top of the wall near him. Finding no other method of access, the ape-man uncoiled his rope and throwing it over the branch of the tree where it projected beyond the wall, was soon climbing with the ease of a monkey to the summit.

There he found that the wall surrounded an enclosed garden in which grew trees and shrubs and flowers in riotous profusion. Without waiting to ascertain whether the garden was empty or contained Ho-don, Waz-don, or wild beasts, Tarzan dropped lightly to the sward on the inside and without further loss of time commenced a systematic investigation of the enclosure.

His curiosity was aroused by the very evident fact that the place was not for general use, even by those who had free access to other parts of the palace grounds and so there was added to its natural beauties an absence of mortals which rendered its exploration all the more alluring to Tarzan since it suggested that in such a place might he hope to come upon the object of his long and difficult search.

In the garden were tiny artificial streams and little pools of water, flanked by flowering bushes, as though it all had been designed by the cunning hand of some master gardener, so faithfully did it carry out the beauties and contours of nature upon a miniature scale.

The interior surface of the wall was fashioned to represent the white cliffs of Pal-ul-don, broken occasionally by small replicas of the verdure-filled gorges of the original.

Filled with admiration and thoroughly enjoying each new surprise which the scene offered, Tarzan moved slowly around the garden, and as always he moved silently. Passing through a miniature forest he came presently upon a tiny area of flower-studded sward and at the same time beheld before him the first Ho-don female he had seen since entering the palace. A young and beautiful woman stood in the center of the little open space, stroking the head of a bird which she held against her golden breastplate with one hand. Her profile was presented to the ape-man and he saw that by the standards of any land she would have been accounted more than lovely.

Seated in the grass at her feet, with her back toward him, was a female Waz-don slave. Seeing that she he sought was not there and apprehensive that an alarm be raised were he discovered by the two women, Tarzan moved back to hide himself in the foliage, but before he had succeeded the Ho-don girl turned quickly toward him as though apprised of his presence by that unnamed sense, the manifestations of which are more or less familiar to us all.

At sight of him her eyes registered only her surprise though there was no expression of terror reflected in them, nor did she scream or even raise her well-modulated voice as she addressed him.

"Who are you," she asked, "who enters thus boldly the For-bidden Garden?"

At sound of her mistress' voice the slave maiden turned quickly, rising to her feet. "Tarzan-jad-guru!" she exclaimed in tones of mingled astonishment and relief.

"You know him?" cried her mistress turning toward the slave and affording Tarzan an opportunity to raise a cautioning finger to his lips lest Pan-at-lee further betray him, for it was Pan-at-lee indeed who stood before him, no less a source of surprise to him than had his presence been to her.

Thus questioned by her mistress and simultaneously admonished to silence by Tarzan, Pan-at-lee was momentarily silenced and then haltingly she groped for a way to extricate herself from her dilemma. "I thought—" she faltered, "but no, I am mistaken—I thought that he was one whom I had seen before near the Kor-ul-gryf."

The Ho-don looked first at one and then at the other an expression of doubt and questioning in her eyes. "But you have not answered me," she continued presently; "who are you?"

"You have not heard then," asked Tarzan, "of the visitor who arrived at your king's court yesterday?"

"You mean," she exclaimed, "that you are the Dor-ul-Otho?" And now the erstwhile doubting eyes reflected naught but awe.

"I am he," replied Tarzan; "and you?"

"I am O-lo-a, daughter of Ko-tan, the king," she replied.

So this was O-lo-a, for love of whom Ta-den had chosen exile rather than priesthood. Tarzan had approached more closely the dainty barbarian princess. "Daughter of Ko-tan," he said, "Jad-ben-Otho is pleased with you and as a mark of his favor he has preserved for you through many dangers him whom you love."

"I do not understand," replied the girl but the flush that mounted to her cheek belied her words. "Bu-lat is a guest in the palace of Ko-tan, my father. I do not know that he has faced any danger. It is to Bu-lat that I am betrothed."

"But it is not Bu-lat whom you love," said Tarzan.

Again the flush and the girl half turned her face away. "Have I then displeased the Great God?" she asked.

"No," replied Tarzan; "as I told you he is well satisfied and for your sake he has saved Ta-den for you."

"Jad-ben-Otho knows all," whispered the girl, "and his son shares his great knowledge."

"No," Tarzan hastened to correct her lest a reputation for omniscience might prove embarrassing. "I know only what Jad-ben-Otho wishes me to know."

"But tell me," she said, "I shall be reunited with Ta-den? Surely the son of god can read the future."

The ape-man was glad that he had left himself an avenue of escape. "I know nothing of the future," he replied, "other than what Jad-ben-Otho tells me. But I think you need have no fear for the future if you remain faithful to Ta-den and Ta-den's friends."

"You have seen him?" asked O-lo-a. "Tell me, where is he?"

"Yes," replied Tarzan, "I have seen him. He was with Om-at, the *gund* of Kor-ul-ja."

"A prisoner of the Waz-don?" interrupted the girl.

"Not a prisoner but an honored guest," replied the ape-man.

"Wait," he exclaimed, raising his face toward the heavens; "do not speak. I am receiving a message from Jad-ben-Otho, my father."

The two women dropped to their knees, covering their faces with their hands, stricken with awe at the thought of the awful nearness of the Great God. Presently Tarzan touched O-lo-a on the shoulder.

"Rise," he said. "Jad-ben-Otho has spoken. He has told me that this slave girl is from the tribe of Kor-ul-ja, where Ta-den is, and that she is betrothed to Om-at, their chief. Her name is Pan-at-lee."

O-lo-a turned questioningly toward Pan-at-lee. The latter nodded, her simple mind unable to determine whether or not she and her mistress were the victims of a colossal hoax. "It is even as he says," she whispered.

O-lo-a fell upon her knees and touched her forehead to Tarzan's feet. "Great is the honor that Jad-ben-Otho has done his poor servant," she cried. "Carry to him my poor thanks for the happiness that he has brought to O-lo-a."

"It would please my father," said Tarzan, "if you were to cause Pan-at-lee to be returned in safety to the village of her people."

"What cares Jad-ben-Otho for such as she?" asked O-lo-a, a slight trace of hauteur in her tone.

"There is but one god," replied Tarzan, "and he is the god of the Waz-don as well as of the Ho-don; of the birds and the beasts and the flowers and of everything that grows upon the earth or beneath the waters. If Pan-at-lee does right she is greater in the eyes of Jad-ben-Otho than would be the daughter of Ko-tan should she do wrong."

It was evident that O-lo-a did not quite understand this interpretation of divine favor, so contrary was it to the teachings of the priesthood of her people. In one respect only did Tarzan's teachings coincide with her belief—that there was but one god. For the rest she had always been taught that he was solely the god of the Ho-don in every sense, other than that other creatures were created by Jad-ben-Otho to serve some useful purpose for the benefit of the Ho-don race. And now to be told by the son of god that she stood no higher in divine esteem than the black handmaiden at her side was indeed a shock to her pride, her vanity, and her faith. But who could question the word of Dor-ul-Otho, especially when she had with her own eyes seen him in actual communion with god in heaven?

"The will of Jad-ben-Otho be done," said O-lo-a meekly, "if it lies within my power. But it would be best, O Dor-ul-Otho, to communicate your father's wish directly to the king."

"Then keep her with you," said Tarzan, "and see that no harm befalls her."

O-lo-a looked ruefully at Pan-at-lee. "She was brought to me but yesterday," she said, "and never have I had slave woman who pleased me better. I shall hate to part with her."

"But there are others," said Tarzan.

"Yes," replied O-lo-a, "there are others, but there is only one Pan-at-lee."

"Many slaves are brought to the city?" asked Tarzan.

"Yes," she replied.

"And many strangers come from other lands?" he asked.

She shook her head negatively. "Only the Ho-don from the other side of the Valley of Jad-ben-Otho," she replied, "and they are not strangers."

"Am I then the first stranger to enter the gates of A-lur?" he asked.

"Can it be," she parried, "that the son of Jad-ben-Otho need question a poor ignorant mortal like O-lo-a?"

"As I told you before," replied Tarzan, "Jad-ben-Otho alone is all-knowing."

"Then if he wished you to know this thing," retorted O-lo-a quickly, "you would know it."

Inwardly the ape-man smiled that this little heathen's astuteness should beat him at his own game, yet in a measure her evasion of the question might be an answer to it. "There have been other strangers here then recently?" he persisted.

"I cannot tell you what I do not know," she replied. "Always is the palace of Ko-tan filled with rumors, but how much fact and how much fancy how may a woman of the palace know?"

"There has been such a rumor then?" he asked.

"It was only rumor that reached the Forbidden Garden," she replied.

"It described, perhaps, a woman of another race?" As he put the question and awaited her answer he thought that his heart ceased to beat, so grave to him was the issue at stake.

The girl hesitated before replying, and then: "No," she said, "I cannot speak of this thing, for if it be of sufficient importance to elicit the interest of the gods then indeed would I be subject to the wrath of my father should I discuss it."

"In the name of Jad-ben-Otho I command you to speak,"

said Tarzan. "In the name of Jad-ben-Otho in whose hands lies the fate of Ta-den!"

The girl paled. "Have mercy!" she cried, "and for the sake of Ta-den I will tell you all that I know."

"Tell what?" demanded a stern voice from the shrubbery behind them. The three turned to see the figure of Ko-tan emerging from the foliage. An angry scowl distorted his kingly features but at sight of Tarzan it gave place to an expression of surprise not unmixed with fear. "Dor-ul-Otho!" he exclaimed, "I did not know that it was you," and then, raising his head and squaring his shoulders he said, "but there are places where even the son of the Great God may not walk and this, the Forbidden Garden of Ko-tan, is one."

It was a challenge but despite the king's bold front there was a note of apology in it, indicating that in his superstitious mind there flourished the inherent fear of man for his Maker. "Come, Dor-ul-Otho," he continued, "I do not know all this foolish child has said to you but whatever you would know Ko-tan, the king, will tell you. O-lo-a, go to your quarters immediately," and he pointed with stern finger toward the opposite end of the garden.

The princess, followed by Pan-at-lee, turned at once and left them.

"We will go this way," said Ko-tan and preceding, led Tarzan in another direction. Close to that part of the wall which they approached Tarzan perceived a grotto in the miniature cliff into the interior of which Ko-tan led him, and down a rocky stairway to a gloomy corridor the opposite end of which opened into the palace proper. Two armed warriors stood at this entrance to the Forbidden Garden, evidencing how jealously were the sacred precincts of the place guarded.

In silence Ko-tan led the way back to his own quarters in the palace. A large chamber just outside the room toward which Ko-tan was leading his guest was filled with chiefs and warriors awaiting the pleasure of their ruler. As the two entered, an aisle was formed for them the length of the chamber, down which they passed in silence.

Close to the farther door and half hidden by the warriors who stood before him was Lu-don, the high priest. Tarzan glimpsed him but briefly but in that short period he was aware of a cunning and malevolent expression upon the cruel countenance that he was subconsciously aware boded him no good, and then with Ko-tan he passed into the adjoining room and the hangings dropped.

At the same moment the hideous headdress of an under priest appeared in the entrance of the outer chamber. Its owner, pausing for a moment, glanced quickly around the interior and then having located him whom he sought moved rapidly in the direction of Lu-don. There was a whispered conversation which was terminated by the high priest.

"Return immediately to the quarters of the princess," he said, "and see that the slave is sent to me at the temple at once." The under priest turned and departed upon his mission while Lu-don also left the apartment and directed his footsteps toward the sacred enclosure over which he ruled.

A half-hour later a warrior was ushered into the presence of Ko-tan. "Lu-don, the high priest, desires the presence of Ko-tan, the king, in the temple," he announced, "and it is his wish that he come alone."

Ko-tan nodded to indicate that he accepted the command which even the king must obey. "I will return presently, Dor-ul-Otho," he said to Tarzan, "and in the meantime my warriors and my slaves are yours to command."

11

The Sentence of Death

B UT it was an hour before the king re-entered the apartment and in the meantime the ape-man had occupied himself in examining the carvings upon the walls and the numerous specimens of the handicraft of Pal-ul-donian artisans which combined to impart an atmosphere of richness and luxury to the apartment.

The limestone of the country, close-grained and of marble whiteness yet worked with comparative ease with crude implements, had been wrought by cunning craftsmen into bowls and urns and vases of considerable grace and beauty. Into the carved designs of many of these virgin gold had been hammered, presenting the effect of a rich and magnificent cloisonné. A barbarian himself the art of barbarians had always appealed to the ape-man to whom they represented a natural expression of man's love of the beautiful to even a greater extent than the studied and artificial efforts of civilization. Here was the real art of old masters, the other the cheap imitation of the chromo.

It was while he was thus pleasurably engaged that Ko-tan returned. As Tarzan, attracted by the movement of the hangings through which the king entered, turned and faced him he was almost shocked by the remarkable alteration of the king's appearance. His face was livid; his hands trembled as with palsy, and his eyes were wide as with fright. His appearance was one apparently of a combination of consuming anger and withering fear. Tarzan looked at him questioningly.

"You have had bad news, Ko-tan?" he asked.

The king mumbled an unintelligible reply. Behind there thronged into the apartment so great a number of warriors that they choked the entrance-way. The king looked apprehensively to right and left. He cast terrified glances at the ape-man and then raising his face and turning his eyes upward he cried: "Jad-ben-Otho be my witness that I do not this thing of my own accord." There was a moment's silence which was again broken by Ko-tan. "Seize him," he cried to the warriors about him, "for Lu-don, the high priest, swears that he is an impostor."

To have offered armed resistance to this great concourse of warriors in the very heart of the palace of their king would have been worse than fatal. Already Tarzan had come far by his wits and now that within a few hours he had had his hopes and his suspicions partially verified by the vague admissions of O-lo-a he was impressed with the necessity of inviting no mortal risk that he could avoid.

"Stop!" he cried, raising his palm against them. "What is the meaning of this?"

"Lu-don claims he has proof that you are not the son of Jad-ben-Otho," replied Ko-tan. "He demands that you be brought to the throneroom to face your accusers. If you are what you claim to be none knows better than you that you need have no fear in acquiescing to his demands, but remember always that in such matters the high priest commands the king and that I am only the bearer of these commands, not their author."

Tarzan saw that Ko-tan was not entirely convinced of his duplicity as was evidenced by his palpable design to play safe.

"Let not your warriors seize me," he said to Ko-tan, "lest Jad-ben-Otho, mistaking their intention, strike them dead." The effect of his words was immediate upon the men in the front rank of those who faced him, each seeming suddenly to acquire a new modesty that compelled him to self-effacement behind those directly in his rear—a modesty that became rapidly contagious.

The ape-man smiled. "Fear not," he said, "I will go willingly to the audience chamber to face the blasphemers who accuse me."

Arrived at the great throneroom a new complication arose. Ko-tan would not acknowledge the right of Lu-don to occupy the apex of the pyramid and Lu-don would not consent to occupying an inferior position while Tarzan, to remain consistent with his high claims, insisted that no one should stand above him, but only to the ape-man was the humor of the situation apparent.

To relieve the situation Ja-don suggested that all three of them occupy the throne, but this suggestion was repudiated by Ko-tan who argued that no mortal other than a king of Pal-uldon had ever sat upon the high eminence, and that furthermore there was not room for three there.

"But who," said Tarzan, "is my accuser and who is my judge?"

"Lu-don is your accuser," explained Ko-tan.

"And Lu-don is your judge," cried the high priest.

"I am to be judged by him who accuses me then," said Tarzan. "It were better to dispense then with any formalities and ask Lu-don to sentence me." His tone was ironical and his sneering face, looking straight into that of the high priest, but caused the latter's hatred to rise to still greater proportions.

It was evident that Ko-tan and his warriors saw the justice of Tarzan's implied objection to this unfair method of dispensing justice. "Only Ko-tan can judge in the throneroom of his palace," said Ja-don, "let him hear Lu-don's charges and the testimony of his witnesses, and then let Ko-tan's judgment be final."

Ko-tan, however, was not particularly enthusiastic over the prospect of sitting in trial upon one who might after all very possibly be the son of his god, and so he temporized, seeking for an avenue of escape. "It is purely a religious matter," he said, "and it is traditional that the kings of Pal-ul-don interfere not in questions of the church."

"Then let the trial be held in the temple," cried one of the chiefs, for the warriors were as anxious as their king to be relieved of all responsibility in the matter. This suggestion was more than satisfactory to the high priest who inwardly condemned himself for not having thought of it before.

"It is true," he said, "this man's sin is against the temple. Let him be dragged thither then for trial."

"The son of Jad-ben-Otho will be dragged nowhere," cried

Tarzan. "But when this trial is over it is possible that the corpse of Lu-don, the high priest, will be dragged from the temple of the god he would desecrate. Think well, then, Lu-don before you commit this folly."

His words, intended to frighten the high priest from his position failed utterly in consummating their purpose. Lu-don showed no terror at the suggestion the ape-man's words implied.

"Here is one," thought Tarzan, "who, knowing more of his religion than any of his fellows, realizes fully the falsity of my claims as he does the falsity of the faith he preaches."

He realized, however, that his only hope lay in seeming indifference to the charges. Ko-tan and the warriors were still under the spell of their belief in him and upon this fact must he depend in the final act of the drama that Lu-don was staging for his rescue from the jealous priest whom he knew had already passed sentence upon him in his own heart.

With a shrug he descended the steps of the pyramid. "It matters not to Dor-ul-Otho," he said, "where Lu-don enrages his god, for Jad-ben-Otho can reach as easily into the chambers of the temple as into the throneroom of Ko-tan."

Immeasurably relieved by this easy solution of their problem the king and the warriors thronged from the throneroom toward the temple grounds, their faith in Tarzan increased by his apparent indifference to the charges against him. Lu-don led them to the largest of the altar courts.

Taking his place behind the western altar he motioned Ko-tan to a place upon the platform at the left hand of the altar and directed Tarzan to a similar place at the right.

As Tarzan ascended the platform his eyes narrowed angrily at the sight which met them. The basin hollowed in the top of the altar was filled with water in which floated the naked corpse of a new-born babe. "What means this?" he cried angrily, turning upon Lu-don.

The latter smiled malevolently. "That you do not know," he replied, "is but added evidence of the falsity of your claim. He who poses as the son of god did not know that as the last rays of the setting sun flood the eastern altar of the temple the lifeblood of an adult reddens the white stone for the edification of Jad-ben-Otho; and that when the sun rises again from the body of its maker it looks first upon this western altar and rejoices in the death of a new-born babe each day, the ghost of which accompanies it across the heavens by day as the ghost of the adult returns with it to Jad-ben-Otho at night.

"Even the little children of the Ho-don know these things, while he who claims to be the son of Jad-ben-Otho knows them not; and if this proof be not enough, there is more. Come, Waz-don," he cried, pointing to a tall slave who stood with a group of other blacks and priests on the temple floor at the left of the altar.

The fellow came forward fearfully. "Tell us what you know of this creature," cried Lu-don, pointing to Tarzan.

"I have seen him before," said the Waz-don. "I am of the tribe of Kor-ul-lul, and one day recently a party of which I was one encountered a few of the warriors of the Kor-ul-ja upon the ridge which separates our villages. Among the enemy was this strange creature whom they called Tarzan-jad-guru; and terrible indeed was he for he fought with the strength of many men so that it required twenty of us to subdue him. But he did not fight as a god fights, and when a club struck him upon the head he sank unconscious as might an ordinary mortal.

"We carried him with us to our village as a prisoner but he escaped after cutting off the head of the warrior we left to guard him and carrying it down into the gorge and tying it to the branch of a tree upon the opposite side."

"The word of a slave against that of a god!" cried Ja-don, who had shown previously a friendly interest in the pseudo godling.

"It is only a step in the progress toward truth," interjected Lu-don. "Possibly the evidence of the only princess of the house of Ko-tan will have greater weight with the great chief from the north, though the father of a son who fled the holy offer of the priesthood may not receive with willing ears any testimony against another blasphemer."

Ja-don's hand leaped to his knife, but the warriors next him laid detaining fingers upon his arms. "You are in the temple of Jad-ben-Otho, Ja-don," they cautioned and the great chief was forced to swallow Lu-don's affront though it left in his heart bitter hatred of the high priest.

And now Ko-tan turned toward Lu-don. "What knoweth my daughter of this matter?" he asked. "You would not bring a princess of my house to testify thus publicly?"

"No," replied Lu-don, "not in person, but I have here one who will testify for her." He beckoned to an under priest. "Fetch the slave of the princess," he said.

His grotesque headdress adding a touch of the hideous to the scene, the priest stepped forward dragging the reluctant Pan-at-lee by the wrist.

"The Princess O-lo-a was alone in the Forbidden Garden with but this one slave," explained the priest, "when there suddenly appeared from the foliage nearby this creature who claims to be the Dor-ul-Otho. When the slave saw him the princess says that she cried aloud in startled recognition and called the creature by name—Tarzan-jad-guru—the same name that the slave from Kor-ul-lul gave him. This woman is not from Kor-ul-lul but from Kor-ul-ja, the very tribe with which the Kor-ul-lul says the creature was associating when he first saw him. And further the princess said that when this woman, whose name is Pan-at-lee, was brought to her yesterday she told a strange story of having been rescued from a Tor-o-don in the Kor-ul-gryf by a creature such as this, whom she spoke of then as Tarzan-jad-guru; and of how the two were pursued in the bottom of the gorge by two monster *gryfs*, and of how the man led them away while Pan-at-lee escaped, only to be taken prisoner in the Kor-ul-lul as she was seeking to return to her own tribe.

"Is it not plain now," cried Lu-don, "that this creature is no god. Did he tell you that he was the son of god?" he almost shouted, turning suddenly upon Pan-at-lee.

The girl shrank back terrified. "Answer me, slave!" cried the high priest.

"He seemed more than mortal," parried Pan-at-lee.

"Did he tell you that he was the son of god? Answer my question," insisted Lu-don.

"No," she admitted in a low voice, casting an appealing look of forgiveness at Tarzan who returned a smile of encouragement and friendship.

"That is no proof that he is not the son of god," cried Jadon. "Dost think Jad-ben-Otho goes about crying 'I am god! I am god!' Hast ever heard him Lu-don? No, you have not. Why should his son do that which the father does not do?"

"Enough," cried Lu-don. "The evidence is clear. The creature is an impostor and I, the head priest of Jad-ben-Otho in the city of A-lur, do condemn him to die." There was a moment's silence during which Lu-don evidently paused for the dramatic effect of his climax. "And if I am wrong may Jad-ben-Otho pierce my heart with his lightnings as I stand here before you all."

The lapping of the wavelets of the lake against the foot of the palace wall was distinctly audible in the utter and almost breathless silence which ensued. Lu-don stood with his face turned toward the heavens and his arms outstretched in the attitude of one who bares his breast to the dagger of an executioner. The warriors and the priests and the slaves gathered in the sacred court awaited the consuming vengeance of their god.

It was Tarzan who broke the silence. "Your god ignores you

Lu-don," he taunted, with a sneer that he meant to still further anger the high priest, "he ignores you and I can prove it before the eyes of your priests and your people."

"Prove it, blasphemer! How can you prove it?"

"You have called me a blasphemer," replied Tarzan, "you have proved to your own satisfaction that I am an impostor, that I, an ordinary mortal, have posed as the son of god. Demand then that Jad-ben-Otho uphold his godship and the dignity of his priesthood by directing his consuming fires through my own bosom."

Again there ensued a brief silence while the onlookers waited for Lu-don to thus consummate the destruction of this presumptuous impostor.

"You dare not," taunted Tarzan, "for you know that I would be struck dead no quicker than were you."

"You lie," cried Lu-don, "and I would do it had I not but just received a message from Jad-ben-Otho directing that your fate be different."

A chorus of admiring and reverential "Ahs" arose from the priesthood. Ko-tan and his warriors were in a state of mental confusion. Secretly they hated and feared Lu-don, but so ingrained was their sense of reverence for the office of the high priest that none dared raise a voice against him.

None? Well, there was Ja-don, fearless old Lion-man of the north. "The proposition was a fair one," he cried. "Invoke the lightnings of Jad-ben-Otho upon this man if you would ever convince us of his guilt."

"Enough of this," snapped Lu-don. "Since when was Ja-don created high priest? Seize the prisoner," he cried to the priests and warriors, "and on the morrow he shall die in the manner that Jad-ben-Otho has willed."

There was no immediate movement on the part of any of the warriors to obey the high priest's command, but the lesser priests on the other hand, imbued with the courage of fanaticism leaped eagerly forward like a flock of hideous harpies to seize upon their prey.

The game was up. That Tarzan knew. No longer could cunning and diplomacy usurp the functions of the weapons of defense he best loved. And so the first hideous priest who leaped to the platform was confronted by no suave ambassador from heaven, but rather a grim and ferocious beast whose temper savored more of hell.

The altar stood close to the western wall of the enclosure. There was just room between the two for the high priest to stand during the performance of the sacrificial ceremonies and only Lu-don stood there now behind Tarzan, while before him were perhaps two hundred warriors and priests.

The presumptuous one who would have had the glory of first laying arresting hands upon the blasphemous impersonator rushed forward with outstretched hand to seize the ape-man. Instead it was he who was seized; seized by steel fingers that snapped him up as though he had been a dummy of straw, grasped him by one leg and the harness at his back and raised him with giant arms high above the altar. Close at his heels were others ready to seize the ape-man and drag him down, and beyond the altar was Lu-don with drawn knife advancing toward him.

There was no instant to waste, nor was it the way of the ape-man to fritter away precious moments in the uncertainty of belated decision. Before Lu-don or any other could guess what was in the mind of the condemned, Tarzan with all the force of his great muscles dashed the screaming hierophant in the face of the high priest, and, as though the two actions were one, so quickly did he move, he had leaped to the top of the altar and from there to a handhold upon the summit of the temple wall. As he gained a footing there he turned and looked down upon those beneath. For a moment he stood in silence and then he spoke.

"Who dare believe," he cried, "that Jad-ben-Otho would forsake his son?" and then he dropped from their sight upon the other side.

There were two at least left within the enclosure whose hearts leaped with involuntary elation at the success of the ape-man's maneuver, and one of them smiled openly. This was Ja-don, and the other, Pan-at-lee.

The brains of the priest that Tarzan had thrown at the head of Lu-don had been dashed out against the temple wall while the high priest himself had escaped with only a few bruises, sustained in his fall to the hard pavement. Quickly scrambling to his feet he looked around in fear, in terror and finally in bewilderment, for he had not been a witness to the ape-man's escape. "Seize him," he cried; "seize the blas-·phemer," and he continued to look around in search of his victim with such a ridiculous expression of bewilderment that more than a single warrior was compelled to hide his smiles beneath his palm.

The priests were rushing around wildly, exhorting the warriors to pursue the fugitive but these awaited now stolidly the command of their king or high priest. Ko-tan, more or less secretly pleased by the discomfiture of Lu-don, waited for that worthy to give the necessary directions which he presently did when one of his acolytes excitedly explained to him the manner of Tarzan's escape.

Instantly the necessary orders were issued and priests and warriors sought the temple exit in pursuit of the ape-man. His departing words, hurled at them from the summit of the temple wall, had had little effect in impressing the majority that his claims had not been disproven by Lu-don, but in the hearts of the warriors was admiration for a brave man and in many the same unholy gratification that had risen in that of their ruler at the discomfiture of Lu-don.

A careful search of the temple grounds revealed no trace of the quarry. The secret recesses of the subterranean chambers, familiar only to the priesthood, were examined by these while the warriors scattered through the palace and the palace grounds without the temple. Swift runners were dispatched to the city to arouse the poeple there that all might be upon the lookout for Tarzan the Terrible. The story of his imposture and of his escape, and the tales that the Waz-don slaves had brought into the city concerning him were soon spread throughout A-lur, nor did they lose aught in the spreading, so that before an hour had passed the women and children were hiding behind barred doorways while the warriors crept apprehensively through the streets expecting momentarily to be pounced upon by a ferocious demon who, bare-handed, did victorious battle with huge *gryfs* and whose lightest pastime consisted in tearing strong men limb from limb.

12

The Giant Stranger

AND while the warriors and the priests of A-lur searched the temple and the palace and the city for the vanished ape-man there entered the head of Kor-ul-ja down the precipitous trail from the mountains, a naked stranger bearing an Enfield upon his back. Silently he moved downward toward the bottom of the gorge and there where the ancient trail unfolded more levelly before him he swung along with easy strides, though always with the utmost alertness against possible dangers. A gentle breeze came down from the mountains behind him so that only his ears and his eyes were of value in detecting the presence of danger ahead. Generally the trail followed along the banks of the winding brooklet at the bottom of the gorge, but in some places where the waters tumbled over a precipitous ledge the trail made a detour along the side of the gorge, and again it wound in and out among rocky outcroppings, and presently where it rounded sharply the projecting shoulder of a cliff the stranger came suddenly face to face with one who was ascending the gorge.

Separated by a hundred paces the two halted simultaneously. Before him the stranger saw a tall white warrior, naked but for a loin cloth, cross belts, and a girdle. The man was armed with a heavy, knotted club and a short knife, the latter hanging in its sheath at his left hip from the end of one of his cross belts, the opposite belt supporting a leathern pouch at his right side. It was Ta-den hunting alone in the gorge of his friend, the chief of Kor-ul-ja. He contemplated the stranger with surprise but no wonder, since he recognized in him a member of the race with which his experience of Tarzan the Terrible had made him familiar and also, thanks to his friendship for the ape-man, he looked upon the newcomer without hostility.

The latter was the first to make outward sign of his intentions, raising his palm toward Ta-den in that gesture which has been a symbol of peace from pole to pole since man ceased to walk upon his knuckles. Simultaneously he advanced a few paces and halted.

Ta-den, assuming that one so like Tarzan the Terrible must be a fellow-tribesman of his lost friend, was more than glad to accept this overture of peace, the sign of which he returned in kind as he ascended the trail to where the other stood. "Who are you?" he asked, but the newcomer only shook his head to indicate that he did not understand.

By signs he tried to carry to the Ho-don the fact that he was following a trail that had led him over a period of many days from some place beyond the mountains and Ta-den was convinced that the newcomer sought Tarzan-jad-guru. He wished, however, that he might discover whether as friend or foe.

The stranger perceived the Ho-don's prehensile thumbs and great toes and his long tail with an astonishment which he sought to conceal, but greater than all was the sense of relief that the first inhabitant of this strange country whom he had met had proven friendly, so greatly would he have been handicapped by the necessity for forcing his way through a hostile land.

Ta-den, who had been hunting for some of the smaller mammals, the meat of which is especially relished by the Ho-don, forgot his intended sport in the greater interest of his new discovery. He would take the stranger to Om-at and possibly together the two would find some way of discovering the true intentions of the newcomer. And so again through signs he apprised the other that he would accompany him and together they descended toward the cliffs of Om-at's people.

As they approached these they came upon the women and children working under guard of the old men and the youths —gathering the wild fruits and herbs which constitute a part of their diet, as well as tending the small acres of growing crops which they cultivate. The fields lay in small level patches that had been cleared of trees and brush. Their farm implements consisted of metal-shod poles which bore a closer resemblance to spears than to tools of peaceful agriculture. Supplementing these were others with flattened blades that were neither hoes nor spades, but instead possessed the appearance of an unhappy attempt to combine the two implements in one.

At first sight of these people the stranger halted and unslung his bow for these creatures were black as night, their bodies entirely covered with hair. But Ta-den, interpreting the doubt in the other's mind, reassured him with a gesture and a smile. The Waz-don, however, gathered around excitedly jabbering questions in a language which the stranger discovered his guide understood though it was entirely unintelligible to the former. They made no attempt to molest him and he was now sure that he had fallen among a peaceful and friendly people.

It was but a short distance now to the caves and when they reached these Ta-den led the way aloft upon the wooden pegs, assured that this creature whom he had discovered would have no more difficulty in following him than had Tarzan the Terrible. Nor was he mistaken for the other mounted with ease until presently the two stood within the recess before the cave of Om-at, the chief.

The latter was not there and it was mid-afternoon before he returned, but in the meantime many warriors came to look upon the visitor and in each instance the latter was more thoroughly impressed with the friendly and peaceable spirit of his hosts, little guessing that he was being entertained by a ferocious and warlike tribe who never before the coming of Ta-den and Tarzan had suffered a stranger among them.

At last Om-at returned and the guest sensed intuitively that he was in the presence of a great man among these people, possibly a chief or king, for not only did the attitude of the

other black warriors indicate this but it was written also in
the mein and bearing of the splendid creature who stood
looking at him while Ta-den explained the circumstances of
their meeting. "And I believe, Om-at," concluded the Ho-don,
"that he seeks Tarzan the Terrible."

At the sound of that name, the first intelligible word that
had fallen upon the ears of the stranger since he had come
among them, his face lightened. "Tarzan!" he cried, "Tarzan
of the Apes!" and by signs he tried to tell them that it was he
whom he sought.

They understood, and also they guessed from the expression
of his face that he sought Tarzan from motives of affection
rather than the reverse, but of this Om-at wished to make sure.
He pointed to the stranger's knife, and repeating Tarzan's
name, seized Ta-den and pretended to stab him, immediately
turning questioningly toward the stranger.

The latter shook his head vehemently and then first placing
a hand above his heart he raised his palm in the symbol of
peace.

"He is a friend of Tarzan-jad-guru," exclaimed Ta-den.

"Either a friend or a great liar," replied Om-at.

"Tarzan," continued the stranger, "you know him? He lives?
O God, if I could only speak your language." And again re-
verting to sign language he sought to ascertain where Tarzan
was. He would pronounce the name and point in different
directions, in the cave, down into the gorge, back toward the
mountains, or out upon the valley below, and each time he
would raise his brows questioningly and voice the universal
"eh?" of interrogation which they could not fail to understand.
But always Om-at shook his head and spread his palms in a
gesture which indicated that while he understood the question
he was ignorant as to the whereabouts of the ape-man, and
then the black chief attempted as best he might to explain
to the stranger what he knew of the whereabouts of Tarzan.

He called the newcomer Jar-don, which in the language of
Pal-ul-don means "stranger," and he pointed to the sun and
said *as*. This he repeated several times and then he held up
one hand with the fingers outspread and touching them one
by one, including the thumb, repeated the word *adenen* until
the stranger understood that he meant five. Again he pointed
to the sun and describing an arc with his forefinger starting
at the eastern horizon and terminating at the western, he repeated again the words *as adenen*. It was plain to the stranger
that the words meant that the sun had crossed the heavens
five times. In other words, five days had passed. Om-at then
pointed to the cave where they stood, pronouncing Tarzan's

name and imitating a walking man with the first and second
fingers of his right hand upon the floor of the recess, sought to
show that Tarzan had walked out of the cave and climbed upward on the pegs five days before, but this was as far as the
sign language would permit him to go.

This far the stranger followed him and, indicating that he
understood he pointed to himself and then indicating the
pegs leading above announced that he would follow Tarzan.

"Let us go with him," said Om-at, "for as yet we have not
punished the Kor-ul-lul for killing our friend and ally."

"Persuade him to wait until morning," said Ta-den, "that
you may take with you many warriors and make a great raid
upon the Kor-ul-lul, and this time, Om-at, do not kill your
prisoners. Take as many as you can alive and from some of
them we may learn the fate of Tarzan-jad-guru."

"Great is the wisdom of the Ho-don," replied Om-at. "It
shall be as you say, and having made prisoners of all the Kor-
ul-lul we shall make them tell us what we wish to know. And
then we shall march them to the rim of Kor-ul-gryf and push
them over the edge of the cliff."

Ta-den smiled. He knew that they would not take prisoner
all the Kor-ul-lul warriors—that they would be fortunate if
they took one and it was also possible that they might even be
driven back in defeat, but he knew too that Om-at would not
hesitate to carry out his threat if he had the opportunity, so
implacable was the hatred of these neighbors for each other.

It was not difficult to explain Om-at's plan to the stranger or
to win his consent since he was aware, when the great black
had made it plain that they would be accompanied by many
warriors, that their venture would probably lead them into a
hostile country and every safeguard that he could employ he
was glad to avail himself of, since the furtherance of his quest
was the paramount issue.

He slept that night upon a pile of furs in one of the com-
partments of Om-at's ancestral cave, and early the next day
following the morning meal they sallied forth, a hundred savage warriors swarming up the face of the sheer cliff and out
upon the summit of the ridge, the main body preceded by two
warriors whose duties coincided with those of the point of
modern military maneuvers, safeguarding the column against
the danger of too sudden contact with the enemy.

Across the ridge they went and down into the Kor-ul-lul and
there almost immediately they came upon a lone and unarmed
Waz-don who was making his way fearfully up the gorge
toward the village of his tribe. Him they took prisoner which,
strangely, only added to his terror since from the moment

that he had seen them and realized that escape was impossible, he had expected to be slain immediately.

"Take him back to Kor-ul-ja," said Om-at, to one of his warriors, "and hold him there unharmed until I return."

And so the puzzled Kor-ul-lul was led away while the savage company moved stealthily from tree to tree in its closer advance upon the village. Fortune smiled upon Om-at in that it gave him quickly what he sought—a battle royal, for they had not yet come in sight of the caves of the Kor-ul-lul when they encountered a considerable band of warriors headed down the gorge upon some expedition.

Like shadows the Kor-ul-ja melted into the concealment of the foliage upon either side of the trail. Ignorant of impending danger, safe in the knowledge that they trod their own domain where each rock and stone was as familiar as the features of their mates, the Kor-ul-lul walked innocently into the ambush. Suddenly the quiet of that seeming peace was shattered by a savage cry and a hurled club felled a Kor-ul-lul.

The cry was a signal for a savage chorus from a hundred Kor-ul-ja throats with which were soon mingled the war cries of their enemies. The air was filled with flying clubs and then as the two forces mingled, the battle resolved itself into a number of individual encounters as each warrior singled out a foe and closed upon him. Knives gleamed and flashed in the mottling sunlight that filtered through the foliage of the trees above. Sleek black coats were streaked with crimson stains.

In the thick of the fight the smooth brown skin of the stranger mingled with the black bodies of friend and foe. Only his keen eyes and his quick wit had shown him how to differentiate between Kor-ul-lul and Kor-ul-ja since with the single exception of apparel they were identical, but at the first rush of the enemy he had noticed that their loin cloths were not of the leopard-marked hides such as were worn by his allies.

Om-at, after dispatching his first antagonist, glanced at Jardon. "He fights with the ferocity of *jato*," mused the chief. "Powerful indeed must be the tribe from which he and Tarzan-jad-guru come," and then his whole attention was occupied by a new assailant.

The fighters surged to and fro through the forest until those who survived were spent with exhaustion. All but the stranger who seemed not to know the sense of fatigue. He fought on when each new antagonist would have gladly quit, and when there were no more Kor-ul-lul who were not engaged, he leaped upon those who stood pantingly facing the exhausted Kor-ul-ja.

And always he carried upon his back the peculiar thing which Om-at had thought was some manner of strange weapon but the purpose of which he could not now account for in view of the fact that Jar-don never used it, and that for the most part it seemed but a nuisance and needless incumbrance since it banged and smashed against its owner as he leaped, catlike, hither and thither in the course of his victorious duels. The bow and arrows he had tossed aside at the beginning of the fight but the Enfield he would not discard, for where he went he meant that it should go until its mission had been fulfilled.

Presently the Kor-ul-ja, seemingly shamed by the example of Jar-don closed once more with the enemy, but the latter, moved no doubt to terror by the presence of the stranger, a tireless demon who appeared invulnerable to their attacks, lost heart and sought to flee. And then it was that at Om-at's command his warriors surrounded a half-dozen of the most exhausted and made them prisoners.

It was a tired, bloody, and elated company that returned victorious to the Kor-ul-ja. Twenty of their number were carried back and six of these were dead men. It was the most glorious and successful raid that the Kor-ul-ja had made upon the Kor-ul-lul in the memory of man, and it marked Om-at as the greatest of chiefs, but that fierce warrior knew that advantage had lain upon his side largely because of the presence of his strange ally. Nor did he hesitate to give credit where credit belonged, with the result that Jar-don and his exploits were upon the tongue of every member of the tribe of Kor-ul-ja and great was the fame of the race that could produce two such as he and Tarzan-jad-guru.

And in the gorge of Kor-ul-lul beyond the ridge the survivors spoke in bated breath of this second demon that had joined forces with their ancient enemy.

Returned to his cave Om-at caused the Kor-ul-lul prisoners to be brought into his presence singly, and each he questioned as to the fate of Tarzan. Without exception they told him the same story—that Tarzan had been taken prisoner by them five days before but that he had slain the warrior left to guard him and escaped, carrying the head of the unfortunate sentry to the opposite side of Kor-ul-lul where he had left it suspended by its hair from the branch of a tree. But what had become of him after, they did not know; not one of them, until the last prisoner was examined, he whom they had taken first—the unarmed Kor-ul-lul making his way from the direction of the Valley of Jad-ben-Otho toward the caves of his people.

This one, when he discovered the purpose of their question-

ing, bartered with them for the lives and liberty of himself
and his fellows. "I can tell you much of this terrible man of
whom you ask, Kor-ul-ja," he said. "I saw him yesterday and
I know where he is, and if you will promise to let me and my
fellows return in safety to the caves of our ancestors I will tell
you all, and truthfully, that which I know."

"You will tell us anyway," replied Om-at, "or we shall kill
you."

"You will kill me anyway," retorted the prisoner, "unless you
make me this promise; so if I am to be killed the thing I know
shall go with me."

"He is right, Om-at," said Ta-den; "promise him that they
shall have their liberty."

"Very well," said Om-at. "Speak Kor-ul-lul, and when you
have told me all, you and your fellows may return unharmed
to your tribe."

"It was thus," commenced the prisoner. "Three days since
I was hunting with a party of my fellows near the mouth of
Kor-ul-lul not far from where you captured me this morning,
when we were surprised and set upon by a large number of
Ho-don who took us prisoners and carried us to A-lur where
a few were chosen to be slaves and the rest were cast into a
chamber beneath the temple where are held for sacrifice the
victims that are offered by the Ho-don to Jad-ben-Otho upon
the sacrificial altars of the temple at A-lur.

"It seemed then that indeed was my fate sealed and that
lucky were those who had been selected for slaves among the
Ho-don, for they at least might hope to escape—those in the
chamber with me must be without hope.

"But yesterday a strange thing happened. There came to
the temple, accompanied by all the priests and by the king and
many of his warriors, one whom all did great reverence, and
when he came to the barred gateway leading to the chamber
in which we wretched ones awaited our fate, I saw to my
surprise that it was none other than that terrible man who had
so recently been a prisoner in the village of Kor-ul-lul—he
whom you call Tarzan-jad-guru but whom they addressed as
Dor-ul-Otho. And he looked upon us and questioned the high
priest and when he was told of the purpose for which we were
imprisoned there he grew angry and cried that it was not the
will of Jad-ben-Otho that his people be thus sacrificed, and
he commanded the high priest to liberate us, and this was
done.

"The Ho-don prisoners were permitted to return to their
homes and we were led beyond the City of A-lur and set upon
our way toward Kor-ul-lul. There were three of us, but many

are the dangers that lie between A-lur and Kor-ul-lul and we were only three and unarmed. Therefore none of us reached the village of our people and only one of us lives. I have spoken."

"That is all you know concerning Tarzan-jad-guru?" asked Om-at.

"That is all I know," replied the prisoner, "other than that he whom they call Lu-don, the high priest at A-lur, was very angry, and that one of the two priests who guided us out of the city said to the other that the stranger was not Dor-ul-Otho at all; that Lu-don had said so and that he had also said that he would expose him and that he should be punished with death for his presumption. That is all they said within my hearing.

"And now, chief of Kor-ul-ja, let us depart."

Om-at nodded. "Go your way," he said, "and Ab-on, send warriors to guard them until they are safely within the Kor-ul-lul.

"Jar-don," he said beckoning to the stranger, "come with me," and rising he led the way toward the summit of the cliff, and when they stood upon the ridge Om-at pointed down into the valley toward the City of A-lur gleaming in the light of the western sun.

"There is Tarzan-jad-guru," he said, and Jar-don understood.

13

The Masquerader

As Tarzan dropped to the ground beyond the temple wall there was in his mind no intention to escape from the City of A-lur until he had satisfied himself that his mate was not a prisoner there, but how, in this strange city in which every man's hand must be now against him, he was to live and prosecute his search was far from clear to him.

There was only one place of which he knew that he might find even temporary sanctuary and that was the Forbidden Garden of the king. There was thick shrubbery in which a man might hide, and water and fruits. A cunning jungle creature, if he could reach the spot unsuspected, might remain concealed there for a considerable time, but how he was to traverse the distance between the temple grounds and the garden unseen was a question the seriousness of which he fully appreciated.

"Mighty is Tarzan," he soliloquized, "in his native jungle, but in the cities of man he is little better than they."

Depending upon his keen observation and sense of location he felt safe in assuming that he could reach the palace grounds by means of the subterranean corridors and chambers of the temple through which he had been conducted the day before, nor any slightest detail of which had escaped his keen eyes. That would be better, he reasoned, than crossing the open grounds above where his pursuers would naturally immediately follow him from the temple and quickly discover him.

And so a dozen paces from the temple wall he disappeared from sight of any chance observer above, down one of the stone stairways that led to the apartments beneath. The way that he had been conducted the previous day had followed the windings and turnings of numerous corridors and apartments, but Tarzan, sure of himself in such matters, retraced the route accurately without hesitation.

He had little fear of immediate apprehension here since he believed that all the priests of the temple had assembled in the court above to witness his trial and his humiliation and his death, and with this idea firmly implanted in his mind he rounded the turn of the corridor and came face to face with an under priest, his grotesque headdress concealing whatever emotion the sight of Tarzan may have aroused.

However, Tarzan had one advantage over the masked votary of Jad-ben-Otho in that the moment he saw the priest he knew his intention concerning him, and therefore was not compelled to delay action. And so it was that before the priest could determine on any suitable line of conduct in the premises a long, keen knife had been slipped into his heart.

As the body lunged toward the floor Tarzan caught it and snatched the headdress from its shoulders, for the first sight of the creature had suggested to his ever-alert mind a bold scheme for deceiving his enemies.

The headdress saved from such possible damage as it must have sustained had it fallen to the floor with the body of its owner, Tarzan relinquished his hold upon the corpse, set the headdress carefully upon the floor and stooping down severed the tail of the Ho-don close to its root. Near by at his right was a small chamber from which the priest had evidently just emerged and into this Tarzan dragged the corpse, the headdress, and the tail.

Quickly cutting a thin strip of hide from the loin cloth of the priest, Tarzan tied it securely about the upper end of the severed member and then tucking the tail under his loin cloth behind him, secured it in place as best he could. Then he fitted the headdress over his shoulders and stepped from the apartment, to all appearances a priest of the temple of Jad-ben-Otho unless one examined too closely his thumbs and his great toes.

He had noticed that among both the Ho-don and the Waz-don it was not at all unusual that the end of the tail be carried in one hand, and so he caught his own tail up thus lest the lifeless appearance of it dragging along behind him should arouse suspicion.

Passing along the corridor and through the various chambers he emerged at last into the palace grounds beyond the temple. The pursuit had not yet reached this point though he was conscious of a commotion not far behind him. He met now both warriors and slaves but none gave him more than a passing glance, a priest being too common a sight about the palace.

And so, passing the guards unchallenged, he came at last to the inner entrance to the Forbidden Garden and there he paused and scanned quickly that portion of the beautiful spot that lay before his eyes. To his relief it seemed unoccupied and congratulating himself upon the ease with which he had so far outwitted the high powers of A-lur he moved rapidly to the opposite end of the enclosure. Here he found a patch of flowering shrubbery that might safely have concealed a dozen men.

Crawling well within he removed the uncomfortable head-dress and sat down to await whatever eventualities fate might have in store for him the while he formulated plans for the future. The one night that he had spent in A-lur had kept him up to a late hour, apprising him of the fact that while there were few abroad in the temple grounds at night, there were yet enough to make it possible for him to fare forth under cover of his disguise without attracting the unpleasant atten-tion of the guards, and, too, he had noticed that the priest-hood constituted a privileged class that seemed to come and go at will and unchallenged throughout the palace as well as the temple. Altogether then, he decided, night furnished the most propitious hours for his investigation—by day he could lie up in the shrubbery of the Forbidden Garden, reasonably free from detection. From beyond the garden he heard the voices of men calling to one another both far and near, and he guessed that diligent was the search that was being prosecuted for him.

The idle moments afforded him an opportunity to evolve a more satisfactory scheme for attaching his stolen caudal appendage. He arranged it in such a way that it might be quickly assumed or discarded, and this done he fell to examining the weird mask that had so effectively hidden his features.

The thing had been very cunningly wrought from a single block of wood, very probably a section of a tree, upon which the features had been carved and afterward the interior hollowed out until only a comparatively thin shell remained. Two semicircular notches had been rounded out from opposite sides of the lower edge. These fitted snugly over his shoulders, aprons of wood extending downward a few inches upon his chest and back. From these aprons hung long tassels or switches of hair tapering from the outer edges toward the center which reached below the bottom of his torso. It required but the most cursory examination to indicate to the ape-man that these ornaments consisted of human scalps, taken, doubtless, from the heads of the sacrifices upon the eastern altars. The headdress itself had been carved to depict in formal design a hideous face that suggested both man and *gryf*. There were the three white horns, the yellow face with the blue bands encircling the eyes and the red hood which took the form of the posterior and anterior aprons.

As Tarzan sat within the concealing foliage of the shrubbery meditating upon the hideous priest-mask which he held in his hands he became aware that he was not alone in the garden. He sensed another presence and presently his trained ears detected the slow approach of naked feet across the sward. At first he suspected that it might be one stealthily searching the Forbidden Garden for him but a little later the figure came within the limited area of his vision which was circumscribed by stems and foliage and flowers. He saw then that it was the princess O-lo-a and that she was alone and walking with bowed head as though in meditation—sorrowful meditation for there were traces of tears upon her lids.

Shortly after his ears warned him that others had entered the garden—men they were and their footsteps proclaimed that they walked neither slowly nor meditatively. They came directly toward the princess and when Tarzan could see them he discovered that both were priests.

"O-lo-a, Princess of Pal-ul-don," said one, addressing her, "the stranger who told us that he was the son of Jad-ben-Otho has but just fled from the wrath of Lu-don, the high priest, who exposed him and all his wicked blasphemy. The temple, and the palace, and the city are being searched and we have been sent to search the Forbidden Garden, since Ko-tan, the king, said that only this morning he found him here, though how he passed the guards he could not guess."

"He is not here," said O-lo-a. "I have been in the garden for some time and have seen nor heard no other than myself. However, search it if you will."

"No," said the priest who had before spoken, "it is not necessary since he could not have entered without your knowledge and the connivance of the guards, and even had he, the priest who preceded us must have seen him."

"What priest?" asked O-lo-a.

"One passed the guards shortly before us," explained the man.

"I did not see him," said O-lo-a.

"Doubtless he left by another exit," remarked the second priest.

"Yes, doubtless," acquiesced O-lo-a, "but it is strange that I did not see him." The two priests made their obeisance and turned to depart.

"Stupid as Buto, the rhinoceros," soliloquized Tarzan, who considered Buto a very stupid creature indeed. "It should be easy to outwit such as these."

The priests had scarce departed when there came the sound of feet running rapidly across the garden in the direction of the princess to an accompaniment of rapid breathing as of one almost spent, either from fatigue or excitement.

"Pan-at-lee," exclaimed O-lo-a, "what has happened? You look as terrified as the doe for which you were named!"

"O Princess of Pal-ul-don," cried Pan-at-lee, "they would have killed him in the temple. They would have killed the wondrous stranger who claimed to be the Dor-ul-Otho."

"But he escaped," said O-lo-a. "You were there. Tell me about it."

"The head priest would have had him seized and slain, but when they rushed upon him he hurled one in the face of Lu-don with the same ease that you might cast your breast-plates at me; and then he leaped upon the altar and from there to the top of the temple wall and disappeared below. They are searching for him, but, O Princess, I pray that they do not find him."

"And why do you pray that?" asked O-lo-a. "Has not one who has so blasphemed earned death?"

"Ah, but you do not know him," replied Pan-at-lee.

"And you do, then?" retorted O-lo-a quickly. "This morning you betrayed yourself and then attempted to deceive me. The slaves of O-lo-a do not such things with impunity. He is then the same Tarzan-jad-guru of whom you told me? Speak woman and speak only the truth."

Pan-at-lee drew herself up very erect, her little chin held high, for was not she too among her own people already as good as a princess? "Panat-lee, the Kor-ul-ja does not lie," she said, "to protect herself."

"Then tell me what you know of this Tarzan-jad-guru," insisted O-lo-a.

"I know that he is a wondrous man and very brave," said Pan-at-lee, "and that he saved me from the Tor-o-don and the *gryf* as I told you, and that he is indeed the same who came into the garden this morning; and even now I do not know that he is not the son of Jad-ben-Otho for his courage and his strength are more than those of mortal man, as are also his kindness and his honor: for when he might have harmed me he protected me, and when he might have saved himself he thought only of me. And all this he did because of his friendship for Om-at, who is *gund* of Kor-ul-ja and with whom I should have mated had the Ho-don not captured me."

"He was indeed a wonderful man to look upon," mused O-lo-a, "and he was not as are other men, not alone in the conformation of his hands and feet or the fact that he was tailless, but there was that about him which made him seem different in ways more important than these."

"And," supplemented Pan-at-lee, her savage little heart loyal to the man who had befriended her and hoping to win for him the consideration of the princess even though it might not avail him; "and," she said, "did he not know all about Ta-den and even his whereabouts. Tell me, O Princess, could mortal know such things as these?"

"Perhaps he saw Ta-den," suggested O-lo-a.

"But how would he know that you loved Ta-den," parried Pan-at-lee. "I tell you, my Princess, that if he is not a god he is at least more than Ho-don or Waz-don. He followed me from the cave of Es-sat in Kor-ul-ja across Kor-ul-lul and two wide ridges to the very cave in Kor-ul-gryf where I hid, though many hours had passed since I had come that way and my bare feet left no impress upon the ground. What mortal man could do such things as these? And where in all Pal-ul-don would virgin maid find friend and protector in a strange male other than he?"

"Perhaps Lu-don may be mistaken—perhaps he is a god,"

said O-lo-a, influenced by her slave's enthusiastic championing of the stranger.

"But whether god or man he is too wonderful to die," cried Pan-at-lee. "Would that I might save him. If he lived he might even find a way to give you your Ta-den, Princess."

"Ah, if he only could," sighed O-lo-a, "but alas it is too late for tomorrow I am to be given to Bu-lot."

"He who came to your quarters yesterday with your father?" asked Pan-at-lee.

"Yes; the one with the awful round face and the big belly," exclaimed the Princess disgustedly. "He is so lazy he will neither hunt nor fight. To eat and to drink is all that Bu-lot is fit for, and he thinks of naught else except these things and his slave women. But come, Pan-at-lee, gather for me some of these beautiful blossoms. I would have them spread around my couch tonight that I may carry away with me in the morning the memory of the fragrance that I love best and which I know that I shall not find in the village of Mo-sar, the father of Bu-lot. I will help you, Pan-at-lee, and we will gather armfuls of them, for I love to gather them as I love nothing else —they were Ta-den's favorite flowers."

The two approached the flowering shrubbery where Tarzan hid, but as the blooms grew plentifully upon every bush the ape-man guessed there would be no necessity for them to enter the patch far enough to discover him. With little exclamations of pleasure as they found particularly large or perfect blooms the two moved from place to place upon the outskirts of Tarzan's retreat.

"Oh, look, Pan-at-lee," cried O-lo-a presently; "there is the king of them all. Never did I see so wonderful a flower—No! I will get it myself—it is so large and wonderful no other hand shall touch it," and the princess wound in among the bushes toward the point where the great flower bloomed upon a bush above the ape-man's head.

So sudden and unexpected her approach that there was no opportunity to escape and Tarzan sat silently trusting that fate might be kind to him and lead Ko-tan's daughter away before her eyes dropped from the high-growing bloom to him. But as the girl cut the long stem with her knife she looked down straight into the smiling face of Tarzan-jad-guru.

With a stifled scream she drew back and the ape-man rose and faced her.

"Have no fear, Princess," he assured her. "It is the friend of Ta-den who salutes you," raising her fingers to his lips.

Pan-at-lee came now excitedly forward. "O Jad-ben-Otho, it is he!"

"And now that you have found me," queried Tarzan, "will you give me up to Lu-don, the high priest?"

Pan-at-lee threw herself upon her knees at O-lo-a's feet. "Princess! Princess!" she beseeched, "do not discover him to his enemies."

"But Ko-tan, my father," whispered O-lo-a fearfully, "if he knew of my perfidy his rage would be beyond naming. Even though I am a princess Lu-don might demand that I be sacrificed to appease the wrath of Jad-ben-Otho, and between the two of them I should be lost."

"But they need never know," cried Pan-at-lee, "that you have seen him unless you tell them yourself for as Jad-ben-Otho is my witness I will never betray you."

"Oh, tell me, stranger," implored O-lo-a, "are you indeed a god?"

"Jad-ben-Otho is not more so," replied Tarzan truthfully.

"But why do you seek to escape then from the hands of mortals if you are a god?" she asked.

"When gods mingle with mortals," replied Tarzan, "they are no less vulnerable than mortals. Even Jad-ben-Otho, should he appear before you in the flesh, might be slain."

"You have seen Ta-den and spoken with him?" she asked with apparent irrelevancy.

"Yes, I have seen him and spoken with him," replied the ape-man. "For the duration of a moon I was with him constantly."

"And—" she hesitated—"he—" she cast her eyes toward the ground and a flush mantled her cheek—"he still loves me?" and Tarzan knew that she had been won over.

"Yes," he said, "Ta-den speaks only of O-lo-a and he waits and hopes for the day when he can claim her."

"But tomorrow they give me to Bu-lot," she said sadly.

"May it be always tomorrow," replied Tarzan, "for tomorrow never comes."

"Ah, but this unhappiness will come, and for all the tomorrows of my life I must pine in misery for the Ta-den who will never be mine."

"But for Lu-don I might have helped you," said the ape-man. "And who knows that I may not help you yet?"

"Ah, if you only could, Dor-ul-Otho," cried the girl, "and I know that you would if it were possible for Pan-at-lee has told me how brave you are, and at the same time how kind."

"Only Jad-ben-Otho knows what the future may bring," said Tarzan. "And now you two go your way lest someone should discover you and become suspicious."

"We will go," said O-lo-a, "but Pan-at-lee will return with

food. I hope that you escape and that Jad-ben-Otho is pleased with what I have done." She turned and walked away and Pan-at-lee followed while the ape-man again resumed his hiding.

At dusk Pan-at-lee came with food and having her alone Tarzan put the question that he had been anxious to put since his conversation earlier in the day with O-lo-a.

"Tell me," he said, "what you know of the rumors of which O-lo-a spoke of the mysterious stranger which is supposed to be hidden in A-lur. Have you too heard of this during the short time that you have been here?"

"Yes," said Pan-at-lee, "I have heard it spoken of among the other slaves. It is something of which all whisper among themselves but of which none dares to speak aloud. They say that there is a strange she hidden in the temple and that Lu-don wants her for a priestess and that Ko-tan wants her for a wife and that neither as yet dares take her for fear of the other."

"Do you know where she is hidden in the temple?" asked Tarzan.

"No," said Pan-at-lee. "How should I know? I do not even know that it is more than a story and I but tell you that which I have heard others say."

"There was only one," asked Tarzan, "whom they spoke of?"

"No, they speak of another who came with her but none seems to know what became of this one."

Tarzan nodded. "Thank you Pan-at-lee," he said. "You may have helped me more than either of us guess."

"I hope that I have helped you," said the girl as she turned back toward the palace.

"And I hope so too," exclaimed Tarzan emphatically.

14

The Temple of the Gryf

___

WHEN night had fallen Tarzan donned the mask and the dead tail of the priest he had slain in the vaults beneath the temple. He judged that it would not do to attempt again to pass the guard, especially so late at night as it would be likely to arouse comment and suspicion, and so he swung into the tree that overhung the garden wall and from its branches dropped to the ground beyond.

Avoiding too grave risk of apprehension the ape-man passed through the grounds to the court of the palace, approaching the temple from the side opposite to that at which he had left it at the time of his escape. He came thus it is true through a portion of the grounds with which he was unfamiliar but he preferred this to the danger of following the beaten track between the palace apartments and those of the temple. Having a definite goal in mind and endowed as he was with an almost miraculous sense of location he moved with great assurance through the shadows of the temple yard.

Taking advantage of the denser shadows close to the walls and of what shrubs and trees there were he came without mishap at last to the ornate building concerning the purpose of which he had asked Lu-don only to be put off with the assertion that it was forgotten—nothing strange in itself but given possible importance by the apparent hesitancy of the priest to discuss its use and the impression the ape-man had gained at the time that Lu-don lied.

And now he stood at last alone before the structure which was three stories in height and detached from all the other temple buildings. It had a single barred entrance which was carved from the living rock in representation of the head of a *gryf*, whose wide-open mouth constituted the doorway. The head, hood, and front paws of the creature were depicted as though it lay crouching with its lower jaw on the ground between its outspread paws. Small oval windows, which were likewise barred, flanked the doorway.

Seeing that the coast was clear, Tarzan stepped into the darkened entrance where he tried the bars only to discover that they were ingeniously locked in place by some device with which he was unfamiliar and that they also were probably too strong to be broken even if he could have risked the noise which would have resulted. Nothing was visible within the darkened interior and so, momentarily baffled, he sought the windows. Here also the bars refused to yield up their secret, but again Tarzan was not dismayed since he had counted upon nothing different.

If the bars would not yield to his cunning they would yield to his giant strength if there proved no other means of ingress, but first he would assure himself that this latter was the case. Moving entirely around the building he examined it carefully. There were other windows but they were similarly barred. He stopped often to look and listen but he saw no one and the sounds that he heard were too far away to cause him any apprehension.

He glanced above him at the wall of the building. Like so many of the other walls of the city, palace, and temple, it was ornately carved and there were too the peculiar ledges that ran sometimes in a horizontal plane and again were tilted at an angle, giving ofttimes an impression of irregularity and even crookedness to the buildings. It was not a difficult wall to climb, at least not difficult for the ape-man.

But he found the bulky and awkward headdress a considerable handicap and so he laid it aside upon the ground at the foot of the wall. Nimbly he ascended to find the windows of the second floor not only barred but curtained within. He did not delay long at the second floor since he had in mind an idea that he would find the easiest entrance through the roof which he had noticed was roughly dome shaped like the throneroom of Ko-tan. Here there were apertures. He had seen them from the ground, and if the construction of the interior resembled even slightly that of the throneroom, bars would not be necessary upon these apertures, since no one could reach them from the floor of the room.

There was but a single question: would they be large enough to admit the broad shoulders of the ape-man.

He paused again at the third floor, and here, in spite of the hangings, he saw that the interior was lighted and simultaneously there came to his nostrils from within a scent that stripped from him temporarily any remnant of civilization that might have remained and left him a fierce and terrible bull of the jungles of Kerchak. So sudden and complete was the metamorphosis that there almost broke from the savage lips the hideous challenge of his kind, but the cunning brute-mind saved him this blunder.

And now he heard voices within—the voice of Lu-don he could have sworn, demanding. And haughty and disdainful came the answering words though utter hopelessness spoke in the tones of this other voice which brought Tarzan to the pinnacle of frenzy.

The dome with its possible apertures was forgotten. Every consideration of stealth and quiet was cast aside as the ape-man drew back his mighty fist and struck a single terrific blow upon the bars of the small window before him, a blow that sent the bars and the casing that held them clattering to the floor of the apartment within.

Instantly Tarzan dove headforemost through the aperture carrying the hangings of antelope hide with him to the floor below. Leaping to his feet he tore the èntangling pelt from about his head only to find himself in utter darkness and in silence. He called aloud a name that had not passed his lips for many weary months. "Jane, Jane," he cried, "where are you?" But there was only silence in reply.

Again and again he called, groping with outstretched hands through the Stygian blackness of the room, his nostrils assailed and his brain tantalized by the delicate effluvia that had first assured him that his mate had been within this very room. And he had heard her dear voice combatting the base demands of the vile priest. Ah, if he had but acted with greater caution! If he had but continued to move with quiet and stealth he might even at this moment be holding her in his arms while the body of Lu-don, beneath his foot, spoke eloquently of vengeance achieved. But there was no time now for idle self-reproaches.

He stumbled blindly forward, groping for he knew not what till suddenly the floor beneath him tilted and he shot downward into a darkness even more utter than that above. He felt his body strike a smooth surface and he realized that he was hurtling downward as through a polished chute while from above there came the mocking tones of a taunting laugh and the voice of Lu-don screamed after him: "Return to thy father, O Dor-ul-Otho!"

The ape-man came to a sudden and painful stop upon a rocky floor. Directly before him was an oval window crossed by many bars, and beyond he saw the moonlight playing on the waters of the blue lake below. Simultaneously he was conscious of a familiar odor in the air of the chamber, which a quick glance revealed in the semidarkness as of considerable proportion.

It was the faint, but unmistakable odor of the *gryf,* and now Tarzan stood silently listening. At first he detected no sounds other than those of the city that came to him through the window overlooking the lake; but presently, faintly, as though from a distance he heard the shuffling of padded feet along a stone pavement, and as he listened he was aware that the sound approached.

Nearer and nearer it came, and now even the breathing of the beast was audible. Evidently attracted by the noise of his descent into its cavernous retreat it was approaching to investigate. He could not see it but he knew that it was not far distant, and then, deafeningly there reverberated through those gloomy corridors the mad bellow of the *gryf.*

Aware of the poor eyesight of the beast, and his own eyes now grown accustomed to the darkness of the cavern, the ape-man sought to elude the infuriated charge which he well knew no living creature could withstand. Neither did he dare risk the chance of experimenting upon this strange *gryf* with the tactics of the Tor-o-don that he had found so efficacious upon that other occasion when his life and liberty had been the stakes for which he cast. In many respects the conditions were dissimilar. Before, in broad daylight, he had been able to approach the *gryf* under normal conditions in its natural state, and the *gryf* itself was one that he had seen subjected to the authority of man, or at least of a manlike creature; but here he was confronted by an imprisoned beast in the full swing of a furious charge and he had every reason to suspect that this *gryf* might never have felt the restraining influence of authority, confined as it was in this gloomy pit to serve likely but the single purpose that Tarzan had already seen so graph-ically portrayed in his own experience of the past few moments.

To elude the creature, then, upon the possibility of discover-ing some loophole of escape from his predicament seemed to the ape-man the wisest course to pursue. Too much was at stake to risk an encounter that might be avoided—an encoun-ter the outcome of which there was every reason to apprehend would seal the fate of the mate that he had just found, only to lose again so harrowingly. Yet high as his disappointment and chagrin ran, hopeless as his present estate now appeared, there tingled in the veins of the savage lord a warm glow of thanks-giving and elation. She lived! After all these weary months of hopelessness and fear he had found her. She lived!

To the opposite side of the chamber, silently as the wraith of a disembodied soul, the swift jungle creature moved from the path of the charging Titan that, guided solely in the semidarkness by its keen ears, bore down upon the spot toward which Tarzan's noisy entrance into its lair had attracted it. Along the further wall the ape-man hurried. Before him now appeared the black opening of the corridor from which the beast had emerged into the larger chamber. Without hesitation Tarzan plunged into it. Even here his eyes, long accustomed to darkness that would have seemed total to you or to me, saw dimly the floor and the walls within a radius of a few feet—enough at least to prevent him plunging into any unguessed abyss, or dashing himself upon solid rock at a sudden turning.

The corridor was both wide and lofty, which indeed it must be to accommodate the colossal proportions of the creature whose habitat it was, and so Tarzan encountered no difficulty in moving with reasonable speed along its winding trail. He was aware as he proceeded that the trend of the passage was downward, though not steeply, but it seemed interminable and he wondered to what distant subterranean lair it might lead. There was a feeling that perhaps after all he might better have remained in the larger chamber and risked all on the chance of subduing the *gryf* where there was at least sufficient room and light to lend to the experiment some slight chance of success. To be overtaken here in the narrow confines of the black corridor where he was assured the *gryf* could not see him at all would spell almost certain death and now he heard the thing approaching from behind. Its thunderous bellows fairly shook the cliff from which the cavernous chambers were excavated. To halt and meet this monstrous incarnation of fury with a futile *whee-oo!* seemed to Tarzan the height of insanity and so he continued along the corridor, increasing his pace as he realized that the *gryf* was overhauling him.

Presently the darkness lessened and at the final turning of the passage he saw before him an area of moonlight. With renewed hope he sprang rapidly forward and emerged from the mouth of the corridor to find himself in a large circular enclosure the towering white walls of which rose high upon every side—smooth perpendicular walls upon the sheer face of which was no slightest foothold. To his left lay a pool of water, one side of which lapped the foot of the wall at this point. It was, doubtless, the wallow and the drinking pool of the *gryf*.

And now the creature emerged from the corridor and Tarzan retreated to the edge of the pool to make his last stand. There was no staff with which to enforce the authority of his voice, but yet he made his stand for there seemed naught else to do. Just beyond the entrance to the corridor the *gryf* paused,

turning its weak eyes in all directions as though searching for
its prey. This then seemed the psychological moment for his
attempt and raising his voice in peremptory command the ape-
man voiced the weird *whee-oo!* of the Tor-o-don. Its effect
upon the *gryf* was instantaneous and complete—with a terrific
bellow it lowered its three horns and dashed madly in the direction of the sound.

To right nor to left was any avenue of escape, for behind
him lay the placid waters of the pool, while down upon him
from before thundered annihilation. The mighty body seemed
already to tower above him as the ape-man turned and dove
into the dark waters.

Dead in her breast lay hope. Battling for life during har-
rowing months of imprisonment and danger and hardship it
had fitfully flickered and flamed only to sink after each renewal
to smaller proportions than before and now it had died out
entirely leaving only cold, charred embers that Jane Clayton
knew would never again be rekindled. Hope was dead as she
faced Lu-don, the high priest, in her prison quarters in the
Temple of the *Gryf* at A-lur. Both time and hardship had
failed to leave their impress upon her physical beauty—the
contours of her perfect form, the glory of her radiant loveli-
ness had defied them, yet to these very attributes she owed the
danger which now confronted her, for Lu-don desired her.
From the lesser priests she had been safe, but from Lu-don,
she was not safe, for Lu-don was not as they, since the high
priestship of Pal-ul-don may descend from father to son.

Ko-tan, the king, had wanted her and all that had so far
saved her from either was the fear of each for the other, but
at last Lu-don had cast aside discretion and had come in the
silent watches of the night to claim her. Haughtily had she
repulsed him, seeking ever to gain time, though what time
might bring her of relief or renewed hope she could not even
remotely conjecture. A leer of lust and greed shone hungrily
upon his cruel countenance as he advanced across the room to
seize her. She did not shrink nor cower, but stood there very
erect, her chin up, her level gaze freighted with the loathing
and contempt she felt for him. He read her expression and
while it angered him, it but increased his desire for possession.
Here indeed was a queen, perhaps a goddess; fit mate for the
high priest.

"You shall not!" she said as he would have touched her.
"One of us shall die before ever your purpose is accomplished."

He was close beside her now. His laugh grated upon her ears. "Love does not kill," he replied mockingly.

He reached for her arm and at the same instant something clashed against the bars of one of the windows, crashing them inward to the floor, to be followed almost simultaneously by a human figure which dove headforemost into the room, its head enveloped in the skin window hangings which it carried with it in its impetuous entry.

Jane Clayton saw surprise and something of terror too leap to the countenance of the high priest and then she saw him spring forward and jerk upon a leather thong that depended from the ceiling of the apartment. Instantly there dropped from above a cunningly contrived partition that fell between them and the intruder, effectively barring him from them and at the same time leaving him to grope upon its opposite side in darkness, since the only cresset the room contained was upon their side of the partition.

Faintly from beyond the wall Jane heard a voice calling, but whose it was and what the words she could not distinguish. Then she saw Lu-don jerk upon another thong and wait in evident expectancy of some consequent happening. He did not have long to wait. She saw the thong move suddenly as though jerked from above and then Lu-don smiled and with another signal put in motion whatever machinery it was that raised the partition again to its place in the ceiling.

Advancing into that portion of the room that the partition had shut off from them, the high priest knelt upon the floor, and down tilting a section of it, revealed the dark mouth of a shaft leading below. Laughing loudly he shouted into the hole: "Return to thy father, O Dor-ul-Otho!"

Making fast the catch that prevented the trapdoor from opening beneath the feet of the unwary until such time as Lu-don chose the high priest rose again to his feet.

"Now, Beautiful One!" he cried, and then; "Ja-don! what do you here?"

Jane Clayton turned to follow the direction of Lu-don's eyes and there she saw framed in the entrance-way to the apartment the mighty figure of a warrior, upon whose massive features sat an expression of stern and uncompromising authority.

"I come from Ko-tan, the king," replied Ja-don, "to remove the beautiful stranger to the Forbidden Garden."

"The king defies me, the high priest of Jad-ben-Otho?" cried Lu-don.

"It is the king's command—I have spoken," snapped Ja-don,

in whose manner was no sign of either fear or respect for the priest.

Lu-don well knew why the king had chosen this messenger whose heresy was notorious, but whose power had as yet protected him from the machinations of the priest. Lu-don cast a surreptitious glance at the thongs hanging from the ceiling. Why not? If he could but maneuver to entice Ja-don to the opposite side of the chamber!

"Come," he said in a conciliatory tone, "let us discuss the matter," and moved toward the spot where he would have Ja-don follow him.

"There is nothing to discuss," replied Ja-don, yet he followed the priest, fearing treachery.

Jane watched them. In the face and figure of the warrior she found reflected those admirable traits of courage and honor that the profession of arms best develops. In the hypocritical priest there was no redeeming quality. Of the two then she might best choose the warrior. With him there was a chance —with Lu-don, none. Even the very process of exchange from one prison to another might offer some possibility of escape. She weighed all these things and decided, for Lu-don's quick glance at the thongs had not gone unnoticed nor uninterpreted by her.

"Warrior," she said, addressing Ja-don, "if you would live enter not that portion of the room."

Lu-don cast an angry glance upon her. "Silence, slave!" he cried.

"And where lies the danger?" Ja-don asked of Jane, ignoring Lu-don.

The woman pointed to the thongs. "Look," she said, and before the high priest could prevent she had seized that which controlled the partition which shot downward separating Lu-don from the warrior and herself.

Ja-don looked inquiringly at her. "He would have tricked me neatly but for you," he said; "kept me imprisoned there while he secreted you elsewhere in the mazes of his temple."

"He would have done more than that," replied Jane, as she pulled upon the other thong. "This releases the fastenings of a trapdoor in the floor beyond the partition. When you stepped on that you would have been precipitated into a pit beneath the temple. Lu-don has threatened me with this fate often. I do not know that he speaks the truth, but he says that a demon of the temple is imprisoned there—a huge *gryf*."

"There is a *gryf* within the temple," said Ja-don. "What with it and the sacrifices, the priests keep us busy supplying them with prisoners, though the victims are sometimes those for whom Lu-don has conceived hatred among our own people. He has had his eyes upon me for a long time. This would have been his chance but for you. Tell me, woman, why you warned me. Are we not all equally your jailers and your enemies?"

"None could be more horrible than Lu-don," she replied; "and you have the appearance of a brave and honorable warrior. I could not hope, for hope has died and yet there is the possibility that among so many fighting men, even though they be of another race than mine, there is one who would accord honorable treatment to a stranger within his gates—even though she be a woman."

Ja-don looked at her for a long minute. "Ko-tan would make you his queen," he said. "That he told me himself and surely that were honorable treatment from one who might make you a slave."

"Why, then, would he make me queen?" she asked.

Ja-don came closer as though in fear his words might be overheard. "He believes, although he did not tell me so in fact, that you are of the race of gods. And why not? Jad-ben-Otho is tailless, therefore it is not strange that Ko-tan should suspect that only the gods are thus. His queen is dead leaving only a single daughter. He craves a son and what more desirable than that he should found a line of rulers for Pal-ul-don descended from the gods?"

"But I am already wed," cried Jane. "I cannot wed another. I do not want him or his throne."

"Ko-tan is king," replied Ja-don simply as though that explained and simplified everything.

"You will not save me then?" she asked.

"If you were in Ja-lur," he replied, "I might protect you, even against the king."

"What and where is Ja-lur?" she asked, grasping at any straw.

"It is the city where I rule," he answered. "I am chief there and of all the valley beyond."

"Where is it?" she insisted, and "is it far?"

"No," he replied, smiling, "it is not far, but do not think of that—you could never reach it. There are too many to pursue and capture you. If you wish to know, however, it lies up the river that empties into Jad-ben-lul whose waters kiss the walls of A-lur—up the western fork it lies with water upon three sides. Impregnable city of Pal-ul-don—alone of all the cities it has never been entered by a foeman since it was built there while Jad-ben-Otho was a boy."

"And there I would be safe?" she asked.

"Perhaps," he replied.

Ah, dead Hope; upon what slender provocation would you seek to glow again! She sighed and shook her head, realizing the inutility of Hope—yet the tempting bait dangled before her mind's eye—Ja-lur!

"You are wise," commented Ja-don interpreting her sigh. "Come now, we will go to the quarters of the princess beside the Forbidden Garden. There you will remain with O-lo-a, the king's daughter. It will be better than this prison you have occupied."

"And Ko-tan?" she asked, a shudder passing through her slender frame.

"There are ceremonies," explained Ja-don, "that may occupy several days before you become queen, and one of them may be difficult of arrangement." He laughed, then.

"What?" she asked.

"Only the high priest may perform the marriage ceremony for a king," he explained.

"Delay!" she murmured; "blessed delay!" Tenacious indeed of life is Hope even though it be reduced to cold and lifeless char—a veritable phoenix.

15

"The King Is Dead!"

As THEY conversed Ja-don had led her down the stone stairway that leads from the upper floors of the Temple of the *Gryf* to the chambers and the corridors that honeycomb the rocky hills from which the temple and the palace are hewn and now they passed from one to the other through a doorway upon one side of which two priests stood guard and upon the other two warriors. The former would have halted Ja-don when they saw who it was that accompanied him for well known throughout the temple was the quarrel between king and high priest for possession of this beautiful stranger.

"Only by order of Lu-don may she pass," said one, placing himself directly in front of Jane Clayton, barring her progress. Through the hollow eyes of the hideous mask the woman could see those of the priest beneath gleaming with the fires of fanaticism. Ja-don placed an arm about her shoulders and laid his hand upon his knife.

"She passes by order of Ko-tan, the king," he said, "and by virtue of the fact that Ja-don, the chief, is her guide. Stand aside!"

The two warriors upon the palace side pressed forward. "We are here, *gund* of Ja-lur," said one, addressing Ja-don, "to receive and obey your commands."

The second priest now interposed. "Let them pass," he admonished his companion. "We have received no direct commands from Lu-don to the contrary and it is a law of the temple and the palace that chiefs and priests may come and go without interference."

"But I know Lu-don's wishes," insisted the other.

"He told you then that Ja-don must not pass with the stranger?"

"No—but——"

"Then let them pass, for they are three to two and will pass anyway—we have done our best."

Grumbling, the priest stepped aside. "Lu-don will exact an accounting," he cried angrily.

Ja-don turned upon him. "And get it when and where he will," he snapped.

They came at last to the quarters of the Princess O-lo-a where, in the main entrance-way, loitered a small guard of palace warriors and several stalwart black eunuchs belonging to the princess, or her women. To one of the latter Ja-don relinquished his charge.

"Take her to the princess," he commanded, "and see that she does not escape."

Through a number of corridors and apartments lighted by stone cressets the eunuch led Lady Greystoke halting at last before a doorway concealed by hangings of *jato* skin, where the guide beat with his staff upon the wall beside the door.

"O-lo-a, Princes of Pal-ul-don," he called, "here is the stranger woman, the prisoner from the temple."

"Bid her enter," Jane heard a sweet voice from within command.

The eunuch drew aside the hangings and Lady Greystoke stepped within. Before her was a low-ceiled room of moderate size. In each of the four corners a kneeling figure of stone seemed to be bearing its portion of the weight of the ceiling upon its shoulders. These figures were evidently intended to represent Waz-don slaves and were not without bold artistic beauty. The ceiling itself was slightly arched to a central dome which was pierced to admit light by day, and air. Upon one side of the room were many windows, the other three walls being blank except for a doorway in each. The princess lay upon a pile of furs which were arranged over a low stone dais in one corner of the apartment and was alone except for a single Waz-don slave girl who sat upon the edge of the dais near her feet.

As Jane entered O-lo-a beckoned her to approach and when she stood beside the couch the girl half rose upon an elbow and surveyed her critically.

"How beautiful you are," she said simply.

Jane smiled, sadly; for she had found that beauty may be a curse.

"That is indeed a compliment," she replied quickly, "from one so radiant as the Princess O-lo-a."

"Ah!" exclaimed the princess delightedly; "you speak my language! I was told that you were of another race and from some far land of which we of Pal-ul-don have never heard."

"Lu-don saw to it that the priests instructed me," explained Jane; "but I am from a far country, Princess; one to which I long to return—and I am very unhappy."

"But Ko-tan, my father, would make you his queen," cried the girl; "that should make you very happy."

"But it does not," replied the prisoner; "I love another to whom I am already wed. Ah, Princess, if you had known what it was to love and to be forced into marriage with an-other you would sympathize with me."

The Princess O-lo-a was silent for a long moment. "I know," she said at last, "and I am very sorry for you; but if the king's daughter cannot save herself from such a fate who may save a slave woman? for such in fact you are."

The drinking in the great banquet hall of the palace of Ko-tan, king of Pal-ul-don had commenced earlier this night than was usual, for the king was celebrating the morrow's be-trothal of his only daughter to Bu-lot, son of Mo-sar, the chief, whose great-grandfather had been king of Pal-ul-don and who thought that he should be king, and Mo-sar was drunk and so was Bu-lot, his son. For that matter nearly all of the warriors, including the king himself, were drunk. In the heart of Ko-tan was no love either for Mo-sar, or Bu-lot, nor did either of these love the king. Ko-tan was giving his daugh-ter to Bu-lot in the hope that the alliance would prevent Mo-sar from insisting upon his claims to the throne, for, next to Ja-don, Mo-sar was the most powerful of the chiefs and while Ko-tan looked with fear upon Ja-don, too, he had no fear that the old Lion-man would attempt to seize the throne, though which way he would throw his influence and his warriors in the event that Mo-sar declare war upon Ko-tan, the king could not guess.

Primitive people who are also warlike are seldom inclined toward either tact or diplomacy even when sober; but drunk they know not the words, if aroused. It was really Bu-lot who started it.

"This," he said, "I drink to O-lo-a," and he emptied his tankard at a single gulp. "And this," seizing a full one from a neighbor, "to her son and mine who will bring back the throne of Pal-ul-don to its rightful owners!"

"The king is not yet dead!" cried Ko-tan, rising to his feet; "nor is Bu-lot yet married to his daughter—and there is yet time to save Pal-ul-don from the spawn of the rabbit breed."

The king's angry tone and his insulting reference to Bu-lot's well-known cowardice brought a sudden, sobering silence upon the roistering company. Every eye turned upon Bu-lot and Mo-sar, who sat together directly opposite the king. The first was very drunk though suddenly he seemed quite sober. He was so drunk that for an instant he forgot to be a coward, since his reasoning powers were so effectually paralyzed by the fumes of liquor that he could not intelligently weigh the consequences of his acts. It is reasonably conceivable that a drunk and angry rabbit might commit a rash deed. Upon no other hypothesis is the thing that Bu-lot now did explicable. He rose suddenly from the seat to which he had sunk after delivering his toast and seizing the knife from the sheath of the warrior upon his right hurled it with terrific force at Ko-tan. Skilled in the art of throwing both their knives and their clubs are the warriors of Pal-ul-don and at this short distance and coming as it did without warning there was no defense and but one possible result—Ko-tan, the king, lunged forward across the table, the blade buried in his heart.

A brief silence followed the assassin's cowardly act. White with terror, now, Bu-lot fell slowly back toward the doorway at his rear, when suddenly angry warriors leaped with drawn knives to prevent his escape and to avenge their king. But Mo-sar now took his stand beside his son.

"Ko-tan is dead!" he cried. "Mo-sar is king! Let the loyal warriors of Pal-ul-don protect their ruler!"

Mo-sar commanded a goodly following and these quickly surrounded him and Bu-lot, but there were many knives against them and now Ja-don pressed forward through those who confronted the pretender.

"Take them both!" he shouted. "The warriors of Pal-ul-don

will choose their own king after the assassin of Ko-tan has paid the penalty of his treachery."

Directed now by a leader whom they both respected and admired those who had been loyal to Ko-tan rushed forward upon the faction that had surrounded Mo-sar. Fierce and terrible was the fighting, devoid, apparently, of all else than the ferocious lust to kill and while it was at its height Mo-sar and Bu-lot slipped unnoticed from the banquet hall.

To that part of the palace assigned to them during their visit to A-lur they hastened. Here were their servants and the lesser warriors of their party who had not been bidden to the feast of Ko-tan. These were directed quickly to gather together their belongings for immediate departure. When all was ready, and it did not take long, since the warriors of Pal-ul-don require but little impedimenta on the march, they moved toward the palace gate.

Suddenly Mo-sar approached his son. "The princess," he whispered. "We must not leave the city without her—she is half the battle for the throne."

Bu-lot, now entirely sober, demurred. He had had enough of fighting and of risk. "Let us get out of A-lur quickly," he urged, "or we shall have the whole city upon us. She would not come without a struggle and that would delay us too long."

"There is plenty of time," insisted Mo-sar. "They are still fighting in the *pal-e-don-so*. It will be long before they miss us and, with Ko-tan dead, long before any will think to look to the safety of the princess. Our time is now—it was made for us by Jad-ben-Otho. Come!"

Reluctantly Bu-lot followed his father, who first instructed the warriors to await them just inside the gateway of the palace. Rapidly the two approached the quarters of the princess. Within the entrance-way only a handful of warriors were on guard. The eunuchs had retired.

"There is fighting in the *pal-e-don-so*," Mo-sar announced in feigned excitement as they entered the presence of the guards. "The king desires you to come at once and has sent us to guard the apartments of the princess. Make haste!" he commanded as the men hesitated.

The warriors knew him and that on the morrow the princess was to be betrothed to Bu-lot, his son. If there was trouble what more natural than that Mo-sar and Bu-lot should be intrusted with the safety of the princess. And then, too, was not Mo-sar a powerful chief to whose orders disobedience might prove a dangerous thing? They were but common fighting men disciplined in the rough school of tribal warfare, but they had learned to obey a superior and so they departed for the banquet hall—the *place-where-men-eat*.

Barely waiting until they had disappeared Mo-sar crossed to the hangings at the opposite end of the entrance-hall and followed by Bu-lot made his way toward the sleeping apartment of O-lo-a and a moment later, without warning, the two men burst in upon the three occupants of the room. At sight of them O-lo-a sprang to her feet.

"What is the meaning of this?" she demanded angrily.

Mo-sar advanced and halted before her. Into his cunning mind had entered a plan to trick her. If it succeeded it would prove easier than taking her by force, and then his eyes fell upon Jane Clayton and he almost gasped in astonishment and admiration, but he caught himself and returned to the business of the moment.

"O-lo-a," he cried, "when you know the urgency of our mission you will forgive us. We have sad news for you. There has been an uprising in the palace and Ko-tan, the king, has been slain. The rebels are drunk with liquor and now on their way here. We must get you out of A-lur at once—there is not a moment to lose. Come, and quickly!"

"My father dead?" cried O-lo-a, and suddenly her eyes went wide. "Then my place is here with my people," she cried. "If Ko-tan is dead I am queen until the warriors choose a new ruler—that is the law of Pal-ul-don. And if I am queen none can make me wed whom I do not wish to wed—and Jad-ben-Otho knows I never wished to wed thy cowardly son. Go!" She pointed a slim forefinger imperiously toward the doorway.

Mo-sar saw that neither trickery nor persuasion would avail now and every precious minute counted. He looked again at the beautiful woman who stood beside O-lo-a. He had never before seen her but he well knew from palace gossip that she could be no other than the godlike stranger whom Ko-tan had planned to make his queen.

"Bu-lot," he cried to his son, "take you your own woman and I will take—mine!" and with that he sprang suddenly forward and seizing Jane about the waist lifted her in his arms, so that before O-lo-a or Pan-at-lee might even guess his purpose he had disappeared through the hangings near the foot of the dais and was gone with the stranger woman struggling and fighting in his grasp.

And then Bu-lot sought to seize O-lo-a, but O-lo-a had her Pan-at-lee—fierce little tiger-girl of the savage Kor-ul-ja—Pan-at-lee whose name belied her—and Bu-lot found that with the two of them his hands were full. When he would have lifted O-lo-a and borne her away Pan-at-lee seized him around the legs and strove to drag him down. Viciously he kicked her, but she would not desist, and finally, realizing that he might not only lose his princess but be so delayed as to invite capture if he did not rid himself of this clawing, scratching she-*jato*, he hurled O-lo-a to the floor and seizing Pan-at-lee by the hair drew his knife and——

The curtains behind him suddenly parted. In two swift bounds a lithe figure crossed the room and before ever the knife of Bu-lot reached its goal his wrist was seized from behind and a terrific blow crashing to the base of his brain dropped him, lifeless, to the floor. Bu-lot, coward, traitor, and assassin, died without knowing who struck him down.

As Tarzan of the Apes leaped into the pool in the *gryf* pit of the temple at A-lur one might have accounted for his act on the hypothesis that it was the last blind urge of self-preservation to delay, even for a moment, the inevitable tragedy in which each some day must play the leading rôle upon his little stage; but no—those cool, gray eyes had caught the sole possibility for escape that the surroundings and the circumstances offered—a tiny, moonlit patch of water glimmering through a small aperture in the cliff at the surface of the pool upon its farther side. With swift, bold strokes he swam for speed alone knowing that the water would in no way deter his pursuer. Nor did it. Tarzan heard the great splash as the huge creature plunged into the pool behind him; he heard the churning waters as it forged rapidly onward in his wake. He was nearing the opening—would it be large enough to permit the passage of his body? That portion of it which showed above the surface of the water most certainly would not. His life, then, depended upon how much of the aperture was submerged. And now it was directly before him and the *gryf* directly behind. There was no alternative—there was no other hope. The ape-man threw all the resources of his great strength into the last few strokes, extended his hands before him as a cutwater, submerged to the water's level and shot forward toward the hole.

Frothing with rage was the baffled Lu-don as he realized how neatly the stranger she had turned his own tables upon him. He could of course escape the Temple of the *Gryf* in which her quick wit had temporarily imprisoned him; but during the delay, however brief, Ja-don would find time to steal her from the temple and deliver her to Ko-tan. But he would have her yet—that the high priest swore in the names of Jad-ben-Otho and all the demons of his faith. He hated Kotan. Secretly he had espoused the cause of Mo-sar, in whom he would have a willing tool. Perhaps, then, this would give him the opportunity he had long awaited—a pretext for inciting the revolt that would dethrone Ko-tan and place Mo-sar in power—with Lu-don the real ruler of Pal-ul-don. He licked his thin lips as he sought the window through which Tarzan had entered and now Lu-don's only avenue of escape. Cautiously he made his way across the floor, feeling before him with his hands, and when they discovered that the trap was set for him an ugly snarl broke from the priest's lips. "The she-devil!" he muttered; "but she shall pay, she shall pay—ah, Jad-ben-Otho; how she shall pay for the trick she has played upon Lu-don!"

He crawled through the window and climbed easily downward to the ground. Should he pursue Ja-don and the woman, chancing an encounter with the fierce chief, or bide his time until treachery and intrigue should accomplish his design? He chose the latter solution, as might have been expected of such as he.

Going to his quarters he summoned several of his priests—those who were most in his confidence and who shared his ambitions for absolute power of the temple over the palace—all men who hated Ko-tan.

"The time has come," he told them, "when the authority of the temple must be placed definitely above that of the palace. Ko-tan must make way for Mo-sar, for Ko-tan has defied your high priest. Go then, Pan-sat, and summon Mo-sar secretly to the temple, and you others go to the city and prepare the faithful warriors that they may be in readiness when the time comes."

For another hour they discussed the details of the coup d'état that was to overthrow the government of Pal-ul-don. One knew a slave who, as the signal sounded from the temple gong, would thrust a knife into the heart of Ko-tan, for the price of liberty. Another held personal knowledge of an officer of the palace that he could use to compel the latter to admit a number of Lu-don's warriors to various parts of the palace. With Mo-sar as the cat's paw, the plan seemed scarce possible of failure and so they separated, going upon their immediate errands to palace and to city.

As Pan-sat entered the palace grounds he was aware of a sudden commotion in the direction of the *pal-e-don-so* and a few minutes later Lu-don was surprised to see him return to the apartments of the high priest, breathless and excited.

"What now, Pan-sat?" cried Lu-don. "Are you pursued by demons?"

"O master, our time has come and gone while we sat here

planning. Ko-tan is already dead and Mo-sar fled. His friends are fighting with the warriors of the palace but they have no head, while Ja-don leads the others. I could learn but little from frightened slaves who had fled at the outburst of the quarrel. One told me that Bu-lot had slain the king and that he had seen Mo-sar and the assassin hurrying from the palace."

"Ja-don," muttered the high priest. "The fools will make him king if we do not act and act quickly. Get into the city, Pan-sat—let your feet fly and raise the cry that Ja-don has killed the king and is seeking to wrest the throne from O-lo-a. Spread the word as you know best how to spread it that Ja-don has threatened to destroy the priests and hurl the altars of the temple into Jad-ben-lul. Rouse the warriors of the city and urge them to attack at once. Lead them into the temple by the secret way that only the priests know and from here we may spew them out upon the palace before they learn the truth. Go, Pan-sat, immediately—delay not an instant."

"But stay," he called as the under priest turned to leave the apartment; "saw or heard you anything of the strange white woman that Ja-don stole from the Temple of the *Gryf* where we have had her imprisoned?"

"Only that Ja-don took her into the palace where he threatened the priests with violence if they did not permit him to pass," replied Pan-sat. "This they told me, but where within the palace she is hidden I know not."

"Ko-tan ordered her to the Forbidden Garden," said Lu-don, "doubtless we shall find her there. And now, Pan-sat, be upon your errand."

In a corridor by Lu-don's chamber a hideously masked priest leaned close to the curtained aperture that led within. Were he listening he must have heard all that passed between Pan-sat and the high priest, and that he had listened was evidenced by his hasty withdrawal to the shadows of a nearby passage as the lesser priest moved across the chamber toward the doorway. Pan-sat went his way in ignorance of the near presence that he almost brushed against as he hurried toward the secret passage that leads from the temple of Jad-ben-Otho, far beneath the palace, to the city beyond, nor did he sense the silent creature following in his footsteps.

16

The Secret Way

I T WAS a baffled *gryf* that bellowed in angry rage as Tarzan's sleek brown body cutting the moonlit waters shot through the aperture in the wall of the *gryf* pool and out into the lake beyond. The ape-man smiled as he thought of the comparative ease with which he had defeated the purpose of the high priest but his face clouded again at the ensuing remembrance of the grave danger that threatened his mate. His sole object now must be to return as quickly as he might to the chamber where he had last seen her on the third floor of the Temple of the *Gryf*, but how he was to find his way again into the temple grounds was a question not easy of solution.

In the moonlight he could see the sheer cliff rising from the water for a great distance along the shore—far beyond the precincts of the temple and the palace—towering high above him, a seemingly impregnable barrier against his return. Swimming close in, he skirted the wall searching diligently for some foothold, however slight, upon its smooth, forbidding surface. Above him and quite out of reach were numerous apertures, but there were no means at hand by which he could reach them. Presently, however, his hopes were raised by the sight of an opening level with the surface of the water. It lay just ahead and a few strokes brought him to it—cautious strokes that brought forth no sound from the yielding waters. At the nearer side of the opening he stopped and reconnoitered. There was no one in sight. Carefully he raised his body to the threshold of the entrance-way, his smooth brown hide glistening in the moonlight as it shed the water in tiny sparkling rivulets.

Before him stretched a gloomy corridor, unlighted save for the faint illumination of the diffused moonlight that penetrated it for but a short distance from the opening. Moving as rapidly as reasonable caution warranted, Tarzan followed the corridor into the bowels of the cave. There was an abrupt turn and then a flight of steps at the top of which lay another corridor running parallel with the face of the cliff. This passage was dimly lighted by flickering cressets set in niches in the walls at considerable distances apart. A quick survey showed the ape-man numerous openings upon each side of the corridor and his quick ears caught sounds that indicated that there were other beings not far distant—priests, he concluded, in some of the apartments letting upon the passageway.

To pass undetected through this hive of enemies appeared quite beyond the range of possibility. He must again seek disguise and knowing from experience how best to secure such he crept stealthily along the corridor toward the nearest doorway. Like Numa, the lion, stalking a wary prey he crept with quivering nostrils to the hangings that shut off his view from the interior of the apartment beyond. A moment later his head disappeared within; then his shoulders, and his lithe body, and the hangings dropped quietly into place again. A moment later there filtered to the vacant corridor without a brief, gasping gurgle and again silence. A minute passed; a second, and a third, and then the hangings were thrust aside and a grimly masked priest of the temple of Jad-ben-Otho strode into the passageway.

With bold steps he moved along and was about to turn into a diverging gallery when his attention was aroused by voices coming from a room upon his left. Instantly the figure halted and crossing the corridor stood with an ear close to the skins that concealed the occupants of the room from him, and him from them. Presently he leaped back into the concealing shadows of the diverging gallery and immediately thereafter the hangings by which he had been listening parted and a priest emerged to turn quickly down the main corridor. The eavesdropper waited until the other had gained a little distance and then stepping from his place of concealment followed silently behind.

The way led along the corridor which ran parallel with the face of the cliff for some little distance and then Pan-sat, taking a cresset from one of the wall niches, turned abruptly into a small apartment at his left. The tracker followed cautiously in time to see the rays of the flickering light dimly visible from an aperture in the floor before him. Here he found a series of steps, similar to those used by the Waz-don in scaling the cliff to their caves, leading to a lower level.

First satisfying himself that his guide was continuing upon his way unsuspecting, the other descended after him and continued his stealthy stalking. The passageway was now both narrow and low, giving but bare headroom to a tall man, and it was broken often by flights of steps leading always downward. The steps in each unit seldom numbered more than six and sometimes there was only one or two but in the aggregate the tracker imagined that they had descended between fifty and seventy-five feet from the level of the upper corridor when the passageway terminated in a small apartment at one side of which was a little pile of rubble.

Setting his cresset upon the ground, Pan-sat commenced hurriedly to toss the bits of broken stone aside, presently revealing a small aperture at the base of the wall upon the opposite side of which there appeared to be a further accumulation of rubble. This he also removed until he had a hole of sufficient size to permit the passage of his body, and leaving the cresset still burning upon the floor the priest crawled through the opening he had made and disappeared from the sight of the watcher hiding in the shadows of the narrow passageway behind him.

No sooner, however, was he safely gone than the other followed, finding himself, after passing through the hole, on a little ledge about halfway between the surface of the lake and the top of the cliff above. The ledge inclined steeply upward, ending at the rear of a building which stood upon the edge of the cliff and which the second priest entered just in time to see Pan-sat pass out into the city beyond.

As the latter turned a nearby corner the other emerged from the doorway and quickly surveyed his surroundings. He was satisfied the priest who had led him hither had served his purpose in so far as the tracker was concerned. Above him, and perhaps a hundred yards away, the white walls of the palace gleamed against the northern sky. The time that it had taken him to acquire definite knowledge concerning the secret passageway between the temple and the city he did not count as lost, though he begrudged every instant that kept him from the prosecution of his main objective. It had seemed to him, however, necessary to the success of a bold plan that he had formulated upon overhearing the conversation between Lu-don and Pan-sat as he stood without the hangings of the apartment of the high priest.

Alone against a nation of suspicious and half-savage enemies he could scarce hope for a successful outcome to the one great issue upon which hung the life and happiness of the creature he loved best. For her sake he must win allies and it was for this purpose that he had sacrificed these precious moments, but now he lost no further time in seeking to regain entrance to the palace grounds that he might search out whatever new prison they had found in which to incarcerate his lost love.

He found no difficulty in passing the guards at the entrance

to the palace for, as he had guessed, his priestly disguise dis-
armed all suspicion. As he approached the warriors he kept
his hands behind him and trusted to fate that the sickly light
of the single torch which stood beside the doorway would not
reveal his un-Pal-ul-donian feet. As a matter of fact so accustomed were they to the comings and goings of the priesthood that they paid scant attention to him and he passed on
into the palace grounds without even a moment's delay.

His goal now was the Forbidden Garden and this he had
little difficulty in reaching though he elected to enter it over
the wall rather than to chance arousing any suspicion on the
part of the guards at the inner entrance, since he could imagine
no reason why a priest should seek entrance there thus late at
night.

He found the garden deserted, nor any sign of her he sought.
That she had been brought hither he had learned from the
conversation he had overheard between Lu-don and Pan-sat,
and he was sure that there had been no time or opportunity
for the high priest to remove her from the palace grounds. The
garden he knew to be devoted exclusively to the uses of the
princess and her women and it was only reasonable to assume
therefore that if Jane had been brought to the garden it could
only have been upon an order from Ko-tan. This being the
case the natural assumption would follow that he would find
her in some other portion of O-lo-a's quarters.

Just where these lay he could only conjecture, but it seemed
reasonable to believe that they must be adjacent to the garden,
so once more he scaled the wall and passing around its end
directed his steps toward an entrance-way which he judged
must lead to that portion of the palace nearest the Forbidden
Garden.

To his surprise he found the place unguarded and then there
fell upon his ear from an interior apartment the sound of
voices raised in anger and excitement. Guided by the sound he
quickly traversed several corridors and chambers until he stood
before the hangings which separated him from the chamber
from which issued the sounds of altercation. Raising the skins
slightly he looked within. There were two women battling
with a Ho-don warrior. One was the daughter of Ko-tan and
the other Pan-at-lee, the Kor-ul-ja.

At the moment that Tarzan lifted the hangings, the warrior
threw O-lo-a viciously to the ground and seizing Pan-at-lee by
the hair drew his knife and raised it above her head. Casting
the encumbering headdress of the dead priest from his shoulders the ape-man leaped across the intervening space and
seizing the brute from behind struck him a single terrible blow.

As the man fell forward dead, the two women recognized Tarzan simultaneously. Pan-at-lee fell upon her knees and would have bowed her head upon his feet had he not, with an impatient gesture, commanded her to rise. He had no time to listen to their protestations of gratitude or answer the numerous questions which he knew would soon be flowing from those two feminine tongues.

"Tell me," he cried, "where is the woman of my own race whom Ja-don brought here from the temple?"

"She is but this moment gone," cried O-lo-a. "Mo-sar, the father of this thing here," and she indicated the body of Bu-lot with a scornful finger, "seized her and carried her away."

"Which way?" he cried. "Tell me quickly, in what direction he took her."

"That way," cried Pan-at-lee, pointing to the doorway through which Mo-sar had passed. "They would have taken the princess and the stranger woman to Tu-lur, Mo-sar's city by the Dark Lake."

"I go to find her," he said to Pan-at-lee, "she is my mate. And if I survive I shall find means to liberate you too and return you to Om-at."

Before the girl could reply he had disappeared behind the hangings of the door near the foot of the dais. The corridor through which he ran was illy lighted and like nearly all its kind in the Ho-don city wound in and out and up and down, but at last it terminated at a sudden turn which brought him into a courtyard filled with warriors, a portion of the palace guard that had just been summoned by one of the lesser palace chiefs to join the warriors of Ko-tan in the battle that was raging in the banquet hall.

At sight of Tarzan, who in his haste had forgotten to recover his disguising headdress, a great shout arose. "Blasphemer!" "Defiler of the temple!" burst hoarsely from savage throats, and mingling with these were a few who cried, "Dor-ul-Otho!" evidencing the fact that there were among them still some who clung to their belief in his divinity.

To cross the courtyard armed only with a knife, in the face of this great throng of savage fighting men seemed even to the giant ape-man a thing impossible of achievement. He must use his wits now and quickly too, for they were closing upon him. He might have turned and fled back through the corridor but flight now even in the face of dire necessity would but delay him in his pursuit of Mo-sar and his mate.

"Stop!" he cried, raising his palm against them. "I am the Dor-ul-Otho and I come to you with a word from Ja-don, who it is my father's will shall be your king now that Ko-tan is

slain. Lu-don, the high priest, has planned to seize the palace
and destroy the loyal warriors that Mo-sar may be made king
—Mo-sar who will be the tool and creature of Lu-don. Follow
me. There is no time to lose if you would prevent the traitors
whom Lu-don has organized in the city from entering the
palace by a secret way and overpowering Ja-don and the
faithful band within."

For a moment they hesitated. At last one spoke. "What
guarantee have we," he demanded, "that it is not you who
would betray us and by leading us now away from the fighting
in the banquet hall cause those who fight at Ja-don's side to
be defeated?"

"My life will be your guarantee," replied Tarzan. "If you
find that I have not spoken the truth you are sufficient in
numbers to execute whatever penalty you choose. But come,
there is not time to lose. Already are the lesser priests gathering their warriors in the city below," and without waiting for
any further parley he strode directly toward them in the direction of the gate upon the opposite side of the courtyard which
led toward the principal entrance to the palace ground.

Slower in wit than he, they were swept away by his greater
initiative and that compelling power which is inherent to all
natural leaders. And so they followed him, the giant ape-man
with a dead tail dragging the ground behind him—a demigod where another would have been ridiculous. Out into the
city he led them and down toward the unpretentious building
that hid Lu-don's secret passageway from the city to the
temple, and as they rounded the last turn they saw before
them a gathering of warriors which was being rapidly augmented from all directions as the traitors of A-lur mobilized
at the call of the priesthood.

"You spoke the truth, stranger," said the chief who marched
at Tarzan's side, "for there are the warriors with the priests
among them, even as you told us."

"And now," replied the ape-man, "that I have fulfilled my
promise I will go my way after Mo-sar, who has done me a
great wrong. Tell Ja-don that Jad-ben-Otho is upon his side,
nor do you forget to tell him also that it was the Dor-ul-Otho
who thwarted Lu-don's plan to seize the palace."

"I will not forget," replied the chief. "Go your way. We
are enough to overpower the traitors."

"Tell me," asked Tarzan, "how I may know this city of
Tu-lur?"

"It lies upon the south shore of the second lake below A-
lur," replied the chief, "the lake that is called Jad-in-lul."

They were now approaching the band of traitors, who evidently thought that this was another contingent of their own party since they made no effort either toward defense or retreat. Suddenly the chief raised his voice in a savage war cry that was immediately taken up by his followers, and simultaneously, as though the cry were a command, the entire party broke into a mad charge upon the surprised rebels.

Satisfied with the outcome of his suddenly conceived plan and sure that it would work to the disadvantage of Lu-don, Tarzan turned into a side street and pointed his steps toward the outskirts of the city in search of the trail that led southward toward Tu-lur.

17

By Jad-bal-lul

AS MO-SAR carried Jane Clayton from the palace of Ko-tan, the king, the woman struggled incessantly to regain her freedom. He tried to compel her to walk, but despite his threats and his abuse she would not voluntarily take a single step in the direction in which he wished her to go. Instead she threw herself to the ground each time he sought to place her upon her feet, and so of necessity he was compelled to carry her though at last he tied her hands and gagged her to save himself from further lacerations, for the beauty and slenderness of the woman belied her strength and courage. When he came at last to where his men had gathered he was glad indeed to turn her over to a couple of stalwart warriors, but these too were forced to carry her since Mo-sar's fear of the vengeance of Ko-tan's retainers would brook no delays.

And thus they came down out of the hills from which A-lur is carved, to the meadows that skirt the lower end of Jad-ben-lul, with Jane Clayton carried between two of Mo-sar's men. At the edge of the lake lay a fleet of strong canoes, hollowed from the trunks of trees, their bows and sterns carved in the semblance of grotesque beasts or birds and vividly colored by some master in that primitive school of art, which fortunately is not without its devotees today.

Into the stern of one of these canoes the warriors tossed their captive at a sign from Mo-sar, who came and stood beside her as the warriors were finding their places in the canoes and selecting their paddles.

"Come, Beautiful One," he said, "let us be friends and you shall not be harmed. You will find Mo-sar a kind master if you do his bidding," and thinking to make a good impression on her he removed the gag from her mouth and the thongs from her wrists, knowing well that she could not escape surrounded as she was by his warriors, and presently, when they were out on the lake, she would be as safely imprisoned as though he held her behind bars.

And so the fleet moved off to the accompaniment of the gentle splashing of a hundred paddles, to follow the windings of the rivers and lakes through which the waters of the Valley of Jad-ben-Otho empty into the great morass to the south. The warriors, resting upon one knee, faced the bow and in the last canoe Mo-sar tiring of his fruitless attempts to win responses from his sullen captive, squatted in the bottom of the canoe with his back toward her and resting his head upon the gunwale sought sleep.

Thus they moved in silence between the verdure-clad banks of the little river through which the waters of Jad-ben-lul emptied—now in the moonlight, now in dense shadow where great trees overhung the stream, and at last out upon the waters of another lake, the black shores of which seemed far away under the weird influence of a moonlight night.

Jane Clayton sat alert in the stern of the last canoe. For months she had been under constant surveillance, the prisoner first of one ruthless race and now the prisoner of another. Since the long-gone day that Hauptmann Fritz Schneider and his band of native German troops had treacherously wrought the Kaiser's work of rapine and destruction on the Greystoke bungalow and carried her away to captivity she had not drawn a free breath. That she had survived unharmed the countless dangers through which she had passed she attributed solely to the beneficence of a kind and watchful Providence.

At first she had been held on the orders of the German High Command with a view of her ultimate value as a hostage and during these months she had been subjected to neither hardship nor oppression, but when the Germans had become hard pressed toward the close of their unsuccessful campaign in East Africa it had been determined to take her further into the interior and now there was an element of revenge in their motives, since it must have been apparent that she could no longer be of any possible military value.

Bitter indeed were the Germans against that half-savage mate of hers who had cunningly annoyed and harassed them with a fiendishness of persistence and ingenuity that had resulted in a noticeable loss in morale in the sector he had chosen for his operations. They had to charge against him the lives of certain officers that he had deliberately taken with his own hands, and one entire section of trench that had made possible a disastrous turning movement by the British. Tarzan had out-generaled them at every point. He had met cunning with cunning and cruelty with cruelties until they feared and loathed his very name. The cunning trick that they had played upon him in destroying his home, murdering his retainers, and covering the abduction of his wife in such a way as to lead him to believe that she had been killed, they had regretted a thousand times, for a thousandfold had they paid the price for their senseless ruthlessness, and now, unable to wreak their vengeance directly upon him, they had conceived the idea of inflicting further suffering upon his mate.

In sending her into the interior to avoid the path of the victorious British, they had chosen as her escort Lieutenant Erich Obergatz who had been second in command of Schneider's company, and who alone of its officers had escaped the consuming vengeance of the ape-man. For a long time Obergatz had held her in a native village, the chief of which was still under the domination of his fear of the ruthless German oppressors. While here only hardships and discomforts assailed her, Obergatz himself being held in leash by the orders of his distant superior but as time went on the life in the village grew to be a veritable hell of cruelties and oppressions practised by the arrogant Prussian upon the villagers and the members of his native command—for time hung heavily upon the hands of the lieutenant and with idleness combining with the personal discomforts he was compelled to endure, his none too agreeable temper found an outlet first in petty interference with the chiefs and later in the practise of absolute cruelties upon them.

What the self-sufficient German could not see was plain to Jane Clayton—that the sympathies of Obergatz' native soldiers lay with the villagers and that all were so heartily sickened by his abuse that it needed now but the slightest spark to detonate the mine of revenge and hatred that the pig-headed Hun had been assiduously fabricating beneath his own person.

And at last it came, but from an unexpected source in the form of a German native deserter from the theater of war. Footsore, weary, and spent, he dragged himself into the village late one afternoon, and before Obergatz was even aware of his presence the whole village knew that the power of Germany in Africa was at an end. It did not take long for the lieutenant's native soldiers to realize that the authority that held them in service no longer existed and that with it had gone the power to pay them their miserable wage. Or at least, so they reasoned. To them Obergatz no longer represented aught else than a powerless and hated foreigner, and short indeed would have been his shrift had not a native woman who had conceived a doglike affection for Jane Clayton hurried to her with word of the murderous plan, for the fate of the innocent white woman lay in the balance beside that of the guilty Teuton.

"Already they are quarreling as to which one shall possess you," she told Jane.

"When will they come for us?" asked Jane. "Did you hear them say?"

"Tonight," replied the woman, "for even now that he has none to fight for him they still fear the white man. And so they will come at night and kill him while he sleeps."

Jane thanked the woman and sent her away lest the suspicion of her fellows be aroused against her when they discovered that the two whites had learned of their intentions. The woman went at once to the hut occupied by Obergatz. She had never gone there before and the German looked up in surprise as he saw who his visitor was.

Briefly she told him what she had heard. At first he was inclined to bluster arrogantly, with a great display of bravado but she silenced him peremptorily.

"Such talk is useless," she said shortly. "You have brought upon yourself the just hatred of these people. Regardless of the truth or falsity of the report which has been brought to them, they believe in it and there is nothing now between you and your Maker other than flight. We shall both be dead before morning if we are unable to escape from the village unseen. If you go to them now with your silly protestations of authority you will be dead a little sooner, that is all."

"You think it is as bad as that?" he said, a noticeable alteration in his tone and manner.

"It is precisely as I have told you," she replied. "They will come tonight and kill you while you sleep. Find me pistols and a rifle and ammunition and we will pretend that we go into the jungle to hunt. That you have done often. Perhaps it will arouse suspicion that I accompany you but that we must chance. And be sure my dear Herr Lieutenant to bluster and curse and abuse your servants unless they note a change in your manner and realizing your fear know that you suspect their intention. If all goes well then we can go out into the jungle to hunt and we need not return.

"But first and now you must swear never to harm me, or otherwise it would be better that I called the chief and turned you over to him and then put a bullet into my own head, for unless you swear as I have asked I were no better alone in the jungle with you than here at the mercies of these degraded blacks."

"I swear," he replied solemnly, "in the names of my God and my Kaiser that no harm shall befall you at my hands, Lady Greystoke."

"Very well," she said, "we will make this pact to assist each other to return to civilization, but let it be understood that there is and never can be any semblance even of respect for you upon my part. I am drowning and you are the straw. Carry that always in your mind, German."

If Obergatz had held any doubt as to the sincerity of her word it would have been wholly dissipated by the scathing contempt of her tone. And so Obergatz, without further parley, got pistols and an extra rifle for Jane, as well as bandoleers of cartridges. In his usual arrogant and disagreeable manner he called his servants, telling them that he and the white *kali* were going out into the brush to hunt. The beaters would go north as far as the little hill and then circle back to the east and in toward the village. The gun carriers he directed to take the extra pieces and precede himself and Jane slowly toward the east, waiting for them at the ford about half a mile distant. The blacks responded with greater alacrity than usual and it was noticeable to both Jane and Obergatz that they left the village whispering and laughing.

"The swine think it is a great joke," growled Obergatz, "that the afternoon before I die I go out and hunt meat for them."

As soon as the gun bearers disappeared in the jungle beyond the village the two Europeans followed along the same trail, nor was there any attempt upon the part of Obergatz' native soldiers, or the warriors of the chief to detain them, for they too doubtless were more than willing that the whites should bring them in one more mess of meat before they killed them.

A quarter of a mile from the village, Obergatz turned toward the south from the trail that led to the ford and hurrying onward the two put as great a distance as possible between them and the village before night fell. They knew from the habits of their erstwhile hosts that there was little danger of pursuit by night since the villagers held Numa, the lion, in too great respect to venture needlessly beyond their stockade during the hours that the king of beasts was prone to choose for hunting.

And thus began a seemingly endless sequence of frightful days and horror-laden nights as the two fought their way toward the south in the face of almost inconceivable hardships, privations, and dangers. The east coast was nearer but Obergatz positively refused to chance throwing himself into the hands of the British by returning to the territory which they now controlled, insisting instead upon attempting to make his way through an unknown wilderness to South Africa where, among the Boers, he was convinced he would find willing sympathizers who would find some way to return him in safety to Germany, and the woman was perforce compelled to accompany him.

And so they had crossed the great thorny, waterless steppe and come at last to the edge of the morass before Pal-ul-don. They had reached this point just before the rainy season when the waters of the morass were at their lowest ebb. At this time a hard crust is baked upon the dried surface of the marsh and there is only the open water at the center to materially impede progress. It is a condition that exists perhaps not more than a few weeks, or even days at the termination of long periods of drought, and so the two crossed the otherwise almost impassable barrier without realizing its latent terrors. Even the open water in the center chanced to be deserted at the time by its frightful denizens which the drought and the receding waters had driven southward toward the mouth of Pal-ul-don's largest river which carries the waters out of the Valley of Jad-ben-Otho.

Their wanderings carried them across the mountains and into the Valley of Jad-ben-Otho at the source of one of the larger streams which bears the mountain waters down into the valley to empty them into the main river just below The Great Lake on whose northern shore lies A-lur. As they had come down out of the mountains they had been surprised by a party of Ho-don hunters. Obergatz had escaped while Jane had been taken prisoner and brought to A-lur. She had neither seen nor heard aught of the German since that time and she did not know whether he had perished in this strange land, or succeeded in successfully eluding its savage denizens and making his way at last into South Africa.

For her part, she had been incarcerated alternately in the palace and the temple as either Ko-tan or Lu-don succeeded in wresting her temporarily from the other by various strokes of cunning and intrigue. And now at last she was in the power of a new captor, one whom she knew from the gossip of the temple and the palace to be cruel and degraded. And she was in the stern of the last canoe, and every enemy back was toward her, while almost at her feet Mo-sar's loud snores gave ample evidence of his unconsciousness to his immediate surroundings.

The dark shore loomed closer to the south as Jane Clayton, Lady Greystoke, slid quietly over the stern of the canoe into the chill waters of the lake. She scarcely moved other than to keep her nostrils above the surface while the canoe was yet discernible in the last rays of the declining moon. Then she struck out toward the southern shore.

Alone, unarmed, all but naked, in a country overrun by savage beasts and hostile men, she yet felt for the first time in many months a sensation of elation and relief. She was free! What if the next moment brought death, she knew again, at least a brief instant of absolute freedom. Her blood tingled to the almost forgotten sensation and it was with difficulty that she restrained a glad triumphant cry as she clambered from the quiet waters and stood upon the silent beach.

Before her loomed a forest, darkly, and from its depths came those nameless sounds that are a part of the night life of the jungle—the rustling of leaves in the wind, the rubbing together of contiguous branches, the scurrying of a rodent, all magnified by the darkness to sinister and awe-inspiring proportions; the hoot of an owl, the distant scream of a great cat, the barking of wild dogs, attested the presence of the myriad life she could not see—the savage life, the free life of which she was now a part. And then there came to her, possibly for the first time since the giant ape-man had come into her life, a fuller realization of what the jungle meant to him, for though alone and unprotected from its hideous dangers she yet felt its lure upon her and an exaltation that she had not dared hope to feel again.

Ah, if that mighty mate of hers were but by her side! What utter joy and bliss would be hers! She longed for no more than this. The parade of cities, the comforts and luxuries of civilization held forth no allure half as insistent as the glorious freedom of the jungle.

A lion moaned in the blackness to her right, eliciting delicious thrills that crept along her spine. The hair at the back of her head seemed to stand erect—yet she was unafraid. The muscles bequeathed her by some primordial ancestor reacted instinctively to the presence of an ancient enemy—that was all. The woman moved slowly and deliberately toward the wood. Again the lion moaned; this time nearer. She sought a low-hanging branch and finding it swung easily into the friendly shelter of the tree. The long and perilous journey with Obergatz had trained her muscles and her nerves to such unaccustomed habits. She found a safe resting place such as Tarzan had taught her was best and there she curled herself, thirty feet above the ground, for a night's rest. She was cold and uncomfortable and yet she slept, for her heart was warm with renewed hope and her tired brain had found temporary surcease from worry.

She slept until the heat of the sun, high in the heavens, awakened her. She was rested and now her body was well as her heart was warm. A sensation of ease and comfort and happiness pervaded her being. She rose upon her gently swaying couch and stretched luxuriously, her naked limbs and lithe body mottled by the sunlight filtering through the foliage above combined with the lazy gesture to impart to her appearance something of the leopard. With careful eye she scrutinized the ground below and with attentive ear she listened for any warning sound that might suggest the near presence of enemies, either man or beast. Satisfied at last that there was nothing close of which she need have fear she clambered to the ground. She wished to bathe but the lake was too exposed and just a bit too far from the safety of the trees for her to risk it until she became more familiar with her surroundings. She wandered aimlessly through the forest searching for food which she found in abundance. She ate and rested, for she had no objective as yet. Her freedom was too new to be spoiled by plannings for the future. The haunts of civilized man seemed to her now as vague and unattainable as the half-forgotten substance of a dream. If she could but live on here in peace, waiting, waiting for—*him*. It was the old hope revived. She knew that he would come some day, if he lived. She had always known that, though recently she had believed that he would come too late. If he lived! Yes, he would come if he lived, and if he did not live she were as well off here as elsewhere, for then nothing mattered, only to wait for the end as patiently as might be.

Her wanderings brought her to a crystal brook and there she drank and bathed beneath an overhanging tree that offered her quick asylum in the event of danger. It was a quiet and beautiful spot and she loved it from the first. The bottom of the brook was paved with pretty stones and bits of glassy obsidian. As she gathered a handful of the pebbles and held them up to look at them she noticed that one of her fingers was bleeding from a clean, straight cut. She fell to searching for the cause and presently discovered it in one of the fragments of volcanic glass which revealed an edge that was almost razor-like. Jane Clayton was elated. Here, God-given to her hands, was the first beginning with which she might eventually arrive at both weapons and tools—a cutting edge. Everything was possible to him who possessed it—nothing without.

She sought until she had collected many of the precious bits of stone—until the pouch that hung at her right side was almost filled. Then she climbed into the great tree to examine them at leisure. There were some that looked like knife blades, and some that could easily be fashioned into spear heads, and many smaller ones that nature seemed to have intended for the tips of savage arrows.

The spear she would essay first—that would be easiest. There was a hollow in the bole of the tree in a great crotch high above the ground. Here she cached all of her treasure except a single knifelike sliver. With this she descended to the ground and searching out a slender sapling that grew arrow-straight she hacked and sawed until she could break it off without splitting the wood. It was just the right diameter for the shaft of a spear—a hunting spear such as her beloved Waziri had liked best. How often had she watched them fashioning them, and they had taught her how to use them, too—them and the heavy war spears—laughing and clapping their hands as her proficiency increased.

She knew the arborescent grasses that yielded the longest and toughest fibers and these she sought and carried to her tree with the spear shaft that was to be. Clambering to her crotch she bent to her work, humming softly a little tune. She caught herself and smiled—it was the first time in all these bitter months that song had passed her lips or such a smile.

"I feel," she sighed, "I almost feel that John is near—my John—my Tarzan!"

She cut the spear shaft to the proper length and removed the twigs and branches and the bark, whittling and scraping at the nubs until the surface was all smooth and straight. Then she split one end and inserted a spear point, shaping the wood until it fitted perfectly. This done she laid the shaft aside and fell to splitting the thick grass stems and pounding and twisting them until she had separated and partially cleaned the fibers. These she took down to the brook and washed and brought back again and wound tightly around the cleft end of the shaft, which she had notched to receive them, and the upper part of the spear head which she had also notched slightly with a bit of stone. It was a crude spear but the best that she

could attain in so short a time. Later, she promised herself,
she should have others—many of them—and they would be
spears of which even the greatest of the Waziri spear-men
might be proud.

18

The Lion Pit of Tu-lur

THOUGH Tarzan searched the outskirts of the city until
nearly dawn he discovered nowhere the spoor of his mate.
The breeze coming down from the mountains brought to
his nostrils a diversity of scents but there was not among them
the slightest suggestion of her whom he sought. The natural
deduction was therefore that she had been taken in some other
direction. In his search he had many times crossed the fresh
tracks of many men leading toward the lake and these he concluded had probably been made by Jane Clayton's abductors.
It had only been to minimize the chance of error by the process
of elimination that he had carefully reconnoitered every other
avenue leading from A-lur toward the southeast where lay Mo-
sar's city of Tu-lur, and now he followed the trail to the shores
of Jad-ben-lul where the party had embarked upon the quiet
waters in their sturdy canoes.

He found many other craft of the same description moored
along the shore and one of these he commandeered for the
purpose of pursuit. It was daylight when he passed through
the lake which lies next below Jad-ben-lul and paddling
strongly passed within sight of the very tree in which his lost
mate lay sleeping.

Had the gentle wind that caressed the bosom of the lake
been blowing from a southerly direction the giant ape-man
and Jane Clayton would have been reunited then, but an un-
kind fate had willed otherwise and the opportunity passed with
the passing of his canoe which presently his powerful strokes
carried out of sight into the stream at the lower end of the
lake.

Following the winding river which bore a considerable distance to the north before doubling back to empty into the

Jad-in-lul, the ape-man missed a portage that would have saved him hours of paddling.

It was at the upper end of this portage where Mo-sar and his warriors had debarked that the chief discovered the absence of his captive. As Mo-sar had been asleep since shortly after their departure from A-lur, and as none of the warriors recalled when she had last been seen, it was impossible to conjecture with any degree of accuracy the place where she had escaped. The concensus of opinion was, however, that it had been in the narrow river connecting Jad-ben-lul with the lake next below it, which is called Jad-bal-lul, which freely translated means the lake of gold. Mo-sar had been very wroth and having himself been the only one at fault he naturally sought with great diligence to fix the blame upon another.

He would have returned in search of her had he not feared to meet a pursuing company dispatched either by Ja-don or the high priest, both of whom, he knew, had just grievances against him. He would not even spare a boatload of his warriors from his own protection to return in quest of the fugitive but hastened onward with as little delay as possible across the portage and out upon the waters of Jad-in-lul.

The morning sun was just touching the white domes of Tu-lur when Mo-sar's paddlers brought their canoes against the shore at the city's edge. Safe once more behind his own walls and protected by many warriors, the courage of the chief returned sufficiently at least to permit him to dispatch three canoes in search of Jane Clayton, and also to go as far as A-lur if possible to learn what had delayed Bu-lot, whose failure to reach the canoes with the balance of the party at the time of the flight from the northern city had in no way delayed Mo-sar's departure, his own safety being of far greater moment than that of his son.

As the three canoes reached the portage on their return journey the warriors who were dragging them from the water were suddenly startled by the appearance of two priests, carrying a light canoe in the direction of Jad-in-lul. At first they thought them the advance guard of a larger force of Lu-don's followers, although the correctness of such a theory was belied by their knowledge that priests never accepted the risks or perils of a warrior's vocation, nor even fought until driven into a corner and forced to do so. Secretly the warriors of Pal-ul-don held the emasculated priesthood in contempt and so instead of immediately taking up the offensive as they would have had the two men been warriors from A-lur instead of priests, they waited to question them.

At sight of the warriors the priests made the sign of peace

and upon being asked if they were alone they answered in the affirmative.

The leader of Mo-sar's warriors permitted them to approach. "What do you here," he asked, "in the country of Mo-sar, so far from your own city?"

"We carry a message from Lu-don, the high priest, to Mo-sar," explained one.

"Is it a message of peace or of war?" asked the warrior.

"It is an offer of peace," replied the priest.

"And Lu-don is sending no warriors behind you?" queried the fighting man.

"We are alone," the priest assured him. "None in A-lur save Lu-don knows that we have come upon this errand."

"Then go your way," said the warrior.

"Who is that?" asked one of the priests suddenly, pointing toward the upper end of the lake at the point where the river from Jad-bal-lul entered it.

All eyes turned in the direction that he had indicated to see a lone warrior paddling rapidly into Jad-in-lul, the prow of his canoe pointing toward Tu-lur. The warriors and the priests drew into the concealment of the bushes on either side of the portage.

"It is the terrible man who called himself the Dor-ul-Otho," whispered one of the priests. "I would know that figure among a great multitude as far as I could see it."

"You are right, priest," cried one of the warriors who had seen Tarzan the day that he had first entered Ko-tan's palace. "It is indeed he who has been rightly called Tarzan-jad-guru."

"Hasten priests," cried the leader of the party. "You are two paddles in a light canoe. Easily can you reach Tu-lur ahead of him and warn Mo-sar of his coming, for he has but only entered the lake."

For a moment the priests demurred for they had no stomach for an encounter with this terrible man, but the warrior insisted and even went so far as to threaten them. Their canoe was taken from them and pushed into the lake and they were all but lifted bodily from their feet and put aboard it. Still protesting they were shoved out upon the water where they were immediately in full view of the lone paddler above them. Now there was no alternative. The city of Tu-lur offered the only safety and bending to their paddles the two priests sent their craft swiftly in the direction of the city.

The warriors withdrew again to the concealment of the foliage. If Tarzan had seen them and should come hither to investigate there were thirty of them against one and naturally they had no fear of the outcome, but they did not consider it necessary to go out upon the lake to meet him since they had been sent to look for the escaped prisoner and not to intercept the strange warrior, the stories of whose ferocity and prowess doubtless helped them to arrive at their decision to provoke no uncalled-for quarrel with him.

If he had seen them he gave no sign, but continued paddling steadily and strongly toward the city, nor did he increase his speed as the two priests shot out in full view. The moment the priests' canoe touched the shore by the city its occupants leaped out and hurried swiftly toward the palace gate, casting affrighted glances behind them. They sought immediate audience with Mo-sar, after warning the warriors on guard that Tarzan was approaching.

They were conducted at once to the chief, whose court was a smaller replica of that of the king of A-lur. "We come from Lu-don, the high priest," explained the spokesman. "He wishes the friendship of Mo-sar, who has always been his friend. Ja-don is gathering warriors to make himself king. Throughout the villages of the Ho-don are thousands who will obey the commands of Lu-don, the high priest. Only with Lu-don's assistance can Mo-sar become king, and the message from Lu-don is that if Mo-sar would retain the friendship of Lu-don he must return immediately the woman he took from the quarters of the Princess O-lo-a."

At this juncture a warrior entered. His excitement was evident. "The Dor-ul-Otho has come to Tu-lur and demands to see Mo-sar at once," he said.

"The Dor-ul-Otho!" exclaimed Mo-sar.

"That is the message he sent," replied the warrior, "and indeed he is not as are the people of Pal-ul-don. He is, we think, the same of whom the warriors that returned from A-lur today told us and whom some call Tarzan-jad-guru and some Dor-ul-Otho. But indeed only the son of god would dare come thus alone to a strange city, so it must be that he speaks the truth."

Mo-sar, his heart filled with terror and indecision, turned questioningly toward the priests.

"Receive him graciously, Mo-sar," counseled he who had spoken before, his advice prompted by the petty shrewdness of his defective brain which, under the added influence of Lu-don's tutorage leaned always toward duplicity. "Receive him graciously and when he is quite convinced of your friendship he will be off his guard, and then you may do with him as you will. But if possible, Mo-sar, and you would win the undying gratitude of Lu-don, the high priest, save him alive for my master."

Mo-sar nodded understandingly and turning to the warrior commanded that he conduct the visitor to him.

"We must not be seen by the creature," said one of the priests. "Give us your answer to Lu-don, Mo-sar, and we will go our way."

"Tell Lu-don," replied the chief, "that the woman would have been lost to him entirely had it not been for me. I sought to bring her to Tu-lur that I might save her for him from the clutches of Ja-don, but during the night she escaped. Tell Lu-don that I have sent thirty warriors to search for her. It is strange you did not see them as you came."

"We did," replied the priests, "but they told us nothing of the purpose of their journey."

"It is as I have told you," said Mo-sar, "and if they find her, assure your master that she will be kept unharmed in Tu-lur for him. Also tell him that I will send my warriors to join with his against Ja-don whenever he sends word that he wants them. Now go, for Tarzan-jad-guru will soon be here."

He signaled to a slave. "Lead the priests to the temple," he commanded, "and ask the high priest of Tu-lur to see that they are fed and permitted to return to A-lur when they will."

The two priests were conducted from the apartment by the slave through a doorway other than that at which they had entered, and a moment later Tarzan-jad-guru strode into the presence of Mo-sar, ahead of the warrior whose duty it had been to conduct and announce him. The ape-man made no sign of greeting or of peace but strode directly toward the chief who, only by the exertion of his utmost powers of will, hid the terror that was in his heart at sight of the giant figure and the scowling face.

"I am the Dor-ul-Otho," said the ape-man in level tones that carried to the mind of Mo-sar a suggestion of cold steel; "I am Dor-ul-Otho, and I come to Tu-lur for the woman you stole from the apartments of O-lo-a, the princess."

The very boldness of Tarzan's entry into this hostile city had had the effect of giving him a great moral advantage over Mo-sar and the savage warriors who stood upon either side of the chief. Truly it seemed to them that no other than the son of Jad-ben-Otho would dare so heroic an act. Would any mortal warrior act thus boldly, and alone enter the presence of a powerful chief and, in the midst of a score of warriors, arrogantly demand an accounting? No, it was beyond reason. Mo-sar was faltering in his decision to betray the stranger by seeming friendliness. He even paled to a sudden thought—Jad-ben-Otho knew everything, even our inmost thoughts. Was it not therefore possible that this creature, if after all it should prove true that he was the Dor-ul-Otho, might even now be reading the wicked design that the priests had implanted in the brain of Mo-sar and which he had entertained so favorably? The chief squirmed and fidgeted upon the bench of hewn rock that was his throne.

"Quick," snapped the ape-man, "Where is she?"

"She is not here," cried Mo-sar.

"You lie," replied Tarzan.

"As Jad-ben-Otho is my witness, she is not in Tu-lur," insisted the chief. "You may search the palace and the temple and the entire city but you will not find her, for she is not here."

"Where is she, then?" demanded the ape-man. "You took her from the palace at A-lur. If she is not here, where is she? Tell me not that harm has befallen her," and he took a sudden threatening step toward Mo-sar, that sent the chief shrinking back in terror.

"Wait," he cried, "if you are indeed the Dor-ul-Otho you will know that I speak the truth. I took her from the palace of Ko-tan to save her for Lu-don, the high priest, lest with Ko-tan dead Ja-don seize her. But during the night she escaped from me between here and A-lur, and I have but just sent three canoes full-manned in search of her."

Something in the chief's tone and manner assured the ape-man that he spoke in part the truth, and that once again he had braved incalculable dangers and suffered loss of time futilely.

"What wanted the priests of Lu-don that preceded me here?" demanded Tarzan chancing a shrewd guess that the two he had seen paddling so frantically to avoid a meeting with him had indeed come from the high priest at A-lur.

"They came upon an errand similar to yours," replied Mo-sar; "to demand the return of the woman whom Lu-don thought I had stolen from him, thus wronging me as deeply, O Dor-ul-Otho, as have you."

"I would question the priests," said Tarzan. "Bring them hither." His peremptory and arrogant manner left Mo-sar in doubt as to whether to be more incensed, or terrified, but ever as is the way with such as he, he concluded that the first consideration was his own safety. If he could transfer the attention and the wrath of this terrible man from himself to Lu-don's priests it would more than satisfy him and if they should conspire to harm it, then Mo-sar would be safe in the eyes of Jad-ben-Otho if it finally developed that the stranger was in reality the son of god. He felt uncomfortable in Tarzan's presence and this fact rather accentuated his doubt, for thus indeed would mortal feel in the presence of a god. Now he saw a way to escape, at least temporarily.

"I will fetch them myself, Dor-ul-Otho," he said, and turning, left the apartment. His hurried steps brought him quickly to the temple, for the palace grounds of Tu-lur, which also included the temple as in all of the Ho-don cities, covered a much smaller area than those of the larger city of A-lur. He found Lu-don's messengers with the high priest of his own temple and quickly transmitted to them the commands of the ape-man.

"What do you intend to do with him?" asked one of the priests.

"I have no quarrel with him," replied Mo-sar. "He came in peace and he may depart in peace, for who knows but that he is indeed the Dor-ul-Otho?"

"We know that he is not," replied Lu-don's emissary. "We have every proof that he is only mortal, a strange creature from another country. Already has Lu-don offered his life to Jad-ben-Otho if he is wrong in his belief that this creature is not the son of god. If the high priest of A-lur, who is the highest priest of all the high priests of Pal-ul-don is thus so sure that the creature in an impostor as to stake his life upon his judgment then who are we to give credence to the claims of this stranger? No, Mo-sar, you need not fear him. He is only a warrior who may be overcome with the same weapons that subdue your own fighting men. Were it not for Lu-don's command that he be taken alive I would urge you to set your warriors upon him and slay him, but the commands of Lu-don are the commands of Jad-ben-Otho himself, and those we may not disobey."

But still the remnant of a doubt stirred within the cowardly breast of Mo-sar, urging him to let another take the initiative against the stranger.

"He is yours then," he replied, "to do with as you will. I have no quarrel with him. What you may command shall be the command of Lu-don, the high priest, and further than that I shall have nothing to do in the matter."

The priests turned to him who guided the destinies of the temple at Tu-lur. "Have you no plan?" they asked. "High indeed will he stand in the counsels of Lu-don and in the eyes of Jad-ben-Otho who finds the means to capture this impostor alive."

"There is the lion pit," whispered the high priest. "It is now vacant and what will hold *ja* and *jato* will hold this stranger if he is not the Dor-ul-Otho."

"It will hold him," said Mo-sar; "doubtless too it would hold a *gryf,* but first you would have to get the *gryf* into it."

The priests pondered this bit of wisdom thoughtfully and then one of those from A-lur spoke. "It should not be difficult," he said, "if we use the wits that Jad-ben-Otho gave us instead of the worldly muscles which were handed down to us from our fathers and our mothers and which have not even the power possessed by those of the beasts that run about on four feet."

"Lu-don matched his wits with the stranger and lost," suggested Mo-sar. "But this is your own affair. Carry it out as you see best."

"At A-lur, Ko-tan made much of this Dor-ul-Otho and the priests conducted him through the temple. It would arouse in his mind no suspicion were you to do the same, and let the high priest of Tu-lur invite him to the temple and gathering all the priests make a great show of belief in his kinship to Jad-ben-Otho. And what more natural then than that the high priest should wish to show him through the temple as did Lu-don at A-lur when Ko-tan commanded it, and if by chance he should be led through the lion pit it would be a simple matter for those who bear the torches to extinguish them suddenly and before the stranger was aware of what had happened, the stone gates could be dropped, thus safely securing him."

"But there are windows in the pit that let in light," interposed the high priest, "and even though the torches were extinguished he could still see and might escape before the stone door could be lowered."

"Send one who will cover the windows tightly with hides," said the priest from A-lur.

"The plan is a good one," said Mo-sar, seeing an opportunity for entirely eliminating himself from any suspicion of complicity, "for it will require the presence of no warriors, and thus with only priests about him his mind will entertain no suspicion of harm."

They were interrupted at this point by a messenger from the palace who brought word that the Dor-ul-Otho was becoming impatient and if the priests from A-lur were not brought to him at once he would come himself to the temple and get them. Mo-sar shook his head. He could not conceive of such brazen courage in mortal breast and glad he was that the plan evolved for Tarzan's undoing did not necessitate his active participation.

And so, while Mo-sar left for a secret corner of the palace by a roundabout way, three priests were dispatched to Tarzan and with whining words that did not entirely deceive him, they acknowledged his kinship to Jad-ben-Otho and begged him in the name of the high priest to honor the temple with a visit, when the priests from A-lur would be brought to him and would answer any questions that he put to them.

Confident that a continuation of his bravado would best serve his purpose, and also that if suspicion against him should crystallize into conviction on the part of Mo-sar and his followers that he would be no worse off in the temple than in the palace, the ape-man haughtily accepted the invitation of the high priest.

And so he came into the temple and was received in a manner befitting his high claims. He questioned the two priests of A-lur from whom he obtained only a repetition of the story that Mo-sar had told him, and then the high priest invited him to inspect the temple.

They took him first to the altar court, of which there was only one in Tu-lur. It was almost identical in every respect with those at A-lur. There was a bloody altar at the east end and the drowning basin at the west, and the grizzly fringes upon the headdresses of the priests attested the fact that the eastern altar was an active force in the rites of the temple. Through the chambers and corridors beneath they led him, and finally, with torch bearers to light their steps, into a damp and gloomy labyrinth at a low level and here in a large chamber, the air of which was still heavy with the odor of lions, the crafty priests of Tu-lur encompassed their shrewd design.

The torches were suddenly extinguished. There was a hurried confusion of bare feet moving rapidly across the stone floor. There was a loud crash as of a heavy weight of stone falling upon stone, and then surrounding the ape-man naught but the darkness and the silence of the tomb.

19

Diana of the Jungle

JANE had made her first kill and she was very proud of it. It was not a very formidable animal—only a hare; but it marked an epoch in her existence. Just as in the dim past the first hunter had shaped the destinies of mankind so it seemed that this event might shape hers in some new mold. No longer was she dependent upon the wild fruits and vegetables for sustenance. Now she might command meat, the giver of the strength and endurance she would require successfully to cope with the necessities of her primitive existence.

The next step was fire. She might learn to eat raw flesh as had her lord and master; but she shrank from that. The thought even was repulsive. She had, however, a plan for fire. She had given the matter thought, but had been too busy to put it into execution so long as fire could be of no immediate use to her. Now it was different—she had something to cook and her mouth watered for the flesh of her kill. She would grill it above glowing embers. Jane hastened to her tree. Among the treasures she had gathered in the bed of the stream were several pieces of volcanic glass, clear as crystal. She sought until she had found the one in mind, which was convex. Then she hurried to the ground and gathered a little pile of powdered bark that was very dry, and some dead leaves and grasses that had lain long in the hot sun. Near at hand she arranged a supply of dead twigs and branches—small and large.

Vibrant with suppressed excitement she held the bit of glass above the tinder, moving it slowly until she had focused the sun's rays upon a tiny spot. She waited breathlessly. How slow it was! Were her high hopes to be dashed in spite of all her clever planning? No! A thin thread of smoke rose gracefully into the quiet air. Presently the tinder glowed and broke suddenly into flame. Jane clasped her hands beneath her chin with a little gurgling exclamation of delight. She had achieved fire!

She piled on twigs and then larger branches and at last dragged a small log to the flames and pushed an end of it into the fire which was crackling merrily. It was the sweetest sound that she had heard for many a month. But she could not wait for the mass of embers that would be required to cook her hare. As quickly as might be she skinned and cleaned her kill, burying the hide and entrails. That she had learned from Tarzan. It served two purposes. One was the necessity for keeping a sanitary camp and the other the obliteration of the scent that most quickly attracts the man-eaters.

Then she ran a stick through the carcass and held it above the flames. By turning it often she prevented burning and at the same time permitted the meat to cook thoroughly all the way through. When it was done she scampered high into the safety of her tree to enjoy her meal in quiet and peace. Never, thought Lady Greystoke, had aught more delicious passed her lips. She patted her spear affectionately. It had brought her this toothsome dainty and with it a feeling of greater confidence and safety than she had enjoyed since that frightful day that she and Obergatz had spent their last cartridge. She would never forget that day—it had seemed one hideous succession of frightful beast after frightful beast. They had not been long in this strange country, yet they thought that they were hardened to dangers, for daily they had had encounters with ferocious creatures; but this day—she shuddered when she thought of it. And with her last cartridge she had killed a black and yellow striped lion-thing with great saber teeth just as it was about to spring upon Obergatz who had futilely emptied his rifle into it—the last shot—his final cartridge. For another day they had carried the now useless rifles; but at last they had discarded them and thrown away the cumbersome bandoleers, as well. How they had managed to survive during the ensuing week she could never quite understand, and then the Ho-don had come upon them and captured her. Obergatz had escaped—she was living it all over again. Doubtless he was dead unless he had been able to reach this side of the valley which was quite evidently less overrun with savage beasts.

Jane's days were very full ones now, and the daylight hours seemed all too short in which to accomplish the many things she had determined upon, since she had concluded that this spot presented as ideal a place as she could find to live until she could fashion the weapons she considered necessary for the obtaining of meat and for self-defense.

She felt that she must have, in addition to a good spear, a knife, and bow and arrows. Possibly when these had been achieved she might seriously consider an attempt to fight her way to one of civilization's nearest outposts. In the meantime it was necessary to construct some sort of protective shelter in which she might feel a greater sense of security by night, for she knew that there was a possiblity that any night she might receive a visit from a prowling panther, although she had as yet seen none upon this side of the valley. Aside from this danger she felt comparatively safe in her aerial retreat.

The cutting of the long poles for her home occupied all of the daylight hours that were not engaged in the search for food. These poles she carried high into her tree and with them constructed a flooring across two stout branches binding the poles together and also to the branches with fibers from the tough arboraceous grasses that grew in profusion near the stream. Similarly she built walls and a roof, the latter thatched with many layers of great leaves. The fashioning of the barred windows and the door were matters of great importance and consuming interest. The windows, there were two of them, were large and the bars permanently fixed; but the door was small, the opening just large enough to permit her to pass through easily on hands and knees, which made it easier to barricade. She lost count of the days that the house cost her; but time was a cheap commodity—she had more of it than of anything else. It meant so little to her that she had not even any desire to keep account of it. How long since she and Obergatz had fled from the wrath of the Negro villagers she did not know and she could only roughly guess at the seasons. She worked hard for two reasons; one was to hasten the completion of her little place of refuge, and the other a desire for such physical exhaustion at night that she would sleep through those dreaded hours to a new day. As a matter of fact the house was finished in less than a week—that is, it was made as safe as it ever would be, though regardless of how long she might occupy it she would keep on adding touches and refinements here and there.

Her daily life was filled with her house building and her hunting, to which was added an occasional spice of excitement contributed by roving lions. To the woodcraft that she had learned from Tarzan, that master of the art, was added a considerable store of practical experience derived from her own past adventures in the jungle and the long months with Obergatz, nor was any day now lacking in some added store of useful knowledge. To these facts was attributable her apparent immunity from harm, since they told her when *ja* was approaching before he crept close enough for a successful charge and, too, they kept her close to those never-failing havens of retreat—the trees.

The nights, filled with their weird noises, were lonely and depressing. Only her ability to sleep quickly and soundly made them endurable. The first night that she spent in her completed house behind barred windows and barricaded door was one of almost undiluted peace and happiness. The night noises seemed far removed and impersonal and the soughing of the wind in the trees was gently soothing. Before, it had carried a mournful note and was sinister in that it might hide the approach of some real danger. That night she slept indeed.

She went further afield now in search of food. So far nothing but rodents had fallen to her spear—her ambition was an antelope, since beside the flesh it would give her, and the gut for her bow, the hide would prove invaluable during the colder

weather that she knew would accompany the rainy season.
She had caught glimpses of these wary animals and was sure
that they always crossed the stream at a certain spot above her
camp. It was to this place that she went to hunt them. With
the stealth and cunning of a panther she crept through the
forest, circling about to get up wind from the ford, pausing
often to look and listen for aught that might menace her—
herself the personification of a hunted deer. Now she moved
silently down upon the chosen spot. What luck! A beautiful
buck stood drinking in the stream. The woman wormed her
way closer. Now she lay upon her belly behind a small bush
within throwing distance of the quarry. She must rise to her
full height and throw her spear almost in the same instant and
she must throw it with great force and perfect accuracy. She
thrilled with the excitement of the minute, yet cool and steady
were her swift muscles as she rose and cast her missile. Scarce
by the width of a finger did the point strike from the spot at
which it had been directed. The buck leaped high, landed
upon the bank of the stream, and fell dead. Jane Clayton
sprang quickly forward toward her kill.

"Bravo!" A man's voice spoke in English from the shrubbery upon the opposite side of the stream. Jane Clayton
halted in her tracks—stunned, almost, by surprise. And then
a strange, unkempt figure of a man stepped into view. At
first she did not recognize him, but when she did, instinctively
she stepped back.

"Lieutenant Obergatz!" she cried. "Can it be you?"

"It can. It is," replied the German. "I am a strange sight,
no doubt; but still it is I, Erich Obergatz. And you? You
have changed too, is it not?"

He was looking at her naked limbs and her golden breastplates, the loin cloth of *jato*-hide, the harness and ornaments
that constitute the apparel of a Ho-don woman—the things
that Lu-don had dressed her in as his passion for her grew.
Not Ko-tan's daughter, even, had finer trappings.

"But why are you here?" Jane insisted. "I had thought you
safely among civilized men by this time, if you still lived."

"Gott!" he exclaimed. "I do not know why I continue to
live. I have prayed to die and yet I cling to life. There is no
hope. We are doomed to remain in this horrible land until we
die. The bog! The frightful bog! I have searched its shores
for a place to cross until I have entirely circled the hideous
country. Easily enough we entered; but the rains have come
since and now no living man could pass that slough of slimy
mud and hungry reptiles. Have I not tried it! And the beasts

that roam this accursed land. They hunt me by day and by night."

"But how have you escaped them?" she asked.

"I do not know," he replied gloomily. "I have fled and fled and fled. I have remained hungry and thirsty in tree tops for days at a time. I have fashioned weapons—clubs and spears —and I have learned to use them. I have slain a lion with my club. So even will a cornered rat fight. And we are no better than rats in this land of stupendous dangers, you and I. But tell me about yourself. If it is surprising that I live, how much more so that you still survive."

Briefly she told him and all the while she was wondering what she might do to rid herself of him. She could not conceive of a prolonged existence with him as her sole companion. Better, a thousand times better, to be alone. Never had her hatred and contempt for him lessened through the long weeks and months of their constant companionship, and now that he could be of no service in returning her to civilization, she shrank from the thought of seeing him daily. And, too, she feared him. Never had she trusted him; but now there was a strange light in his eye that had not been there when last she saw him. She could not interpret it—all she knew was that it gave her a feeling of apprehension—a nameless dread.

"You lived long then in the city of A-lur?" he said, speaking in the language of Pal-ul-don.

"You have learned this tongue?" she asked. "How?"

"I fell in with a band of half-breeds," he replied, "members of a proscribed race that dwells in the rock-bound gut through which the principal river of the valley empties into the morass. They are called Waz-ho-don and their village is partly made up of cave dwellings and partly of houses carved from the soft rock at the foot of the cliff. They are very ignorant and superstitious and when they first saw me and realized that I had no tail and that my hands and feet were not like theirs they were afraid of me. They thought that I was either god or demon. Being in a position where I could neither escape them nor defend myself, I made a bold front and succeeded in impressing them to such an extent that they conducted me to their city, which they call Bu-lur, and there they fed me and treated me with kindness. As I learned their language I sought to impress them more and more with the idea that I was a god, and I succeeded, too, until an old fellow who was something of a priest among them, or medicine-man, became jealous of my growing power. That was the beginning of the end and came near to being the end in fact. He told them that if I was a god I would not bleed if a knife was stuck into me

—if I did bleed it would prove conclusively that I was not a god. Without my knowledge he arranged to stage the ordeal before the whole village upon a certain night—it was upon one of those numerous occasions when they eat and drink to Jad-ben-Otho, their pagan deity. Under the influence of their vile liquor they would be ripe for any bloodthirsty scheme the medicine-man might evolve. One of the women told me about the plan—not with any intent to warn me of danger, but prompted merely by feminine curiosity as to whether or not I would bleed if stuck with a dagger. She could not wait, it seemed, for the orderly procedure of the ordeal—she wanted to know at once, and when I caught her trying to slip a knife into my side and questioned her she explained the whole thing with the utmost naïveté. The warriors already had commenced drinking—it would have been futile to make any sort of appeal either to their intellects or their superstitions. There was but one alternative to death and that was flight. I told the woman that I was very much outraged and offended at this reflection upon my godhood and that as a mark of my disfavor I should abandon them to their fate.

" 'I shall return to heaven at once!' I exclaimed.

"She wanted to hang around and see me go, but I told her that her eyes would be blasted by the fire surrounding my departure and that she must leave at once and not return to the spot for at least an hour. I also impressed upon her the fact that should any other approach this part of the village within that time not only they, but she as well, would burst into flames and be consumed.

"She was very much impressed and lost no time in leaving, calling back as she departed that if I were indeed gone in an hour she and all the village would know that I was no less than Jad-ben-Otho himself, and so they must thank me, for I can assure you that I was gone in much less than an hour, nor have I ventured close to the neighborhood of the city of Bu-lur since," and he fell to laughing in harsh, cackling notes that sent a shiver through the woman's frame.

As Obergatz talked Jane had recovered her spear from the carcass of the antelope and commenced busying herself with the removal of the hide. The man made no attempt to assist her, but stood by talking and watching her, the while he continually ran his filthy fingers through his matted hair and beard. His face and body were caked with dirt and he was naked except for a torn greasy hide about his loins. His weapons consisted of a club and knife of Waz-don pattern, that he had stolen from the city of Bu-lur; but what more greatly concerned the woman than his filth or his armament were his cackling laughter and the strange expression in his eyes.

She went on with her work, however, removing those parts of the buck she wanted, taking only as much meat as she might consume before it spoiled, as she was not sufficiently a true jungle creature to relish it beyond that stage, and then she straightened up and faced the man.

"Lieutenant Obergatz," she said, "by a chance of accident we have met again. Certainly you would not have sought the meeting any more than I. We have nothing in common other than those sentiments which may have been engendered by my natural dislike and suspicion of you, one of the authors of all the misery and sorrow that I have endured for endless months. This little corner of the world is mine by right of discovery and occupation. Go away and leave me to enjoy here what peace I may. It is the least that you can do to amend the wrong that you have done me and mine."

The man stared at her through his fishy eyes for a moment in silence, then there broke from his lips a peal of mirthless, uncanny laughter.

"Go away! Leave you alone!" he cried. "I have found you. We are going to be good friends. There is no one else in the world but us. No one will ever know what we do or what becomes of us and now you ask me to go away and live alone in this hellish solitude." Again he laughed, though neither the muscles of his eyes or his mouth reflected any mirth—it was just a hollow sound that imitated laughter.

"Remember your promise," she said.

"Promise! Promise! What are promises? They are made to be broken—we taught the world that at Liége and Louvain. No, no! I will not go away. I shall stay and protect you."

"I do not need your protection," she insisted. "You have already seen that I can use a spear."

"Yes," he said; "but it would not be right to leave you here alone—you are but a woman. No, no; I am an officer of the Kaiser and I cannot abandon you."

Once more he laughed. "We could be very happy here together," he added.

The woman could not repress a shudder, nor, in fact, did she attempt to hide her aversion.

"You do not like me?" he asked. "Ah, well; it is too sad. But some day you will love me," and again the hideous laughter.

The woman had wrapped the pieces of the buck in the hide and this she now raised and threw across her shoulder. In her other hand she held her spear and faced the German.

"Go!" she commanded. "We have wasted enough words. This is my country and I shall defend it. If I see you about again I shall kill you. Do you understand?"

An expression of rage contorted Obergatz' features. He raised his club and started toward her.

"Stop!" she commanded, throwing her spear-hand backward for a cast. "You saw me kill this buck and you have said truthfully that no one will ever know what we do here. Put these two facts together, German, and draw your own conclusions before you take another step in my direction."

The man halted and his club-hand dropped to his side. "Come," he begged in what he intended as a conciliatory tone. "Let us be friends, Lady Greystoke. We can be of great assistance to each other and I promise not to harm you."

"Remember Liége and Louvain," she reminded him with a sneer. "I am going now—be sure that you do not follow me. As far as you can walk in a day from this spot in any direction you may consider the limits of my domain. If ever again I see you within these limits I shall kill you."

There could be no question that she meant what she said and the man seemed convinced for he but stood sullenly eyeing her as she backed from sight beyond a turn in the game trail that crossed the ford where they had met, and disappeared in the forest.

20

Silently in the Night

IN A-LUR the fortunes of the city had been tossed from hand to hand. The party of Ko-tan's loyal warriors that Tarzan had led to the rendezvous at the entrance to the secret passage below the palace gates had met with disaster. Their first rush had been met with soft words from the priests. They had been exhorted to defend the faith of their fathers from blasphemers. Ja-don was painted to them as a defiler of temples, and the wrath of Jad-ben-Otho was prophesied for those who embraced his cause. The priests insisted that Lu-don's only wish was to prevent the seizure of the throne by Ja-don until a new king could be chosen according to the laws of the Ho-don.

The result was that many of the palace warriors joined their fellows of the city, and when the priests saw that those whom they could influence outnumbered those who remained loyal to the palace, they caused the former to fall upon the latter with the result that many were killed and only a handful succeeded in reaching the safety of the palace gates, which they quickly barred.

The priests led their own forces through the secret passageway into the temple, while some of the loyal ones sought out Ja-don and told him all that had happened. The fight in the banquet hall had spread over a considerable portion of the palace grounds and had at last resulted in the temporary defeat of those who had opposed Ja-don. This force, counseled by under priests sent for the purpose by Lu-don, had withdrawn within the temple grounds so that now the issue was plainly marked as between Ja-don on the one side and Lu-don on the other.

The former had been told of all that had occurred in the apartments of O-lo-a to whose safety he had attended at the first opportunity and he had also learned of Tarzan's part in leading his men to the gathering of Lu-don's warriors.

These things had naturally increased the old warrior's former inclinations of friendliness toward the ape-man, and now he regretted that the other had departed from the city.

The testimony of O-lo-a and Pan-at-lee was such as to strengthen whatever belief in the godliness of the stranger Ja-don and others of the warriors had previously entertained, until presently there appeared a strong tendency upon the part of this palace faction to make the Dor-ul-otho an issue of their original quarrel with Lu-don. Whether this occurred as the natural sequence to repeated narrations of the ape-man's exploits, which lost nothing by repetition, in conjunction with Lu-don's enmity toward him, or whether it was the shrewd design of some wily old warrior such as Ja-don, who realized the value of adding a religious cause to their temporal one, it were difficult to determine; but the fact remained that Ja-don's followers developed bitter hatred for the followers of Lu-don because of the high priest's antagonism to Tarzan.

Unfortunately however Tarzan was not there to inspire the followers of Ja-don with the holy zeal that might have quickly settled the dispute in the old chieftain's favor. Instead, he was miles away and because their repeated prayers for his presence were unanswered, the weaker spirits among them commenced to suspect that their cause did not have divine favor. There was also another and a potent cause for defection from the ranks of Ja-don. It emanated from the city where the friends and relatives of the palace warriors, who were largely also the friends and relatives of Lu-don's forces, found the means, urged on by the priesthood, to circulate throughout the palace pernicious propaganda aimed at Ja-don's cause.

The result was that Lu-don's power increased while that of Ja-don waned. Then followed a sortie from the temple which resulted in the defeat of the palace forces, and though they were able to withdraw in decent order withdraw they did, leaving the palace to Lu-don, who was now virtually ruler of Pal-ul-don.

Ja-don, taking with him the princess, her women, and their slaves, including Pan-at-lee, as well as the women and children of his faithful followers, retreated not only from the palace but from the city of A-lur as well and fell back upon his own city of Ja-lur. Here he remained, recruiting his forces from the surrounding villages of the north which, being far removed from the influence of the priesthood of A-lur, were enthusiastic partizans in any cause that the old chieftain espoused, since for years he had been revered as their friend and protector.

And while these events were transpiring in the north, Tarzan-jad-guru lay in the lion pit at Tu-lur while messengers passed back and forth between Mo-sar and Lu-don as the two dickered for the throne of Pal-ul-don. Mo-sar was cunning enough to guess that should an open breach occur between himself and the high priest he might use his prisoner to his own advantage, for he had heard whisperings among even his own people that suggested that there were those who were more than a trifle inclined to belief in the divinity of the stranger and that he might indeed be the Dor-ul-Otho. Lu-don wanted Tarzan himself. He wanted to sacrifice him upon the eastern altar with his own hands before a multitude of people, since he was not without evidence that his own standing and authority had been lessened by the claims of the bold and heroic figure of the stranger.

The method that the high priest of Tu-lur had employed to trap Tarzan had left the ape-man in possession of his weapons though there seemed little likelihood of their being of any service to him. He also had his pouch, in which were the various odds and ends which are the natural accumulation of all receptacles from a gold meshbag to an attic. There were bits of obsidian and choice feathers for arrows, some pieces of flint and a couple of steel, an old knife, a heavy bone needle, and

strips of dried gut. Nothing very useful to you or me, perhaps; but nothing useless to the savage life of the ape-man.

When Tarzan realized the trick that had been so neatly
played upon him he had awaited expectantly the coming of
the lion, for though the scent of *ja* was old he was sure that
sooner or later they would let one of the beasts in upon him.
His first consideration was a thorough exploration of his prison.
He had noticed the hide-covered windows and these he immediately uncovered, letting in the light, and revealing the
fact that though the chamber was far below the level of the
temple courts it was yet many feet above the base of the hill
from which the temple was hewn. The windows were so
closely barred that he could not see over the edge of the thick
wall in which they were cut to determine what lay close in
below him. At a little distance were the blue waters of Jad-in-
lul and beyond, the verdure-clad farther shore, and beyond
that the mountains. It was a beautiful picture upon which
he looked—a picture of peace and harmony and quiet. Nor
anywhere a slightest suggestion of the savage men and beasts
that claimed this lovely landscape as their own. What a
paradise! And some day civilized man would come and—
spoil it! Ruthless axes would raze that age-old wood; black,
sticky smoke would rise from ugly chimneys against that azure
sky; grimy little boats with wheels behind or upon either side
would churn the mud from the bottom of Jad-in-lul, turning
its blue waters to a dirty brown; hideous piers would project
into the lake from squalid buildings of corrugated iron, doubtless, for of such are the pioneer cities of the world.

But would civilized man come? Tarzan hoped not. For
countless generations civilization had ramped about the globe;
it had dispatched its emissaries to the North Pole and the
South; it had circled Pal-ul-don once, perhaps many times,
but it had never touched her. God grant that it never would.
Perhaps He was saving this little spot to be always just as He
had made it, for the scratching of the Ho-don and the Waz-
don upon His rocks had not altered the fair face of Nature.

Through the windows came sufficient light to reveal the
whole interior to Tarzan. The room was fairly large and there
was a door at each end—a large door for men and a smaller
one for lions. Both were closed with heavy masses of stone
that had been lowered in grooves running to the floor. The
two windows were small and closely barred with the first iron
that Tarzan had seen in Pal-ul-don. The bars were let into
holes in the casing, and the whole so strongly and neatly contrived that escape seemed impossible. Yet within a few minutes of his incarceration Tarzan had commenced to undertake

his escape. The old knife in his pouch was brought into requisition and slowly the ape-man began to scrape and chip away the stone from about the bars of one of the windows. It was slow work but Tarzan had the patience of absolute health.

Each day food and water were brought him and slipped quickly beneath the smaller door which was raised just sufficiently to allow the stone receptacles to pass in. The prisoner began to believe that he was being preserved for something beside lions. However that was immaterial. If they would but hold off for a few more days they might select what fate they would—he would not be there when they arrived to announce it.

And then one day came Pan-sat, Lu-don's chief tool, to the city of Tu-lur. He came ostensibly with a fair message for Mo-sar from the high priest at A-lur. Lu-don had decided that Mo-sar should be king and he invited Mo-sar to come at once to A-lur and then Pan-sat, having delivered the message, asked that he might go to the temple of Tu-lur and pray, and there he sought the high priest of Tu-lur to whom was the true message that Lu-don had sent. The two were closeted alone in a little chamber and Pan-sat whispered into the ear of the high priest.

"Mo-sar wishes to be king," he said, "and Lu-don wishes to be king. Mo-sar wishes to retain the stranger who claims to be the Dor-ul-Otho and Lu-don wishes to kill him, and now," he leaned even closer to the ear of the high priest of Tu-lur, "if you would be high priest at A-lur it is within your power."

Pan-sat ceased speaking and waited for the other's reply. The high priest was visibly affected. To be high priest at A-lur! That was almost as good as being king of all Pal-ul-don, for great were the powers of him who conducted the sacrifices upon the altars of A-lur.

"How?" whispered the high priest. "How may I become high priest at A-lur?"

Again Pan-sat leaned close: "By killing the one and bringing the other to A-lur," replied he. Then he rose and departed knowing that the other had swallowed the bait and could be depended upon to do whatever was required to win him the great prize.

Nor was Pan-sat mistaken other than in one trivial consideration. This high priest would indeed commit murder and treason to attain the high office at A-lur; but he had misunderstood which of his victims was to be killed and which to be delivered to Lu-don. Pan-sat, knowing himself all the details of the plannings of Lu-don, had made the quite natural error of assuming that the other was perfectly aware that only by publicly sacrificing the false Dor-ul-Otho could the high priest at A-lur bolster his waning power and that the assassination of Mo-sar, the pretender, would remove from Lu-don's camp the only obstacle to his combining the offices of high priest and king. The high priest at Tu-lur thought that he had been commissioned to kill Tarzan and bring Mo-sar to A-lur. He also thought that when he had done these things he would be made high priest at A-lur; but he did not know that already the priest had been selected who was to murder him within the hour that he arrived at A-lur, nor did he know that a secret grave had been prepared for him in the floor of a subterranean chamber in the very temple he dreamed of controlling.

And so when he should have been arranging the assassination of his chief he was leading a dozen heavily bribed warriors through the dark corridors beneath the temple to slay Tarzan in the lion pit. Night had fallen. A single torch guided the footsteps of the murderers as they crept stealthily upon their evil way, for they knew that they were doing the thing that their chief did not want done and their guilty consciences warned them to stealth.

In the dark of his cell the ape-man worked at his seemingly endless chipping and scraping. His keen ears detected the coming of footsteps along the corridor without—footsteps that approached the larger door. Always before had they come to the smaller door—the footsteps of a single slave who brought his food. This time there were many more than one and their coming at this time of night carried a sinister suggestion. Tarzan continued to work at his scraping and chipping. He heard them stop beyond the door. All was silence broken only by the scrape, scrape, scrape of the ape-man's tireless blade.

Those without heard it and listening sought to explain it. They whispered in low tones making their plans. Two would raise the door quickly and the others would rush in and hurl their clubs at the prisoner. They would take no chances, for the stories that had circulated in A-lur had been brought to Tu-lur—stories of the great strength and wonderful prowess of Tarzan-jad-guru that caused the sweat to stand upon the brows of the warriors, though it was cool in the damp corridor and they were twelve to one.

And then the high priest gave the signal—the door shot upward and ten warriors leaped into the chamber with poised clubs. Three of the heavy weapons flew across the room toward a darker shadow that lay in the shadow of the opposite wall, then the flare of the torch in the priest's hand lighted the interior and they saw that the thing at which they had flung their clubs was a pile of skins torn from the windows and that except for themselves the chamber was vacant.

One of them hastened to a window. All but a single bar was gone and to this was tied one end of a braided rope fashioned from strips cut from the leather window hangings.

To the ordinary dangers of Jane Clayton's existence was now added the menace of Obergatz' knowledge of her whereabouts. The lion and the panther had given her less cause for anxiety than did the return of the unscrupulous Hun, whom she had always distrusted and feared, and whose repulsiveness was now immeasurably augmented by his unkempt and filthy appearance, his strange and mirthless laughter, and his unnatural demeanor. She feared him now with a new fear as though he had suddenly become the personification of some nameless horror. The wholesome, outdoor life that she had been leading had strengthened and rebuilt her nervous system yet it seemed to her as she thought of him that if this man should ever touch her she should scream, and, possibly, even faint. Again and again during the day following their unexpected meeting the woman reproached herself for not having killed him as she would *ja* or *jato* or any other predatory beast that menaced her existence or her safety. There was no attempt at self-justification for these sinister reflections—they needed no justification. The standards by which the acts of such as you or I may be judged could not apply to hers. We have recourse to the protection of friends and relatives and the civil soldiery that upholds the majesty of the law and which may be invoked to protect the righteous weak against the unrighteous strong; but Jane Clayton comprised within herself not only the righteous weak but all the various agencies for the protection of the weak. To her, then, Lieutenant Erich Obergatz presented no different problem than did *ja,* the lion, other than that she considered the former the more dangerous animal. And so she determined that should he ignore her warning there would be no temporizing upon the occasion of their next meeting—the same swift spear that would meet *ja's* advances would meet his.

That night her snug little nest perched high in the great tree seemed less the sanctuary that it had before. What might resist the sanguinary intentions of a prowling panther would prove no great barrier to man, and influenced by this thought she slept less well than before. The slightest noise that broke the monotonous hum of the nocturnal jungle startled her into alert wakefulness to lie with straining ears in an attempt to classify the origin of the disturbance, and once she was awakened thus by a sound that seemed to come from something moving in her own tree. She listened intently—scarce breathing. Yes, there it was again. A scuffing of something soft against the hard bark of the tree. The woman reached out in the darkness and grasped her spear. Now she felt a slight sagging of one of the limbs that supported her shelter as though the thing, whatever it was, was slowly raising its weight to the branch. It came nearer. Now she thought that she could detect its breathing. It was at the door. She could hear it fumbling with the frail barrier. What could it be? It made no sound by which she might identify it. She raised herself upon her hands and knees and crept stealthily the little distance to the doorway, her spear clutched tightly in her hand. Whatever the thing was, it was evidently attempting to gain entrance without awakening her. It was just beyond the pitiful little contraption of slender boughs that she had bound together with grasses and called a door—only a few inches lay between the thing and her. Rising to her knees she reached out with her left hand and felt until she found a place where a crooked branch had left an opening a couple of inches wide near the center of the barrier. Into this she inserted the point of her spear. The thing must have heard her move within for suddenly it abandoned its efforts for stealth and tore angrily at the obstacle. At the same moment Jane thrust her spear forward with all her strength. She felt it enter flesh. There was a scream and a curse from without, followed by the crashing of a body through limbs and foliage. Her spear was almost dragged from her grasp, but she held to it until it broke free from the thing it had pierced.

It was Obergatz; the curse had told her that. From below came no further sound. Had she, then, killed him? She prayed so—with all her heart she prayed it. To be freed from the menace of this loathsome creature were relief indeed. During all the balance of the night she lay there awake, listening. Below her, she imagined, she could see the dead man with his hideous face bathed in the cold light of the moon—lying there upon his back staring up at her.

She prayed that *ja* might come and drag it away, but all during the remainder of the night she heard never another sound above the drowsy hum of the jungle. She was glad that he was dead, but she dreaded the gruesome ordeal that awaited her on the morrow, for she must bury the thing that had been Erich Obergatz and live on there above the shallow grave of the man she had slain.

She reproached herself for her weakness, repeating over and over that she had killed in self-defense, that her act was justified; but she was still a woman of today, and strong upon her were the iron mandates of the social order from which she had sprung, its interdictions and its superstitions.

At last came the tardy dawn. Slowly the sun topped the distant mountains beyond Jad-in-lul. And yet she hesitated to loosen the fastenings of her door and look out upon the thing below. But it must be done. She steeled herself and untied the rawhide thong that secured the barrier. She looked down and only the grass and the flowers looked up at her. She came from her shelter and examined the ground upon the opposite side of the tree—there was no dead man there, nor anywhere as far as she could see. Slowly she descended, keeping a wary eye and an alert ear ready for the first intimation of danger.

At the foot of the tree was a pool of blood and a little trail of crimson drops upon the grass, leading away parallel with the shore of Jad-ben-lul. Then she had not slain him! She was vaguely aware of a peculiar, double sensation of relief and regret. Now she would be always in doubt. He might return; but at least she would not have to live above his grave.

She thought some of following the bloody spoor on the chance that he might have crawled away to die later, but she gave up the idea for fear that she might find him dead nearby, or, worse yet badly wounded. What then could she do? She could not finish him with her spear—no, she knew that she could not do that, nor could she bring him back and nurse him, nor could she leave him there to die of hunger or of thirst, or to become the prey of some prowling beast. It were better then not to search for him for fear that she might find him.

That day was one of nervous starting to every sudden sound. The day before she would have said that her nerves were of iron; but not today. She knew now the shock that she had suffered and that this was the reaction. Tomorrow it might be different, but something told her that never again would her little shelter and the patch of forest and jungle that she called her own be the same. There would hang over them always the menace of this man. No longer would she pass restful nights of deep slumber. The peace of her little world was shattered forever.

That night she made her door doubly secure with additional thongs of rawhide cut from the pelt of the buck she had slain the day that she met Obergatz. She was very tired for she had lost much sleep the night before; but for a long time she lay with wide-open eyes staring into the darkness. What saw she there? Visions that brought tears to those brave and beautiful eyes—visions of a rambling bungalow that had been home to her and that was no more, destroyed by the same cruel force that haunted her even now in this remote, uncharted corner of the earth; visions of a strong man whose protecting arm would never press her close again; visions of a tall, straight son who looked at her adoringly out of brave, smiling eyes that were like his father's. Always the vision of the crude simple bungalow rather than of the stately halls that had been as much a part of her life as the other. But *he* had loved the bungalow and the broad, free acres best and so she had come to love them best, too.

At last she slept, the sleep of utter exhaustion. How long it lasted she did not know; but suddenly she was wide awake and once again she heard the scuffing of a body against the bark of her tree and again the limb bent to a heavy weight. He had returned! She went cold, trembling as with ague. Was it he, or, O God! had she killed him then and was this—? She tried to drive the horrid thought from her mind, for this way, she knew, lay madness.

And once again she crept to the door, for the thing was outside just as it had been last night. Her hands trembled as she placed the point of her weapon to the opening. She wondered if it would scream as it fell.

21

The Maniac

THE last bar that would make the opening large enough to permit his body to pass had been removed as Tarzan heard the warriors whispering beyond the stone door of his prison. Long since had the rope of hide been braided. To secure one end to the remaining bar that he had left for this purpose was the work of but a moment, and while the warriors whispered without, the brown body of the ape-man slipped through the small aperture and disappeared below the sill.

Tarzan's escape from the cell left him still within the walled area that comprised the palace and temple grounds and buildings. He had reconnoitered as best he might from the window after he had removed enough bars to permit him to pass his head through the opening, so that he knew what lay immediately before him—a winding and usually deserted alleyway leading in the direction of the outer gate that opened from the palace grounds into the city.

The darkness would facilitate his escape. He might even pass out of the palace and the city without detection. If he could elude the guard at the palace gate the rest would be easy. He strode along confidently, exhibiting no fear of detection, for he reasoned that thus would he disarm suspicion. In the darkness he easily could pass for a Ho-don and in truth, though he passed several after leaving the deserted alley, no one accosted or detained him, and thus he came at last to the guard of a half-dozen warriors before the palace gate. These he attempted to pass in the same unconcerned fashion and he might have succeeded had it not been for one who came running rapidly from the direction of the temple shouting: "Let no one pass the gates! The prisoner has escaped from the *pal-ul-ja!*"

Instantly a warrior barred his way and simultaneously the fellow recognized him. *"Xot tor!"* he exclaimed: "Here he is now. Fall upon him! Fall upon him! Back! Back before I kill you."

The others came forward. It cannot be said that they rushed forward. If it was their wish to fall upon him there was a noticeable lack of enthusiasm other than that which directed their efforts to persuade someone else to fall upon him. His fame as a fighter had been too long a topic of conversation for the good of the morale of Mo-sar's warriors. It were safer to stand at a distance and hurl their clubs and this they did, but the ape-man had learned something of the use of this weapon since he had arrived in Pal-ul-don. And as he learned great had grown his respect for this most primitive of arms. He had come to realize that the black savages he had known had never appreciated the possibilities of their knob sticks, nor had he, and he had discovered, too, why the Pal-ul-dons had turned their ancient spears into plowshares and pinned their faith to the heavy-ended club alone. In deadly execution it was far more effective than a spear and it answered, too, every purpose of a shield, combining the two in one and thus reducing the burden of the warrior. Thrown as they throw it, after the manner of the hammer-throwers of the Olympian games, an ordinary shield would prove more a weakness than a strength while one that would be strong enough to prove a protection would be too heavy to carry. Only another club, deftly wielded to deflect the course of an enemy missile, is in any way effective against these formidable weapons and, too, the war club of Pal-ul-don can be thrown with accuracy a far greater distance than any spear.

And now was put to the test that which Tarzan had learned from Om-at and Ta-den. His eyes and his muscles trained by a lifetime of necessity moved with the rapidity of light and his brain functioned with an uncanny celerity that suggested nothing less than prescience, and these things more than compensated for his lack of experience with the war club he handled so dexterously. Weapon after weapon he warded off and always he moved with a single idea in mind—to place himself within reach of one of his antagonists. But they were wary for they feared this strange creature to whom the superstitious fears of many of them attributed the miraculous powers of deity. They managed to keep between Tarzan and the gateway and all the time they bawled lustily for reinforcements. Should these come before he had made his escape the ape-man realized that the odds against him would be unsurmountable, and so he redoubled his efforts to carry out his design.

Following their usual tactics, two or three of the warriors were always circling behind him collecting the thrown clubs when Tarzan's attention was directed elsewhere. He himself retrieved several of them which he hurled with such deadly effect as to dispose of two of his antagonists, but now he heard the approach of hurrying warriors, the patter of their bare feet upon the stone pavement and then the savage cries which were to bolster the courage of their fellows and fill the enemy with fear.

There was no time to lose. Tarzan held a club in either hand and, swinging one he hurled it at a warrior before him and as the man dodged he rushed in and seized him, at the same time casting his second club at another of his opponents. The Ho-don with whom he grappled reached instantly for his knife but the ape-man grasped his wrist. There was a sudden twist, the snapping of a bone and an agonized scream, then the warrior was lifted bodily from his feet and held as a shield between his fellows and the fugitive as the latter backed through the gateway. Beside Tarzan stood the single torch that lighted the entrance to the palace grounds. The warriors were advancing to the succor of their fellow when the ape-man raised his captive high above his head and flung him full in the face of the foremost attacker. The fellow went down and two directly behind him sprawled headlong over their companion as the ape-man seized the torch and cast it back

into the palace grounds to be extinguished as it struck the
bodies of those who led the charging reinforcements.

In the ensuing darkness Tarzan disappeared in the streets
of Tu-lur beyond the palace gate. For a time he was aware
of sounds of pursuit but the fact that they trailed away and
died in the direction of Jad-in-lul informed him that they were
searching in the wrong direction, for he had turned south out
of Tu-lur purposely to throw them off his track. Beyond the
outskirts of the city he turned directly toward the northwest,
in which direction lay A-lur.

In his path he knew lay Jad-bal-lul, the shore of which he
was compelled to skirt, and there would be a river to cross at
the lower end of the great lake upon the shores of which lay
A-lur. What other obstacles lay in his way he did not know
but he believed that he could make better time on foot than by
attempting to steal a canoe and force his way up stream with
a single paddle. It was his intention to put as much distance
as possible between himself and Tu-lur before he slept for he
was sure that Mo-sar would not lightly accept his loss, but
that with the coming of day, or possibly even before, he would
dispatch warriors in search of him.

A mile or two from the city he entered a forest and here at
last he felt such a measure of safety as he never knew in open
spaces or in cities. The forest and the jungle were his birth-
right. No creature that went upon the ground upon four feet,
or climbed among the trees, or crawled upon its belly had any
advantage over the ape-man in his native heath. As myrrh
and frankincense were the dank odors of rotting vegetation
in the nostrils of the great Tarmangani. He squared his broad
shoulders and lifting his head filled his lungs with the air that
he loved best. The heavy fragrance of tropical blooms, the
commingled odors of the myriad-scented life of the jungle
went to his head with a pleasurable intoxication far more potent than aught contained in the oldest vintages of civilization.

He took to the trees now, not from necessity but from pure
love of the wild freedom that had been denied him so long.
Though it was dark and the forest strange yet he moved with
a surety and ease that bespoke more a strange uncanny sense
than wondrous skill. He heard *ja* moaning somewhere ahead
and an owl hooted mournfully to the right of him—long familiar sounds that imparted to him no sense of loneliness as
they might to you or to me, but on the contrary one of companionship for they betokened the presence of his fellows of
the jungle, and whether friend or foe it was all the same to the
ape-man.

He came at last to a little stream at a spot where the trees

did not meet above it so he was forced to descend to the
ground and wade through the water and upon the opposite
shore he stopped as though suddenly his godlike figure had
been transmuted from flesh to marble. Only his dilating nostrils bespoke his pulsing vitality. For a long moment he stood
there thus and then swiftly, but with a caution and silence
that were inherent in him he moved forward again, but now
his whole attitude bespoke a new urge. There was a definite
and masterful purpose in every movement of those steel muscles rolling softly beneath the smooth brown hide. He moved
now toward a certain goal that quite evidently filled him with
far greater enthusiasm than had the possible event of his return to A-lur.

And so he came at last to the foot of a great tree and there
he stopped and looked up above him among the foliage where
the dim outlines of a roughly rectangular bulk loomed darkly.
There was a choking sensation in Tarzan's throat as he raised
himself gently into the branches. It was as though his heart
were swelling either to a great happiness or a great fear.

Before the rude shelter built among the branches he paused
listening. From within there came to his sensitive nostrils the
same delicate aroma that had arrested his eager attention at
the little stream a mile away. He crouched upon the branch
close to the little door.

"Jane," he called, "heart of my heart, it is I."

The only answer from within was as the sudden indrawing
of a breath that was half gasp and half sigh, and the sound of
a body falling to the floor. Hurriedly Tarzan sought to release
the thongs which held the door but they were fastened from
the inside, and at last, impatient with further delay, he seized
the frail barrier in one giant hand and with a single effort tore
it completely away. And then he entered to find the seemingly
lifeless body of his mate stretched upon the floor.

He gathered her in his arms; her heart beat; she still
breathed, and presently he realized that she had but swooned.

When Jane Clayton regained consciousness it was to find
herself held tightly in two strong arms, her head pillowed upon
the broad shoulder where so often before her fears had been
soothed and her sorrows comforted. At first she was not sure
but that it was all a dream. Timidly her hand stole to his
cheek.

"John," she murmured, "tell me, is it really you?"

In reply he drew her more closely to him. "It is I," he replied. "But there is something in my throat," he said haltingly,
"that makes it hard for me to speak."

She smiled and snuggled closer to him. "God has been good to us, Tarzan of the Apes," she said.

For some time neither spoke. It was enough that they were reunited and that each knew that the other was alive and safe. But at last they found their voices and when the sun rose they were still talking, so much had each to tell the other; so many questions there were to be asked and answered.

"And Jack," she asked, "where is he?"

"I do not know," replied Tarzan. "The last I heard of him he was on the Argonne Front."

"Ah, then our happiness is not quite complete," she said, a little note of sadness creeping into her voice.

"No," he replied, "but the same is true in countless other English homes today, and pride is learning to take the place of happiness in these."

She shook her head, "I want my boy," she said.

"And I too," replied Tarzan, "and we may have him yet. He was safe and unwounded the last word I had. And now," he said, "we must plan upon our return. Would you like to re-build the bungalow and gather together the remnants of our Waziri or would you rather return to London?"

"Only to find Jack," she said. "I dream always of the bunga-low and never of the city, but John, we can only dream, for Obergatz told me that he had circled this whole country and found no place where he might cross the morass."

"I am not Obergatz," Tarzan reminded her, smiling. "We will rest today and tomorrow we will set out toward the north. It is a savage country, but we have crossed it once and we can cross it again."

And so, upon the following morning, the Tarmangani and his mate went forth upon their journey across the Valley cf Jad-ben-Otho, and ahead of them were fierce men and savage beasts, and the lofty mountains of Pal-ul-don; and beyond the mountains the reptiles and the morass, and beyond that the arid, thorn-covered steppe, and other savage beasts and men and weary, hostile miles of untracked wilderness between them and the charred ruins of their home.

Lieutenant Erich Obergatz crawled through the grass upon all fours, leaving a trail of blood behind him after Jane's spear had sent him crashing to the ground beneath her tree. He made no sound after the one piercing scream that had ac-knowledged the severity of his wound. He was quiet because of a great fear that had crept into his warped brain that the devil woman would pursue and slay him. And so he crawled away like some filthy beast of prey, seeking a thicket where he might lie down and hide.

He thought that he was going to die, but he did not, and with the coming of the new day he discovered that his wound was superficial. The rough obsidian-shod spear had entered the muscles of his side beneath his right arm inflicting a painful, but not a fatal wound. With the realization of this fact came a renewed desire to put as much distance as possible between himself and Jane Clayton. And so he moved on, still going upon all fours because of a persistent hallucination that in this way he might escape observation. Yet though he fled his mind still revolved muddily about a central desire—while he fled from her he still planned to pursue her, and to his lust of possession was added a desire for revenge. She should pay for the suffering she had inflicted upon him. She should pay for rebuffing him, but for some reason which he did not try to explain to himself he would crawl away and hide. He would come back though. He would come back and when he had finished with her, he would take that smooth throat in his two hands and crush the life from her.

He kept repeating this over and over to himself and then he fell to laughing out loud, the cackling, hideous laughter that had terrified Jane. Presently he realized his knees were bleeding and that they hurt him. He looked cautiously behind. No one was in sight. He listened. He could hear no indications of pursuit and so he rose to his feet and continued upon his way a sorry sight—covered with filth and blood, his beard and hair tangled and matted and filled with burrs and dried mud and unspeakable filth. He kept no track of time. He ate fruits and berries and tubers that he dug from the earth with his fingers. He followed the shore of the lake and the river that he might be near water, and when *ja* roared or moaned he climbed a tree and hid there, shivering.

And so after a time he came up the southern shore of Jadben-lul until a wide river stopped his progress. Across the blue water a white city glimmered in the sun. He looked at it for a long time, blinking his eyes like an owl. Slowly a recollection forced itself through his tangled brain. This was A-lur, the City of Light. The association of ideas recalled Bu-lur and the Waz-ho-don. They had called him Jad-ben-Otho. He commenced to laugh aloud and stood up very straight and strode back and forth along the shore. "I am Jad-ben-Otho," he cried, "I am the Great God. In A-lur is my temple and my high priests. What is Jad-ben-Otho doing here alone in the jungle?"

He stepped out into the water and raising his voice shrieked

loudly across toward A-lur. "I am Jad-ben-Otho!" he
screamed. "Come hither slaves and take your god to his
temple." But the distance was great and they did not hear
him and no one came, and the feeble mind was distracted by
other things—a bird flying in the air, a school of minnows
swimming around his feet. He lunged at them trying to catch
them, and falling upon his hands and knees he crawled
through the water grasping futilely at the elusive fish.

Presently it occurred to him that he was a sea lion and he
forgot the fish and lay down and tried to swim by wriggling
his feet in the water as though they were a tail. The hardships, the privations, the terrors, and for the past few weeks
the lack of proper nourishment had reduced Erich Obergatz
to little more than a gibbering idiot.

A water snake swam out upon the surface of the lake and
the man pursued it, crawling upon his hands and knees. The
snake swam toward the shore just within the mouth of the
river where tall reeds grew thickly and Obergatz followed,
making grunting noises like a pig. He lost the snake within
the reeds but he came upon something else—a canoe hidden
there close to the bank. He examined it with cackling laughter. There were two paddles within it which he took and
threw out into the current of the river. He watched them for
a while and then he sat down beside the canoe and commenced to splash his hands up and down upon the water. He
liked to hear the noise and see the little splashes of spray.
He rubbed his left forearm with his right palm and the dirt
came off and left a white spot that drew his attention. He
rubbed again upon the now thoroughly soaked blood and
grime that covered his body. He was not attempting to wash
himself; he was merely amused by the strange results. "I am
turning white," he cried. His glance wandered from his body
now that the grime and blood were all removed and caught
again the white city shimmering beneath the hot sun.

"A-lur—City of Light!" he shrieked and that reminded him
again of Tu-lur and by the same process of associated ideas
that had before suggested it, he recalled that the Waz-ho-don
had thought him Jad-ben-Otho.

"I am Jad-ben-Otho!" he screamed and then his eyes fell
again upon the canoe. A new idea came and persisted. He
looked down at himself, examining his body, and seeing the
filthy loin cloth, now water soaked and more bedraggled than
before, he tore it from him and flung it into the lake. "Gods
do not wear dirty rags," he said aloud. "They do not wear
anything but wreaths and garlands of flowers and I am a god

—I am Jad-ben-Otho—and I go in state to my sacred city of A-lur."

He ran his fingers through his matted hair and beard. The water had softened the burrs but had not removed them. The man shook his head. His hair and beard failed to harmonize with his other godly attributes. He was commencing to think more clearly now, for the great idea had taken hold of his scattered wits and concentrated them upon a single purpose, but he was still a maniac. The only difference being that he was now a maniac with a fixed intent. He went out on the shore and gathered flowers and ferns and wove them in his beard and hair—blazing blooms of different colors—green ferns that trailed about his ears or rose bravely upward like the plumes in a lady's hat.

When he was satisfied that his appearance would impress the most casual observer with his evident deity he returned to the canoe, pushed it from shore and jumped in. The impetus carried it into the river's current and the current bore it out upon the lake. The naked man stood erect in the center of the little craft, his arms folded upon his chest. He screamed aloud his message to the city: "I am Jad-ben-Otho! Let the high priest and the under priests attend upon me!"

As the current of the river was dissipated by the waters of the lake the wind caught him and his craft and carried them bravely forward. Sometimes he drifted with his back toward A-lur and sometimes with his face toward it, and at intervals he shrieked his message and his commands. He was still in the middle of the lake when someone discovered him from the palace wall, and as he drew nearer, a crowd of warriors and women and children were congregated there watching him and along the temple walls were many priests and among them Lu-don, the high priest. When the boat had drifted close enough for them to distinguish the bizarre figure standing in it and for them to catch the meaning of his words Lu-don's cunning eyes narrowed. The high priest had learned of the escape of Tarzan and he feared that should he join Ja-don's forces, as seemed likely, he would attract many recruits who might still believe in him, and the Dor-ul-Otho, even if a false one, upon the side of the enemy might easily work havoc with Lu-don's plans.

The man was drifting close in. His canoe would soon be caught in the current that ran close to shore here and carried toward the river that emptied the waters of Jad-ben-lul into Jad-bal-lul. The under priests were looking toward Lu-don for instructions.

"Fetch him hither!" he commanded. "If he is Jad-ben-Otho I shall know him."

The priests hurried to the palace grounds and summoned warriors. "Go, bring the stranger to Lu-don. If he is Jad-ben-Otho we shall know him."

And so Lieutenant Erich Obergatz was brought before the high priest at A-lur. Lu-don looked closely at the naked man with the fantastic headdress.

"Where did you come from?" he asked.

"I am Jad-ben-Otho," cried the German. "I came from heaven. Where is my high priest?"

"I am the high priest," replied Lu-don.

Obergatz clapped his hands. "Have my feet bathed and food brought to me," he commanded.

Lu-don's eyes narrowed to mere slits of crafty cunning. He bowed low until his forehead touched the feet of the stranger. Before the eyes of many priests, and warriors from the palace he did it.

"Ho, slaves!" he cried, rising; "fetch water and food for the Great God," and thus the high priest acknowledged before his people the godhood of Lieutenant Erich Obergatz, nor was it long before the story ran like wildfire through the palace and out into the city and beyond that to the lesser villages all the way from A-lur to Tu-lur.

The real god had come—Jad-ben-Otho himself, and he had espoused the cause of Lu-don, the high priest. Mo-sar lost no time in placing himself at the disposal of Lu-don, nor did he mention aught about his claims to the throne. It was Mo-sar's opinion that he might consider himself fortunate were he allowed to remain in peaceful occupation of his chieftainship at Tu-lur, nor was Mo-sar wrong in his deductions. But Lu-don could still use him and so he let him live and sent word to him to come to A-lur with all his warriors, for it was rumored that Ja-don was raising a great army in the north and might soon march upon the City of Light.

Obergatz thoroughly enjoyed being a god. Plenty of food and peace of mind and rest partially brought back to him the reason that had been so rapidly slipping from him; but in one respect he was madder than ever, since now no power on earth would ever be able to convince him that he was not a god. Slaves were put at his disposal and these he ordered about in godly fashion. The same portion of his naturally cruel mind met upon common ground the mind of Lu-don, so that the two seemed always in accord. The high priest saw in the stranger a mighty force wherewith to hold forever his power over all Pal-ul-don and thus the future of Obergatz was assured so long as he cared to play god to Lu-don's high priest.

A throne was erected in the main temple court before the eastern altar where Jad-ben-Otho might sit in person and behold the sacrifices that were offered up to him there each day at sunset. So much did the cruel, half-crazed mind enjoy these spectacles that at times he even insisted upon wielding the sacrificial knife himself and upon such occasions the priests and the people fell upon their faces in awe of the dread deity.

If Obergatz taught them not to love their god more he taught them to fear him as they never had before, so that the name of Jad-ben-Otho was whispered in the city and little children were frightened into obedience by the mere mention of it. Lu-don, through his priests and slaves, circulated the information that Jad-ben-Otho had commanded all his faithful followers to flock to the standard of the high priest at A-lur and that all others were cursed, especially Ja-don and the base impostor who had posed as the Dor-ul-Otho. The curse was to take the form of early death following terrible suffering, and Lu-don caused it to be published abroad that the name of any warrior who complained of a pain should be brought to him, for such might be deemed to be under suspicion, since the first effects of the curse would result in slight pains attacking the unholy. He counseled those who felt pains to look carefully to their loyalty. The result was remarkable and immediate—half a nation without a pain, and recruits pouring into A-lur to offer their services to Lu-don while secretly hoping that the little pains they had felt in arm or leg or belly would not recur in aggravated form.

22

A Journey on a Gryf

TARZAN and Jane skirted the shore of Jad-bal-lul and crossed the river at the head of the lake. They moved in leisurely fashion with an eye to comfort and safety, for the ape-man, now that he had found his mate, was determined to court no chance that might again separate them, or delay or prevent their escape from Pal-ul-don. How they were to re-

cross the morass was a matter of little concern to him as yet—
it would be time enough to consider that matter when it became of more immediate moment. Their hours were filled with
the happiness and content of reunion after long separation;
they had much to talk of, for each had passed through many
trials and vicissitudes and strange adventures, and no important hour might go unaccounted for since last they met.

It was Tarzan's intention to choose a way above A-lur and
the scattered Ho-don villages below it, passing about midway
between them and the mountains, thus avoiding, in so far as
possible, both the Ho-don and Waz-don, for in this area lay
the neutral territory that was uninhabited by either. Thus he
would travel northwest until opposite the Kor-ul-ja where he
planned to stop to pay his respects to Om-at and give the *gund*
word of Pan-at-lee, and a plan Tarzan had for insuring her safe
return to her people. It was upon the third day of their
journey and they had almost reached the river that passes
through A-lur when Jane suddenly clutched Tarzan's arm and
pointed ahead toward the edge of a forest that they were approaching. Beneath the shadows of the trees loomed a great
bulk that the ape-man instantly recognized.

"What is it?" whispered Jane.

"A *gryf*," replied the ape-man, "and we have met him in the
worst place that we could possibly have found. There is not
a large tree within a quarter of a mile, other than those among
which he stands. Come, we shall have to go back, Jane; I
cannot risk it with you along. The best we can do is to pray
that he does not discover us."

"And if he does?"

"Then I shall have to risk it."

"Risk what?"

"The chance that I can subdue him as I subdued one of his
fellows," replied Tarzan. "I told you—you recall?"

"Yes, but I did not picture so huge a creature. Why, John,
he is as big as a battleship."

The ape-man laughed. "Not quite, though I'll admit he
looks quite as formidable as one when he charges."

They were moving away slowly so as not to attract the attention of the beast.

"I believe we're going to make it," whispered the woman,
her voice tense with suppressed excitement. A low rumble
rolled like distant thunder from the wood. Tarzan shook his
head.

" 'The big show is about to commence in the main tent,' "
he quoted, grinning. He caught the woman suddenly to his
breast and kissed her. "One can never tell, Jane," he said.

"We'll do our best—that is all we can do. Give me your spear, and—don't run. The only hope we have lies in that little brain more than in us. If I can control it—well, let us see."

The beast had emerged from the forest and was looking about through his weak eyes, evidently in search of them. Tarzan raised his voice in the weird notes of the Tor-o-don's cry; "Whee-oo! Whee-oo! Whee-oo!" For a moment the great beast stood motionless, his attention riveted by the call. The ape-man advanced straight toward him, Jane Clayton at his elbow. "Whee-oo!" he cried again peremptorily. A low rumble rolled from the *gryf's* cavernous chest in answer to the call, and the beast moved slowly toward them.

"Fine!" exclaimed Tarzan. "The odds are in our favor now. You can keep your nerve?—but I do not need to ask."

"I know no fear when I am with Tarzan of the Apes," she replied softly, and he felt the pressure of her soft fingers on his arm.

And thus the two approached the giant monster of a forgotten epoch until they stood close in the shadow of a mighty shoulder. "Whee-oo!" shouted Tarzan and struck the hideous snout with the shaft of the spear. The vicious side snap that did not reach its mark—that evidently was not intended to reach its mark—was the hoped-for answer.

"Come," said Tarzan, and taking Jane by the hand he led her around behind the monster and up the broad tail to the great, horned back. "Now will we ride in the state that our forebears knew, before which the pomp of modern kings pales into cheap and tawdry insignificance. How would you like to canter through Hyde Park on a mount like this?"

"I am afraid the Bobbies would be shocked by our riding habits, John," she cried, laughingly.

Tarzan guided the *gryf* in the direction that they wished to go. Steep embankments and rivers proved no slightest obstacle to the ponderous creature.

"A prehistoric tank, this," Jane assured him, and laughing and talking they continued on their way. Once they came unexpectedly upon a dozen Ho-don warriors as the *gryf* emerged suddenly into a small clearing. The fellows were lying about in the shade of a single tree that grew alone. When they saw the beast they leaped to their feet in consternation and at their shouts the *gryf* issued his hideous, challenging bellow and charged them. The warriors fled in all directions while Tarzan belabored the beast across the snout with his spear in an effort to control him, and at last he succeeded, just as the *gryf* was almost upon one poor devil that it seemed to have singled out for its special prey. With an angry grunt the *gryf* stopped and the man, with a single backward glance that showed a face white with terror, disappeared in the jungle he had been seeking to reach.

The ape-man was elated. He had doubted that he could control the beast should it take it into its head to charge a victim and had intended abandoning it before they reached the Kor-ul-ja. Now he altered his plans—they would ride to the very village of Om-at upon the *gryf,* and the Kor-ul-ja would have food for conversation for many generations to come. Nor was it the theatric instinct of the ape-man alone that gave favor to this plan. The element of Jane's safety entered into the matter for he knew that she would be safe from man and beast alike so long as she rode upon the back of Pal-ul-don's most formidable creature.

As they proceeded slowly in the direction of the Kor-ul-ja, for the natural gait of the *gryf* is far from rapid, a handful of terrified warriors came panting into A-lur, spreading a weird story of the Dor-ul-Otho, only none dared call him the Dor-ul-Otho aloud. Instead they spoke of him as Tarzan-jad-guru and they told of meeting him mounted upon a mighty *gryf* beside the beautiful stranger woman whom Ko-tan would have made queen of Pal-ul-don. This story was brought to Lu-don who caused the warriors to be hailed to his presence, when he questioned them closely until finally he was convinced that they spoke the truth and when they had told him the direction in which the two were traveling, Lu-don guessed that they were on their way to Ja-lur to join Ja-don, a contingency that he felt must be prevented at any cost. As was his wont in the stress of emergency, he called Pan-sat into consultation and for long the two sat in close conference. When they arose a plan had been developed. Pan-sat went immediately to his own quarters where he removed the headdress and trappings of a priest to don in their stead the harness and weapons of a warrior. Then he returned to Lu-don.

"Good!" cried the latter, when he saw him. "Not even your fellow-priests or the slaves that wait upon you daily would know you now. Lose no time, Pan-sat, for all depends upon the speed with which you strike and—remember! Kill the man if you can; but in any event bring the woman to me here, alive. You understand?"

"Yes, master," replied the priest, and so it was that a lone warrior set out from A-lur and made his way northwest in the direction of Ja-lur.

The gorge next above Kor-ul-ja is uninhabited and here the wily Ja-don had chosen to mobilize his army for its descent upon A-lur. Two considerations influenced him—one being the fact that could he keep his plans a secret from the enemy he would have the advantage of delivering a surprise attack upon the forces of Lu-don from a direction that they would not expect attack, and in the meantime he would be able to keep his men from the gossip of the cities where strange tales were already circulating relative to the coming of Jad-ben-Otho in person to aid the high priest in his war against Ja-don. It took stout hearts and loyal ones to ignore the implied threats of divine vengeance that these tales suggested. Already there had been desertions and the cause of Ja-don seemed tottering to destruction.

Such was the state of affairs when a sentry posted on the knoll in the mouth of the gorge sent word that he had observed in the valley below what appeared at a distance to be nothing less than two people mounted upon the back of a *gryf*. He said that he had caught glimpses of them, as they passed open spaces, and they seemed to be traveling up the river in the direction of the Kor-ul-ja.

At first Ja-don was inclined to doubt the veracity of his informant; but, like all good generals, he could not permit even palpably false information to go uninvestigated and so he determined to visit the knoll himself and learn precisely what it was that the sentry had observed through the distorting spectacles of fear. He had scarce taken his place beside the man ere the fellow touched his arm and pointed. "They are closer now," he whispered, "you can see them plainly." And sure enough, not a quarter of a mile away Ja-don saw that which in his long experience in Pal-ul-don he had never before seen—two humans riding upon the broad back of a *gryf*.

At first he could scarce credit even this testimony of his own eyes, but soon he realized that the creatres below could be naught else than they appeared, and then he recognized the man and rose to his feet with a loud cry.

"It is he!" he shouted to those about him. "It is the Dor-ul-Otho himself."

The *gryf* and his riders heard the shout though not the words. The former bellowed terrifically and started in the direction of the knoll, and Ja-don, followed by a few of his more intrepid warriors, ran to meet him. Tarzan, loath to enter an unnecessary quarrel, tried to turn the animal, but as the beast was far from tractable it always took a few minutes to force the will of its master upon it; and so the two parties were quite close before the ape-man succeeded in stopping the mad charge of his furious mount.

Ja-don and his warriors, however, had come to the realization that this bellowing creature was bearing down upon them with evil intent and they had assumed the better part of valor and taken to trees, accordingly. It was beneath these trees that Tarzan finally stopped the *gryf*. Ja-don called down to him.

"We are friends," he cried. "I am Ja-don, Chief of Ja-lur. I and my warriors lay our foreheads upon the feet of Dor-ul-Otho and pray that he will aid us in our righteous fight with Lu-don, the high priest."

"You have not defeated him yet?" asked Tarzan. "Why I thought you would be king of Pal-ul-don long before this."

"No," replied Ja-don. "The people fear the high priest and now that he has in the temple one whom he claims to be Jad-ben-Otho many of my warriors are afraid. If they but knew that the Dor-ul-Otho had returned and that he had blessed the cause of Ja-don I am sure that victory would be ours."

Tarzan thought for a long minute and then he spoke. "Ja-don," he said, "was one of the few who believed in me and who wished to accord me fair treatment. I have a debt to pay to Ja-don and an account to settle with Lu-don, not alone on my own behalf, but principally upon that of my mate. I will go with you Ja-don to mete to Lu-don the punishment he deserves. Tell me, chief, how may the Dor-ul-Otho best serve his father's people?"

"By coming with me to Ja-lur and the villages between," replied Ja-don quickly, "that the people may see that it is indeed the Dor-ul-Otho and that he smiles upon the cause of Ja-don."

"You think that they will believe in me more now than before?" asked the ape-man.

"Who will dare doubt that he who rides upon the great *gryf* is less than a god?" returned the old chief.

"And if I go with you to the battle at A-lur," asked Tarzan, "can you assure the safety of my mate while I am gone from her?"

"She shall remain in Ja-lur with the Princess O-lo-a and my own women," replied Ja-don. "There she will be safe for there I shall leave trusted warriors to protect them. Say that you will come, O Dor-ul-Otho, and my cup of happiness will be full, for even now Ta-den, my son, marches toward A-lur with a force from the northwest and if we can attack, with the Dor-ul-Otho at our head, from the northeast our arms should be victorious."

"It shall be as you wish, Ja-don," replied the ape-man; "but first you must have meat fetched for my *gryf*."

"There are many carcasses in the camp above," replied Ja-don, "for my men have little else to do than hunt."

"Good," exclaimed Tarzan. "Have them brought at once."

And when the meat was brought and laid at a distance the ape-man slipped from the back of his fierce charger and fed him with his own hand. "See that there is always plenty of flesh for him," he said to Ja-don, for he guessed that his mastery might be short-lived should the vicious beast become over-hungry.

It was morning before they could leave for Ja-lur, but Tarzan found the *gryf* lying where he had left him the night before beside the carcasses of two antelope and a lion; but now there was nothing but the *gryf*.

"The paleontologists say that he was herbivorous," said Tarzan as he and Jane approached the beast.

The journey to Ja-lur was made through the scattered villages where Ja-don hoped to arouse a keener enthusiasm for his cause. A party of warriors preceded Tarzan that the people might properly be prepared, not only for the sight of the *gryf* but to receive the Dor-ul-Otho as became his high station. The results were all that Ja-don could have hoped and in no village through which they passed was there one who doubted the deity of the ape-man.

As they approached Ja-lur a strange warrior joined them, one whom none of Ja-don's following knew. He said he came from one of the villages to the south and that he had been treated unfairly by one of Lu-don's chiefs. For this reason he had deserted the cause of the high priest and come north in the hope of finding a home in Ja-lur. As every addition to his forces was welcome to the old chief he permitted the stranger to accompany them, and so he came into Ja-lur with them.

There arose now the question as to what was to be done with the *gryf* while they remained in the city. It was with difficulty that Tarzan had prevented the savage beast from attacking all who came near it when they had first entered the camp of Ja-don in the uninhabited gorge next to the Kor-ul-ja, but during the march to Ja-lur the creature had seemed to become accustomed to the presence of the Ho-don. The latter, however, gave him no cause for annoyance since they kept as far from him as possible and when he passed through the streets of the city he was viewed from the safety of lofty windows and roofs. However tractable he appeared to have become there would have been no enthusiastic seconding of a suggestion to turn him loose within the city. It was finally suggested that he be turned into a walled enclosure within the palace grounds and this was done, Tarzan driving him in after Jane had dismounted. More meat was thrown to him and he was left to his own devices, the awe-struck inhabitants of the palace not even venturing to climb upon the walls to look at him.

Ja-don led Tarzan and Jane to the quarters of the Princess O-lo-a who, the moment that she beheld the ape-man, threw herself to the ground and touched her forehead to his feet. Pan-at-lee was there with her and she too seemed happy to see Tarzan-jad-guru again. When they found that Jane was his mate they looked with almost equal awe upon her, since even the most skeptical of the warriors of Ja-don were now convinced that they were entertaining a god and a goddess within the city of Ja-lur, and that with the assistance of the power of these two, the cause of Ja-don would soon be victorious and the old Lion-man set upon the throne of Pal-ul-don.

From O-lo-a Tarzan learned that Ta-den had returned and that they were to be united in marriage with the weird rites of their religion and in accordance with the custom of their people as soon as Ta-den came home from the battle that was to be fought at A-lur.

The recruits were now gathering at the city and it was decided that the next day Ja-don and Tarzan would return to the main body in the hidden camp and immediately under cover of night the attack should be made in force upon Ludon's forces at A-lur. Word of this was sent to Ta-den where he awaited with his warriors upon the north side of Jad-ben-lul, only a few miles from A-lur.

In the carrying out of these plans it was necessary to leave Jane behind in Ja-don's palace at Ja-lur, but O-lo-a and her women were with her and there were many warriors to guard them, so Tarzan bid his mate good-bye with no feelings of apprehension as to her safety, and again seated upon the *gryf* made his way out of the city with Ja-don and his warriors.

At the mouth of the gorge the ape-man abandoned his huge mount since it had served its purpose and could be of no further value to him in their attack upon A-lur, which was to be made just before dawn the following day when, as he could not have been seen by the enemy, the effect of his entry to the city upon the *gryf* would have been totally lost. A couple of sharp blows with the spear sent the big animal rumbling and growling in the direction of the Kor-ul-gryf nor was the ape-man sorry to see it depart since he had never known at what instant its short temper and insatiable appetite for flesh might turn it upon some of his companions.

Immediately upon their arrival at the gorge the march on A-lur was commenced.

23

Taken Alive

A S NIGHT fell a warrior from the palace of Ja-lur slipped into the temple grounds. He made his way to where the lesser priests were quartered. His presence aroused no suspicion as it was not unusual for warriors to have business within the temple. He came at last to a chamber where several priests were congregated after the evening meal. The rites and ceremonies of the sacrifice had been concluded and there was nothing more of a religious nature to make call upon their time until the rites at sunrise.

Now the warrior knew, as in fact nearly all Pal-ul-don knew, that there was no strong bond between the temple and the palace at Ja-lur and that Ja-don only suffered the presence of the priests and permitted their cruel and abhorrent acts because of the fact that these things had been the custom of the Ho-don of Pal-ul-don for countless ages, and rash indeed must have been the man who would have attempted to interfere with the priests or their ceremonies. That Ja-don never entered the temple was well known, and that his high priest never entered the palace, but the people came to the temple with their votive offerings and the sacrifices were made night and morning as in every other temple in Pal-ul-don.

The warriors knew these things, knew them better perhaps than a simple warrior should have known them. And so it was here in the temple that he looked for the aid that he sought in the carrying out of whatever design he had.

As he entered the apartment where the priests were he greeted them after the manner which was customary in Pal-ul-don, but at the same time he made a sign with his finger that might have attracted little attention or scarcely been noticed at all by one who knew not its meaning. That there were those within the room who noticed it and interpreted it was quickly apparent, through the fact that two of the priests rose and came close to him as he stood just within the doorway and each of them, as he came, returned the signal that the warrior had made.

The three talked for but a moment and then the warrior turned and left the apartment. A little later one of the priests who had talked with him left also and shortly after that the other.

In the corridor they found the warrior waiting, and led him to a little chamber which opened upon a smaller corridor just beyond where it joined the larger. Here the three remained in whispered conversation for some little time and then the warrior returned to the palace and the two priests to their quarters.

The apartments of the women of the palace at Ja-lur are all upon the same side of a long, straight corridor. Each has a single door leading into the corridor and at the opposite end several windows overlooking a garden. It was in one of these rooms that Jane slept alone. At each end of the corridor was a sentinel, the main body of the guard being stationed in a room near the outer entrance to the women's quarters.

The palace slept for they kept early hours there where Ja-don ruled. The *pal-e-don-so* of the great chieftain of the north knew no such wild orgies as had resounded through the palace of the king at A-lur. Ja-lur was a quiet city by comparison with the capital, yet there was always a guard kept at every entrance to the chambers of Ja-don and his immediate family as well as at the gate leading into the temple and that which opened upon the city.

These guards, however, were small, consisting usually of not more than five or six warriors, one of whom remained awake while the others slept. Such were the conditions then when two warriors presented themselves, one at either end of the corridor, to the sentries who watched over the safety of Jane Clayton and the Princess O-lo-a, and each of the newcomers repeated to the sentinels the stereotyped words which announced that they were relieved and these others sent to watch in their stead. Never is a warrior loath to be relieved of sentry duty. Where, under different circumstances he might ask numerous questions he is now too well satisfied to escape the monotonies of that universally hated duty. And so these two men accepted their relief without question and hastened away to their pallets.

And then a third warrior entered the corridor and all of the newcomers came together before the door of the ape-man's slumbering mate. And one was the strange warrior who had met Ja-don and Tarzan outside the city of Ja-lur as they had approached it the previous day; and he was the same warrior who had entered the temple a short hour before, but the faces of his fellows were unfamiliar, even to one another, since it is seldom that a priest removes his hideous headdress in the presence even of his associates.

Silently they lifted the hangings that hid the interior of the room from the view of those who passed through the corridor, and stealthily slunk within. Upon a pile of furs in a far corner lay the sleeping form of Lady Greystoke. The bare feet of the intruders gave forth no sound as they crossed the stone floor toward her. A ray of moonlight entering through a window near her couch shone full upon her, revealing the beautiful contours of an arm and shoulder in cameo-distinctness against the dark furry pelt beneath which she slept, and the perfect profile that was turned toward the skulking three.

But neither the beauty nor the helplessness of the sleeper aroused such sentiments of passion or pity as might stir in the breasts of normal men. To the three priests she was but a lump of clay, nor could they conceive aught of that passion which had aroused men to intrigue and to murder for possession of this beautiful American girl, and which even now was influencing the destiny of undiscovered Pal-ul-don.

Upon the floor of the chamber were numerous pelts and as the leader of the trio came close to the sleeping woman he stooped and gathered up one of the smaller of these. Standing close to her head he held the rug outspread above her face. "Now," he whispered and simultaneously he threw the rug over the woman's head and his two fellows leaped upon her, seizing her arms and pinioning her body while their leader stifled her cries with the furry pelt. Quickly and silently they bound her wrists and gagged her and during the brief time that their work required there was no sound that might have been heard by occupants of the adjoining apartments.

Jerking her roughly to her feet they forced her toward a window but she refused to walk, throwing herself instead upon the floor. They were very angry and would have resorted to cruelties to compel her obedience but dared not, since the wrath of Lu-don might fall heavily upon whoever mutilated his fair prize.

And so they were forced to lift and carry her bodily. Nor was the task any sinecure since the captive kicked and struggled as best she might, making their labor as arduous as possible. But finally they succeeded in getting her through the window and into the garden beyond where one of the two priests from the Ja-lur temple directed their steps toward a small barred gateway in the south wall of the enclosure. Immediately beyond this a flight of stone stairs led downward toward the river and at the foot of the stairs were moored several canoes. Pan-sat had indeed been fortunate in enlisting aid from those who knew the temple and the palace so well, or otherwise he might never have escaped from Ja-lur with his captive. Placing the woman in the bottom of a light canoe Pan-sat entered it and took up the paddle. His companions unfastened the moorings and shoved the little craft out into the current of the stream. Their traitorous work completed they turned and retraced their steps toward the temple, while Pan-sat, paddling strongly with the current, moved rapidly down the river that would carry him to the Jad-ben-lul and A-lur.

The moon had set and the eastern horizon still gave no hint of approaching day as a long file of warriors wound stealthily through the darkness into the city of A-lur. Their plans were all laid and there seemed no likelihood of their miscarriage. A messenger had been dispatched to Ta-den whose forces lay northwest of the city. Tarzan, with a small contingent, was to enter the temple through the secret passageway, the location of which he alone knew, while Ja-don, with the greater proportion of the warriors, was to attack the palace gates.

The ape-man, leading his little band, moved stealthily through the winding alleys of A-lur, arriving undetected at the building which hid the entrance to the secret passageway. This spot being best protected by the fact that its existence was unknown to others than the priests, was unguarded. To facilitate the passage of his little company through the narrow winding, uneven tunnel, Tarzan lighted a torch which had been brought for the purpose and preceding his warriors led the way toward the temple.

That he could accomplish much once he reached the inner chambers of the temple with his little band of picked warriors the ape-man was confident since an attack at this point would bring confusion and consternation to the easily overpowered priests, and permit Tarzan to attack the palace forces in the rear at the same time that Ja-don engaged them at the palace gates, while Ta-den and his forces swarmed the northern walls. Great value had been placed by Ja-don on the moral effect of the Dor-ul-Otho's mysterious appearance in the heart of the temple and he had urged Tarzan to take every advantage of the old chieftain's belief that many of Lu-don's warriors still wavered in their allegiance between the high priest and the Dor-ul-Otho, being held to the former more by the fear which he engendered in the breasts of all his followers than by any love or loyalty they might feel toward him.

There is a Pal-ul-donian proverb setting forth a truth similar to that contained in the old Scotch adage that "The best laid schemes o' mice and men gang aft a-gley." Freely translated it might read, "He who follows the right trail sometimes reaches the wrong destination," and such apparently was the fate that lay in the footsteps of the great chieftain of the north and his godlike ally.

Tarzan, more familiar with the windings of the corridors than his fellows and having the advantage of the full light of the torch, which at best was but a dim and flickering affair, was some distance ahead of the others, and in his keen anxiety to close with the enemy he gave too little thought to those who were to support him. Nor is this strange, since from childhood the ape-man had been accustomed to fight the battles of life single-handed so that it had become habitual for him to depend solely upon his own cunning and prowess.

And so it was that he came into the upper corridor from which opened the chambers of Lu-don and the lesser priests far in advance of his warriors, and as he turned into this corridor with its dim cressets flickering somberly, he saw another enter it from a corridor before him—a warrior half carrying, half dragging the figure of a woman. Instantly Tarzan recognized the gagged and fettered captive whom he had thought safe in the palace of Ja-don at Ja-lur.

The warrior with the woman had seen Tarzan at the same instant that the latter had discovered him. He heard the low beastlike growl that broke from the ape-man's lips as he sprang forward to wrest his mate from her captor and wreak upon him the vengeance that was in the Tarmangani's savage heart. Across the corridor from Pan-sat was the entrance to a smaller chamber. Into this he leaped carrying the woman with him.

Close behind came Tarzan of the Apes. He had cast aside his torch and drawn the long knife that had been his father's. With the impetuosity of a charging bull he rushed into the chamber in pursuit of Pan-sat to find himself, when the hangings dropped behind him, in utter darkness. Almost immediately there was a crash of stone on stone before him followed a moment later by a similar crash behind. No other evidence was necessary to announce to the ape-man that he was again a prisoner in Lu-don's temple.

He stood perfectly still where he had halted at the first sound of the descending stone door. Not again would he easily be precipitated to the *gryf* pit, or some similar danger, as had occurred when Lu-don had trapped him in the Temple of the *Gryf*. As he stood there his eyes slowly grew accustomed to the darkness and he became aware that a dim light was entering the chamber through some opening, though it was several minutes before he discovered its source. In the roof of the chamber he finally discerned a small aperture, possibly three feet in diameter and it was through this that what was really only a lesser darkness rather than a light was penetrating its Stygian blackness of the chamber in which he was imprisoned.

Since the doors had fallen he had heard no sound though his keen ears were constantly strained in an effort to discover a clue to the direction taken by the abductor of his mate. Presently he could discern the outlines of his prison cell. It was a small room, not over fifteen feet across. On hands and knees, with the utmost caution, he examined the entire area of the floor. In the exact center, directly beneath the opening in the roof, was a trap, but otherwise the floor was solid. With this knowledge it was only necessary to avoid this spot in so far as the floor was concerned. The walls next received his attention. There were only two openings. One the doorway through which he had entered, and upon the opposite side that through which the warrior had borne Jane Clayton. These were both closed by the slabs of stone which the fleeing warrior had released as he departed.

Lu-don, the high priest, licked his thin lips and rubbed his bony white hands together in gratification as Pan-sat bore Jane Clayton into his presence and laid her on the floor of the chamber before him.

"Good, Pan-sat!" he exclaimed. "You shall be well rewarded for this service. Now, if we but had the false Dor-ul-Otho in our power all Pal-ul-don would be at our feet."

"Master, I have him!" cried Pan-sat.

"What!" exclaimed Lu-don, "you have Tarzan-jad-guru? You have slain him perhaps. Tell me, my wonderful Pan-sat, tell me quickly. My breast is bursting with a desire to know."

"I have taken him alive, Lu-don, my master," replied Pan-sat. "He is in the little chamber that the ancients built to trap those who were too powerful to take alive in personal encounter."

"You have done well, Pan-sat, I——"

A frightened priest burst into the apartment. "Quick, master, quick," he cried, "the corridors are filled with the warriors of Ja-don."

"You are mad," cried the high priest. "My warriors hold the palace and the temple."

"I speak the truth, master," replied the priest, "there are warriors in the corridor approaching this very chamber, and they come from the direction of the secret passage which leads hither from the city."

"It may be even as he says," exclaimed Pan-sat. "It was from that direction that Tarzan-jad-guru was coming when I discovered and trapped him. He was leading his warriors to the very holy of holies."

Lu-don ran quickly to the doorway and looked out into the corridor. At a glance he saw that the fears of the frightened priest were well founded. A dozen warriors were moving along the corridor toward him but they seemed confused and far from sure of themselves. The high priest guessed that deprived of the leadership of Tarzan they were little better than lost in the unknown mazes of the subterranean precincts of the temple.

Stepping back into the apartment he seized a leathern thong that depended from the ceiling. He pulled upon it sharply and through the temple boomed the deep tones of a metal gong. Five times the clanging notes rang through the corridors, then he turned toward the two priests. "Bring the woman and follow me," he directed.

Crossing the chamber he passed through a small doorway, the others lifting Jane Clayton from the floor and following him. Through a narrow corridor and up a flight of steps they went, turning to right and left and doubling back through a maze of winding passageways which terminated in a spiral staircase that gave forth at the surface of the ground within the largest of the inner altar courts close beside the eastern altar.

From all directions now, in the corridors below and the grounds above, came the sound of hurrying footsteps. The five strokes of the great gong had summoned the faithful to the defense of Lu-don in his private chambers. The priests who knew the way led the less familiar warriors to the spot and presently those who had accompanied Tarzan found themselves not only leaderless but facing a vastly superior force. They were brave men but under the circumstances they were helpless and so they fell back the way they had come, and when they reached the narrow confines of the smaller passageway their safety was assured since only one foeman could attack them at a time. But their plans were frustrated and possibly also their entire cause lost, so heavily had Ja-don banked upon the success of their venture.

With the clanging of the temple gong Ja-don assumed that Tarzan and his party had struck their initial blow and so he launched his attack upon the palace gate. To the ears of Lu-don in the inner temple court came the savage war cries that announced the beginning of the battle. Leaving Pan-sat and the other priest to guard the woman he hastened toward the palace personally to direct his force and as he passed through the temple grounds he dispatched a messenger to learn the outcome of the fight in the corridors below, and other messengers to spread the news among his followers that the false Dor-ul-Otho was a prisoner in the temple.

As the din of battle rose above A-lur, Lieutenant Erich Obergatz turned upon his bed of soft hides and sat up. He rubbed his eyes and looked about him. It was still dark without.

"I am Jad-ben-Otho," he cried, "who dares disturb my slumber?"

A slave squatting upon the floor at the foot of his couch shuddered and touched her forehead to the floor. "It must be that the enemy have come, O Jad-ben-Otho." She spoke soothingly for she had reason to know the terrors of the mad frenzy into which trivial things sometimes threw the Great God.

A priest burst suddenly through the hangings of the doorway and falling upon his hands and knees rubbed his forehead against the stone flagging. "O Jad-ben-Otho," he cried, "the warriors of Ja-don have attacked the palace and the temple. Even now they are fighting in the corridors near the quarters of Lu-don, and the high priest begs that you come to the palace and encourage your faithful warriors by your presence."

Obergatz sprang to his feet. "I am Jad-ben-Otho," he screamed. "With lightning I will blast the blasphemers who dare attack the holy city of A-lur."

For a moment he rushed aimlessly and madly about the room, while the priest and the slave remained upon hands and knees with their foreheads against the floor.

"Come," cried Obergatz, planting a vicious kick in the side of the slave girl. "Come! Would you wait here all day while the forces of darkness overwhelm the City of Light?"

Thoroughly frightened as were all those who were forced to serve the Great God, the two arose and followed Obergatz towards the palace.

Above the shouting of the warriors rose constantly the cries of the temple priests: "Jad-ben-Otho is here and the false Dor-ul-Otho is a prisoner in the temple." The persistent cries reached even to the ears of the enemy as it was intended that they should.

T HE sun rose to see the forces of Ja-don still held at the palace gate. The old warrior had seized the tall structure that stood just beyond the palace and at the summit of this he kept a warrior stationed to look toward the northern wall of the palace where Ta-den was to make his attack; but as the minutes wore into hours no sign of the other force appeared, and now in the full light of the new sun upon the roof of one of the palace buildings appeared Lu-don, the high priest, Mo-sar, the pretender, and the strange, naked figure of a man, into whose long hair and beard were woven fresh ferns and flowers. Behind them were banked a score of lesser priests who chanted in unison: "This is Jad-ben-Otho. Lay down your arms and surrender." This they repeated again and again, alternating it with the cry: "The false Dor-ul-Otho is a prisoner."

In one of those lulls which are common in battles between forces armed with weapons that require great physical effort in their use, a voice suddenly arose from among the followers of Ja-don: "Show us the Dor-ul-Otho. We do not believe you!"

"Wait," cried Lu-don. "If I do not produce him before the sun has moved his own width, the gates of the palace shall be opened to you and my warriors will lay down their arms."

He turned to one of his priests and issued brief instructions.

The ape-man paced the confines of his narrow cell. Bitterly he reproached himself for the stupidity which had led him into this trap, and yet was it stupidity? What else might he have done other than rush to the succor of his mate? He wondered how they had stolen her from Ja-lur, and then suddenly there flashed to his mind the features of the warrior whom he had just seen with her. They were strangely familiar. He racked his brain to recall where he had seen the man before and then it came to him. He was the strange warrior who had joined Ja-don's forces outside of Ja-lur the day that Tarzan had ridden upon the great *gryf* from the uninhabited gorge next to the Kor-ul-ja down to the capital city of the chieftain of the north. But who could the man be? Tarzan knew that never before that other day had he seen him.

Presently he heard the clanging of a gong from the corridor without and very faintly the rush of feet, and shouts. He guessed that his warriors had been discovered and a fight was in progress. He fretted and chafed at the chance that had denied him participation in it.

Again and again he tried the doors of his prison and the trap in the center of the floor, but none would give to his utmost endeavors. He strained his eyes toward the aperture above but he could see nothing, and then he continued his futile pacing to and fro like a caged lion behind its bars.

The minutes dragged slowly into hours. Faintly sounds came to him as of shouting men at a great distance. The battle was in progress. He wondered if Ja-don would be victorious and should he be, would his friends ever discover him in this hidden chamber in the bowels of the hill? He doubted it.

And now as he looked again toward the aperture in the roof there appeared to be something depending through its center. He came closer and strained his eyes to see. Yes, there was something there. It appeared to be a rope. Tarzan wondered if it had been there all the time. It must have, he reasoned, since he had heard no sound from above and it was so dark within the chamber that he might easily have overlooked it.

He raised his hand toward it. The end of it was just within his reach. He bore his weight upon it to see if it would hold him. Then he released it and backed away, still watching it, as you have seen an animal do after investigating some unfamiliar object, one of the little traits that differentiated Tarzan from other men, accentuating his similarity to the savage beasts of his native jungle. Again and again he touched and tested the braided leather rope, and always he listened for any warning sound from above.

He was very careful not to step upon the trap at any time and when finally he bore all his weight upon the rope and took his feet from the floor he spread them wide apart so that if he fell he would fall astride the trap. The rope held him. There was no sound from above, nor any from the trap below.

Slowly and cautiously he drew himself upward, hand over hand. Nearer and nearer the roof he came. In a moment his eyes would be above the level of the floor above. Already his extended arms projected into the upper chamber and then something closed suddenly upon both his forearms, pinioning them tightly and leaving him hanging in mid-air unable to advance or retreat.

Immediately a light appeared in the room above him and presently he saw the hiedous mask of a priest peering down upon him. In the priest's hands were leathern thongs and these he tied about Tarzan's wrists and forearms until they were completely bound together from his elbows almost to his fingers. Behind this priest Tarzan presently saw others and soon several lay hold of him and pulled him up through the hole.

Almost instantly his eyes were above the level of the floor he understood how they had trapped him. Two nooses had lain encircling the aperture into the cell below. A priest had waited at the end of each of these ropes and at opposite sides of the chamber. When he had climbed to a sufficient height upon the rope that had dangled into his prison below and his arms were well within the encircling snares the two priests had pulled quickly upon their ropes and he had been made an easy captive without any opportunity of defending himself or inflicting injury upon his captors.

And now they bound his legs from his ankles to his knees and picking him up carried him from the chamber. No word did they speak to him as they bore him upward to the temple yard.

The din of battle had risen again as Ja-don had urged his forces to renewed efforts. Ta-den had not arrived and the forces of the old chieftain were revealing in their lessened efforts their increasing demoralization, and then it was that the priests carried Tarzan-jad-guru to the roof of the palace and exhibited him in the sight of the warriors of both factions.

"Here is the false Dor-ul-Otho," screamed Lu-don.

Obergatz, his shattered mentality having never grasped fully the meaning of much that was going on about him, cast a casual glance at the bound and helpless prisoner, and as his eyes fell upon the noble features of the ape-man, they went wide in astonishment and fright, and his pasty countenance turned a sickly blue. Once before had he seen Tarzan of the Apes, but many times had he dreamed that he had seen him and always was the giant ape-man avenging the wrongs that had been committed upon him and his by the ruthless hands of the three German officers who had led their native troops in the ravishing of Tarzan's peaceful home. Hauptmann Fritz Schneider had paid the penalty of his needless cruelties; Unter-lieutenant von Goss, too, had paid; and now Obergatz, the last of the three, stood face to face with the Nemesis that had trailed him through his dreams for long, weary months. That he was bound and helpless lessened not the German's terror—he seemed not to realize that the man could not harm him. He but stood cringing and jibbering and Lu-don saw and was filled with apprehension that others might see and seeing realize that this bewhiskered idiot was no god—that of the two Tarzan-jad-guru was the more godly figure. Already the high priest noted that some of the palace warriors standing near were whispering together and pointing. He stepped closer to Obergatz. "You are Jad-ben-Otho," he whispered, "denounce him!"

The German shook himself. His mind cleared of all but his great terror and the words of the high priest gave him the clue to safety.

"I am Jad-ben-Otho!" he screamed.

Tarzan looked him straight in the eye. "You are Lieutenant Obergatz of the German Army," he said in excellent German. "You are the last of the three I have sought so long and in your putrid heart you know that God has not brought us together at last for nothing."

The mind of Lieutenant Obergatz was functioning clearly and rapidly at last. He too saw the questioning looks upon the faces of some of those around them. He saw the opposing warriors of both cities standing by the gate inactive, every eye turned upon him, and the trussed figure of the ape-man. He realized that indecision now meant ruin, and ruin, death. He raised his voice in the sharp barking tones of a Prussian officer, so unlike his former maniacal screaming as to quickly arouse the attention of every ear and to cause an expression of puzzlement to cross the crafty face of Lu-don.

"I am Jad-ben-Otho," snapped Obergatz. "This creature is no son of mine. As a lesson to all blasphemers he shall die upon the altar at the hand of the god he has profaned. Take him from my sight, and when the sun stands at zenith let the faithful congregate in the temple court and witness the wrath of this divine hand," and he held aloft his right palm.

Those who had brought Tarzan took him away then as Obergatz had directed, and the German turned once more to the warriors by the gate. "Throw down your arms, warriors of Ja-don," he cried, "lest I call down my lightnings to blast you where you stand. Those who do as I bid shall be forgiven. Come! Throw down your arms."

The warriors of Ja-don moved uneasily, casting looks of appeal at their leader and of apprehension toward the figures upon the palace roof. Ja-don sprang forward among his men. "Let the cowards and knaves throw down their arms and enter the palace," he cried, "but never will Ja-don and the warriors of

Ja-lur touch their foreheads to the feet of Lu-don and his false god. Make your decision now," he cried to his followers.

A few threw down their arms and with sheepish looks passed through the gateway into the palace, and with the example of these to bolster their courage others joined in the desertion from the old chieftain of the north, but staunch and true around him stood the majority of his warriors and when the last weakling had left their ranks Ja-don voiced the savage cry with which he led his followers to the attack, and once again the battle raged about the palace gate.

At times Ja-don's forces pushed the defenders far into the palace ground and then the wave of combat would recede and pass out into the city again. And still Ta-den and the reinforcements did not come. It was drawing close to noon. Lu-don had mustered every available man that was not actually needed for the defense of the gate within the temple, and these he sent, under the leadership of Pan-sat, out into the city through the secret passageway and there they fell upon Ja-don's forces from the rear while those at the gate hammered them in front.

Attacked on two sides by a vastly superior force the result was inevitable and finally the last remnant of Ja-don's little army capitulated and the old chief was taken a prisoner before Lu-don. "Take him to the temple court," cried the high priest. "He shall witness the death of his accomplice and perhaps Jad-ben-Otho shall pass a similar sentence upon him as well."

The inner temple court was packed with humanity. At either end of the western altar stood Tarzan and his mate, bound and helpless. The sounds of battle had ceased and presently the ape-man saw Ja-don being led into the inner court, his wrists bound tightly together before him. Tarzan turned his eyes toward Jane and nodded in the direction of Ja-don. "This looks like the end," he said quietly. "He was our last and only hope."

"We have at least found each other, John," she replied, "and our last days have been spent together. My only prayer now is that if they take you they do not leave me."

Tarzan made no reply for in his heart was the same bitter thought that her own contained—not the fear that they would kill him but the fear that they would not kill her. The ape-man strained at his bonds but they were too many and too strong. A priest near him saw and with a jeering laugh struck the defenseless ape-man in the face.

"The brute!" cried Jane Clayton.

Tarzan smiled. "I have been struck thus before, Jane," he said, "and always has the striker died."

"You still have hope?" he asked.

"I am still alive," he said as though that were sufficient answer. She was a woman and she did not have the courage of this man who knew no fear. In her heart of hearts she knew that he would die upon the altar at high noon for he had told her, after he had been brought to the inner court, of the sentence of death that Obergatz had pronounced upon him, and she knew too that Tarzan knew that he would die, but that he was too courageous to admit it even to himself.

As she looked upon him standing there so straight and wonderful and brave among his savage captors her heart cried out against the cruelty of the fate that had overtaken him. It seemed a gross and hideous wrong that that wonderful creature, now so quick with exuberant life and strength and purpose should be presently naught but a bleeding lump of clay—and all so uselessly and wantonly. Gladly would she have offered her life for his but she knew that it was a waste of words since their captors would work upon them whatever it was their will to do—for him, death; for her—she shuddered at the thought.

And now came Lu-don and the naked Obergatz, and the high priest led the German to his place behind the altar, himself standing upon the other's left. Lu-don whispered a word to Obergatz, at the same time nodding in the direction of Ja-don. The Hun cast a scowling look upon the old warrior.

"And after the false god," he cried, "the false prophet," and he pointed an accusing finger at Ja-don. Then his eyes wandered to the form of Jane Clayton.

"And the woman, too?" asked Lu-don.

"The case of the woman I will attend to later," replied Obergatz. "I will talk with her tonight after she has had a chance to meditate upon the consequences of arousing the wrath of Jad-ben-Otho."

He cast his eyes upward at the sun. "The time approaches," he said to Lu-don. "Prepare the sacrifice."

Lu-don nodded to the priests who were gathered about Tarzan. They seized the ape-man and lifted him bodily to the altar where they laid him upon his back with his head at the south end of the monolith, but a few feet from where Jane Clayton stood. Impulsively and before they could restrain her the woman rushed forward and bending quickly kissed her mate upon the forehead. "Good-bye, John," she whispered.

"Good-bye," he answered, smiling.

The priests seized her and dragged her away. Lu-don handed the sacrificial knife to Obergatz. "I am the Great God," cried the German, "thus falleth the divine wrath upon all my enemies!" He looked up at the sun and then raised the knife high above his head.

"Thus die the blasphemers of God!" he screamed, and at the same instant a sharp staccato note rang out above the silent, spell-bound multitude. There was a screaming whistle in the air and Jad-ben-Otho crumpled forward across the body of his intended victim. Again the same alarming noise and Lu-don fell, a third and Mo-sar crumpled to the ground. And now the warriors and the people, locating the direction of this new and unknown sound turned toward the western end of the court.

Upon the summit of the temple wall they saw two figures— a Ho-don warrior and beside him an almost naked creature of the race of Tarzan-jad-guru, across his shoulders and about his hips were strange broad belts studded with beautiful cylinders that glinted in the mid-day sun, and in his hands a shining thing of wood and metal from the end of which rose a thin wreath of blue-gray smoke.

And then the voice of the Ho-don warrior rang clear upon the ears of the silent throng. "Thus speaks the true Jad-ben-Otho," he cried, "through this his Messenger of Death. Cut the bonds of the prisoners. Cut the bonds of the Dor-ul-Otho and of Ja-don, King of Pal-ul-don, and of the woman who is the mate of the son of god."

Pan-sat, filled with the frenzy of fanaticism saw the power and the glory of the régime he had served crumpled and gone. To one and only one did he attribute the blame for the disaster that had but just overwhelmed him. It was the creature who lay upon the sacrificial altar who had brought Lu-don to his death and toppled the dreams of power that day by day had been growing in the brain of the under priest.

The sacrificial knife lay upon the altar where it had fallen from the dead fingers of Obergatz. Pan-sat crept closer and then with a sudden lunge he reached forth to seize the handle of the blade, and even as his clutching fingers were poised above it, the strange thing in the hands of the strange creature upon the temple wall cried out its crashing word of doom and Pan-sat the under priest, screaming, fell back upon the dead body of his master.

"Seize all the priests," cried Ta-den to the warriors, "and let none hesitate lest Jad-ben-Otho's messenger send forth still other bolts of lightning."

The warriors and the people had now witnessed such an exhibition of divine power as might have convinced an even less superstitious and more enlightened people, and since many of them had but lately wavered between the Jad-ben-Otho of Lu-

don and the Dor-ul-Otho of Ja-don it was not difficult for
them to swing quickly back to the latter, especially in view of
the unanswerable argument in the hands of him whom Ta-den
had described as the Messenger of the Great God.

And so the warriors sprang forward now with alacrity and
surrounded the priests, and when they looked again at the
western wall of the temple court they saw pouring over it a
great force of warriors. And the thing that startled and ap-
palled them was the fact that many of these were black and
hairy Waz-don.

At their head came the stranger with the shiny weapon and
on his right was Ta-den, the Ho-don, and on his left Om-at,
the black *gund* of Kor-ul-ja.

A warrior near the altar had seized the sacrificial knife and
cut Tarzan's bonds and also those of Ja-don and Jane Clayton,
and now the three stood together beside the altar and as the
newcomers from the western end of the temple court pushed
their way toward them the eyes of the woman went wide in
mingled astonishment, incredulity, and hope. And the stranger,
slinging his weapon across his back by a leather strap, rushed
forward and took her in his arms.

"Jack!" she cried, sobbing on his shoulder. "Jack, my son!"

And Tarzan of the Apes came then and put his arms around
them both, and the King of Pal-ul-don and the warriors and
the people kneeled in the temple court and placed their foreheads to the ground before the altar where the three stood.

25

Home

WITHIN an hour of the fall of Lu-don and Mo-sar, the
chiefs and principal warriors of Pal-ul-don gathered in
the great throneroom of the palace at A-lur upon the
steps of the lofty pyramid and placing Ja-don at the apex proclaimed him king. Upon one side of the old chieftain stood
Tarzan of the Apes, and upon the other Korak, the Killer,
worthy son of the mighty ape-man.

And when the brief ceremony was over and the warriors

with upraised clubs had sworn fealty to their new ruler, Ja-don dispatched a trusted company to fetch O-lo-a and Pan-at-lee and the women of his own household from Ja-lur.

And then the warriors discussed the future of Pal-ul-don and the question arose as to the administration of the temples and the fate of the priests, who practically without exception had been disloyal to the government of the king, seeking always only their own power and comfort and aggrandizement. And then it was that Ja-don turned to Tarzan. "Let the Dor-ul-Otho transmit to his people the wishes of his father," he said.

"Your problem is a simple one," said the ape-man, "if you but wish to do that which shall be pleasing in the eyes of God. Your priests, to increase their power, have taught you that Jad-ben-Otho is a cruel god; that his eyes love to dwell upon blood and upon suffering. But the falsity of their teachings has been demonstrated to you today in the utter defeat of the priesthood.

"Take then the temples from the men and give them instead to the women that they may be administered in kindness and charity and love. Wash the blood from your eastern altar and drain forever the water from the western.

"Once I gave Lu-don the opportunity to do these things but he ignored my commands, and again is the corridor of sacrifice filled with its victims. Liberate these from every temple in Pal-ul-don. Bring offerings of such gifts as your people like and place them upon the altars of your god. And there he will bless them and the priestesses of Jad-ben-Otho can distribute them among those who need them most."

As he ceased speaking a murmur of evident approval ran through the throng. Long had they been weary of the avarice and cruelty of the priests and now that authority had come from a high source with a feasible plan for ridding themselves of the old religious order without necessitating any change in the faith of the people they welcomed it.

"And the priests," cried one. "We shall put them to death upon their own altars if it pleases the Dor-ul-Otho to give the word."

"No," cried Tarzan. "Let no more blood be spilled. Give them their freedom and the right to take up such occupations as they choose."

That night a great feast was spread in the *pal-e-don-so* and for the first time in the history of ancient Pal-ul-don black warriors sat in peace and friendship with white. And a pact was sealed between Ja-don and Om-at that would ever make his tribe and the Ho-don allies and friends.

It was here that Tarzan learned the cause of Ta-den's failure to attack at the stipulated time. A messenger had come from Ja-don carrying instructions to delay the attack until noon, nor had they discovered until almost too late that the messenger was a disguised priest of Lu-don. And they had put him to death and scaled the walls and come to the inner temple court with not a moment to spare.

The following day O-lo-a and Pan-at-lee and the women of Ja-don's family arrived at the palace at A-lur and in the great throneroom Ta-den and O-lo-a were wed, and Om-at and Pan-at-lee.

For a week Tarzan and Jane and Korak remained the guests of Ja-don, as did Om-at and his black warriors. And then the ape-man announced that he would depart from Pal-ul-don. Hazy in the minds of their hosts was the location of heaven and equally so the means by which the gods traveled between their celestial homes and the haunts of men and so no questionings arose when it was found that the Dor-ul-Otho with his mate and son would travel overland across the mountains and out of Pal-ul-don toward the north.

They went by way of the Kor-ul-ja accompanied by the warriors of that tribe and a great contingent of Ho-don warriors under Ta-den. The king and many warriors and a multitude of people accompanied them beyond the limits of A-lur and after they had bid them good-bye and Tarzan had invoked the blessings of God upon them the three Europeans saw their simple, loyal friends prostrate in the dust behind them until the cavalcade had wound out of the city and disappeared among the trees of the nearby forest.

They rested for a day among the Kor-ul-ja while Jane investigated the ancient caves of these strange people and then they moved on, avoiding the rugged shoulder of Pastar-ul-ved and winding down the opposite slope toward the great morass. They moved in comfort and in safety, surrounded by their escort of Ho-don and Waz-don.

In the minds of many there was doubtless a question as to how the three would cross the great morass but least of all was Tarzan worried by the problem. In the course of his life he had been confronted by many obstacles only to learn that he who will may always pass. In his mind lurked an easy solution of the passage but it was one which depended wholly upon chance.

It was the morning of the last day that, as they were breaking camp to take up the march, a deep bellow thundered from a nearby grove. The ape-man smiled. The chance had come. Fittingly then would the Dor-ul-Otho and his mate and their son depart from unmapped Pal-ul-don.

He still carried the spear that Jane had made, which he had prized so highly because it was her handiwork that he had caused a search to be made for it through the temple in A-lur after his release, and it had been found and brought to him. He had told her laughingly that it should have the place of honor above their hearth as the ancient flintlock of her Puritan grandsire had held a similar place of honor above the fireplace of Professor Porter, her father.

At the sound of the bellowing the Ho-don warriors, some of whom had accompanied Tarzan from Ja-don's camp to Ja-lur, looked questioningly at the ape-man while Om-at's Waz-don looked for trees, since the *gryf* was the one creature of Pal-ul-don which might not be safely encountered even by a great multitude of warriors. Its tough, armored hide was impregnable to their knife thrusts while their thrown clubs rattled from it as futilely as if hurled at the rocky shoulder of Pastar-ul-ved.

"Wait," said the ape-man, and with his spear in hand he advanced toward the *gryf*, voicing the weird cry of the Tor-o-don. The bellowing ceased and turned to low rumblings and presently the huge beast appeared. What followed was but a repetition of the ape-man's previous experience with these huge and ferocious creatures.

And so it was that Jane and Korak and Tarzan rode through the morass that hems Pa-ul-don, upon the back of a prehistoric triceratops while the lesser reptiles of the swamp fled hissing in terror. Upon the opposite shore they turned and called back their farewells to Ta-den and Om-at and the brave warriors they had learned to admire and respect. And then Tarzan urged their titanic mount onward toward the north, abandoning him only when he was assured that the Waz-don and the Ho-don had had time to reach a point of comparative safety among the craggy ravines of the foothills.

Turning the beast's head again toward Pal-ul-don the three dismounted and a sharp blow upon the thick hide sent the creature lumbering majestically back in the direction of its native haunts. For a time they stood looking back upon the land they had just quit—the land of Tor-o-don and *gryf;* of *ja* and *jato;* of Waz-don and Ho-don; a primitive land of terror and sudden death and peace and beauty; a land that they all had learned to love.

And then they turned once more toward the north and with light hearts and brave hearts took up their long journey toward the land that is best of all—home.

Glossary

From conversations with Lord Greystoke and from his notes, there have been gleaned a number of interesting items relative to the language and customs of the inhabitants of Pal-ul-don that are not brought out in the story. For the benefit of those who may care to delve into the derivation of the proper names used in the text, and thus obtain some slight insight into the language of the race, there is appended an incomplete glossary taken from some of Lord Greystoke's notes.

A point of particular interest hinges upon the fact that the names of all male hairless pithecanthropi begin with a consonant, have an even number of syllables, and end with a consonant, while the names of the females of the same species begin with a vowel, have an odd number of syllables, and end with a vowel. On the contrary, the names of the male hairy black pithecanthropi while having an even number of syllables begin with a vowel and end with a consonant; while the females of this species have an odd number of syllables in their names which begin always with a consonant and end with a vowel.

A. Light.

ab. Boy.

Ab-on. Acting *gund* of Kor-ul-ja.

Ad. Three.

Adad. Six.

Adadad. Nine.

Adaden. Seven.

Aden. Four.

Adenaden. Eight.

Adenen. Five.

A-lur. City of light.

An. Spear.

An-un. Father of Pan-at-lee.

As. The sun.

At. Tail.

Bal. Gold or golden.

Bar. Battle.

Ben. Great.

Bu. Moon.

Bu-lot (moon face). Son of chief Mo-sar.

Bu-lur (moon city). The city of the Waz-ho-don.

Dak. Fat.

Dak-at (fat tail). Chief of a Hodon village.

Dak-lot. One of Ko-tan's palace warriors.

Dan. Rock.

Den. Tree.

Don. Man.

Dor. Son.

Dor-ul-Otho (son of god). Tarzan.

E. Where.

Ed. Seventy.

El. Grace or graceful.

En. One.

Enen. Two.

Es. Rough.

Es-sat (rough skin). Chief of Om-at's tribe of hairy blacks.

Et. Eighty.

Fur. Thirty.

Ged. Forty.

Go. Clear.

Gryf. "Triceratops. A genus of huge herbivorous dinosaurs of the group Ceratopsia. The skull had two large horns above the eyes, a median horn on the nose, a horny beak, and a great bony hood or transverse crest over the neck. Their toes, five in front and three behind, were provided with hoofs, and the tail was large and strong." Webster's Dict. The *gryf* of Pal-ul-don is similar except that it is omniverous, has strong, powerfully armed jaws and talons instead of hoofs. Coloration: face yellow with blue bands encircling the eyes; hood red on top, yellow underneath; belly yellow; body a dirty, slate blue; legs same. Bony protuberances yellow except along the spine—these are red. Tail conforms with body and belly. Horns, ivory.

Gund. Chief.

Guru. Terrible.

Het. Fifty.

Ho. White.

Ho-don. The hairless white men of Pal-ul-don.

Id. Silver.

Id-an. One of Pan-at-lee's two brothers.

In. Dark.

In-sad. Kor-ul-ja warrior accompanying Tarzan, Om-at, and Ta-den in search of Pan-at-lee.

In-tan. Kor-ul-lul left to guard Tarzan

Ja. Lion.

Jad. The.

Jad-bal-lul. The golden lake.

Jad-ben-lul. The big lake.

Jab-ben-Otho. The Great God.

Jad-guru-don. The terrible man.

Jad-in-lul. The dark lake.

Ja-don (the lion-man). Chief of a Ho-don village and father of Ta-den.

Jad Pele ul Jad-ben-Otho. The valley of the Great God.

Ja-lur (lion city). Ja-don's capital.

Jar. Strange.

Jar-don. Name given Korak by Om-at.

Jato. Saber-tooth hybrid.

Ko. Mighty.

Kor. Gorge.

Kor-ul-gryf. Gorge of the *gryf.*

Kor-ul-ja. Name of Es-sat's gorge and tribe.

Kor-ul-lul. Name of another Waz-don gorge and tribe.

Ko-tan. King of the Ho-don.

Lav. Run or running.

Lee. Doe.

Lo. Star.

Lot. Face.

Lu. Fierce.

Lu-don (fierce man). High priest of A-lur.

Lul. Water.

Lur. City.

Ma. Child.

Mo. Short.

Mo-sar (short nose). Chief and pretender.

Mu. Strong.

No. Brook.

O. Like or similar.

Od. Ninety.

O-dan. Kor-ul-ja warrior accompanying Tarzan, Om-at, and Ta-den in search of Pan-at-lee.

Og. Sixty.

O-lo-a (like-star-light). Ko-tan's daughter.

Om. Long.

Om-at (long tail). A black.

On. Ten.

Otho. God.

Pal. Place; land; country.

Pal-e-don-so (place where men eat). Banquet hall.

Pal-ul-don (land of man). Name of the country.

Pal-ul-ja. Place of lions.

Pan. Soft.

Pan-at-lee. Om-at's sweetheart.

Pan-sat (soft skin). A priest.

Pastar. Father.

Pastar-ul-ved. Father of Mountains.

Pele. Valley.

Ro. Flower.

Sad. Forest.

San. One hundred

Sar. Nose.

Sat. Skin.

So. Eat.

Sod. Eaten.

Sog. Eating.

Son. Ate.

Ta. Tall.

Ta-den (tall tree). A white.

Tan. Warrior.

Tarzan-jad-guru. Tarzan the Terrible.

To. Purple.

Ton. Twenty.

Tor. Beast.

Tor-o-don. Beastlike man.

Tu. Bright.

Tu-lur (bright city). Mo-sar's city.

Ul. Of.

Un. Eye.

Ut. Corn.

Ved. Mountain.

Waz. Black.

Waz-don. The hairy black men of Pal-ul-don.

Waz-ho-don (black white men). A mixed race.

Xot. One thousand.

Yo. Friend.

Za. Girl.

ABOUT EDGAR RICE BURROUGHS

Edgar Rice Burroughs is one of the world's most popular authors. With no previous experience as an author, he wrote and sold his first novel—*A Princess of Mars*—in 1912. In the ensuing thirty-eight years until his death in 1950, Burroughs wrote 91 books and a host of short stories and articles. Although best known as the creator of the classic *Tarzan of the Apes* and *John Carter of Mars,* his restless imagination knew few bounds. Burroughs' prolific pen ranged from the American West to primitive Africa and on to romantic adventure on the moon, the planets, and even beyond the farthest star.

No one knows how many copies of ERB books have been published throughout the world. It is conservative to say, however, that of the translations into 32 known languages, including Braille, the number must run into the hundreds of millions. When one considers the additional world-wide following of the Tarzan newspaper feature, radio programs, comic magazines, motion pictures and television, Burroughs must have been known and loved by literally a thousand million or more.

Attesting to the unparalleled holding power Edgar Rice Burroughs maintains upon his readers are the many ERB fan clubs existing today. Established by dedicated Burroughs admirers, some of these groups publish their own fan magazines devoted exclusively to all facets of the Burroughs legend.

Interested admirers of Mr. Burroughs' literary works are cordially invited to write to the secretaries of these fan clubs for detailed information regarding membership and availability of their excellent Burroughs fan publications.

Readers in other parts of the world wishing to establish ERB fan clubs may write to Edgar Rice Burroughs, Inc., Tarzana, California, U.S.A., 91356, who will give every possible assistance.

Following are a few of the long-established fan groups:

The Burroughs Bibliophiles
6657 Locust St.
Kansas City, Missouri 64131

ERB-dom Magazine
Post Office Box 550
Evergreen, Colorado 80439

Erbania
8001 Fernview Lane
Tampa, Florida 33615

Jasoomian
Post Office Box 1305
Yuba City, California 95991

ORDER YOUR SET OF TARZAN TITLES
FROM BALLANTINE BOOKS

TARZAN OF THE APES

The original great classic in which Tarzan is rescued by the great apes of Africa and grows to manhood with the tribe of Kerchak.

THE RETURN OF TARZAN

In which Tarzan finds a mate and almost loses her on the cruel sacrificial altars of Opar.

THE BEASTS OF TARZAN

In which Tarzan rescues his baby son John and his wife Jane from kidnappers, helped by his friends Sheeta, the panther, and Akut, the ape.

THE SON OF TARZAN

In which young John Greystoke learns from the faithful Akut how to live in the jungle—and earns the title Korak the Killer.

TARZAN AND THE JEWELS OF OPAR

In which Tarzan discovers hidden vaults under the dread city of Opar—and almost loses his life.

JUNGLE TALES OF TARZAN

Stories of Tarzan's young manhood in the jungle before he met civilized man.

TARZAN THE UNTAMED
The veneer of civilization is stripped from Tarzan as he seeks vengeance for the loss of his beloved wife Jane.

TARZAN THE TERRIBLE
In which Tarzan journeys across an impenetrable swamp in search of the lost Jane, to find prehistoric monsters and an ancient civilization.

TARZAN AND THE GOLDEN LION
In which Tarzan trains a magnificent golden lion which fights by his side in the strange lands beyond Opar.

TARZAN AND THE ANT MEN
In which Tarzan penetrates mile-wide thorn forests to discover a race of knee-high men who use miniature deer as horses.

TARZAN, LORD OF THE JUNGLE
Tarzan orders an American hunter and an Arab slave to leave his country, and gets involved in one of the most fantastic adventures he has yet encountered.

TARZAN AND THE LOST EMPIRE
Tarzan alone tackles the armed might of a strange civilization descended from ancient Rome.

**The authorized Ballantine Editions of Tarzan
are complete and unabridged.**

To order by mail, send 95¢ per book plus 10¢ for handling to Dept. CS, Ballantine Books, 36 West 20th Street, New York, N.Y. 10003